NEVER TOO LATE

A COMPLETE CONTEMPORARY ROMANCE SECOND CHANCE COLLECTION

ALEXIS WINTER

Copyright 2021 by Alexis Winter - All rights reserved.

In no way is it legal to reproduce, duplicate, or transmit any part of this document in either electronic means or in printed format. Recording of this publication is strictly prohibited and any storage of this document is not allowed unless with written permission from the publisher. All rights reserved.

Respective authors own all copyrights not held by the publisher.

ELLA AND LOGAN'S STORY

ONE

ELLA

"Mom! Have you seen my cap and gown?" my daughter, Erin, yells from up in her bedroom.

"Check the laundry room," I shout back as I pour coffee into my to-go cup.

She comes running down the stairs, into the kitchen, and to the laundry room at record speed.

I laugh and shake my head when her sock-covered feet cause her to slide across the floor, making her look like a cartoon character who's spinning out.

I catch a glimpse of my reflection in the glass of the microwave that's positioned above the stove, and my smile falls. I get lost as I stare at the reflection of a woman I don't even know anymore. How'd I get here? It seems like it was only yesterday when I was eighteen, full of excitement for the promise of a bright future. Now I'm forty years old, have crow's feet around my eyes, and my only child is graduating from high school.

Erin comes back into the kitchen with her cap and gown in hand. She tosses them down onto the table with her books, and she grabs her shoes. "Did you remember the bake sale tomorrow to help the new senior cheerleaders pay for their uniforms?"

I nod. "I'll pick something up after your ceremony," I promise.

A horn honks, and I look out the bay window in the front of the house to see Erin's boyfriend, Brock, waiting in the driveway.

"Got to go, Mom," Erin says, standing and grabbing her things.

"Hey, wait." I put down my coffee and take the few steps to her.

"What?" Her eyes are wide and her brows are raised. She's anxious to get to school, to say goodbye to her high school years.

"Slow down a moment and let me look at you." I push her blond hair behind her shoulders so I can clearly view her beautiful face. She looks so much like I did at her age. Her blue eyes match mine but hers aren't surrounded by wrinkles. Her pink lips are full and plump, and her smile can stop anyone in their tracks. She has a bright future, and it's only a matter of time before she leaves me and our small town in Illinois to join some of the brightest minds in the world at Harvard University.

"Mom, I'm going to be late," she complains, rolling her striking blue eyes, but she can't hide that smile.

I laugh. "You're late every day," I point out. "Plus, who cares? It's your last day. What are they going to do, withhold your diploma?"

Her eyes grow wide, and her back gets ramrod straight as panic sets in. "Can they do that?"

I laugh. "No." I pull her in for a hug. "I just wanted to remind you to go slow today, to take it all in. This is the last day. Your life is about to change in so many ways, and you'll never get this back."

She pulls back with a sweet smile, clearly more relaxed now. "Thanks, Mom. I love you."

"I love you too." I step back and pick up my coffee.

"Hey, is Dad going to make it to graduation tonight?"

I shrug. "I haven't talked to him all week. I guess we'll just have to wait and see."

She smiles before tugging open the door. I stand and watch out the window as she runs across the yard to the awaiting truck. Her boyfriend leans across the cab and opens the door for her. She climbs up, and they meet in the middle for a quick kiss. Seconds later, they're backing out of the drive, ready to finish their last day of high school.

With the house now empty, I grab my purse and keys and shut off the lights as I make my way to the front door. I set the alarm and pull the door closed behind me, spinning around to lock it. I turn and walk off the porch and down the sidewalk to my black Audi parked in the driveway. I can't help but notice how well the roses are blooming along the front of the house and how the landscaper did an amazing job at trimming the hedges to make the house look like the perfect family home.

That's what everyone thinks, anyway. This is the perfect home for the perfect family. All they see is the nice house, nice cars, our beautiful, smart daughter who's about to leave for an Ivy League college, and my husband who has a good job and makes lots of money. They don't see that he's gone more times than he's home, leaving a wife and daughter behind to live life without him. They don't see the fights we have because of that job. And they most definitely don't see the regret I have when I look at my life and the way it turned out.

I push all thoughts away, and I get behind the wheel and drive over to the flower shop I own. I inherited it when I was nineteen when my mother passed away of stomach cancer. I've been working at the place since I was old enough to hold a pair of sheers. I walk in and the bell above the door rings. Lisa, my employee and best friend, has already opened for the day.

"Hi, love. How's your morning?" she asks from behind the counter.

"I think I'm on the verge of a mental breakdown, but I'm here," I reply as I'm placing my purse under the counter and pulling out my apron to tie around myself.

She giggles. "It's the day, huh?"

I nod. "Yep."

"Is Tom going to make it home?" She knows that Tom is a sore subject, so her tone isn't as strong as usual. It's slightly shaky, unsure.

I shrug. "I haven't talked to Tom since last week."

"What?" she asks, confused.

I plop down on the wooden stool behind the counter. "I think he's going to ask for a divorce."

"What? Why in the world would you think that?" She's suddenly concerned. Like most people in this town, Lisa doesn't know the full extent of our problems. She knows more than most, but I've shielded that part of my life away from her as much as I could.

"Things haven't been good for a long time," I confess. "We hardly ever talk anymore, and when we do, we just argue. He's been living at his apartment in London. If it wasn't for Erin's graduation today, I don't think he'd be coming home now... if he even is. I don't know anymore." I feel a sob make its way up my chest. "What am I going to do, Lisa? I'm forty years old, and I'm going to be going through a divorce? It's too late to start over. I haven't been single in twenty years. I haven't gone on a date since I was nineteen. I don't even know how to date anymore." Tears are quickly filling my eyes and falling over the rims. My heart is pounding hard, threatening to beat out of my chest, and my lungs feel like they've suddenly forgotten how to work.

"Shhhh. Oh, honey. You're going to be just fine," Lisa says, coming to wrap me up in a warm hug. She holds me close, slightly rocking me back and forth while *shhhh*-ing me. "Everything will be great, you'll see. You are a beautiful, sexy, successful woman. Any man in town would be more than happy to have you on his arm."

I snort. "Like who?"

"Well, let's see." She steps back to think it over. "What about Jack?"

I laugh. "Jack, really? He's been married four times, Lisa," I remind her, rolling my eyes.

"But he's going through a divorce," she points out.

"Next."

Her eyes roll up as she thinks again. "Tony?"

I shake my head. "He's twenty years older than me and just suffered a heart attack."

"Damn, El. I didn't know you were so picky!"

I laugh.

"I guess we could always track down Lo—"

"Don't you dare say his name," I nearly yell, cutting her off. I haven't seen him since he left for college without me when we were eighteen.

He's the one that got away. The real love of my life. The one that left for the college that we were both supposed to attend—that is, until my mom got sick and I had to stay home to run the store. I was to join him the following year, but we lost touch. The calls between us dwindled down to nothing. The letters stopped coming, and the visits never came through. The worst part is, I don't even know why.

"It's been years, El. I don't think saying his name is like Beetlejuice or anything. He's not going to magically appear if I say it out loud," she points out.

"Well, I never thought I'd be forty, with my only child about to leave home, and going through a divorce either, but here I am, Lisa!" Okay, I may be a little irritable at the moment.

She laughs, knowing not to take my tone as serious as it sounds. "You don't even know that. Tom isn't home yet. Just... calm down and see how the evening goes. Enjoy your daughter's graduation."

Easier said than done. But the one thing I can do is control my thoughts. I push myself up off the stool and move to the back to start on the orders that need to go out today. I can't control what's going on in my life, but I can control these arrangements and I can control my thoughts. Staying busy is the best option at this point.

I turn the radio on and get busy, listening to the old '90s alternative station on Pandora as I gather the needed materials for the day. I go through my checklist and have everything out and ready. I get to work, singing along with all my favorite songs and keeping everything outside of this room out of my head.

By lunch, I almost feel normal again. I put things away and head back out onto the sales floor. Lisa is behind the counter, dusting. There isn't much to do around here if you're not making arrangements or waiting on a customer.

"I'm going to grab a salad for lunch. Want anything?"

"Oh, make it two. And a glass of wine wouldn't hurt," she jokes.

I laugh. "There's a six-pack back in the cooler," I say, walking out the door and heading across the square for the diner.

TWO

LOGAN

I can't believe I'm doing this—going home after twenty-two years. It's something I said I'd never do, not after ruining the lives of everyone I knew. I look down at the letter in my hand from the city of Herrin, Illinois. It states that if my father's property, now mine, isn't dealt with soon, they will have no choice but to condemn it and tear it down. I haven't been in that house since I left it at the age of eighteen. I can't help but think back on the last day.

"Please don't cry, El." I raise my hands and cup her cheeks, wiping her tears away with my thumbs.

She nods and forces a smile. "It's just so unfair. I was supposed to be going with you. This was supposed to be our new start."

I pull her against my chest. "I know, but it won't change anything, baby. I promise, I'll wait for you. We'll talk every day. We can send each other love letters. And Tom will still be here if you need anything. He's my best friend. You can trust him just like you do me. In a year, you'll come to school, and it will be like no time at all has passed."

"Promise?" she asks, looking up at me with her big blue eyes full of tears.

"I promise. I love you, El. We're going to spend the rest of our lives *together." I lean in, pressing my mouth to hers, and she kisses me like I'm the air she needs to breathe.*

Pulling away from her and getting behind the wheel is the hardest thing I've ever had to do, but I manage. I have no choice. My dad's health isn't doing good, and I need this degree to take over his business. He's counting on me. Not to mention, El will need someone to take care of her too. Getting this degree is the first step at getting my future with her.

I shake the memory from my head, cursing myself at how wrong I was. I didn't know the future that I would get. I didn't know I'd end up here, alone at forty and still desperately in love with my high school sweetheart, the girl I left behind. She never did come to school, not that I know of anyway. Hell, she could've, but I would have already been gone. Truth be told, I haven't even talked to her since my father passed away three months after I left for college. He didn't make it long and neither did I.

The bus stops at the center of town and I climb off, almost expecting something to change, but everything looks the same as the day I left. The town square still has its big white gazebo in the center with all the little shops and restaurants scattered around it. This town really does look like it's taken from a picture in a storybook with its perfectly planted flowers, school spirit decorations, and little shops. It was something I hated growing up.

I hike my duffel bag up higher on my shoulder and push onward, not wanting to run into anyone from my past. I'm sure that will only bring up the question: where have you been? And that's not something I'm really prepared to answer. If I owe anyone an answer to that question, it's El.

I walk past the diner, peeking inside to see the older citizens of town in there, having their morning coffee, eating their donuts, and reading the morning paper that probably contains nothing but good news. I pass the antique store and see Mrs. Mary through the window and behind the counter. I'm surprised she's still alive. She had to be close to a hundred when I left. But she sees me and her smile falls. Her eyes watch as I move across the window and out of sight. I'm sure she's surprised to see me back here. Then I walk by the flower store that El's mother owned. I peek in the window but find a woman I don't recognize. I'm sure El probably sold it after her mother passed so she could get on with her life.

I round the corner and can breathe a little easier now since I haven't run into anyone. I keep walking down the sidewalk that leads to the house I grew up in. I find it funny and strange that nothing in this town has changed over the years. All the houses are the same as I remember them. They all have perfectly manicured lawns, flags flying in their front yards, and white picket fences. All of them except this house, my dad's house.

I come to a stop on the sidewalk and turn to face it. I look it over, noticing how rundown the place has become. The yard is overgrown with weeds, the wooden privacy fence in the backyard has a section that's already fallen down, and the flowers and scrubs that used to line the walkways are dead or grown out of control. The old tree in the front yard has a broken branch that's now lying in the grass, and the garage door is hanging on by one hinge. It's amazing the place doesn't have any broken windows or any other signs of vandalism, but this is the perfect town after all.

I walk up to the front door, kicking rocks and weeds out of the way of the sidewalk. I bend down and pick up the small concrete turtle, finding the key just where I'd left it.

"Huh." I laugh and place the turtle back in its spot. I open the screen door, and it squeals in protest. I make a mental note to oil it later as I slide the key into the doorknob. The door opens inward, and the smell of dust, mildew, and old house fills my nose. I go to step inside, but the screen door decides to give out, its bottom hinge breaking. I catch the door, now only hanging by the top hinge, and pull it closed. With a sense of dread and sadness, I journey though the old house that used to be called home.

The entryway is completely bare, all but the old rug and staircase that leads to the second floor. The living room is to my right, and I peek my head inside to see it almost just as empty as the entryway. When Dad passed, I couldn't bring myself to come back here to clean it out, so I called a company here in town and told them to take anything they wanted and to send me a check in the mail. The only things left are the pictures on the walls and Dad's old lounge chair that I assume was too worn for resale.

I try to remain detached as I turn and walk farther down the hall to the kitchen. The table is no longer there, but everything else looks intact. The old refrigerator and stove are in the same spot, doors open and empty. There are a few cabinets with the doors hanging off, but the shelves are still lined with dishes and glasses. Everything is covered in a thick layer or dust, but all it needs is a good cleaning.

I open the back door and step outside onto the porch. It's still good and solid but the backyard is completely overgrown and in need of care. The rose garden that used to be Mom's baby is destroyed, dead and covered in debris. The swing that used to hang from the roof has fallen down on one side, and I move to hang it back upright. I pick up the chain and raise it to the hook. I move around it to have a seat, sitting slowly in case it gives out, but it doesn't. I bounce gently a couple of times, and when I don't fall on my ass, I feel a little more at ease.

As I swing slowly back and forth, I look out over the yard, but instead of seeing what is, I see what used to be: Mom's rose garden, green and flourishing; the neatly mowed grass; the bird house that I made in grade school that used to hang from that tree in the far corner of the yard; the area next to the garage that used to be paved with lawn furniture; and a grill for our family barbecues. And I see her. El. We used to hang out here all the time. We'd drag a chair over to the corner of the garage and make out behind it where my parents couldn't see. I smile at the memory and feel my lips tingle as I remember those kisses.

"You swear your dad won't find us back here?" she asks, moving to sit on my lap.

I pull her down on me. "He's inside, asleep in his recliner. He's out." *I place my hands on her cheeks and direct her lips to mine.*

Kissing her is like heaven. Her lips are soft and meld to mine perfectly. She tastes of strawberries and a sweetness that is all her own. Her heat sinks into me, making me want to take this make-out session further. Always wanting to take it further. Always needing more from her. But with my dad in the house, it's hard to get away with having sex in my bedroom. If we don't wake him going up the stairs, the squeaking of my bed directly over his head will for sure.

My hand is on her hip, and I'm squeezing it gently. I wish we had our own little place to go to be together like this, together alone, where there are no prying eyes or controlling parents.

She breaks our kiss and looks into my eyes. "Let's go to your room. We can be quiet."

I smile, happy that she seems to need me as much as I need her. "Okay, but we have to be quiet," *I tell her.*

She agrees and stands up. I take her hand in mine, and we walk across the yard and in through the back door, sneaking past my dad in the living room and up the stairs to my room. The moment the door closes behind us, I spin around, my lips pressing against hers once again. I walk her backward to my bed and just our weight on it makes it cry out in protest.

"This will never work," *I whisper.* "The bed is too loud."

"The floor then," *she says, pushing me away and walking around the bed, sitting on the floor. Even if Dad walks in, he won't see us behind the bed. I laugh and shake my head but waste no time in going to her, giving her what she needs, even if it means getting myself grounded for the rest of my life.*

THREE

ELLA

"Are you sure you don't need anything else before I go?" I ask Lisa as I gather my things.

"I'm sure. Go, have fun. Enjoy your baby graduating," she says, shooing me toward the door.

"Okay, I'm going." I pull the door open and step out into the warm day. I walk over to my car and open the passenger side door to put my purse inside along with the dozen roses that I got for Erin for graduating. As I'm standing back up to close the door, I bump into Mrs. Mary.

"Oh," I say, covering my heart with my hand. "You scared me, Mrs. Mary. What can I do for you?"

"It's not what you can do for me, dear. It's what I can do for you," she says with a knowing look on her face.

"And what's that?" I ask, feeling my heart still racing inside my chest.

"A warning."

Goosebumps prickle my skin. "Excuse me?"

"That no good boy Logan is back in town, dear. I just thought I'd warn you so you're not taken off guard if you bump into him, dear."

She places her soft, wrinkly hand on my arm as if she's saying to be strong.

My mouth opens, but no words come out. She must be confused. Logan hasn't been in this town since the day he left it at eighteen years old. There's no way he's coming back now. "I think you must be confused, Mrs. Mary. Have you seen your doctor lately?"

She rolls her eyes. "Why is it that you reach a certain age and everyone thinks you're crazy? Yes, dear. I am certain of what I saw. It was Logan. He got off the bus over there"—she points to the corner—"and he walked in front of the diner, my place, then your place, and rounded this corner like he was going back to his old home."

I swallow and nod. "Okay, well, thanks for the heads-up, Mrs. Mary. I'm sorry to cut this short, but Erin is graduating today, so I need to be getting home and getting cleaned up."

"Oh, I can't believe that our cute little Erin is already so grown. You go on, dear. Enjoy yourself," she says, shuffling back to her antique store.

I round the car and climb behind the wheel. I wonder if she actually saw what she thinks she did. There's only one way to find out. Instead of driving around the square to go to my house, I turn on the nearest corner and drive down the street I practically used to live on. I drive slowly, taking in all the houses and the ways they've changed. I haven't driven down this road in years, always avoiding it to keep the memories at bay.

I approach his house, and to my surprise, the front door is standing open. Someone is in there. But that doesn't mean it's him. He could've finally sold the house, and the new owners are fixing the place up. Memories flash before my eyes of the two of us climbing on his motorcycle, which was always parked in front of the garage door. I can hear the way he used to make me giggle and the way he always whispered I love you.

I shake the memories from my head as I pass by the house. Now's not the time to take a walk down memory lane. Right now, I have to focus on getting through this day, seeing my only child graduate high school and seeing my husband for the first time in months. I go around the block and start in the right direction to get me home. I try to envision what my life may look like in the near future. Erin will be leaving for college, and Tom probably still won't be here. If he even comes, I'm sure he will leave first thing in the morning to go back to London where his real life is. For the first time in twenty-two years, I'll be all alone. What will I do with myself? Who will I be if I'm not Mom?

I pull the car into the drive and let myself into the house. I go straight to my bedroom to get changed. I push the door open and find Tom standing in front of the dresser, adjusting his tie.

"Oh, you scared me," I say as my heart pounds too hard for the second time today. "I wasn't sure if you were going to make it."

He scoffs. "Of course I'm coming. This is my daughter's graduation day."

"Well, you never returned any of my calls..." I set my purse down on the bed and move to the closet to get my dress. "How's work?"

"Work is work," he replies, always short and to the point. "I'm ready to go. I'll be downstairs." He walks out, leaving me alone in the bedroom.

Nice to see you too. Thanks for the warm greeting. It's not like we haven't seen one another in months.

I quickly change into a nice cream-colored dress and slip on my heels. I move to the dresser to put in my earrings and notice that he left his phone on the dresser. I'll take it down to him when I go. I put in my earrings and reach for my perfume on the corner when his phone chimes. I glance down at the screen to see the message.

Lilly: Hope you have a good trip. I'll miss you. Hurry back, my love.

My eyes nearly bug out of my skull when I see it, although I can't say that I'm really surprised. We haven't been a real married couple in a long time. I've had my suspicions that he's been having an affair for months now, but there was no way to find out for sure. And honestly, I'm not even sure if I care. We've been trapped in this loveless marriage for years now. Mentally, I prepare myself for what's to come, but right now, it's time to focus on Erin and her big day.

I grab the phone and head downstairs, finding him in his office. I walk in and set the phone down. The screen lights up when I do, and he sees it. He knows that I know. He looks at me and I look at him, but nothing is said as I turn and walk out.

I go into the kitchen and put the roses into a vase, arranging them and tying a bow around the glass. I pull the card out of my purse and place it in the front. Moments later, Tom joins me.

"Are you ready to go?"

"I am." I pick up my purse and head to the door.

The drive to the school isn't normally long, but with the silence filling the car, it feels like we've driven miles already and we've barely made it out of the driveway. He doesn't mention the message on his phone and neither do I. I just wait. I know this marriage of ours is stacked on a pile of lies that's bound to come tumbling down at any minute. All I can do is prepare myself to salvage anything that's left.

We make it to the school, and we climb out of the car. The graduating seniors are all standing in front of the gym, snapping pictures with their friends, talking, and celebrating their graduation. We find Erin and we walk over.

"Daddy!" she squeals when she sees us. She comes running over, wrapping her arms around her dad who she hasn't seen in months. "I'm so happy you made it," she says, pulling away.

"I wouldn't miss it for the world, baby girl." He pulls an envelope out of his breast pocket and hands it over. "Just something that says how proud of you I am."

She opens it up, and her eyes stretch wide as her mouth drops open. "Oh my God, Dad! Seriously?"

He nods, smile in place.

"Mom! Look at this," she says, coming closer to show me what it is she's holding. It's a picture of an Audi, almost like the one he bought me, but this one is brand new and a pretty silver color.

"We'll go pick it up in the morning before I leave," he promises her.

"Thank you, Daddy!" she says, pulling him back in for another hug. She tucks the picture away in the envelope and hands it over to me. "Mom, can you put this in your purse? I don't want to hold it for the whole ceremony."

I take the envelope and put it in my purse.

"I'll catch up with you guys after. Go find your seats." She gives us both one more quick hug before running off to be with her friends.

The ceremony is pretty traditional. After everything wraps up, we meet with Erin outside for our family photos. "Feel like going to your favorite Italian restaurant to celebrate?" I ask her.

"Actually, I was hoping to go to a party with a couple of friends. Is that okay? I'll be home by midnight," she says, hopeful.

"Well, your dad is leaving in the morning, honey. Don't you want to spend time with him?"

"It's fine, El. Let the girl be a kid a little while longer. We'll just wake up early and go to breakfast before picking up the car. How's that sound?"

She smiles wide. "Thank you, Daddy." She hugs him and pulls away. "Love you both," she says, rushing off.

"Be careful," I shout after her, knowing my concern has fallen on deaf ears.

Tom and I turn and make our way back to his car where I suffer another silent ride home. The moment we make it to the house, he goes straight into his office and I go to the bedroom to change into something a little more comfortable. I pull on a pair of black yoga pants and a loose-fitting T-shirt. I slide my feet into a pair of flip-flops and go back downstairs. I poke my head into his office.

"Want me to order us anything for dinner?"

"I'm fine. I have a lot of things to go over before I leave in the morning," he says, not bothering to look up from whatever he's working on. It's in this moment I can see how much he's really changed over the years, how his raven-colored hair now has streaks of gray around his temples and his once firm body has gotten soft and more rounded.

I leave his office, thinking about all the things that have changed that can't be seen. He used to want to spend time with me. Now, I couldn't pay him to. He used to love me. Now, I'm not even sure if he knows who I am. Hell, I don't know if I know who I am.

I pour a glass of wine and fix myself a snack to take out to the patio. I cut some cheese into cubes, add some hard salami, and a little fruit. I take my tray of food and my glass of wine out to the patio. I take a sip of my wine and pop a grape into my mouth as I think about all the changes we've been through over the years and all the change to come.

In a way, I've somehow managed to lose the woman I once was. No longer am I driven to escape this town and find a life I'll love. Now, I'm stuck, living the life I managed to scrape together after Logan left me with nothing but broken promises.

Tom walks out the door with a file folder in his hands. "Ahh, there you are," he says, sitting down in the empty chair next to me.

"El, what I have to say isn't easy," he starts. "So, I'm just going to come out with it."

I brace myself for the words we're both desperate to say.

"I want a divorce," he says, and it feels like the weight of the world has been lifted from my shoulders. "We haven't really been together in years and I think, now that Erin is going off to college, it would be a good time for a fresh start for all of us. Don't you think?"

I look over at him but am partially frozen. I don't know what to say. I'm not surprised or angry in the least. I knew this was coming, but having the words out there now, it makes it all so real. Before it was just a thought that my future was going to change. Now, it's going to happen. It's no longer an idea. What will I do with myself?

I clear my throat and nod. "I think you're right, Tom."

He presses his mouth into a thin line, then sets the folder down on the table at my side. "You can look over everything and sign when you're ready. It's a straightforward agreement. Things get a little more simple when you don't have any children that are minors. If there is something in there that you don't agree with, just let me know and we can work it out."

"Okay," I agree, looking over at the pool instead of at him.

He stands and walks back into the house, leaving me alone. A part of me feels sad, broken, and lost. I mean, what am I going to do with myself? But another part of me feels excited, like my future is now wide open. It's almost like I'm eighteen again, getting to plan out my life the way I want it instead of dealing with what's being offered. I don't know where I'll end up, but something tells me that everything will be fine.

There will be an adjustment period, I'm sure. I'll have to learn how to live life all over again. I will no longer have to make sure that dinner is on the table, that Erin wakes up on time, or double-check her homework. There will be no long talks with Tom in the evenings, although we haven't had those in quite a while. Everything will be all about me now, and that thought frightens me a little. For so long, I've ignored my own life and focused on being the best wife and mother I could be. I wanted to honor my mother that way. But my life is very different from how hers was. We're different people, living in different times. I wonder if the life I've lived would make her proud of me, or if the life I'm about to have would make her look down at me?

Surely, she's proud of me, wherever she is. I've put my own wants and needs aside for too long. I took care of her when she needed me, and I've stepped up and taken care of my family as long as they've needed me. Now, it's my time.

FOUR

LOGAN

This house is so old that I can't get any power to the place until all the electrical has been updated, inspected, and approved, so I lock up the house to go to the market and hardware store for supplies. Luckily, everything in this town is within walking distance and anything heavy I can have delivered. I go by the hardware store first and put in my order for a new breaker box, wire to rewire the house, and a few tools that I'll need to do the job. They promise to deliver within the hour, and I'll be able to start work today. If I keep my head in the game, I'll probably be able to have the power turned on in a day or two.

I go by the market next and stock up on cleaning supplies, water, and some food to keep me going. With my arms loaded down with bags, I make the journey back to the house. The ice that I got is nearly melted by the time I make it back, but I grab Dad's old fishing cooler off the top of the fridge and load it down with the food and water before pouring the ice on top. My order from the hardware store gets delivered, and I'm able to immediately start on rewiring the house. I change out the breaker box first and make a call to have it inspected. I check over the wires that I can see, but they look to be in good shape, so I set the wire aside and wait to see if changing out the old fuse box will be good enough to get everything turned back on.

With the sun going down and no place to sleep in the house, I head out to the backyard and set up my tent that I brought with me. I build a fire and get to fixing me some dinner from the food in the cooler. I eat three hot dogs, some beans, and a bag of chips for dinner before crawling into my tent and crashing for the night.

I wake in the morning with my back hurting and cracking as I climb out into the early morning sun. The fire has died down overnight, so I have a power bar and a bottle of water for breakfast before getting back to work on the house. This is going to be a long process, but I'm the only one who can do it. I'm going to fix this place up and put it on the market faster than you can say *sold*. While I wait for the inspector to arrive, I go to the water department and have the water turned back on. By the time I get back to the house, the water is ready to go. I turn on the kitchen sink and air sputters out of the line, spraying bits of dirty water the longer I let it run. Eventually, the water starts to pour out, becoming clearer the longer I leave it running. With running water, I'm able to get to work. I start by stripping out the old carpet in the living room and throwing it all into a burn pile in the backyard, along with Dad's chair. I rip the rug out of the hallway and off the stairs as well. With the old carpeting out, I turn my attention to the old paneled walls. I'm lost to my work when the inspector arrives, but he approves my work and promises to have the power on by morning.

I finish painting the living room walls and ceiling and decide that's enough for today. I'm going to shower, go for a cold beer, and order the things I'll need online from my phone.

Gentry's bar is just down the road, so I make the walk and have a seat in the darkened corner. The waitress takes my order and leaves to go retrieve it while I pull out my phone and shop around online. I order enough laminate flooring to cover the living room and hallway. I haven't even ventured upstairs yet to check it out, and I don't plan on doing much to the kitchen other than cleaning it up. The floor in the kitchen is still in pretty good shape, and the cabinets need some new hardware, but other than that, they look good too. The small downstairs bathroom has seen better days, but the basics are there and they work. I only plan on replacing the floor and painting the walls to freshen it up.

My beer gets placed in front of me, and I drink it a little too quickly but order another as I'm enjoying the AC. After a few beers, I get up to use the restroom, and when I come out, I go right to the bar for one last beer. It's pushing nine o'clock now, and I have another long day ahead of me tomorrow. I need as much sleep as I can get.

IN THE MORNING, I wake up and crawl out of the tent. The first thing that I see is what used to be Mom's rose garden. Dad built it up so it's elevated off the ground by bricks. I walk over to it and start pulling out all the fallen leaves and sticks. There isn't anything growing in here anymore, and I hate that. Mom loved these rose bushes. If there is anything in this house that I want to keep, it's this flower garden.

I can't do much around the house other than paint until my flooring comes in, so after breakfast and a shower, I head out to go to the flower store to buy some rose bushes. Luckily, the place is run by someone other than El now, otherwise I'd never even consider it. I walk into the store, and the woman I saw before is back behind the counter. The bell above the door rings when it opens, and she looks up at me. "Hey, can I help you with anything?"

"Yes, I'm looking to buy some rose bushes to plant."

"Okay, follow me," she says, stepping out from behind the counter as she leads me to the back door and outside to the closed in patio. "This is our selection of outdoor plants. Here are all the roses bushes we have, and other greenery and flowers are all over there. Let me know if you need anything else," she says before walking away.

"Thanks," I mumble but have no idea if she heard me or not. I'm blown away by how everything is still the exact same. I used to help El's mom unload the trucks back when I was in high school, and this is exactly how she had everything set up. But I guess if you buy an already running and operating store, there isn't much point in changing things around.

I grab four roses bushes and take them back inside to the counter. The woman starts ringing me up. "Are you new to town? I haven't seen you around here before," she says as she scans in the plants.

"Um, well… I grew up here but left years ago. I just came back to take care of some family property to get it on the market."

"Oh, well, that's nice. How long ago did you move?" she asks, just to make pleasant chitchat.

"Um… I guess it was around twenty years ago or so."

"Really? Wow, that long?" She takes my card and swipes it. "Hey, if you lived here back then, I bet you probably know my boss." She turns her head to face the swinging door behind the counter that leads to the back area where the flower arranging is done. I know because El and I had many make-out sessions back there.

"Hey, El. I think you might know this person," she shouts.

My blood runs cold. Did she say El? As in Ella James? The girl who I left standing heartbroken on the side of the road while I drove off and never came back or gave her an explanation?

The door opens faster than my head can process and out walks Ella James, still just as beautiful as the day I left her. Her blond locks are pulled back into a ponytail, and her wispy bangs frame her icy-blue eyes that are wide with alarm, just like mine are, I'm sure. Her plump lips are parted as she takes me in. It feels like time has frozen completely for the both of us as we take in the other.

Time has been kind to her. She doesn't look any older than the day I left her standing on the side of the road. She's still tall and thin but round in all the best places. Her breasts that I've memorized seem to have only gotten bigger with age. Her stomach is still toned and flat, but her hips are more rounded, maybe from having children. I notice her hands, and while there is a tan line on her ring finger, there is no ring there. She could have taken it off for work, or maybe she's no longer married. I wonder who she ended up with after all these years.

"Hey, El," I manage to get out.

"Logan?" she asks, taking a step closer, like she can't believe I'm standing here.

I'm sure she's confused. The last time she laid eyes on me I was eighteen. I've aged quite a bit over the years. My brown hair is no longer short and styled, and now it has a little gray peppered through. My once smooth jaw is now covered in overgrown hair, and I'm sure I have a few more wrinkles on my face than she remembers.

"How ya doing, El?"

"I can't believe it's you," she says, rushing toward me. She throws herself against me and pulls me in for a long overdue hug. "I thought Mrs. Mary was losing her mind when she said she saw you." She pulls away but keeps her arms around my neck while she studies my face.

I laugh. "Well, to be fair, Mrs. Mary lost her mind years ago." I notice that my hands are still on her hips, and I let them fall back to my sides. "You look good, El."

She gives me that breathtaking smile of hers and steps back, looking me over. "You, too, a little more rugged than I remember." That smile of hers has a way of lighting up her eyes and damn near making them glow. Her ivory cheeks start to turn pink as her eyes linger a little longer on my body.

I may be old, but I'm in damn good shape. The military helped me out with that.

"What are you doing back in town?" she asks, drawing her brows together as she crosses her arms over her chest, causing her breasts to press closer and giving me a nice shot of cleavage from her low-cut shirt.

"I got a letter from the city that said if I didn't clean up Dad's property, they would condemn it and tear it down. So, I'm back in town, cleaning shit up and remodeling. I'm planning to put it on the market."

"Oh, so you're not staying?"

I shrug, only now noticing the woman behind the counter has my card in her hand, but she's just standing frozen, watching us. "For the time being, I guess. I don't know what my plans are after this." I look at the woman and point toward my card. "You done with that?"

She jumps. "Oh, yeah. Sorry." She hands it back with the receipt.

I take both and put it into my wallet. "Well, I have a lot of work to do. I should probably be getting back."

She nods. "You need help? My car is right outside." She peeks around me to see that her car is the only car outside, meaning I'm on foot.

"Ugh, yeah, I guess so," I agree. I owe her more than I owe anyone in this town, and I don't want to be rude. I'm sure she's looking for a moment alone with me to get into all the details, and I don't want to deny her that.

I take three of the rose bushes, and she grabs one as we head toward the door.

"Lisa, I'll be back in a few."

She smiles. "Take your time. I know you need it." She winks, and I can't help but wonder if this woman knows of me or not. My bet, she does.

I hold the door open for her with my foot, and she's just about to step through it, but she pauses and looks back at the woman. "Not like Beetlejuice, huh?"

FIVE

ELLA

Seeing him has sent my mind spinning. I'm at a loss for words. I don't know what to say or how to act. All I know is that I have to say something, because his house isn't far from the shop and time is limited. All these years, I've imagined this moment, the moment when he came back into this town. I imagined many different ways that I could run into him, none of them being at the flower shop. I never thought he'd step foot in there. So why did he? Didn't he know that's where I'd be?

"What made you come in today?" I ask as I back out of my parking spot.

He seems uncomfortable as he sits in the passenger seat of my Audi. "Mom's rose garden in the backyard is gone, and I wanted to replace it. When I walked by the other day, I saw that woman behind the counter and thought you sold the place."

"So you didn't come in there looking for me then?" I look at him from the corner of my eye. He almost looks like he's afraid to touch anything. His hands are in his lap, and he's sitting completely still.

"I figured that you'd done moved on and would be happy in life, and I didn't want to screw that up for you. So no, I didn't come looking for you."

I pull into his drive and shift into park. I get out and grab one of the rose bushes, heading to the backyard to set it down. I hear him climb out after me. About the time I'm setting the rose bush down beside where it will be planted, he's walking through the back gate.

"El, there's a lot to be said and address between us. If you want to talk about it, I'm okay with that. But if you want to pretend like I never existed, I completely understand. Just so you know, it's up to you and I'll honor whatever you decide."

I snort. "Oh, now you're honoring my wishes? Too bad you didn't do that twenty-two years ago, huh?"

The anger I've been holding back all these years is finally bubbling over, and I have no control over it. The anger I hold toward him has been a seed in my belly for all these years, a seed that was watered the moment he walked into my shop, and now, it's growing uncontrollably. There's no stopping it. It will grow until I can no longer contain it.

"I understand why you're mad, and I'd be mad too," he starts.

"Mad? You think I'm mad?" I point at my chest. "Mad doesn't even begin to cover the years of hell I've lived through because you didn't love me enough to come back." He looks pained, like my words are a sharp sword that's just sliced through him. "And you know what? Now you get to know what it feels like to be ran away from." I don't say another word as I push my way forward, leaving him behind.

I almost run to my car and get behind the wheel. I look back at the gate I just walked through as I shift into reverse. He's not coming after me. That almost makes me feel sadder. I wasn't worth coming back for, and I'm not worth chasing after. Or maybe he's giving me what he thinks I want: the chance to walk away from him.

When I get back to the shop I walk in and Lisa is behind the counter. She stands up quickly. "That was him, wasn't it? The one you're in love with that never came back? How'd it go?" she asks, following me into the back room.

"I yelled at him and ran away," I confess, walking around the table and putting both my hands flat on it while I lean forward, hanging my head. "I've had twenty-two years to think of what I'd say to him if he showed up, but did I say any of that? No! I yelled at him. What the fuck is wrong with me?" My eyes fall closed as I stand upright, letting my head fall back like I'm looking up at the ceiling.

"It's okay. Now you know where he's at. You can gather your thoughts and go to him when you're ready."

I shake my head. "No, I can't go to him. Are you crazy? He left me... with no reason why, no call or letter. Nothing. How does he deserve a second chance?"

"I'm not saying to give him a second chance, El. I'm just saying that maybe hearing him out will help you heal a little and let go. And there's no better time than now. You're about to start a new chapter of your life. Erin will be leaving for college, you and Tom are... well, to be frank, you're over. You need to be able to move forward freely. Put everything in the past and let it go."

Maybe she's right. Logan and I, our chapter hasn't been finished yet, and I need everything finished and wrapped up into a little bow before I can move forward.

———

IT'S GOING on seven o'clock. I'm at the house all alone. Erin has better things to do, like spend the summer with her friends before leaving for college, and Tom took off soon after he took Erin to breakfast and to pick up her new car. I'm sitting at the patio table with a glass of white wine and the papers. It's time to read over them and sign them, to end this chapter of my life once and for all.

The papers state that everything will be split fifty-fifty. I get to keep my car while he keeps his. He keeps his apartment in London, and I keep the house here. Our checking and savings account will be split down the middle along with all other assets. My flower shop is mine and will always be mine. He wouldn't have any interest in it anyway. Since there are no children under the age of eighteen, this divorce is rather simple, unless I wanted to fight for more. But he didn't give me much of anything throughout our marriage. It would be silly for me to ask for more now. Not to mention, I don't want anything. I don't want to fight for more. I have everything I need. I have my own money, my own car, house, and business. More than anything, I just want to be done with him.

I sign the papers and close the folder, almost feeling a sense of empowerment. I slide the folder into an envelope and seal it before taking it to the mailbox to be sent to London. Putting that envelope in the mailbox and closing the lid is like closing the lid on the casket that holds our marriage. It's done—not officially—but done. I'm free. I can be whoever I want to be now. I breathe in fresh air and almost feel like it's given me strength. I'm strong, braver, more ready to take on the world as a newly single woman.

I go back to the table and sip my wine while watching the birds fly around the feeder hanging on the other side of the pool. My mind seems to take on a life of its own, and before I know it, I'm thinking about Logan and how good he looked today.

He was wearing a pair of jeans, dirty work boots, and a black Henley shirt that fit him snugly. He had the sleeves pushed up to his elbows and a few dark tattoos on his forearms. They were toned and tanned. He's so different from how he used to be. He was always on the skinnier side as a teen. He was tall and thin but toned from playing sports and working in the garage. He didn't have any tattoos or long hair or scruff on his face like he does now. Now, he seems hard and dangerous. Tempting.

I finish off my glass of wine and pour another. And then another. The wine only adds to my confusion about him and why he left, why he never came home or called. What kept him away from me? Did he leave and find another girl? Did he fall in love with someone else?

Did he never really love me at all? I need these questions answered so I can finally put them to rest.

I grab my phone and call Lisa. She's always my voice of reason.

"Hello?" she answers, sounding sweet and happy.

"I'm thinking of doing something really dumb, and I need you to talk me down."

"Oh, fun," she says around a giggle. "What's up?"

"I want to go over there, talk to him, force him to answer my questions. That's dumb, right? I should just leave well enough alone. The only thing that matters is that he left and now we have two separate lives, right?"

"What? No!" she yells into the phone. "I told you to go to him. Figure this all out. Listen to what he has to say. What if you're meant to be together, El? Are you really going to turn your back on true love?"

I laugh. "True love? If we were meant to be together, don't you think he would've come back for me, Lisa? It wouldn't have taken him twenty-two years!"

"You don't know that. Maybe he's been held hostage and hasn't been able to come back for you. You don't know his story."

I roll my eyes. "Really? Held hostage? Aren't you supposed to be on my side? This guy broke your best friend's heart. Take my side, damn it."

"Sorry, I would if I could, but something tells me that things happened for a reason, and he is your Prince Charming, coming to rescue you right when you need it most. Go to him and don't call me back until you do!" She hangs up the phone and I growl.

I get up and walk into my kitchen through the double glass doors. I grab my bottle of wine and go to pour another glass, but something comes over me. I need answers more than I need wine, and Lisa thinks it's a good idea. Why not?

I grab my keys and jump in the car. I'm about to drive over to his place, which is only a few blocks away before deciding to walk with the amount of wine I've had. I walk the few blocks to his house and make my way down the driveway heading toward the door, but I notice smoke in the sky, and it looks like it's coming from the backyard, so I pass the door and instead open the gate to the privacy fence. He's there, sitting by the fire with a tent in the background. Was that there earlier?

He sees me coming at him, and he stands to greet me. "Did you bring me a bottle of wine as a housewarming gift?" He smirks, and it's only now that I realize that I'm still holding my bottle of wine from the house.

"No, I didn't. This is mine," I say, lifting it up and taking a much-needed swig straight from the bottle. "I want to know why, Logan. Why did you leave me the way you did? Why didn't you come back? Why didn't you call or write? Why?" The words leave me in a rush that I can't hold back, and when they finish, I feel breathless as my heart beats wildly out of control. His eyes level on me and his jaw flexes. Then he takes a deep breath and motions toward the bench.

SIX

LOGAN

I look up when I hear the sound of my gate being opened. The sun is starting its descent from the sky, but there's more than enough light to see her clearly. She's breathtaking, even to this day. She's wearing a pair of short black shorts and a white long-sleeve top that looks light and airy. She has the sleeves pushed up to her elbows, and it has a wide neck, so it hangs off one of her sun-kissed shoulders. She's wearing these pumps that make her long, tan legs look good and shapely. God, what I wouldn't give to feel them wrapped around my hips again.

I want to laugh when I see that determination in her eyes and the bottle of wine in her hand. Then she stops just before me and I make a joke, but it seems like I've only reminded her that it's there. She takes a swig and finally asks all the questions I knew she would.

I take a deep breath. "Want to have a seat?" I motion toward the bench I dragged out of the garage. She looks from me, to the wooden bench, and back. I wonder if she remembers how many times we made out on this thing.

"I can't believe that thing is still here," she says, moving to take a seat. She takes a drink of her wine and looks up at me.

I sit down, wiping my sweaty palms down the front of my jeans. "So, what have you been up to these last twenty-two years?"

She snorts. "Really? Still not going to answer my questions?"

"I will," I promise, "but first, I want to know how your life has been. Get to know one another again."

She rolls her eyes. "My daughter just graduated and will be leaving me in the fall, and I'm going through a divorce. So, not great as you can imagine."

Okay, first things first. "You have a daughter? That's great. What's her name?"

"Erin."

"Where's she going to school?" I'm honestly interested in her life and the woman she's become. I'm not the same kid that left here. I don't expect her to be the same girl I left.

"Harvard to become a lawyer. She's really smart… and beautiful. She's a good girl, and I couldn't have asked for a better kid."

"You only have the one?"

She nods. "Yep. Tom was never around long enough to make a second. Not to mention, I didn't want to raise two kids on my own, so…"

"Whoa, wait." I have to wrap my head around this. "Tom? My old best friend, Tom?"

She nods with her eyebrows raised. "Yeah, Tom West. My name is Ella West. Didn't you know?"

I shake my head. "How would I have known?"

She takes a deep breath, letting it out slowly. "After you left, and after your dad passed away, Tom was the only one who you'd talk to. He was the reason I knew you were still out there and not dead or something."

"Tom never told me, but it all makes sense now…" I mumble more to myself than her. I stand up and start pacing. She watches me, confused. I can't answer her questions right now because I have questions of my own. Why would my best friend do this to me? I talked to Tom a lot. He's the only one whose advice I'd listen to. He's always considered me more of a brother than a friend. Why would he lead me in the wrong direction? Was it all over El? Was he secretly in love with my girl and I didn't even know it? Did I waste the last twenty-two years of my life because he wanted what I had?

"Logan, what's going on?" she asks, but her voice is off, like she isn't buying this load of bullshit I'm trying to sell her to get out of answering her questions.

I stop my pacing and turn to face her. "Fuck, I'm sorry, El," I breathe out as my hands come up to rub my eyes and temples. I fall back onto the bench at her side.

"What? Just tell me," she demands.

I nod and take a deep breath, trying to figure out where I should start. I guess at the beginning. "When I left here, El, I had every intention of keeping our promise. I thought that you'd stay back one more year, that we'd spend every break together, that you'd be joining me the following year, and we'd spend our lives together."

"Then what happened?"

"My dad died," I state. "It really fucked me up. After losing my mom at such a young age, my dad was all I had. I had this plan to go to college and get my degree in business so I could come back and run the store for him. We knew he was sick and that he wasn't doing so good, but nobody saw his passing coming so soon. So when he died, I didn't know what to do. His lawyers contacted me and stated that the business had to be sold because it wasn't left to me in his will yet since I didn't have a degree. It was to be sold to pay off any money that he still owed, like the house. He wanted to leave this place to me so I'd always be able to come home, even if he wasn't here. When I lost him and lost the business, I lost everything. I thought, what's the point in staying in school when everything I was working for is gone now?

"So, I ended up skipping a bunch of classes, staying out, and drinking. I failed and dropped out. I was prepared to come home to you and tell you everything, that I'd fucked up. I ruined our future, our plans. But I talked to Tom, and he told me that after all the months that I'd been AWOL, that you'd moved on. That you'd finally forgotten about me and was over me, but he wouldn't tell me who it was with. He said it would only make things worse for me and that if I loved you at all, that I would leave you alone to finally be happy. So that's what I did. I joined the military and have spent the last twenty-two years moving up in the ranks. But I thought of you every step of the way, El. I had no idea that Tom was manipulating me to get to you." I turn to face her, and she seems to be staring off into space, thinking over my words.

She nods. "When you left, Tom started hanging around me a lot more. He'd come into the flower shop just to talk. He said you made him promise that he'd keep an eye on me."

"I did," I confirm.

"So when your dad died and you stopped calling and writing, I didn't know what was going on. I asked Tom if he'd heard from you, and he said that the two of you talked nearly every day. He said that you were having a hard time dealing with his death and that you just didn't have it in you to deal with me. As time passed, our friendship grew, and every time I brought you up, he'd say something more and more horrible. Things like you wanted to break up with me, that you had found someone else, that you didn't want me anymore. You weren't there to argue your point, so I had no choice but to believe him. The last time I asked about you, I cried and he kissed me. After that, things between us just blossomed. We went from friends to dating to getting married and having our daughter."

I shake my head and grind my teeth together, silently vowing to beat the shit out of him if I ever see him again. "Where is he now? You said you're getting divorced?"

She nods. "He's in London with the woman he's been seeing behind my back. He works there and lives there."

I take a deep breath. I can't believe he did this, and all so he could end up hurting her anyway? "Can I get his number? I have a few things to talk to him about."

She lets out a short giggle but nods her head as she raises the bottle to her lips. "I can't believe this. We could've been made for one another, and we got cheated out of our lives by a guy we both trusted who ended up screwing us both over." She laughs.

"I'm going to kill him," I think out loud.

"He's not worth the effort, Logan." She holds up the bottle of wine and I take it, downing a big swig.

I swallow it down and turn to face her. Her eyes lock on mine, and I see can the reflection of the fire dancing in her irises. "You have to know that I would've come back for you. I loved you, El. There's never been another that even came close to you."

Her lips part, but nothing comes out. Her eyes fall down to my lips before slowly moving back to my eyes. It feels as if we're being pulled together. Her scent engulfs me, only clouding my head more. We're only an inch apart now. I can practically taste her sweet lips already. Just as her eyes fall closed and I'm about to press my lips to hers, her phone rings.

Her eyes pop open, and she pulls the phone from her pocket. "Hello?" she answers, still looking at me with as close as we are.

"Yes, honey. I've already taken care of it. There's a check at home waiting for you. It's on top of the mantel in the living room." There's a pause. "Swimming? I don't know, Erin. I have to work tomorrow, and I don't want kept up by a pool party." Another long pause. "Okay, you and Emily. That's it. Okay, I'll see you at home." She hangs up the phone, but the moment between us is gone.

"I'm sorry. I should probably go. My daughter is needing..." Her sentence breaks off as she stands up. "But thanks for answering my questions. Hopefully, it helps us both to put things in the past." She holds up her hand and waves goodbye before walking across the lawn and exiting through the fence.

I can't do anything but sit back and watch her walk away from me for the second time today. Each and every time she walks away, it breaks my heart just a little more. How could I have ever believed Tom? It was a miracle I managed to stay away from her as long as I did, and that was only because I was telling myself it was in her best interest. How am I going to keep my distance now that's she's only a few blocks away?

If she wanted to be with me now, she would've stayed right? But she took the first excuse she could to get away from me. That has to mean something. If she wanted that kiss, she would have left the phone in her pocket. But she was looking for an out and she found it.

I run my hand through my hair and let out a long breath. My chest feels hollow, missing the most important piece of me. I'm sure she just took my heart with her, or maybe she's had it all along. It's been far too long since I've felt that strong beat in my chest.

SEVEN
ELLA

My heart is racing as I'm walking away from him. We almost kissed. If it hadn't been for that phone call, I'm sure we would have kissed. Would we have been able to stop after just one kiss after all these years of longing? Just the thought alone is enough to have every muscle in my body tightening to hold off the flood of yearning that's been consuming me for all these years. I feel almost giddy and excited. My time spent there with him wasn't nearly long enough. I want more. I need more after this long of a wait. Deep down, even when I was happy with Tom, I've always believed that I was meant to be with Logan.

When Erin was born, I wished that he could have seen her. When she turned one, and then two, and then all the birthdays to come, I wished he was there by my side. When my mother passed away and Tom was the one holding my hand, I wished it was Logan. When I got married, I almost left the church, knowing that I should've been marrying Logan and not Tom. In the happiest moments with Tom, Logan was still there, in the back of my mind.

But now, Tom is out of the picture, and at the same time, Logan is back. Maybe this is fate giving us a second chance. Maybe this is where our story really starts. Maybe I'm not finishing an old chapter. Maybe I'm starting a new one.

When I get home, Erin and Emily are already here, and judging by the sounds of loud music, splashing, and squealing, they're already in the pool. I walk up the drive and head in the front door, locking it behind me. I set my things on the island in the kitchen and walk out the double glass doors that have been left open. The patio lights are on, lighting up the dark outdoor area.

"Hey, Mom," Erin says.

"Hi, Mrs. West," Emily says, waving from her spot in the deep end.

"Hi, girls. I'm just going to get cleaned up and get to bed. I need that music turned down and the squeals to stop, please."

"Will do," Erin says, getting out of the pool and grabbing the remote to turn down the music.

"Honey, is Emily staying the night?"

She looks over at Emily, and she bobs her head. "If it isn't too much trouble, Mrs. West."

I roll my eyes. "You know it's not. Please lock the patio door and set the alarm when you come in, sweetie."

"I will, Mom," Erin agrees, diving back into the pool.

I head back inside and straight upstairs to shower and get ready for bed. Forty-five minutes later, I'm clean, bare of all hair, lotioned up, and got my skin routine done. I go to my walk-in closet to get dressed.

I pull on a pair of panties, some shorts, and a tank top to sleep in. I brush out my hair at my vanity in the walk-in closet. As I'm sitting and tugging at the tangles, I catch the reflection of a pink box at the top of my closet. I put the brush away and go to pull down the box. The top is dusty, and I'm careful not to touch it against my clothes as I sit with it on the floor of my closet. Even though it's been over twenty years since I've opened this box, I know exactly everything I'll find inside.

I pull off the top, and the first thing that I see is the corsage I wore to our senior prom. The flowers were once full of life and beauty, but now they're old, dried up, and brown. I gingerly set it aside, careful not to crush it. There are pictures of Logan and me in high school, from prom, football games, and random times spent together. Then I find pictures that I took after he'd gone. Things I wanted to be sure to tell him about when I saw him again. At first, I took a lot. Pictures of things that reminded me of him. There's one of me at the age of eighteen. I'm holding up the calendar that said it was our anniversary. There's one of me at the pizza shack we always used to go to. We'd always get a shake with two straws. The first time I went in there alone, I ordered a shake and it came with two straws, so I took a picture of me, drinking the shake with the second straw hanging out of the glass.

There are pictures of our friends from the parties I went to without him, pictures of Tom and me together, his two best friends at the time. Looking back now, I can see all the ways Tom manipulated me. I didn't see it then. Didn't or couldn't... maybe even didn't want to. I'm not sure. But knowing the truth now, it doesn't make any of this any easier.

You'd think I'd just be able to throw my marriage away and jump into Logan's arms. I mean, hey, we're meant to be, right? But that's not how I feel. I wonder about what Erin would think. She doesn't even know about the divorce yet, and what kind of woman goes from signing divorce papers to immediately sleeping with another man? What would the town think? I always hated when my mother would say things like that, and now here I am, saying them. But honestly, my business is in this town. If I tarnish my reputation here, I could lose everything. And for what? A quick fling with an old love, someone who left me and didn't come back until twenty years later?

If Tom finds out about Logan, will it make him want to change the divorce papers in any way? Will he be angry and suddenly want to fight over my house and shop? Is it too late to change any of that now that I've signed the papers and mailed them? I don't know. I don't know any of the answers to the millions of questions I have. All I know is that deep down, that young girl who was desperately in love with Logan still exists. I just wonder how strong she is after being silenced for all these years.

Sleep doesn't find me easily. I keep thinking about the divorce, breaking the news to Erin, and the fact that Logan is back in town and we almost kissed. I love my daughter to the moon and back, but girl has some bad timing. If she could've waited five more minutes... We may never know.

In the morning, I wake up and get ready for work, wearing a pair of skinny jeans, my favorite white tennis shoes, and an oversized white T-shirt with a breast pocket. I leave my blond hair down since it's curled into nice natural beach waves from me going to sleep with it wet, and I finish the look with a little bit of makeup to brighten my eyes. I head downstairs and find Erin already up, eating a bowl of cereal while watching TV.

"It's summer. Shouldn't you be sleeping in?" I joke.

"Still stuck on school schedule," she responds, not taking her eyes off of something on MTV.

I sit on the opposite end of the couch and take the remote, hitting the pause button on the TV.

"Hey," she whines, finally turning to look at me.

"We need to talk."

She reads the seriousness on my face and sits up straight. "What's up, Mom?" She places her bowl of cereal on the coffee table and gives me her full attention.

"I'm sure this won't come as any more of a surprise to you as it did me, but your father has asked for a divorce... and I think it's for the best at this point."

Her mouth drops open and her eyes get wide. "A divorce? Really?"

I nod. "You're not a child anymore, Erin. Surely, you see that he's never here. He missed most of your life. And with you leaving for college, I'm going to be all alone. It'll be good for me to move on, too, and find someone who wants to be with me."

The corners of her mouth begin to turn up. "Mom, you got the hots for some guy in town?" She nudges me.

I laugh. "No, I haven't checked out a man in I don't know how long. I've been married. But now, I'm single and who knows. I might find me someone special. Someone who will stay around."

She picks her cereal back up. "I think it's great. If you're happy, I'm happy."

"Really?"

She nods. "Wait, am I going to lose my car?"

I laugh and smack her knee. "No, of course not."

"What about the house? Is Dad taking it in the divorce, or are you planning on selling it to split?"

"Nope, the house will be mine. He's taking his London apartment."

"So, nothing will really change, other than Dad won't pop in every six months?"

"Pretty much," I confirm.

She shrugs. "Then I think it's great."

I stand up, kiss her head, and say, "I'm grabbing some coffee and I'm off to work."

"Bye, love you."

I'm the happiest I've been in a long time as I drive to work. I have the support of my daughter, and my horrible marriage will be ending soon enough. Not to mention, Logan is back, and I get to explore that option as well. Things are finally looking up just when I thought they were falling apart.

The moment I walk into the shop, Lisa is all over me. "So, how'd it go? I'm dying to know."

"Can I at least set my things down before you attack me?"

"Fine. Sorry," she says, backing up and waiting until the exact moment I no longer have my coffee and purse in my hands. "So, how'd it go? Did you guys make out like you were eighteen again?"

I laugh and shake my head. "What? No! We totally would've,

though, had Erin not called at the perfect time. Ugh, that kid has always had horrendous timing," I joke.

She grabs ahold of my wrists and pulls out two wooden stools. "Tell me everything. Leave nothing out!"

I roll my eyes. "It's really not that exciting."

"I'll be the judge of that," she states matter-of-factly.

"Well, here's one thing I did find interesting. It turns out that Logan never meant to leave me and not come back. Tom had told him that I'd moved on and was seeing someone else, but he wouldn't tell him who. With Logan out of the picture, that was when Tom started asking me out."

She gasps. "So Tom totally broke you two up and kept you for himself. Oh, that's low... even for Tom! Have you called him out on his bullshit?"

"No, what's the point? What's done is done. There's no going back and changing things now."

"So, where does that leave you and Logan?" Her eyes are wide, like she's watching a dramatic scene play out on some soap opera.

I shrug. "That's when he told me that he's always loved me and there's never been another like me before or since. We started moving in for the epic kiss, and my phone rang. It was Erin, so I left."

"Ugh! God! Talk about a cliffhanger. So when does act two come into play?"

"What the hell, Lisa? This isn't some TV show or book. This is my life, and I don't know. I want to explore my feelings for Logan, but at the same time, I feel like I just need to take some time for myself. I mean, my daughter will be leaving soon, my twenty-year marriage is ending, and I'm still not sure where I see myself alone in a year, let alone in another relationship. I just... I need time."

"Twenty-two years isn't enough time for you to figure out how you feel about this guy?" Lisa argues. "He's hot. Hotter than anything you're going to find around here. You better scoop him up before Tammy does."

Ugh. Tammy. I hate Tammy and have always hated Tammy.

Tammy is a woman who Logan and I went to school with. She was always trying to seduce Logan into hooking up with her when I wasn't looking. He never did, but that didn't stop her from trying. If she finds out he's back in town, I'm sure she'll try luring him in just like she does every other single, sexy, or divorced man around here.

"God, Lisa. Don't fucking jinx me like that."

She giggles at the use of my F-bomb. "Time's a wastin', honey. Shit or get off the pot. That's what I always say."

I bust out laughing. "You literally never say that."

She shrugs. "Well, I do now. Figure it out and jump on it. Get laid for the both of us."

I stand up and move to go to the back room to work on today's orders, but while I work, I can't help but wonder if she's right.

Would being with Logan now feel as good as it did all those years ago? Would it feel better? Worse? Different at all? There's only one way to find out. But that way scares me. Am I ready to be with another man? I like the idea of it all but there's been twenty years between us. He isn't the same guy he was. I guess before I know anything, I need to get to know him again, the man he's grown to be. And he needs to get to know me, the woman I am, not the girl I was. I'm no longer concerned with college classes, lip gloss, and dates. Now, I'm a woman who has a full-grown daughter, a business to run, and a messy life to figure out.

EIGHT
LOGAN

I wake in the morning with a big smile on my face just from remembering how close we got last night. I sit up to crawl out of the tent, and my back is stiff and screams in protest. I groan needing to stand up and stretch it out. I'm getting that living room livable today. I can't take another night on the hard ground. The flooring I ordered should be in today, and the walls are painted. My plan is to install the flooring and hit up the furniture store to buy a couch with a pull-out bed. That way, I'll at least have a decent place to crash while I finish up the rest of the house. I go for a shower, and while I wait for the delivery, I get to work with cleaning up the kitchen.

I take everything out of the cabinets and put it all on the countertops while I clean out the cabinets. While the wood dries, I wash the dusty, dirty dishes that were left behind. After everything is washed, dried, and put back in its rightful place, I fix the broken cabinet doors and start cleaning the countertop. I work my way from the top of the room to the bottom of the room, ceiling to floor. I get lucky and find a dolly in the garage, which I use to take out the old refrigerator and stove.

While I sit in the backyard eating a sandwich for lunch, I order new kitchen appliances. Not only will it make the house sell for more, it will help me out while I'm living here. I've been so preoccupied with fixing this place up and running into El that I haven't given much thought to my plans when I'm done here. A beach sounds nice, maybe a quiet island in Hawaii where I can live off the land and bathe in the ocean every morning, spend my days hunting, fishing, and gardening. A simple life where I can live out the rest of my days enjoying time spent on the earth rather than working myself to death just to survive. With the money I have now and the money I get for selling this house, I should have more than enough to live the rest of my life if I do so wisely. What more could a lonely guy ask for?

I hear the sound of a truck out front, and I walk around to the front yard to find the UPS truck parked against the curb. He greets me as he lowers the pallet of flooring to the ground.

"Let me help," I insist, grabbing a few boxes of the flooring and carrying them inside the front door. The delivery man makes the run, setting each box on the front stoop, and I move them into the house until we're all done.

"Thanks." I wave him off after the last load.

"Have a good day, sir," he replies, climbing back into his truck.

I look at all the flooring I have to install and rub my hands together, ready to get to work.

A little while later, I have about half the living room floor done as loud music fills the room around me. I'm elbow deep in work, keeping my head in the game with only one thought: get it finished. I spin around when someone lowers my music. It's El.

"I knocked, but you obviously couldn't hear me," she says, walking farther into the living room. Her eyes glance around, taking in the room. "I haven't been in here in so long. It looks different."

"Yeah, I painted over the old, wood paneling and ripped up the old carpet."

"Can you show me the rest?"

"Yeah," I nod, getting up off my knees. I walk her back toward the entryway and down the hall. "I'm going to be putting the same flooring in here," I say, opening the door to the small bathroom. "I painted in here, but that's pretty much all I plan on doing. The floor, while outdated, is still in good condition, and everything works." I step out and walk farther down the hall to the kitchen. "I just cleaned in here. The cabinets are in good shape, and so is the floor. I'm just going to put a new fridge and stove in here and call it good."

She spins in a circle, taking in the place. "What about upstairs? Is it weird walking back into your old bedroom?"

I laugh. "I haven't even been up there yet."

"What? Really?"

I nod.

"Let's go." She holds out her hand, begging me to take it.

I look from her, to her outstretched hand, and back. Her eyes are shining, and her lips are turned up in the corners. I can't resist, so I slide my hand into hers. She leads me back down the hallway and up the stairs. She leads me straight to my door and pushes it open.

Stepping into this room with her, it's like a time warp. I'm seventeen again, sneaking her up here to make out without my dad finding out. The room is exactly the same. Everything is a little dustier and dirtier, but nothing has changed. There are still posters hanging on the walls even though they're curling up on the edges. Some have even fallen down or are only hanging on by one corner. My twin bed is still in the same spot with its red-checkered bedspread. My dresser, desk, and bedside tables still hold a mess of papers, books, CDs, and trash. Hell, there's even an old empty beer bottle knocked off onto the floor. It's safe to say that Dad didn't open this door once I left.

"So weird," she mumbles as she walks over to my desk, looking down at its contents. She picks up a piece of paper, smiles, and then hands it over.

I take the paper and look down. It reads: *I will miss you, but we'll be together soon. Love, El.* The ink is pink and it's fading but still visible.

"I wrote that the night before you left. Remember that night?"

Do I remember that night? It's burned in my memory.

"Do you think your dad knows I'm up here?" she asks as I cradle her naked body against my chest.

A puff of air leaves my lips. "I'm pretty sure he saw you walking up here. But I'm leaving tomorrow. There isn't much point in trying to keep us apart now." I press my lips to her shoulder, slowly kissing my way up to her neck.

"For a minute, I almost forgot what tomorrow will bring," she replies, wrapping her arms around my neck.

I move until I'm on top of her. My hips are between her parted legs, and my face is only an inch from hers. "Don't think about tomorrow. Stay here, right here in this moment." I close the space between our lips and kiss her like it's the last time. Our kiss turns rushed and heated, and my body comes alive as I press against her center. She lets out a whimper as I push myself forward, sliding into her, right where I'm meant to be.

Just thinking about that memory has my body exploding in tingles. God, that seems like forever ago but also just yesterday at the same time. Her eyes are glazed over and hooded as she watches me with her parted lips.

"Of course I remember that night. That night has kept me going on more than one occasion."

She smiles and tugs her eyes from mine as she looks at the note again. "You want to come over for dinner?"

I feel my brows pull together.

"It's just that, I have this box of stuff... stuff like this, that you might want to see. And, well, you're not eating very good here with no fridge or stove, so two birds, one stone." She offers up that breathtaking smile and she has me. I'm convinced that just a simple smile from her could get me to do anything she wanted.

"Sure," I say.

Her smile widens. "Okay." She grabs a pencil off the desk and turns the note over. "Here's my address. Say... seven?" She hands it over as she passes me by on her way to the door.

"Seven it is," I reply, tucking the note into my pocket as I watch her walk away.

HER PLACE IS ONLY a few blocks from mine, so after finishing up work for the day and taking a shower, I start on my journey. I can't help but notice the way the houses are getting more and more fancy the closer I get. This has always been the nicer side of town even when I was growing up. But now, the houses have only gotten bigger, nicer, more expensive. There's one house off in the distance that catches my eye even as far away as I am. It's a big two-story home. The front yard is open, but there's a brick wall around the entire back. Her black Audi is sitting in the drive, not even in the garage. I knew from the look of her car that she was used to having nicer things in life, so at least she's got that going for her. I'm sure her life wouldn't be anything like it is now if we had stayed together.

The green grass is perfectly manicured, mowed in a way that you can see the straight lines that form diamonds. The plants and bushes that line the house are well taken care of, but that doesn't surprise me since she seemed to inherit her mom's green thumb for all things living. I walk up the few steps and knock on the door. Moments later, she answers it, her blond curls blowing in the soft breeze.

"Hey, you made it," she says around a smile as she pulls me in for a hug.

I hug her lightly but am feeling all kinds of emotion that I can't put into words. I never imagined myself here, in the home she shares with her daughter and my ex-best friend who stole her from me.

I walk inside, and she closes the door behind me. I look around, taking in the house. The entryway is huge with a grand staircase. There's a long hall with the kitchen and living room on either side. Everything is crisp and white, clean and classy.

"Would you like a drink?"

"Yeah, sure," I agree, following her into the kitchen.

The kitchen is no different. It has a breakfast nook with a small table. There's an island in the center of the room with white granite countertops. All the appliances are a shiny stainless steel. There are a set of double glass doors that look out onto a beautiful patio and in-ground pool.

"I hope you don't mind, but I'm not much of a cook, so I ordered in."

"Any hot meal is a good meal for me," I say, taking the glass of wine she offers.

"Would you like to come sit on the patio? It's my favorite place in the whole house." She opens one of the glass doors and walks out with me following along behind her. There's a table to the left with a pink box on the top. We both sit down, and she pushes the box closer to me.

"Go ahead. Open it."

My hands are shaking as I raise them to take off the lid, and I hope she doesn't notice. If she does, she doesn't mention it as I set it aside to find her prom corsage on top.

I gently pick it up, careful not to crush it as I set it aside. "I can't believe you kept this, or that it hasn't completely fallen apart by now."

Under it are a stack of pictures from our past. I go through them, noticing how beautiful she was, how young I looked. There are pictures of us together starting at the age of fourteen up until I left at eighteen. After I flip through them, I find more pictures, but I'm not in any of these.

"I decided that I'd take pictures of things I wanted to talk to you about. At first, it was meant to only last a year. I was going to bring you all of these photos when I joined you at college to show you how I'd spent our year apart, but when that didn't work out, I started taking them anytime something happened that I wish you could've seen, things I wished you'd have been in my life for."

I nod as I listen to her words and look at the pictures. There are pictures of her and Tom together, and it makes my stomach tighten in anger, so much that the acid within starts to bubble up into my throat. I toss the pictures back into the box, sick of looking at them already.

"What's the point of this, El?" I don't mean for the words to come out as sharp as they did, but now they're out there and I can't get them back. Her back straightens, and the expression on her face shows nothing but surprise at my hard tone.

NINE

ELLA

"What's the point in all this, El?" he asks, seeming a little more tense than he has been in the days prior. "Is the point to show me how great your life is? Because trust me, I see it." He motions toward the pool and house.

My mouth drops open, but I'm speechless. How dare he think that I'm the type of person who would consider myself better than anyone. And for what? Because I have a nice house? Car? He doesn't know that the down payment on this house was a wedding gift from my mother. He doesn't know that I paid it off with the money I got from her insurance. This house wasn't bought for me by Tom, which is another reason he isn't trying to take it in the divorce. My nice car wasn't just given to me either. I worked and saved for that car, and I'll be proud of myself when I make the final payment in two years. None of this was just given to me, and if he thinks it's made up for the hell I've lived all these years, he's dead wrong.

"Fuck you, Logan," I breathe out in exasperation, shaking my head. "If that's what you think me, why are you even here?"

He just sits, looking at me with his back stiff and his mouth held in a straight line.

"I didn't ask you to come here to rub anything in your face. I invited you over here because I wanted to show you this box. It's something I've thought about doing since the moment you left. And you know, I thought it might be nice to catch up, get to know one another again, but honestly, I'm not sure if I even like the guy you've grown into. The old Logan never would have said something like that to me."

He lets out a long breath and dips his head forward. "I'm sorry, El." He shakes his head, clearing it. "It's just that..." He stands and starts to pace in front of me. "Being back here, it's fucking with me and I knew it would. I knew the moment I stepped foot back in this town, all this old shit that I've put off for too long would take me down. And then running into you and finding out the truth about Tom and now seeing the way you guys lived, it's just overwhelming. I mean, I'm mad that Tom fucked me over and stole you right out from under me, but then I see all this and think, maybe you made the better choice. I never would have been able to give you all of this." He seems broken, sad.

I stand up and stop in front of him. "Please, don't let this house be the defining factor of the life I've lived. It can't tell you that from the time that Tom and I got married, I was alone. He took that job with his father and he was gone. We got two weeks after getting married, and that's when I got pregnant with Erin. If it weren't for her, I don't know what I would've done. I don't know if I would have stuck around here, waiting on him. He was never around, never. I raised her on my own, and he came home for a weekend a month. And the longer he worked there, the less frequent those trips home were until they eventually stopped altogether. Tom and I, we never had a real marriage, and now it's over anyway. I signed the papers and he's living in London."

"There must have been some happy times. You must have loved him at some point. I saw the pictures in there. It looks like the two of you had the perfect life together."

"I worked very hard at convincing others and myself at one point in time that we did have the perfect life together. It's all just an illusion, Logan. None of it was real." I stop and take a breath, getting the courage I need. "Honestly, I don't know if I've felt anything real since the day you left."

I look up and our eyes lock. Something is being exchanged as his chest starts rising and falling faster. He wets his lips and breathes out, "Fuck, El." His hands grab me, and he pulls me to his chest where our lips finally meet.

The kiss starts slow and timid, but something breaks between us, and years of love and passion come pouring out. As his lips move with mine, his hands travel up to tangle into my hair, pulling me so close. I feel his teeth nip my lip, and it sets free the wild side that's been building up inside me of, the wild side that hasn't been unleashed or explored in years. She's finally free, the teenage girl I used to be. And the longer I stand here in his arms, the stronger she's getting.

His tongue makes its way into my mouth, and he tastes just like I remember. It makes my stomach tighten as tingles flood my body. He picks me up against him and carries me over a few feet to press my back against the brick wall of the awning. With me in place, his hands move to cup my cheeks, deepening the kiss. With my eyes closed, it's easy to imagine that it's not the Logan of today. It's the Logan that drove away from me that day. The eighteen-year-old boy who knew exactly how to set my soul on fire. I don't feel like the forty-year-old woman I am either. I feel eighteen again, ready to throw caution to the wind and take a leap of faith with him.

"Mom?" Erin's voice cuts through our moment, and I break the kiss while he sets me on my feet. He keeps his back turned on her while I rush her inside the house.

I open the door, let us in, and close it behind me.

"Who the hell is that?" she asks with wide eyes and a smile playing on her lips.

I take a deep breath, needing to calm down. "That's Logan."

"Logan? Who in the hell is Logan?" she asks as I walk her through the house, toward the front door.

"Remember, years ago, when you asked me if Daddy was the only man I ever loved and how I told you that there was a guy when I was in high school?"

Her mouth drops open as our feet stop moving. "That's him? That's your first love?"

I nod. "Mm-hmm, and you're kind of ruining the moment, so if you would…" I motion toward the front door.

She giggles. "I don't have anywhere to go or anything to do. I'm broke."

I grab my purse off the entryway table and pull out a wad of cash. "Here, take it. Go shopping for your dorm room or something."

She laughs but gladly takes the money I'm giving her and exits out the front door.

I feel breathless as I turn and make my way back to the patio where Logan is back at the table. "Sorry about that," I say, walking over to take my seat.

He lets out a nervous laugh. "We used to have to worry about parents catching us. Now we're worrying about kids catching us," he jokes.

I pick up my glass of wine and take a sip. "Yeah, but now I give the orders instead of taking them," I point out.

My phone goes off, and I pick it up to see that it's a notification from the local Italian restaurant. "Oh, food is here. Be right back."

I go retrieve the food and take everything back to the patio table. "Hope you still like baked ziti because that's what I ordered," I say, emptying the bags.

"Love it. Italian is still my favorite."

I set his dish down in front of him and mine in front of me. I open the breadsticks and leave them in the middle for the both of us. He takes a bite and points at it with his fork. "This is amazing."

I smile and nod. "Mm-hmm, they've been around for a few years. It's Erin's favorite."

"So, do I ever get to meet her? I mean, under better pretenses that is?"

I smile. "I'd like that. I've told her about you, you know?"

He smirks, and it gives my heart wings that flutter in my chest. "Really? Like what?"

I shrug one shoulder as I poke at my food. "I told her that you were my first love and I thought that we'd end up married and together forever. I told her about our prom and all the stupid, silly things we used to do, like riding around on that deathtrap of yours without helmets, getting drunk at the football games, and carving our initials into the table at our favorite pizza place on the square."

"That place closed down I noticed."

"Yeah, it did a couple of years after you left. It's been opened several times under new ownership, but it never lasts for long. I haven't been in there since, but all the same tables are still in there, so I bet we could find ours if we looked."

"Let's go," he says, a look of determination forming in his eyes.

"What? Like now?"

He nods, still grinning.

I laugh. "I meant, get in touch with the owner and see if he'd let us in. There's nobody there now. What are we supposed to do, break in?"

He nods, his eyes now wide, like he's saying, *duh*.

"What? No way! I'm a mother. I can't be getting arrested for breaking and entering."

He rolls his eyes. "We won't get caught. Come on. Let's do it." He stands and takes my hand.

"Logan, no. We can't," I argue as he drags me to the door.

Finally, he stops and spins me around to face him. "Have I ever got you into trouble before?"

"No."

"Have I ever led you in the wrong direction before?"

"No, but..."

"Then trust me. You used to trust me, remember?" And then he leans in and kisses me, and I'm done for.

I don't know what it is about him, but when we're together, I feel like we're still just a couple of kids. A couple of kids who don't care about getting into trouble or the consequences. A couple of kids who just want to be together. And right now, that's all I want. I just want to be with him. I don't care what we do.

TEN

LOGAN

We park at her store, then walk through the quiet square to the old pizza place. We round the building twice, going into the back alley and up to the old back door. The dumpster used to sit beside the door, but over the years, it's seemed to migrate. Now it's a good three feet from the building but right in front of the door, which provides the perfect cover.

I open the old screen door and work at the lock on the door while she keeps a lookout. She's bouncing from foot to foot, clearly nervous and scared that we'll get caught.

"Hurry up," she whispers rather loudly.

I chuckle. "It's fine. Almost got it," I say, picking the lock. After a few more seconds, I feel the click of the lock, and the handle turns easily. "Got it."

I push the door open as far as it will go, which isn't much because a stack of chairs has been knocked over, and we both slip inside. I take her hand and lead her through the kitchen, which is surprisingly clean other than the fact that everything is covered in a layer of dust. I push open the swinging door that separates the kitchen from the lobby and walk inside the place I haven't seen since I was a kid.

Everything is still pretty much in order. All the tables and booths are still here, but the tables have been pushed up against one wall. The chairs to the tables are gone, being stacked up in the kitchen for easy cleaning I'd guess. I release her hand, and she goes to sit in the booth in the corner that we claimed as ours. I walk over to the far wall where all the booth tables have been pushed. I look over each of their corners, rubbing the dust off as I go. The last one I come to is it. I rub the dust off the corner and feel the grooves of our initials beneath my hand. "Found it," I say, picking it up and carrying it over to the booth she's sitting in. I put the table into place and then sit beside her, looking the place over.

Even though it's slightly dark and everything is dirty, I still see the way the place used to be. There were red-and-white-checkered tablecloths on every table, the plastic ones, not the cloth so they could be easily wiped down. There used to be an old-fashioned jukebox in the front corner with seating for people who had to wait for a table. And I can still see signs of where decor hung on the walls, one I remember being an old Pepsi sign. I remember it because there was a picture of a blond model on it, and I always teased El by saying it looked just like her.

"It's still here," she says, running her fingers over the spot that reads: *E.J + L.M.*

"I can't believe they didn't sand it down and refinish it."

"I can't believe we're back here," she says, wrapping her hands around my arm as her eyes find mine.

"It's been too long," I reply, moving in for another kiss that I can feel deep in my bones. Her hands move up, wrapping around the back of my neck as she kisses me. My hands find her hips, and I pull her on top of me so she's straddling me. Even after all these years, she still feels amazing pressed against me. Our kiss is slow and full of blinding passion. I find myself getting lost in her. Connecting again like this, after so many years, it feels like no time has passed. I'm still the kid that's hell-bent on getting out of this town, and she's still the girl who loves me blindly and believes in me the most.

I let my lips fall from hers, kissing my way across her jaw and down to her neck. She lets her head fall back, exposing her soft skin to me. I kiss and softly nip her neck all the way down to her collarbone. My hands move up her back, and she arches into me where my lips find the swell of her breast. She lets out a soft moan that has my body coming to life in ways it hasn't in years.

There's a banging sound coming from the back, and the next thing I know, someone is yelling, "Who's in there?"

She gasps and straightens up.

"Shhh," I say, holding my finger to my lips as I urge her to get off me. We quickly walk to the front door, unlock it, and escape, running back over to her store where she parked the car. Moments later, a man walks out the front door we just escaped.

"You two happen to see anyone over here?" he yells from across the street.

"A couple of kids ran off that way," I say, pointing down the road.

He waves and says, "Thanks," before turning around and going back inside.

El is clinging to my arm and giggling like crazy. "Come on, let's go in here and get a drink." She pulls her keys from her pocket and lets us into the flower shop. She locks the door behind us and leads me to the back room. She flips on the light and moves to a fridge that's holding flowers, but she pulls two beers out, handing me one.

"Hiding the alcohol, huh?"

She smiles and takes a sip. "It's a trick that my mama taught me. The flowers can only be more beautiful through drunk goggles, thank you."

I laugh and set my beer on the table in the center of the room.

She's sitting on a stool at the end of the table, and I move between her legs, my hands slowly moving up her outer thighs. "You have no idea how many times I dreamt about taking you in here, right under your overprotective mother's nose."

She giggles and wraps her arms around my neck. "Oh, I

remember you telling me. That's why we snuck in here to make out, remember?"

I grin. "Oh, I remember," I say, moving back in for a kiss.

This time, there is no stopping us, and she makes sure of it by running her hands up under my shirt, working it up my stomach and chest until our kiss breaks and I pull it off completely.

When our lips find one another again, it's no longer slow and sweet. Now it's rushed and hard. It's urgent. My hands start pulling her pink top off as my lips fall back down to her chest. I unclasp her bra and it falls down, allowing me to kiss further until I can suck her hard nipple into my mouth. Her fingers thread through my hair, and she tugs at the strands, but she doesn't pull me away. She's pulling me closer.

I pick her up against me and set her on the table. She lies back and allows me to kiss down her stomach to the top of her jeans. I make quick work of removing them, and she sits back up, her lips on mine while she pushes my jeans down my hips. I spring free and she catches me in her hand, wrapping her fingers around my girth and working me up and down.

I'm painfully hard, needing to be back inside her. There have been many women since her, but none that ever meant a damn thing, and none of them had me feeling like I was about to burst apart at the seams. No, that's something that only she can do to me. With her, everything is different and always has been. There's a tingle in my body that I couldn't understand before, but now I know it's the mark she's left on my soul. She's bringing it back to life just like she is my body.

I pull her closer to the edge of the table as we kiss, and I position myself at her entrance. I pause, wanting to make sure that she's absolutely certain. "Are you sure you don't want to wait?"

"I think twenty years is enough waiting, don't you?" she asks against my lips.

That's all I needed to hear. I push forward, sliding into her and filling every inch. She lets out a moan that makes my dick twitch inside her, and I'm ready to come already. She's so hot, tight, welcoming. I'm easily lost in her, wanting to hear her moan, whimper, and scream my name while I make her remember who she really belongs to. It's sure as shit not Tom. She was mine first and she's always been mine.

I thrust into her as hard as I can, wanting to make sure she remembers me with every step she takes tomorrow. The table is screeching off the floor as it moves inch by inch. Her nails dig into my back as her breathing picks up, and her moans grow louder as she shatters around me. Feeling her muscles convulsing around my dick feels too good, and it pushes me over the edge with her. I pump harder and faster, my hips taking up a more erratic rhythm as I empty myself inside her.

I ride out every last wave until I have nothing to give. My hips slow and my breathing is loud and labored as I come to a stop. She's holding on to me and I'm holding on to her, like we'd both fall over without the other's support. Frozen, we wait to regain control of our bodies.

I start to remove myself from her, but her hand comes up to cup my jaw, making me stop and look into her eyes. "There you are," she whispers.

I don't even have to ask what she means by that because I already know. The years I've lived without her have transformed me into the man I am today. By being with her again, the old me is starting to shine through. But who will I be in the future?

———

WE END up going back to her place, and I help her clean up the food we didn't eat and the wineglasses from the wine we drank. After cleaning up, we end up back out on the patio with another glass of wine, talking about old times and what we've both been doing since we last saw one another.

"When did your mom pass?" I ask, knowing that her sick mother is the only reason she didn't leave with me that day.

"She made it about another year after you left. When it happened, I remember being sad but also relieved because it meant that it was finally time to live my life. Unfortunately, I hadn't heard from you in so long, I didn't know how to live my life."

"Was there ever a moment these last twenty years when you thought about me, like really thought about me?"

"Only one? I thought about you all the time. I'd wonder where you were in the world. When we'd go on vacations, I dreamed about running into you. I wondered if you ever found the one or if you were living with second best like I was doing. Did you ever think of me?" She looks over at me, and her blue eyes light up the night.

I take her hand in mine and press a kiss to the back. "I thought about you every single day even when I was in the military and running from bullets that seemed to come out of nowhere. I hoped that you got everything you ever wanted out of life. But I never allowed myself to think about who you could be with, and I'm glad I didn't. I never would've guessed it was Tom, of all people."

There's noise from inside the house. and El stands up to peek around the door. "Erin, come meet an old friend," she says, waving her out.

The girl who walks out the door couldn't possibly be her daughter, she looks like her sister. She looks like El made over. Everything about this girl, from her height, her build, her long blond curls and blue eyes, to the way she smiles and the tone of voice she uses remind me of her. I swear I'm looking at an eighteen-year-old El.

"It's nice to meet you," she says, holding out her hand. "Mom has told me a little about you over the years."

I snap out of my daze and shake her hand. "It's nice to meet you too. You look just like your mom. Lucky for you, because I know your dad," I joke, and she laughs.

She bumps El's shoulder with her own. "Yeah, I get all the good stuff from my mom." She turns to face her. "I'm going to go up to bed.

Don't forget to lock the doors and set the alarm," she says around a smile.

El rolls her eyes. "That's what I always tell her. She's probably been dying for her chance to say it back." She comes to sit back down, and I take my seat across from her.

"She really does look like you. That's crazy. Are you sure you didn't make her yourself?"

She laughs. "As much time as I spent alone, I very well could have, I'm sure. But she's a good girl. Really smart and always has been. She's better than I ever was. But I think that's the point, right? For our children to have more than we did?"

I nod, completely unsure of anything having to do with children.

"She has this boyfriend though..."

"Oh."

She nods. "He's a cute boy. He actually reminds me a lot of you, so I see why she likes him. I just hope that they can agree to part on good terms when the time comes. I don't want to see her hold back or not give it her all because of him."

"Better watch it. You're starting to sound like your mom," I tease.

She gasps and throws a grape at me as giggles bubble out of her.

I catch the grape and throw it back, throwing her off guard.

The grape goes rolling off into the distance, so she picks up another and tosses it at me. This time, I move just in time to catch it in my mouth.

She laughs and shakes her head. "You think you're such a big shot, always have."

I shrug. "I kind of am," I joke.

She picks up her wine and takes a sip as her eyes take in the pool in front of us. "Want to swim?"

I shrug and look down at myself. "I didn't exactly bring a suit."

She snorts and rolls her eyes as she stands up and pulls off her top. "Underwear is basically swimwear. Didn't you teach me that?" she asks, kicking off her jeans and jumping into the pool in her red lace bra and thong.

Seeing that perfect ass shining in the air, I stand up and start pulling off my own clothes. I dive in and swim over to her, coming up out of the water as my arms engulf her. She laughs and giggles and wraps her arms around my neck.

"Aren't you worried that your daughter might be watching?"

She glances toward the house and then back to me. "She's a smart girl. She probably doesn't want to see what she thinks is going on down here." She brings her lips to mine, and her legs wrap around my waist. I move us to the side of the pool and press her against the side so my hands can come up to cup her cheeks. The overwhelming smell of chlorine dulls her sweetness a bit, but her lips are still just as soft and welcoming as always. I was never able to get over her before. It's going to be damn near impossible to now.

As our kiss grows in intensity, so does the urge in my body. I haven't had enough of her yet, and I doubt I ever will. I have to admit, the thought of taking her back in her own home that she shared with Tom only makes the whole thing sweeter. He took her from me, but I'm taking her back. And this time, I'm going to keep her.

Her hand moves up my neck and into my hair, tugging and pulling me closer. My body comes alive, and more than anything, I need to feel her wrapped around me again. I start pulling off her panties, and she lets her legs drop from around me to take them off. I catch her thigh in one hand and put it back around my hip, the other following suit. Now that we're back in position, my hips move forward, pressing right against her center. I slide in easily, and she lets out a soft moan that fills my ears.

As I thrust into her, my hand moves up to cup her breast, feeling the weight of it in my hands and running my thumb over her nipple. It hardens with my touch, coming alive in my hands just like she's always seemed to. I nip the soft skin of her neck, and her thighs tighten around my hips.

"Fuck, you're perfect," I breathe out, moving back in to kiss her. "It's like you were made just for me."

I feel her starting to tighten around me, and I know she's

preparing for her release. I move my hips faster, with as much force as I can in the water, and it's only moments before she's coming undone again.

When she finishes, her eyes open and lock on mine. She wets her lips. "I was made for you, Logan. Nobody else." She shakes her head, and I feel my own release rising to the surface.

My hips take on a rhythm of their own, working harder and faster until I'm spilling everything I have into her. All movement stops as we both try to come down from our recent high. My heart is pounding against my chest, and our loud breathing is all that fills the night around us.

"It feels like I never left," I tell her, picking her up as I remove myself from her and set her on her feet. "When I'm with you, it feels like these last twenty years didn't even happen."

She nods. "I know. I feel the same way."

I pull her in for one last kiss, feeling the world stop spinning. Being together, it's always stopped all time. The world revolves around us now.

ELEVEN
ELLA

A week passes quickly with Logan back in town, and we spend every free moment together that our schedules allow. I work at the flower shop, spending more time telling Lisa all the details of our meetings than I do arranging flowers, and when the workday ends, I go over to see the day's progress on the house he's fixing up. Since the day of our dinner, we've had dinner together every night at my place or his. We've gone out a couple of times, but news of the divorce hasn't made its way through the town yet, so I put a halt to those for now. I haven't talked to Tom at all since Erin's graduation, but I have received a few more legal documents to sign when it comes to changing his beneficiary and other insurance type papers.

Erin has been spending more and more time with her boyfriend before she has to leave, and since I'm left all alone, I've been spending more and more time with Logan. Things are great between us. In a way, it's like being together makes us eighteen again. It's almost like he never left. And while we're having fun recreating our youth, we haven't exactly grown up enough to talk about what all this means, the bigger picture.

I have so many unanswered questions that I'm afraid to ask, like what happens when you sell the house? Are you leaving, or are you staying? Do you see any kind of future with me, or am I just a fun way to pass the time? Are you with me because you still love me, or is this all just a way to get a little piece of your youth back? Questions upon questions with no answers. And I know that if I ask them, he will give me an answer. He's never been the kind of guy to change the topic avoid any hard talks. But I'm also afraid of his answers. What if he says he's leaving when the house sells? Will that affect the time I have with him now? I'm not sure I can keep doing this if I know it's just going to end soon. So for now, I plan to just enjoy my time with him, knowing that eventually, these questions will answer themselves.

A part of me feels like he thinks the same way I do. He's as much afraid of my answers as I'm afraid of his. So for now, we both keep our questions locked away inside and just focus on enjoying the time we do have together.

Lisa and I lock up the flower shop at five sharp, and I get behind the wheel to go see the progress on the house like I've been doing every day. When I walk in, I don't find him. The living room is officially done, with new flooring, fresh paint, and a couch. The hallway floor is done, and the downstairs bathroom and kitchen are completely clean with a new fridge and stove. I peek out the kitchen window to find him out back, tending to the yard. I walk out the back door and stop to watch him for a moment. I burn the image into my brain of him in his loose-fitting jeans as he drags a rake across the ground shirtless, his back and biceps flexing with every movement.

I let out a loud whistle, giving him a little catcall, and he turns around to see me with a smile. "Like what you see?"

I shrug, playing indifferent. "Did I mention I'm looking for a gardener for my place? Uniform is similar to what you're wearing now," I tease, motioning up and down his body as I walk closer.

He laughs and pulls me in for a kiss. "Did you see the upstairs?"

I pull back, flashing him a look. "Are you hitting on me? 'Cause that's a must for anyone I hire."

He laughs and rolls his eyes. "No, seriously. I tore everything out today."

"Ohhh, I must see. Show me your bedroom, Logan." I say it all flirty and breathy.

He laughs but drops the rake to take me inside.

He leads me up the stairs, and already, it looks different. The old carpet has been torn out and is down to the bare, unfinished hardwood. The photos have been taken off the walls, and both the bedroom doors and bathroom door are standing open, rooms completely empty.

"What'd you do with all the stuff?" I ask, walking into what used to be his room.

"Pitched it. Well, not all of it. Some of the stuff I packed up into boxes and stashed in the downstairs closet."

I spin in a circle, taking in the empty room. "So, how long until you have the whole thing finished?"

He shrugs as he leans against the doorframe. "If I keep this pace, another week or two. But if something slows me down..." he says, walking closer. "There's no telling how long it could take. Hell, it may never get finished." He wraps his arms around me and pulls me to his chest.

I squeal from the quick movement, but I wrap my arms around his neck and kiss his delicious lips. I don't know what it is about him, but when we're together, everything else falls away. I don't think about the last twenty-two years. I don't think about my daughter going off to college or the divorce I'm going through. The whole world just falls away, and we stay protected in our own little bubble. Holding me against the wall, he pushes my dress up my hips and moves my panties to the side. Even though we were in this exact position just yesterday, I can't help but want him again. When we're together, I feel like I'm home.

"MY PLACE FOR DINNER?" I ask as I fix my clothing after we've finished. "I think Erin is going to be home, so it'll just be the three of us."

He pulls his jeans up his hips and tightens his belt. "Yeah, okay. I need to shower first though."

I motion for him to go ahead. "Be my guest."

He smirks as he walks past me, back downstairs to the only finished shower in the house. An idea hits me, and I giggle as I head down after him. After I hear the water come on, I strip out of my clothes in the hallway and walk into the tiny bathroom. I pull back the curtain and step in behind him. His head is bowed forward as he washes his hair. When he turns around, he has water dripping into his eyes and he's squinting, but it doesn't stop him from checking me out.

"Ready for round two already, huh?" His hands find my hips, and he pulls me against his chest.

I shrug. "It just occurred to me that I haven't seen you fully naked since we were kids."

He releases me and takes a step back, holding out his arms as if he's saying, *Check out the goods*. He smirks and spins in a circle so I can get the full view of him and all of his hard muscles as water runs over them. I have to say, he is quite sexy. His arms are completely covered in black tattoos, from his shoulders to his wrists. He has another black-and-white tattoo of the American flag on his pecs, just above his nipple, and a tattoo of an eagle in the center of his upper back, just below his neck. But the rest of him is untouched.

"Do you approve?" he asks, smirk still in place.

I smile. "I do. And you?" I ask, spinning in a circle like he did.

His smirk is now a full-blown smile. "You know I do," he says, moving in for a kiss.

I kiss him quickly but pull away to ask. "Where'd you get all these tattoos?"

He shrugs. "Wherever I was at the time. I was stationed in

Germany for a while, but I stayed mostly in the US. Texas, North Carolina, Hawaii."

"I've never really been attracted to tattoos before, but I don't know. They look good on you."

He laughs. "I'm glad you approve. Maybe it's time to brand that pretty skin of yours." He trails his fingers along my collarbone, and I shudder.

"I don't know about that. My mom would kill me."

He rolls his eyes. "Your mom is gone, and I think it's time you start living the way you want. If you want one, get it. If not, tell me to fuck off."

"Can I say... fuck me instead?" I flash him a smile.

"Oh, sweetheart. I hope you say that one a lot."

WE'RE BACK at my place, and the three of us are lounging in the living room. Erin is sitting in the oversized lounge chair while Logan and I are on the couch. We each have a plate in our hands that contains pizza, bread sticks, and hot wings. Erin and Logan picked out the movie we're watching. A horror flick, of course. She did it so she can laugh at me when I get scared. She knows I never watch anything scary, but of course, horror is Logan's favorite movie genre too. If she hadn't been born years after he'd left, I'd wonder if she belongs to him. She has more in common with Logan than she does her own father, but I guess that's because he wasn't actually around much.

I butt out of their conversation as they talk all things horror and give each other spoilers—whatever that means—on movies the other hasn't seen yet. Even though I couldn't care less about the movie or what they're talking about, I do enjoy seeing them interact together. Erin really seems to open up to him, almost like she's known him her whole life, but I guess I've told her so much about him over the years that she probably feels like she does. And

Logan, while being a little awkward toward her at first, really begins to warm up. It's like it took him a minute to wrap his mind around the thought that I have an eighteen-year-old daughter, the same age I was when he last saw me. But he shows her nothing but respect and really listens when she talks where most guys would tune her out.

He laughs and she giggles and they get along like they're the best of friends. By the end of the night, she decides to head up to bed and pulls me into the kitchen.

"What's up?" I ask, carrying in empty pizza boxes.

"I just wanted to let you know that I support you. I think Logan is a good guy, and I think he'll really keep you company and take care of you after I leave."

"Aw, hun. Thank you," I say pulling her in for a hug.

"I love you, Mom. And I didn't want you to think that I was feeling weird or anything about the whole divorce thing and now this guy hanging around. I like him, so it's cool," she says, pulling away.

"Thank you. That's means a lot to me."

She starts to walk off but spins back around. "But if you think I want to have a sibling at the age of eighteen, you're crazy. Condoms are in the bathroom drawer." She flashes me a smile and takes off for her room.

Logan walks into the kitchen with the plates and glasses from dinner. "What was that about?"

"Oh, that was just my daughter reminding me that she doesn't want a little brother or sister and telling me to use condoms." I laugh about the last part.

"What?" Logan says, his eyes wide and suddenly on high alert, causing me to laugh.

"She just has a weird sense of humor. Takes after her mom 'cause we both know her dad doesn't have a sense of humor at all," I say, wrapping him up in my arms and looking up at him. "Want to stay here tonight?"

"With your daughter in the house?" He looks up at the ceiling.

"What? It's not like we're going to be swinging from the light fixtures or something. Just a harmless sleepover."

"Thank you for the offer, but I have an early delivery coming in the morning, and I have to be there to sign for it or they'll ship it back. And I'm not paying double shipping on a shower." He leans in and presses his lips to mine. "Want me to help you clean up?"

"No, I'm fine. I'll just throw these boxes out and throw everything else in the dishwasher."

"You sure?"

"I'm good. Get home to your sofa since you're rejecting my big, soft, warm bed with me in it naked."

He rolls his eyes. "You're killing me."

I laugh and show him the door. "See you tomorrow."

"Bye," he says, giving me one last kiss before walking out.

TWELVE
LOGAN

On my walk home, I can't help but think about how happy I am. It's been a long time since I've felt any kind of positive emotion. For the last twenty-two years, I've felt nothing but sadness, guilt, anger, and hostility. I never thought I'd come back here because I was sure that El hated me. But coming back set things in motion. It made me open my eyes to the world around me and not just stay tucked away in the bubble I've been living in. I found out secrets from my past and made my way back into her heart.

El and I have been having the time of our lives acting like we're still just kids, but we're not kids anymore. We're adults with real lives. We haven't talked much about what this could mean for our future, and I'm not sure if that's on purpose or not. Is she afraid to talk about the future because she isn't sure I'll be in it? Do I want to be in it? Can I live the rest of my life here, in our hometown? It's a long way from living in a hut on a remote island in Hawaii. Not only that, but living in the house that she has shared with him for the last twenty years? Sleep in his room, in his bed? I guess it should've all been mine anyways.

Does El even want to stay here after her daughter leaves? She used to have big plans of going off to college, and then she wanted to travel the world before settling down anywhere. And this little town wasn't on the list of anywhere. She wanted out just as badly as I did. Is that still the case, or has she given up on that dream long ago?

I imagine being able to travel the world with her by my side. We could live in Hawaii together, watching the sunset every night. I could show her New York, California, and everything in between. Surely, she has a friend here who could take care of things while she's gone. Suddenly, I just want to do everything we said we'd do all those years ago. Every promise is at the forefront of my mind, ready to be acted upon.

———

IN THE MORNING, I receive my final shipment. This is the last order I'll be making, and soon, this house will be done, and there will be nothing holding me here. Except her. In this shipment, I get all the flooring to complete the upstairs. I get the new tub and shower combo for the bathroom, new toilet, vanity, and sink. I get a few sheets of drywall that need replacing and the items needed to patch a leak in the roof. The leak is why I had to rip out of the carpeting and replace the drywall. But for as long as this house sat empty, it's still in good shape. I guess Dad knew what he was doing when he built it.

I start with the flooring in the hallway and follow it into the master bedroom. By noon, the heat of the day gets unbearable, and I have to take a break to cool down and get something in my stomach. I retreat out to the backyard under the big shade tree to drink some water and have a sandwich for lunch.

As I eat, I look over the space that I've slowly been working on when I'm not in the house. The lawn has been cleaned up of all sticks, leaves, and overgrown grass. It's been raked, mowed, and raked again. The rose bushes are really taking off, and the fallen section of fence has been rehung and replaced. It's just like I remember it being when I was a kid, other than the missing grill and patio furniture, but I have no plans of replacing those things since I plan on selling. I've given the old swing on the porch a fresh set of white paint, and I've pressure-washed the back of the house so the light-blue siding is fresh and clean, sparkling against the white trim and door.

After lunch, I decide to take a break from the house for a while since the heat is only getting worse in there. I go to the front yard to straighten it up. I do the usual routine of raking and then mowing with the lawn mower I borrowed from the neighbor's kid. Next, I weed around the house, garage, and unkept flower beds that line the front of the house. After that, the sun is starting to go down, but I use what little light I have to rake up the clippings and bag them all to set on the curb.

I notice the time on my watch reads 7:57, so I head inside for a shower, wondering why El didn't stop by after work like she usually does. After showering and dressing, I bag up all my clothes and throw them over my shoulder to hit up the laundromat. I get the washers started and run across the street to the diner to grab some dinner.

I sit in the corner booth and look over the menu, ordering the special of all-you-can-eat fish with fries, hush puppies, beans, and slaw. I'm just tucking the menu back behind the napkin holder when someone says my name.

"Logan? Is that you?"

I look up in time to see a woman walking closer. She looks familiar, but I can't for the life of me remember her name.

"It is you, isn't it?" she asks when she comes to a stop at my table.

"Yeah, and you are?"

She laughs like I'm trying to play a trick on her. "I'm Tammy. Tammy Melville, remember me? We went to school together."

"Oh, right. Of course. How have you been?" I ask, racking my brain to try and pull up any memory I have of her.

"I'm great, but forget about me. How have you been? Where have you been?" she asks, pushing her brown hair behind her ear as she sits down in my booth, across from me.

"I joined the military and have been stationed all over these last twenty years."

Her eyes are wide and she's wearing a big smile. "I've always had a thing for a man in uniform," she says, but when I don't reply, she adds on, "What's brought you back to town?"

"My father's house, actually. The city said if I didn't do something with it, then they would demolish it. So I'm here, working on it with plans to sell it when I finish."

The waitress sets my plate down in front of me, and I grab my rolled-up silverware to begin eating.

"Well, isn't this a nice surprise. Have you seen El yet? Did you know that she married Tom?"

I laugh. "I have seen El, and yes, I did know that. A lot of changes in twenty years. I didn't expect her to sit around and wait on me to get my shit together." I pick up a piece of fish and take a bite.

"Seems to me like you have your shit together just fine." She flashes me a smile and leans forward, reaching for my hand while giving me a glimpse down her shirt. Her hand takes mine while the other skims her fingers across the top. I look down at our hands and back to her.

Now I remember her. She was always the girl that kept trying to get me to cheat on El when she wasn't around. I can't believe she hasn't changed.

I tug my hand away from hers. "Looks like not everything changes after all."

"What?" She smiles. "You're not with El anymore, right?"

"I'm actually just trying to enjoy my meal. So, if you wouldn't mind..."

The waitress is back, filling up my drink, and she looks over at Tammy. "Leave the poor guy alone, Tammy. Don't make me kick you out for harassing the customers again."

Tammy rolls her eyes. "Fine, but I wasn't harassing him. He's an old friend, and something tells me we have unfinished business." She stands and leaves the restaurant.

I flash the waitress a smile. "Thank you."

She laughs. "No problem. You're not the first guy Tammy has attached herself to in here." She turns and walks away, leaving me to eat in peace.

After I finish up, I go back to the laundromat and move my laundry from the washers to the dryers. I sit down with a magazine by the window to kill some time. I lose interest in the magazine after a few minutes, and I look out the window, noticing a small light in the flower shop that's been left on. Upon closer inspection, I see El's car still parked outside.

I stand up and toss the magazine down onto the table before walking out the door and over to the shop. I tug on the handle. The door is locked and doesn't budge, but I can see a light coming from the back room. I raise my hand and knock a couple of times. Just as I'm about to turn around and leave, thinking that maybe the light was left on accidentally, the swinging door opens and El comes walking out. She unlocks the door and opens it with a smile. "Hey," she greets me.

"Hey, working late?"

She nods as she locks the door behind me. "Yes, I've been asked to donate the flower arrangements for the Summer Bash this weekend in the town square." She heads back to the back room with me following along behind her.

"They still do that?"

"Every year. Right along with the Winter Wonderland Festival, the Spring Fling Celebration, and the Fall Harvest." She turns and smiles over her shoulder at me.

"Still no carnival rides for the kids?" I ask, remembering how we used to get bummed because the town never did anything fun, causing us to always travel to other towns.

"Nope. There will be food and vendors selling their handmade jewelry, clothes, home decor, and toys. All the top favorites will be there, like the caramel popcorn stand, Mrs. Mary's homemade candy apples, and funnel cakes. Plus, there is the auction, the dance contest, and all the homemade games. I always enjoy it," she admits.

"Well, if you enjoy it, let's go together," I say, pulling her against my chest and enjoying the way my heart pounds when we touch.

"Yeah?" she asks, wrapping her arms around my neck.

"Yeah," I agree, moving in to press my lips to hers.

THIRTEEN
ELLA

I wake in the morning still tired. I worked too late last night, trying to get all the arrangements done for this weekend. I didn't get home until after midnight, and it's only going on six now. That isn't enough sleep for this fragile mind. I trudge to the shower and wash off. After I get out, I find that I have horrible dark circles under my eyes, so after brushing my hair, I cover them up with concealer, add some mascara and lip gloss, and pull on some clothes.

Erin is still asleep when I grab my coffee and head out the door. I'm at the store by seven and let myself in. I came in an hour early to get back to work on the arrangements. I lock the door behind me and go into the back to see the two dozen arrangements I've already made of tiger lilies, sunflowers, lavender, orange roses, and greenery.

I walk around the table and try making room in the fridge, but there's no luck. I might be able to squeeze in one more arrangement, but I highly doubt it without taking a chance on smashing them. I walk out onto the sales floor and look at the coolers in there that hold the grab-and-go arrangements, but I just filled them earlier this week. While there are a few spots open, it's nothing compared to the space I'll need.

Lisa unlocks the door and walks in. "Hey, hon. Whatcha doing?"

"I came in early to get back to work for the Summer Bash, but I'm out of room." I motion toward the cooler.

"Hmmm," she says, walking around the counter to put her things down.

"You should call Mrs. Mary. She has all those antique coolers in her store. Maybe she'll turn them on for you to use. I mean, she's just as into the town festivities as the rest of us."

"That's a good idea," I say, going for the door to walk over to the antique store. The store doesn't open until eight, but I have a feeling she's already in there and setting up. I knock on the door, and it takes her a while to answer given she's close to two hundred years old. She unlocks it and opens it with a smile.

"What can I do for you, Ella?"

"Good morning, Mrs. Mary. I have a favor to ask."

She laughs. "Well, I don't know what I can do, but ask away."

"I'm in charge of providing the flowers for the Summer Bash…"

"Oh, I know, dear. Your flowers are so beautiful. You're just as talented as your mother was. I'm sure everything will be breathtaking."

I nod. "I'm sure it will, too, if I can keep the flowers from dying."

"Huh?"

"Well, that's why I'm here, Mrs. Mary. I've run out of space in the coolers that I'm using to store the arrangements for the big day. Is there any way I could talk you into turning on those antique coolers to use until Friday? There's no way I can make all those arrangements the day they're due, but if I don't have some place to store them, they'll be dead before the big day comes."

"Oh, well… I guess we can try. Come in and help me, would ya?"

I follow her into the store. She has four big coolers, all of them different brands. I plug them in and watch as the compressor kicks on, cooling down the inside.

"Will Tom make it home for the bash, dear?" Mrs. Mary asks as she opens her register.

"Uhh, no, I don't think he will," I say, keeping my attention on the cooler.

"What a shame. That man just works too hard."

"Yeah, actually, Mrs. Mary," I say, walking over to the counter, "Tom and I... we're actually going through a divorce right now. I don't know if he will be returning to this town as he's living in London with his new girlfriend."

She gasps. "Oh, honey. I'm so sorry."

I hold up my hand. "Please, don't be. It's been a long time coming. He was never home, and I was on my own more than anything anyway."

She nods. "That's right. And you're a strong, smart woman who doesn't need a man to take care of her. You're just like I was."

I smile. "Well... if you wouldn't mind spreading the word, this isn't the kind of conversation I want to keep having if you know what I mean."

"Of course, honey. Consider it done."

"Thank you, Mrs. Mary. I'm going to let these cool off, and I'll bring over some of the arrangements in a bit."

"Okay, dear. I'll be here," she says as I'm walking out.

I walk back into the shop. "I got cooler space!"

"Woo-hoo," Lisa cheers as I walk into the back room to start on more arrangements.

The day passes quickly with how busy I am, and I end up staying long into the night just like the night before. Around nine, there's a knock on the door, and I go to answer it with an idea of who it may be. On the other side of the glass is Logan, wearing a sweet smile.

"Hey," I say, opening the door and allowing him to step inside.

He holds up his hands, which are holding a brown paper bag and a drink carrier with two drinks. "Thought you could use some dinner."

I smile as I shut the door and lock it. "Thank you. I'm starving." I lead him back, and he places the bag of food on the table and starts removing the drinks from their holder. I drag both stools over to the table.

"How many arrangements did you make today?" he asks, handing over a burger and some fries.

"I made twelve yesterday and sixteen today. That means that I have to make another twenty-two by tomorrow evening when the party starts."

"Wow. You think you'll get it all done?"

"Oh, I'll get it all done. I just ran to the store across the street and stocked up on Red Bull to pull an all-nighter. I figured I'd work through the night, leave early in the morning, sleep the day away, and wake up in time to hand over the arrangements and attend the party."

He whistles. "Damn, living like you're seventeen again, huh?"

I laugh. "You know how long it's been since I pulled an all-nighter? Ugh, years. I guess Erin was probably still a baby and not sleeping through the night. She seemed to have her days and nights mixed up. She'd stay up most of the night, and I'd have to be here working the whole next day. But I was lucky and had a lot of help from the town. I used to have a little playpen set up in that corner for her."

His eyes widen. "You had to bring her to work with you?"

I nod. "I had to. Tom was gone working weeks at a time, and my mom had already passed. There wasn't anyone else. It was rough for a while, but we made it."

"I hate that you had to live like that," he says quietly, "and all because I listened to Tom when I should have listened to my heart."

I reach over and place my hand on his. "You're here now. That's all that matters."

MY HARD WORK and good planning paid off, because it's going on five o'clock and I've handed all of the arrangements over to be set up. I'm also fully dressed and ready to attend the Summer Bash just outside the shop doors. Looking out the window fills me with joy and excitement. Seeing all the flowers in place, the strung-up lights, and handmade booths set up almost feels magical. I turn to face Lisa. "How do I look?" I spin around, giving her a full view of my white summer dress that has a pink flower pattern. It fits snugly across my chest and stomach and flows around my legs, down below my knees. It's sleeveless and makes my tanned skin look that much tanner and richer. I paired the dress with a pair of wedged sandals and left my hair down in soft curls.

"You look hot! Logan is going to eat you up tonight."

My face blushes as I wave off her comment.

"How are things going with him anyway? Are you hitting it off like old times?"

"Things are good. We've somehow managed to push the past away and just focus on the here and now."

"And what does Tom think of this newly rekindled relationship of yours?"

I frown. "How would Tom know? We barely spoke when we were married. Going through a divorce hasn't changed that any."

The bell above the door rings, and I spin around to find Logan standing there with a six-pack. He smiles and hands it over. "I was going to bring you flowers, but I figured you had enough of those. So this can go in your hidden stash for our next late night."

I smile, a giggle slipping out. "Thank you. That's very thoughtful." I turn around and hand it to Lisa. "Would you put this in the cooler for me?"

"Sure. Have fun, you two."

Logan holds out his elbow, and I slip my arm around his as he leads me outside and to the center of the square.

We walk around, just taking everything in. There are homemade carnival games, like popping the balloon with a dart, throwing a softball at stacked milk jugs, and tossing the ping pong ball into little bowls to win a fish. There are homemade snack stands offering up hot chocolate, candy apples, caramel popcorn, and the rest of the typical carnival food. There are little stands set up, mostly the vendors from town, selling jewelry, accessories, and home decor. And there's a band playing in the center of it all on the gazebo. There are tables scattered around it so you can watch a live show while you eat, and everything is lit up with white lights and decorated beautifully with my flowers.

Logan and I find a table and have a seat. Erin happens to be walking by with her boyfriend, and they stop to say hi.

"The flowers look beautiful, Mom."

I smile as I gaze around at them. "They really do, don't they," I agree.

"We're going for a candy apple and some hot chocolate," she says, taking her boyfriend's hand.

"That sounds like a good combination," I joke as they walk away.

"You remember the last time we were at this thing?" Logan asks, taking my hand in his.

I think back on it. "I do," I say around a smile. "We danced to the band, shared a stolen glass of wine, and ended up making love behind the candy apple stand."

He laughs. "I remember getting home and finding these sticky spots all over me. I couldn't figure out what it was until I realized it was the sticky candy they coat the apples with."

I laugh. "Oh my God. Me too! Why was it so sticky back there?"

He laughs and shrugs. "No idea. That stuff was like wax though. I lost more body hair that night than I had grown," he jokes, only making me laugh harder. "Want a drink?"

"I'd love one."

He's back moments later with two glasses of wine, and we sit and watch the band play while drinking and talking about the good times. Time passes quickly, and the wine goes down smoothly. We talk, laugh, joke, and tease. It's one of the best nights I've had in a long time. I'm feeling a good buzz when he stands up and holds out his hand. "Dance with me for old time's sake?"

I smile, sliding my hand into his, and let him walk me up to the empty grass space in front of the gazebo. He spins me around and pulls me to his chest as we start swaying back and forth.

I'm having fun being in the moment with him, but I can't help but wonder what the town is thinking, seeing me drinking and dancing with a man who isn't my husband. I wonder how far Mrs. Mary's gossip got. But the thought slips away when I notice more and more people gathering around us to dance as well.

It seems like the whole crowd has taken a hint from us, and they've all abandoned their tables to join us on the dance floor.

"You're beautiful, you know that?" Logan whispers in my ear, and I let my eyes fall closed to enjoy the way his warm breath feels blowing against my soft skin.

"You always say that."

"And I always mean it. You're as beautiful as the day I met you. And I can't help but feel myself falling a little more in love with you every single day." His lips move to mine, and he kisses me soft and slow. It's not hard or rushed in any way. This is him taking his time, being in the moment with me, and showing me how much he still cares. It causes my heart to race and the butterflies in my stomach to take flight. Goosebumps prickle my skin, and a shiver races over my spine. The kiss breaks and we go back to just holding one another close and moving to the beat of the soft song. When it ends, he keeps my hand in his and leads me back to the table.

"Another round?" he asks and of course I agree.

As he walks off to get us some more wine, I can't help but think back on the last twenty-two years of my life without him. If we had somehow managed to stay together back then, would we be doing what we're doing right now? Would I still be head over heels in love with him? There's no way to know for sure, but something tells me yes. We were meant to be.

FOURTEEN
LOGAN

I leave her at the table while I go to get us two more glasses of wine. I'm standing in line, waiting for my turn, when a man stops at my side. I turn to look over at him. It's Tom.

"Logan, what are you doing back here?" he asks me, sliding his hands into his suit pants. He's changed quite a bit over the years. He used to be tall and thin but fairly built and toned. His dark hair was always long and messy. Now, he's gained some weight, getting a little round around the belly, and his hair is short and styled with some gray peppering the strands.

"Tom, didn't think I'd run into you... here of all places. I think we have some things to talk about after all these years."

He nods and runs a hand across his jaw. "Yeah, I thought you might say that."

I get out of line, and we walk off to the side to have a few minutes alone. He spins around to face me. "You have to understand something," he starts, but I cut him off. He doesn't get to talk first this time.

"No, it's my turn to talk. You did all the talking back then, and look where we are." I motion around us. "How could you do that to me, man? You were supposed to be my best friend. You were supposed to keep an eye on her and make sure she was okay, not steal her the first time I had my back turned."

"Your back turned?" he asks, his eyes wide. "You didn't just have your back turned, Logan, and we both know it. You left, and when you left, you changed. You weren't the same guy after your dad passed, and we both knew it. I knew that if you came back to her in the condition you were in, you'd only hurt her. So I did what I had to do. I stepped up. I was there for her. I did what you couldn't or didn't want to do. I made her happy when she was crying over you."

"No, what you did was manipulate us both. You were in her ear telling her I didn't want her. And you were in mine telling me she had found someone new and to move on. These last twenty years have been nothing but a lie fed to us by you. And for what? So you could stay gone for work and never be there for her? So it could end up in divorce right when she needs you the most?"

He doesn't reply. He just cocks his jaw in anger because he knows that everything I'm saying is right.

"You know what, Logan? It all boils down to this. You weren't here, and she was going to move on one way or another. If it wasn't with me, it would've been with someone else. And yes, our marriage hadn't been perfect and it fell apart, but that's something that happens. You honestly think you can tell me that if you'd come back and gotten with her then, that you'd still be together today?" He laughs. "I mean, she's good, but she's not that good." And I know exactly what he means by that, and it pisses me off. I can't hold back my anger anymore. It's been buried too long. It's time he gets what he deserves.

I pull my fist back and send it flying forward, hitting him square in the jaw. It stuns him for a moment, but he shakes it off, and he changes from the old man he is now to the young kid I used to know in an instant. He comes flying at me, wrapping his arms around my stomach and tackling me to the ground.

We're drawing attention now, and people are yelling and gathering around us as we roll around on the ground, both of us fighting for our place on top. He swings and lands a hit to my side, but it's doesn't even faze me. I buck my hips upward and he falls over, allowing me to climb on top and send another punch to his gut. He groans with the force of the hit, but unfortunately, neither of us get another shot in because I'm being pulled off by another man.

"Chill, man. Calm down," he says as he holds me in an arm bar, allowing Tom to climb to his feet.

"I'm good. Let me go," I demand.

The guy releases me and I stand, watching as Tom stays bent over, trying to recover from the gut punch.

"If you think you're coming back for her, you've lost your mind. You left this time and now I'm here. She's mine and I'm taking her back," I tell him, going to get back in line to get our wine.

I dust my clothes off and get us two glasses of wine. I go back to our table where she's still sitting, talking to Erin.

"Thank you," she says when I set down her glass of wine. "Was the line long? What took so long?"

"Tom's here," I state, taking a drink of my wine and trying my best to calm down.

"Tom's here?" she asks, quickly followed by Erin asking, "Daddy? Where?" She starts looking around.

"He was over by the wine stand," I tell them, pointing in that direction.

Erin gets up and starts heading over. I watch her go, and when I turn my head, I find El looking at me. "What?"

"What happened? I know if the two you saw one another, something must have gone down."

I shrug. "A couple punches. Nothing too crazy."

Her eyes double in size and her mouth falls open. "You two got into a fight?" She seems to have forgotten who I am.

I let out a long breath and sit up straight. "Look, we were talking, and he was saying some really shitty stuff. When he insulted you, I couldn't help it. I lost my temper. I'm sorry, but the asshole got what he deserved after all these years. And it wasn't a big deal. I punched him, he punched me, someone pulled me off, and it was over."

I almost expect her to yell at me. I'm surprised when her lips turn up into a smile, and she laughs. "Man, I always miss the good stuff."

"You're not mad?" I ask, a smile starting to spread.

"No. It couldn't have been too bad. I didn't notice. Plus, if he was being an ass, it's about time someone punched him for it. He's gone too long without being put in his place."

I lean over and cup her cheeks, bringing her lips to mine.

The two of us don't let the altercation ruin our good time. In fact, the night only gets better. We drink, talk, laugh, and dance. By the time the band is wrapping up, we're both a little too buzzed to drive. She decides to leave her car at the shop, and the two of us walk back to my place. I've made big promises to pull out the double bed on the couch.

On the walk, she calls Erin.

"Hey, hun. You find your dad?" There's a long pause. "Well, that's just like your dad to interrogate you about me. He couldn't be an adult and ask me himself," she says, taking a jab at him. "Are you good there, or do you have a friend you can stay with? I think I'm going to avoid the fight tonight and stay somewhere else." She waits another minute before saying, "Okay, hun. Call me if you need me. Love you too." She hangs up the phone and puts it in her purse.

"Well?" I ask.

"Well, Tom is at the house, packing up his office, Erin says. He interrogated her, wanting to know when you got into town, whether or not you've been to the house, if we're seeing one another or not."

"What did she tell him?"

"Oh, Erin doesn't lie, so she told the truth, which is fine. I would never ask my daughter to lie for me. I did nothing wrong. I've been faithful for years, which is more than I can say for him. And this thing between us, it didn't start until after I signed the divorce papers. My conscience is clean."

"But you think there will be a fight?"

She shrugs as I tug open the screen door and unlock the front door. "I don't expect him to be here and not give me a hard time over this. I'm sure he's been expecting me to be a mess and lost without him. He doesn't realize that I've lived on my own for twenty years, so this divorce isn't really any different. But enough about him," she says, spinning around to face me while wrapping her arms around my neck. "Tonight is about you and me. Now, I believe you promised me a pull-out bed?" She gives me that smile of hers, and everything else in my head flies right out the window.

I pull out the hideaway bed and get the blankets and pillows out of the closet. I toss the pillows down at the top of the mattress and lay the blanket out across the bed. When I turn around, she's already kicked off her shoes and is pulling her dress above her head, revealing her sexy lace panties and bright-white bra.

I feel my body come alive from watching her. I tug my shirt over my head as I cross the room, pulling her against me. Our lips find one another's and they lock together, creating the perfect moment. My hands move up to tangle in her hair as I lay her back across the bed. My lips break free to pepper her soft, tan skin with kisses. My lips travel from her neck, down her chest, and to the junction between her legs, stripping off clothes as I go.

I run my tongue between her folds and spread her wetness. She lets out a muffled cry as her hands fist the sheets. I flick my tongue against her clit, and her hips lift up off the mattress. When I suck her hard nub into my mouth, she comes undone in my hands. Her cries grow louder and her body becomes uncontrollable. She's wiggling beneath me, moving her hips up and down with my movements. Her thighs are squeezing my head, making it impossible to breathe, but I don't mind. I'd die to pleasure her.

When her body goes limp, I pull back, kissing my way back up her body. She's so wet for me that I slip in with little effort. Connecting as one makes my entire body hard, and it's difficult to hold myself back when all I want to do is bury myself deep inside her over and over until neither of us can move.

"Logan," she whispers from beneath me.

My eyes find hers in the darkened room.

"I still love you," she whispers, lifting her head up to kiss me.

FIFTEEN

ELLA

I wake in the morning, feeling sore, tired, and partially hungover, but completely satisfied. Even with as rough as my body is feeling, my mind, heart, and soul are happy. I don't move or open my eyes. I want to lie here a little while longer, just soaking everything in.

Logan rolls over and kisses my shoulder. "Good morning, beautiful."

A smile forms on its own, and I roll over to my back. When I open my eyes, he's hovering above me looking hot as hell. Since it's bright and early and he hasn't gotten out of bed yet, he has a dark five-o'clock shadow growing on his angular jaw.

"Mmm, anyone every tell you how sexy you look first thing in the morning?" I ask.

He smirks. "Me? What about you with your dirty sex hair and fuck-me eyes?" he asks, leaning down and kissing me.

I break our kiss. "So, are you going to listen to my eyes, or do I have to say it out loud?"

His smirk grows. "I think I'd like to hear you say it." He kisses my neck in a teasing way.

"Fuck me, Logan," I whisper into his ear, knowing that the softness of my words and the feeling of my breath against his skin will tease him more than anything.

His mouth smashes against mine as he positions himself on top of me. One roll of his hips is all it takes to have me seeing stars. After twenty-two years, I'm finally home.

———

LEAVING his house feels like leaving a dream world. I could have stayed locked inside a little longer by letting him walk me back to my car, but it seemed pointless when it's only a block away. I make it back to the car quickly, and I get inside to make the drive home. The whole way, I'm secretly praying that Tom has gotten his things and left already.

I pull into the drive and find Erin's car, but Tom's is nowhere to be seen. A part of me wonders if he took his spot in the garage like he always did before, but I don't bother checking. I'm sure walking in the house will tell me everything I need to know.

When I walk in, the place is quiet. Erin is on the couch, eating her breakfast, and she turns her head to look at me from over her shoulder.

"Is your dad still here?" I ask.

She nods. "He's in the office and he wants to see you."

Ugh. I feel defeated. I'm not in the mood to argue today. Not after my perfect night and morning. I should've stayed locked inside my dream world a little longer.

I walk in through his open office door. "You wanted to see me?" I ask, dropping my purse onto his desk and sitting in the chair in front of him.

"I've gathered all of my things in the office and the bedroom. I also took a few items that I would include in my half of the belongings. Here's a detailed list," he says, passing it over.

What the hell? This isn't the way things are done. We're supposed to go through stuff together, not just take what we want and write it on a piece of paper. As happy as I am to be ending things with Tom, I was actually looking forward to sitting down with him, sorting things out, talking about memories, and giving both of us the closure we need.

I don't want a reason to start a fight, though, so I take the paper and look over the list. He's already packed up the antique ship that sits on the mantel in the living room—thank God—the silver candlestick holders his mother gave us when we got married—kinda bummed but I guess they belong in his family—and his crystal brandy glasses that always stayed in his office—big whoop. My eyes scan the list, but there's nothing on here that I want or that is worth fighting over, so I look up at him and say, "Okay."

"Please sign it so I can deliver it to my lawyer." He hands over a pen.

I roll my eyes but take the pen and scratch my name across the paper. I hand him both items when I'm done. "So, that's it, huh? Twenty years of marriage wiped out with a couple of signatures."

"Pretty much," he agrees. "I've already paid the property taxes and the insurance for the year, so you don't have to worry about that. Erin's car is paid off, and I will keep up with the insurance payments along with her tuition for school. But everything else is falling on you. If she needs money, that's your job."

"Fine, Tom. I don't expect you to pay for everything."

He nods as he stands and tucks the papers into his briefcase. "Just make sure you remember that when Logan bleeds you dry." He grabs his briefcase and starts toward the door.

"Tom?" I ask, spinning around in my chair to face him.

He stops and looks at me with no emotion.

"Why'd you do it? All those years ago. Why lie to me and to Logan?"

He shrugs and lets out a deep breath like he's already tired of this conversation.

"Tell me, please. After everything, it's the least you could do."

He lets out another long breath that makes his shoulders fall. "Because I loved you, and I had always been jealous of him."

"Why?"

He shrugs. "He had it all. He was tall and good-looking, and all the girls wanted him, including you. He was popular, always invited to the parties, and the center of everyone's attention. And he was going to college on his own. It wasn't because his father was pulling strings like mine was. But what pissed me off the most was that he had you, the most beautiful girl in school. I couldn't take anything else from him, but I could take you. And I did." His lips turn up in the corners slightly.

I shake my head, not completely wrapping my head around it all. "You had plenty of girlfriends back in school. And if I remember correctly, you attended most parties."

He nods. "The girls were just using me to get close to him. And the parties, I wasn't invited. But people knew that if they invited Logan, I'd be coming, too, so they dealt with it. Goodbye, Ella. I hope you finally find the happiness you deserve after all these years." With that, he turns and walks away.

I hear Erin telling him goodbye from the living room, but I don't get up to see him out. Instead, I think back on everything he just told me. He ruined our lives for twenty-two years and all because he was a jealous kid? How could he even live with himself this long? Now, more than ever, I'm glad for this marriage to be over.

The moment I hear the door softly click behind him, I see everything in a whole new light. This room, it's no longer his office. All signs of him have been erased. His brandy and glasses are no longer on the cart in the corner. His shoes are no longer in the closet. His stupid antique ship is no longer on the mantle. This house is officially mine, all mine, and it's time I make some changes around here.

I switch chairs so I'm sitting behind the computer and am surprised to see that he's even erased all signs of him from the screen. I bring up the internet browser and check my accounts. Between savings and checking,

I have more than enough to give this place a little spruce. I pull up an online design tool and upload pictures of the office. It allows me to take things away and add things as I see fit. Instead of a boring home office, I'm going to create something I've always wanted. My own private library.

I call Logan and ask him to come over. By the time he gets here, I already have everything pulled off the walls and either set aside or thrown in the trash. He knocks on the door as he walks in. He takes in the sight before him.

"Whoa, what happened here?"

"I talked with Tom. Turns out the reason he lied to the both of us is because he was jealous of you in school. He took me because he said it was the only thing he could take from you. Can you believe that?" I ask, looking over my shoulder at him.

"I meant, what happened to the room?"

"Tom happened," I answer, "and it's time I erase him from this house and my life. I want to turn this room into my own private library. What do you think?" I set down the shelf I took down and walk over to him. "Would it be hard?"

He looks around. "Not at all. We could build some bookcases or buy them. However you want to do it."

I move to a corner of the room. "I want this corner to be my reading nook. I want a comfy chair and a table with a lamp. A room that's all mine and just for me."

He takes my hand and spins me around to face him, catching me in his arms. "If you want it, we'll do it." His lips press against mine, and for the first time all day, I can breathe. I no longer feel as if I'm being suffocated or held down. I'm free.

THREE MONTHS LATER...

The summer comes to an end, and it's time to see Erin off. I get up from my reading chair in my library and walk into the kitchen where she's packing her road trip snacks.

"Are you sure you don't want me to come with you?"

She laughs. "Mom, that's silly. You'd just have to turn around and fly back. Plus, Sarah's riding with me. She got accepted after another student pulled out."

I feel a little sad letting her go, but I know it's time. It's time for her to do something I never got the chance to. "Okay. Call me. A lot. Call me every morning before you get on the road and every night when you stop until you get there. And then call me every day so I know you're okay."

She smiles. "I will, Mom." She wraps her arms around my neck and pulls me in for a hug. I breathe her in deeply, already missing her. The house is going to be so quiet and empty without her.

"I'm going to miss you, kid."

She pulls back. "I have a feeling you'll be very well taken care of. Right, Logan?"

He's just walked into the room and comes up to stand behind me, placing his hands on my hips like he knows I need his strength.

"I swear," he replies, kissing the top of my head.

"Okay, guys. I'm burning daylight."

The three of us walk her out to the car and watch her climb behind the wheel. For the second time in my life, I watch my heart drive away to college, leaving me behind.

"Everything will be okay," he says from behind me.

"I know," I blubber. "I'm just sad. She's my baby and she's all grown up."

He spins me around to face him, his hands landing firmly on my hips. "Yeah, but now we're all alone again... just like we like," he reminds me with a kiss.

I never would have thought that I'd be getting married for a second time in my forties, but now that I have Logan and this ring on my finger, I wouldn't have it any other way. Sure, we may be rushing it a bit considering we've only been together for three months, but my heart has belonged to him for over twenty years, and I don't want to waste one more day of our lives together.

EPILOGUE
ELLA

"Ready to head out?" Logan asks, handing over a motorcycle helmet as I come to a stop at his side.

"Let's do it," I agree, taking the helmet and pulling it on. He takes his seat on the bike, and I climb on behind him. He kicks the motor over and it roars loudly, cutting through the silence of our small town.

He turns the bike around and we're off, ready to see the world like we always planned to do. Lisa has agreed to take care of the flower shop, and she's been with me for years so there is no better person to handle the job.

As we make our way through town, I can't help but view it through the eyes of the eighteen-year-old girl who stood on the side of the road and watched her heart drive away without her. In this moment, I'm not a forty-year-old woman with a daughter in college. I'm eighteen again, running away with the boy I love. Although now, the world doesn't seem so big and scary.

It doesn't matter where we end up because I know that I'll have him by my side for the rest of my life. And even though we've been cheated out of many years, something is better than nothing at all.

My arms are wrapped around his stomach as we drive around

the square, and I tighten my hold on him, enjoying this moment between us. Lisa is standing outside the store, sweeping the sidewalk, and she looks up with a smile and waves. Then we make a left turn, and we're officially on our way out of town. Finally, I get to go with him.

We drive the whole day, only stopping long enough to eat, use the bathroom, and refill the tank with gas. The sun is finally setting, and he pulls out the tent that's rolled up in the saddle bag. While I assemble it, he starts a fire, and we hunker down in front of it.

"I promise it won't be camping every night, but we're nowhere near a hotel tonight." He hands me a hot dog, and I put it on my stick to roast.

I laugh. "I don't mind. I like thinking that we're eighteen again, and this is exactly what we would've done. We wouldn't have had money for a hotel every night or fancy dinners. We're getting our youth back." I bump his shoulder with mine.

He smiles. "I like that. Maybe later we can sneak a few drinks and accidentally impregnate you," he jokes.

I smack his chest. "I don't think so, mister. I may be pretending to be eighteen, but I've figured out what causes that by now. Plus, Erin already said she doesn't want to be a big sister at this age. Now, had you been around when she was five, she would've been all for it," I joke, "but no, I want to spend our time just the two of us and get back every minute that was stolen from us."

"I like that too," he agrees, wrapping his arm around me as we roast our hot dogs in the fire. While we eat our food off of sticks, we pass a bottle of vodka back and forth. By the end of the night, I'm buzzed enough to sleep anywhere.

We cuddle up together in the tent on the hard ground, but he gives me all the softness I need. I rest my head against his chest, and the deep rhythm of his heart lulls me to sleep. I wake in the morning with a groan, now almost on top of him completely. He's wide awake, staring at the top of the tent.

I push my way off him. "Sorry," I mumble, rubbing my eyes.

He takes a deep breath and lets it out. "I was starting to get a little high from lack of oxygen."

I laugh and smack his arm. "Why didn't you wake me?"

He shrugs as he sits up. "You seemed comfortable."

"I was," I agree. "The ground was too hard."

"But my collarbone was as soft as a pillow," he teases. "We might want to stick to hotels from now on."

"Shut up. You enjoyed it."

"Yes, I did," he says, pressing a kiss to my lips before unzipping the tent.

We have a quick breakfast of eggs and bacon, which he fried over the fire with a cast iron skillet, then we pack up and head for the shower houses. I wash off quickly, with water so cold I had to. Then we meet back up at the tent to start on another day of riding into the sunset together.

As we ride, I think about how doing this back then would be different from doing it now. I'm sure my mother would have lost her mind knowing I was living on the road like a nomad. But now, I'm an adult and can enjoy it far more than I would've at eighteen. This time, there is nothing holding me back. I'm free for the first time in my life since I was eighteen, and even though I love my daughter more than the world itself, I enjoy finding little things about myself that I'd forgotten. Like, you don't have to have a well-balanced meal every day. Sometimes, just getting something edible in your system is all you need. You don't have to make your bed every morning. Today, we rolled it all away and stuffed it into a little pouch. And a cold shower isn't always bad, especially if you have someone there to keep you warm. The last twenty years of my life have been spent one way, and now, it's time for me to unlearn it and find out what works for me.

We hop back on the bike and hit the road again. The sights are beautiful. The sunset, spectacular. The night sky as I'm alone in the forest with the man I love suddenly seems different. Before, when I'd look up and see that black blanket covered in tiny little holes, I felt alone. But now, I don't feel alone anymore. It's no longer a blanket shutting me out from the world. Now, my whole world is under that blanket, and it's keeping us safe.

We do nothing but ride during the days and camp at night, learning about one another all over again. We talk about the old times we had together and about our time apart, and we discuss our future. We make a plan every night for where tomorrow will lead, but almost always, something derails our plans. It's too hot, it rains, we get a flat tire—

something always throws us off, but even in times like those, it teaches me an important lesson.

Life can't be planned. There's always going to be something that gets in the way. But what's important is that you never let it get you down. You have to keep working, keep fighting in order to get and keep what you want. And I know that I'll never again let something come between the two of us.

A week on the road turns into a month, and a month turns into three. We travel the country and see the sights, not coming home until early December. When we pull back into the driveway at my house, I feel like I could collapse. I let us in and everything is perfect, just like I knew it would be with Lisa keeping a close eye on everything. I fall onto the couch, and Logan walks in behind me, laughing.

"You seem glad to be home."

"I am," I say, but it's muffled by the couch cushion.

"I thought tonight at dinner we could plan our next adventure."

I roll over and look up at him. "Yeah, dinner... in five years, we'll do that."

He laughs but comes around the couch to sit beside me. "That's too bad. 'Cause I was thinking that now that we've seen the US, we could move on to Canada? Then maybe Europe. Just travel country to country, seeing the world like we always planned to."

I smile as I rest my head against his shoulder. "I do like the sound of that."

"So, dinner tonight?"

I nod in agreement. "Dinner tonight," I agree, "but first..." I stand up and take his hand in mine. "A hot shower!" I pull him along behind me, up the stairs and to my room. By the time I hit the door, I'm already stripping out of my clothes and tossing them on the floor behind me. I step into the shower and turn the water on. It's cold at first, but I don't even jump. I'm far too used to it now. The water heats quickly, though, and I turn around, letting my head fall back.

"Oh, this is amazing," I nearly moan, and he lets out a laugh as he steps in to join me.

"And I have all my shampoo and conditioners, hair masks, and shower lotions. Ahhh, I didn't know I was so spoiled."

He shakes his head. "Maybe on the next trip, we'll do it a little better. We'll fly and stay in hotels."

"Or we could get an RV. How cool would that be?"

He nods. "It would work for Canada, but I don't know how we'd get it across the ocean. Surely that would cost a pretty penny."

I shrug. "One vacation at a time."

His hand moves up to cup my jaw. "We have our whole lives. There's no need to rush." He presses his lips against mine, and just like always, I'm lost in him completely.

I wrap my arms around his neck and pull him underneath the water with me, his bare chest pressing against mine. His hands land on my hips and then move around to my lower back, dipping down further to squeeze my ass.

"We're clean enough, right?" he asks, picking me up against him and carrying me to bed.

OVER THE YEARS, we travel to some pretty amazing places. We've seen all of the US, and we've been through Canada, Europe, Germany, and Australia. But we always come back home to our little town. Even all these years later, I run the flower shop, and Logan has started his own construction company. He managed to flip his father's house, selling it for three times what his father bought it for.

Erin is doing well. She graduated from Harvard and moved to New York to become a lawyer for some fancy company. She loves the job and she travels constantly. She met a man soon after she graduated, and they fell in love and got married. I have a feeling the traveling will begin to slow with her since my first grandchild is due this summer.

And my ex-husband, well, he's as good as he's always been. After our divorce, he rushed back to marry his mistress, but word around town is that their marriage didn't last long at all. No sooner were the papers filed than he had found another mistress. The old mistress wasn't happy about the turn of events and filed for divorce. Since it was a rushed process, there was no prenup, meaning she took him for everything she could. I never wish ill will on anyone, but in this case, he got exactly what he deserved. He's still working and traveling, trying to keep up with the appearance that his life is as good as it's always been, but I know the truth. He travels on the company's dime, and he's sold all his fancy cars and valuable watches. He lives a much more normal life. Who would've thought all it would take was two divorces and losing everything?

But Logan and I don't like to focus on the negative. We've managed to forgive him for manipulating us both and stealing years of our lives. All that matters is that we're together now and will be for the rest of our lives.

I walk into the flower shop, and Lisa's head pops up. Her eyes stretch wide and her mouth drops open. "You're back!" she yells, running at me with her arms held out.

She pulls me in for a hug, and I can't help but laugh.

"You'd think I'd been gone for years," I joke.

"You basically have," she says, pulling back. "Tell me everything about Australia. Were the spiders big? Did you see those cute famous brothers?" She takes me behind the counter and forces me onto the stool.

"I did not meet Thor or his brother," I state, "but it was beautiful there, Lisa. Magical, almost. I loved it. And the men with their accents. If I weren't so deeply in love, I would've stayed just for the men alone!"

"Speaking of being in love, when is the big day? You guys have been engaged for years now."

I laugh. "We were taking it slow."

She rolls her eyes. "Seriously? You're almost fifty! You can't take it much slower, Grandma. Are you scared of breaking a hip?" she teases.

"Hey, you're the same age I am," I remind her.

"Shhh, don't remind me. I still feel like I'm in my thirties."

"But to answer your question, we're getting married tomorrow. In the town square. It's nothing big or fancy, but you are invited, and you have to help me with the arrangements."

She jumps up and down, squealing. "Yes! Finally!"

I laugh. "Alright, let's go get started."

Lisa and I make a dozen flower arrangements, and I make my bouquet. It's not a formal wedding, but I do want it to look beautiful and timeless. I have a dress. It's not bright white but more of an aged white lace. Logan is wearing khakis and a white dress shirt. Erin will be my maid of honor, and with her current size, a formal dress didn't seem fitting. Instead, she's wearing a pale-blue dress that fits in with the spring weather.

We put the arrangements into the cooler and walk back out onto the sales floor. The bell above the door rings and I spin around to see Logan walking in. He walks up to me slowly, a small smile on his lips. He places his hands on my hips and pulls me against his chest. "Everything ready for tomorrow?"

"Mm-hmm," I say, looking up to meet his eyes. "The flowers are done, and Lisa is prepared to bear witness. Erin and Jordan are on their way. They should arrive tonight and will be staying in her room. I've picked up my dress. There's nothing left to do but wait."

"There's one more thing," he says, pulling away and catching my hand in his.

"There is?" I ask, following him out of the store.

He leads me across the street and around the square, pausing in front of the old pizza place we used to eat at, the one we broke into when he first got back into town.

"What's this about?" I ask, looking from him, to the old building, and back.

"I have a wedding present for you," he says, reaching for the door.

I don't expect it to budge, but it pulls open easily. He leads me inside, and I gasp as I look around the room. Everything is exactly the way I remember it being when we were kids, from the red-and-white-checkered tablecloths to the signs and advertisements on the walls.

He leads me over to our old booth. My eyes automatically find our initials he carved in it. "I bought this place, and it's going to open on Monday."

"You?" I ask, still looking around, my eyes taking in every aspect. It feels like we've traveled through time.

He nods. "Remember how I said to let me plan the dinner after the wedding?"

I nod.

"Tomorrow is going to be the trial run for the restaurant. I know pizza isn't usually wedding food"—he shrugs—"but it seemed fitting for us."

"No, I love it. I can't believe you did all of this!"

"You like it?"

"I love it!" I pull him against me for a hug. I breathe him in and his scent soothes me. "This is perfect," I breathe out, still gazing around the room.

He pulls back, his hands cupping my face. "I love you, El. I wish we could've gotten to spend our whole lives together, but this is better than I ever imagined. We may not have gotten it all, but we got this, and it means more than anything else." He leans in and presses a kiss to my lips, a soft, slow kiss that tells me everything he can't put into words. It's all the promises from the past, finally brought back to life and projected into our future. We will get our happily ever after. We will spend our lives together. We really do have it all.

I move to straddle him in the booth, and his hands land on my thighs, squeezing.

"Wanna take this to the office?" he asks against my lips.

I nod. "Mm-hmm."

He quickly stands up, taking me with him, carrying me back to the office.

MIA AND BEN'S STORY

ONE
MIA

"Good morning, sunshine," my best friend and roommate, Lucy, says as I stumble out of my room and into the living room.

I flop down on the couch and grunt a response.

Her brows raise as a smile spreads across her face. "Late night?"

I don't respond. I just nod.

"Too much fun? Please tell me you had a date," she pleads, her brows nearly reaching her blond hairline now.

What's with all the questions? She knows more than anyone that I'm not a morning person. "No," I finally speak. "I was up late grading papers so I can have everything turned in for the end of the year."

She snorts. "You're a kindergarten teacher. What's there to grade?"

I roll my eyes, then reach out and take the cup of coffee from her hands. I take a sip, and the smooth sweetness makes a smile form on my face. "Lots of stuff," I reply, deciding to keep her coffee for myself.

She shakes her head. "You seriously need to get a life. I mean, when's the last time you went out?"

I think back, trying to remember. Surely, it wasn't that long ago, was it?

She laughs as she watches me trying to figure out the answer.

"See, you don't even know. That's it. Tonight, we're going out."

I take a deep breath, preparing for the fight that's sure to come. "No, I have too much stuff to do. I have to do my laundry, plus I still have a stack of papers that need my attention. I was planning on ordering some Chinese food and eating it in my pajamas in bed while grading papers."

"Mia, it's Saturday! You're not eating alone in bed tonight. We're going out. Don't worry, we won't go far. We'll just hit up Gordy's, watch whatever band is playing, eat some fried food, and have a few beers. We'll be home early enough that you might even squeeze in a few papers."

I take long breath. "You're going to fight me on this, aren't you?"

"Yep," she says with a wide smile and a big nod of her head.

"Fine, whatever," I mumble, handing her the cup back as I force myself to get up.

"Where you going?" she calls out after me.

"If I'm going to be spending my Saturday night acting like a teenager again, I have a lot of work to get done before we go. Don't try using the washer—I'm calling it today!" I point at her and give her my serious face before turning to go back into my room to gather up my laundry.

After dumping a load into the washer, I fix a bowl of oatmeal and take it back to my desk in my room where I get started on grading more papers. She's right for the most part. I am a kindergarten teacher, so the work I have to grade is pretty mindless. It's not like I'm reading term paper after term paper. I just have to look over every single paper and correct capital As. I stick stickers on all the ones that need no corrections.

My brain feels numb after looking at messy letters and numbers all day even though I've gotten up several times to transfer over my laundry or to put it away. The work keeps my hands busy but not so much for the brain. It leaves my brain wide open to think of other things. Things such as going to Gordy's tonight with Lucy.

I haven't been to Gordy's since I was in high school, when I was dating Ben.

"I'm nervous. I mean, what if they ask for my ID?" I ask, hanging out at the back of the van the band uses to lug their equipment around.

Ben stops what he's doing and turns to face me, taking my hands in his. "You're with us. They won't. Plus, you don't even drink. If you don't order a drink, they won't have any reason to card you," he says, sounding completely sure and not nervous in the slightest.

Just having his hands in mine calms all of my negative emotions. I take a deep breath and let it out slowly, nodding my head as I do so.

With that, he smiles and wets his lips, moving in quickly to press them against mine.

Ben and I have been dating since our freshmen year of high school. We've kissed a thousand times over the last three years, but every time, it's like the first time. When our lips touch, it's like an explosion going off inside of me. My body buzzes and comes to life, making every inch tingle with need and desire. I can feel this kiss all the way down to the tips of my toes. I wiggle them in my shoes, enjoying the feeling that only he can cause.

I shake that memory from my head and focus on the sloppy 4 that's been traced onto the paper before me. Somehow, it shifts. It's no longer a number on a piece of paper. It's him. Ben.

Back then, I couldn't get enough of him. He was tall and thin, but his muscles were cut. When he held me in his arms, there was no doubt that he was the strongest man on earth. His dark hair was curly, always a sloppy mess that hung in front of his impossibly deep green eyes. His face grew angular as he got older but still held a baby roundness that I found adorable. And his hands, don't get me started on those. He played the guitar like a seasoned pro, even at our young age. Like the guitar, he played me just as well, knowing exactly where to touch to have me falling to my knees before him.

I thought Ben would be my happily ever after. After high school, we had plans of going off to college together, graduating, getting married, and starting our family. But not all plans work out. They're not all meant to be. Our last summer before starting college, his band was discovered by a music rep at Gordy's. He had to make the biggest decision of his life: continue with our plan or give this whole music thing a shot.

"I don't know what to do, Mia. I mean, I can't let the band down. We've worked hard for this for years. But at the same time, I can't let you down either. We have a plan. What should I do?" he asks, flopping down onto the couch next to me.

I know what I have to say, but can I say it? I know forcing these words out will only end us, but this isn't about me. This is about him and his big shot. If he passes on it now, it will never come around again. He might grow to resent me for asking him to pass up this opportunity.

"You have to go, Ben. This isn't about us or me. This is about you and all the hard work you've put in to get here. You can't turn your back on it now."

His shimmering green eyes meet mine, but he doesn't reply. I can see the questions in his eyes.

"Just go hear them out. See what they have to say. Try it out. You know I'll always be here waiting for you." I offer up a smile, and it brings one out in him too.

"Come here," he says, reaching out for me and pulling me into his lap, where our mouths meet.

My lips burn and tingle from remembering that kiss. If I had known then what I know now, would my response have been the same? As much as I hate that we broke up, as much as I miss him, my response would still be the same, and I know that without a doubt. No way could I take away everything he's accomplished. Who cares if I can't listen to the radio in fear of hearing his voice. Who cares if I can't watch the VMAs because I'm too afraid of seeing him perform.

Ben's band has blown up over the years. The moment he signed that contract, he was shipped off to record. Once the album was done, they opened for bigger bands while people fell in love with them. Then they started headlining their own shows. He hasn't been back here in almost ten years, and it's been ten years since I've felt like a whole person. All these years, I've been walking around with half my heart, half my soul.

Even though I want to hate him for all this pain I've felt all these years, I can't. Because deep down, I know that I still belong to him. And because of that, I've completely given up on love. There's no way I'll ever find someone like him again. Nobody has ever made me feel the way he did. Nobody can make me as happy; nobody can make me laugh the way he did. Most importantly, nobody can bring my body to life in their hands the way he did. I know. I've tried being with other men. None of them compare.

"Okay, time's up," Lucy says, sticking her head into my room.

I snap out of my daze and look at the last paper beneath my hand. To my surprise, it's graded and corrected, ready to hand back out next week. I look up at her, and she's still standing there, smiling.

"Go, get ready," she says, waving me on.

With a roll of my eyes, I push my chair away from my desk and stand up with a sigh. At least I got my work done.

It takes me another hour to shower and get ready. I check myself over in the mirror. The skinny jeans I picked hug my curves nicely, and the black long-sleeve shirt is cute but not revealing. I look up at my dark hair that's curled modestly, just a flip here or a curl there. Nothing about me screams "look at me," and that's how I like it. At least lately anyway. There was once upon a time when I liked to get dressed up and go out, looking for men's attention. But I gave that up the day I gave up on falling in love again. As I'm looking myself over, Lucy walks into my room. When she sees me, she scrunches up her nose. "What in the world are you wearing?" she asks, walking a circle around me. "I mean, it's like you're trying to look bad on purpose."

Our eyes meet in the mirror, and she gives me a challenging look. "What's wrong with it? I've worn this top a hundred times, and you never said anything about it before."

She frowns. "That was when you were going to work with a bunch of kindergarteners. We're going out! You need to look hot! Come on, let's find you something else," she starts, but I grab ahold of her wrist, not letting her go anywhere.

"Oh, no. I agreed to go out. I did not agree to being your own doll. This is what I'm wearing. Take me or leave me." I smile proudly.

She rolls her eyes. "Fine," she agrees. "Let's go."

TWO

BEN

"Ten years, my friend," Quinton says, slapping me on the shoulder as he flops down onto the couch next to me on our tour bus.

I have a guitar in my hands, strumming. I'm not playing anything in particular. I'm just trying to find some inspiration to write a new song, something I like to do with all the downtime we have when we're on the road. I nod in his direction, knowing exactly how long it's been.

He leans forward, resting his elbows on his knees as he looks over at me. "You going to be able to handle going back?"

"I'll be fine."

"Grant says that the show has been sold out," he says with excitement.

"Every show we do is sold out. This one is no different," I point out.

He leans back and kicks his foot up onto the table. "This one is kinda different. I mean, we haven't been back home in a decade. We haven't played our favorite stage in a decade. We haven't seen the people we went to high school with, and you haven't seen Mi—"

"Don't fucking go there, Quin," I grind out between my clenched teeth.

He shakes his head. "And that right there," he says, pointing in my direction, "is why I'm asking if you'll be okay."

I roll my eyes, tired of his concern. "I'll be fine. I mean, the chances of her still being there are slim, right?"

He nods. "Yeah, I guess so. But she grew up there. She has family there, friends. Who's to say she doesn't go there all the time?"

Mike comes out from the back and sits across from us. "What are you two talking about?"

Quin nods toward me. "I was just talking about the homecoming show with Ben."

Mike smiles. "I'm kind of excited about it. I mean, we get to go back home, the place where this all started." He looks up. "I wonder if Lucy is still around." His eyes glaze over. "Damn, she was hot and a lot of fun." His smile is wide as he nods his head. Then he looks at me. "Oh, and Mia," he says, pointing.

My eyes jump up to his, and my jaw flexes with anger. It's been ten years since I've heard her name, seen her face, tasted her sweet lips. "It doesn't matter if they are still around. We treated those girls like shit, and I'm sure they never want to see either of us again."

He frowns. "What do you mean? Lucy loved me, and I know Mia was in love with you."

That only fuels the fire. "Exactly, and what did we do? We left them behind while we went and lived our dream. I'll do this show," I say, standing up, "but that's it. The moment it's over, I'm going to the airport and going home." I put my guitar back on its stand and leave the front of the bus. I push my way past the curtain and into the tiny bathroom. I place my hands on the counter and hang my head. My eyes flutter closed as the first memory I have of her surfaces.

I'm on a makeshift stage at a party in someone's living room. I look out over the crowd and see everyone dancing in front of me, all dressed up for homecoming. I step up to the microphone and sing. My eyes fall closed as I feel every line that leaves my lips. When I open my eyes, they land on a girl standing in the middle of the crowd. She isn't dancing like the rest of them. She isn't with a date or a friend. She's just standing completely still with her eyes on me while the world passes us by. Her blue eyes seem welded to mine as they burn and smolder. The depth of her eyes is stunning. They're dark around the outside, so dark they may just be black, but closer to the center, they get lighter. The center of her irises are icy blue, nearly white. Her eyes remind me of the ocean. They reflect dark skies and choppy waters while also holding a coldness, a hardness, like ice.

Her lips turn up into a flirty smile just before she spins around to walk away, her raven-colored hair fanning out around her with the action.

No, wait. I'm not done yet. I need more.

I need to find her. I need to see more of her. Her ivory skin, stunning eyes, and dark hair are so perfect, too perfect. She may as well be an angel or some kind of vision that I can't touch. Was she even real? She turned and vanished so quickly.

We finish the song we're playing and take a break. I put the guitar down and hop off the stage, walking through the crowd of people to find a beer. I walk into the kitchen and stop by the guy operating the keg. He hands me a full cup of foamy beer, and I tip it up, taking a long drink. I'm still not sure if the girl was real or not, but she's all I can think of.

I bring down the cup and turn to leave, bumping into the angel.

"Oh, I'm sorry," she says, and her voice is sweet, like a song.

I'm sure I look like a freak right now. My eyes are wide in surprise, and my mouth is hanging open. She giggles, and it causes a wave of need to wash over me.

"You're in the band, right?" she asks, wrinkling her nose, probably wondering why I'm not talking.

I nod my head and clear my throat. "Yeah, I saw you when I was on stage."

Her cheeks turn a light shade of pink, and I swear, I'm ready to fall to my knees before her.

Her smile widens. "I saw you too. You're really good. The band, I mean."

"Thanks."

"I'm Mia." She holds out her hand.

"Ben," I reply, slipping my hand into hers as I look up and down her light-blue dress. The shade only brings out the true color of her eyes, making them burn hotter.

"You go to school here?" I ask, wondering why I'm only now noticing her.

She nods. "I just started last month. I'm a sophomore."

"I'm a junior," I reply. That's why I haven't noticed her. I don't have any underclassmen in any of my classes.

"So, how long have you been playing music?" She's swaying from side to side, looking nervous. The way her dress dances around her legs teases me. Suddenly, I can't think of anything but pushing it up her thighs as my calloused hands skim her soft skin.

"Since I was a kid, but we started the band a couple years ago."

Her eyes are wide as she takes me in, the corners of her mouth lifted into a smile, face still burning with heat. Everything about her draws me in. "You wanna dance?" she asks, motioning toward the dance floor where everyone is dancing to the stereo that got turned on.

"I only have a few minutes, and I have to get back on stage."

"Oh, okay. Maybe later then?"

I smile and nod. "Yeah, later."

I shake the memory from my head and look at my face in the mirror. My eyes are bloodshot from lack of sleep. Being in a rock band means holding down a crazy schedule. Between the shows, the traveling, and the uncomfortable bunk on the bus, I never get enough sleep. I feel like I've been tired for the past ten years. There are dark circles under them and a thick layer of scruff covering my jaw. I look haggard as fuck. My hair is longer than I usually let it grow. It's curly and messy, but I enjoy the way it falls into my eyes, blocking out the rest of the world when I need it to. Looking at myself in the mirror now, I wonder how I've become the man I am today. It doesn't feel like it was that long ago that I was eighteen and had the love of my life in my arms. But on the other hand, it feels like it's been an eternity since I've seen her, heard her, touched her. Just remembering the feeling of her soft skin under my rough hand causes goosebumps to prickle my skin.

A chill races up my spine, and I stand up straight, turning away from the mirror and going directly to my bunk. I pull the curtain closed and bask in the darkness. I know pretty much everyone would say I'm lucky, that I'm living a dream only few get to, but it leaves me wondering, what am I doing it for? Back then, it was for the guys. It was for her. I wanted to show her what I could do, give her a reason to be proud of me. But now, what's it all for? I have nobody to share my life with. The only woman I've ever loved is gone.

I place my arm across my closed eyes and think back on a better time of my life, a time when I wasn't famous, a time when I wasn't the lead singer and guitarist for one of the most popular rock bands in the country, a time when I was just a regular kid who knew exactly what he wanted: her.

Sleep finds me easily, and I don't bother fighting it off. I know I'll only get a few hours at best. Then the bus will hit a bump in the road, and I'll be awake while everyone else sleeps like a baby. That's the time I hate the most. Being alone. When there's nothing else to distract me, when there is nobody to talk to and nowhere to go because I'm stuck on a bus, that's when everything hits me hard. I think about every decision I've ever made and how I chose wrong. This, what I'm doing with my life—it doesn't mean anything. Not without her.

AS I WARM up for the show that's in a few hours, I look at the calendar on the wall of the bus. The 27th is circled in red marker—the day of our homecoming show. I count the days in between. Twelve days. Less than two weeks. I'm dreading it. I'm dreading the moment I have to look into her striking blue eyes and tell her how badly I fucked up and beg for her forgiveness. I don't expect her to take me back. There may have been a time when she would've taken me back, but that time is long gone now. All I can hope is that she forgives me, and with that forgiveness, I hope that I feel a little resolve. All the booze in the world can't erase the guilt I feel for leaving her the way I did.

As my fingers move over the strings of my guitar, my eyes fall closed. And like always, she's what I see. Raven-colored locks, creamy skin that's as soft as velvet, striking blue eyes that can stop any man, especially me, dead in their tracks, and crimson lips that taste sweeter than any fruit. Goosebumps cover my body, and a chill runs up my spine. My fingers stop as I lean back on the couch, damaged, broken, dead inside.

THREE
MIA

"Have a good summer," I say, smiling and waving to the kids as they rush from the classroom for the last time this school year. The last little one runs out, and the room is suddenly silent. I lean against my desk and look around my room, which is now quiet and empty. I've already started taking things down and putting them away, so the room doesn't look anything like it usually does. A kindergarten class with no kids looks sad, and it causes a pain to throb in my chest.

I sit at my desk and do the last few things that need to be done. After that, I shut down the computer and gather my things. Most teachers are happy on the last day of school, but it always makes me sad. Three months off is a long time when you don't have a life outside of teaching. It means boring days, lonely nights, and way too much time on my hands to think about unpleasant things. Not to mention, this time of year is always hard for me. It always takes me back to eighteen and watching him drive away. My teeth clench when I think of it, and it causes a bout of pain to shoot through my jaw. I force myself to relax, and the pain eases.

The drive home isn't long, and when I walk in, I'm surprised to see Lucy already home. She looks up from her place on the couch and offers a sad smile. She knows how I feel today. "How was your day?" she asks as I set my things down and plop down next to her.

I shrug. "It was alright, I guess. I didn't cry." Crying wouldn't be unusual. Saying goodbye to my kids is never easy. I remind myself that I'll see them next year, even if it is from down the hall.

"You didn't cry? You are making progress!" She smiles wide.

I laugh and roll my eyes.

"Guess what," she says, sitting up higher.

"What?"

"I scored two tickets off the radio to go to Gordy's tonight."

I frown. "Since when do you need tickets to go to Gordy's?"

Her eyes stretch wide. "Please tell me you know about this."

"Know about what?"

She shakes her head. "How is it possible? I mean, I know you don't listen to the radio, but how have you not heard people talking about it or seen the flyers around town?"

"Luce, what are you talking about?" I'm getting annoyed. *Just tell me already*. Of course I don't listen to the radio, and the only place I go around town is to the school and the gym. She does all of our shopping. And hear people talk about it? Ha, I'm with kindergarteners all day. The only thing I hear are about video games and YouTube influencers.

She levels her eyes on me. "You have to get tickets to go to Gordy's tonight because Escaping the Darkness is playing there for their homecoming show to celebrate their tenth anniversary."

I take in her words, thinking over each one slowly. I think about it for so long that each word loses its meaning. It's not until I put the sentence back together that I understand. "Ben is going to be back in town," I say, but it sounds like a question.

She nods. "And I have tickets!" She starts bouncing up and down on the couch. "We're going!"

I don't remember getting up, but the next thing I know, I'm

pacing back and forth across the floor on the verge of a panic attack. My thoughts are racing.

Ben is back. He's here and he's performing. And Lucy has tickets and says we're going. No, I'm not going. I can't face him, not after all these years. But ugh, what would it feel like to look into his green eyes again? What would it feel like to see him up on stage, performing like the night I met him?

Lucy watches me pace back and forth for a long while before speaking. Finally, she breaks her silence. "Okay, hear me out. First of all, you don't have shit to do. School is out. You need to celebrate. Get drunk and stop being so sad. And second, you need this. You need to see him, put him in the past where he belongs so you can move on. Being this caught up over your high school boyfriend isn't healthy, honey. It just isn't. And we can hang out in the back so he doesn't even see you if you want. Although, I say get dressed up and look super hot and show him what he's missing." She smiles.

I shake my head, not sure if it's at her or myself, and sit down on the couch, thinking everything over. "I don't know, Luce," I breathe out and she rolls her eyes. "I mean, how can I face him? He knows how I felt about him. He chose this. He's the one who went away and stopped calling. He's the one who never came back for me."

"Exactly. Make him look you in the eye and regret every decision he's ever made." Her evil smile spreads across her face.

"I need wine. I can't think with you playing the little devil on my shoulder," I say, standing up and moving to the fridge.

I pour a large glass, pick it up, and take a swig. I take a deep breath and let it out slowly. Maybe she's right. All this time, I've felt like I've been waiting for him to come back, and now he has. Am I really going to let this opportunity get away from me?

The whole time I'm standing at the kitchen island drinking my wine and thinking over the situation, Lucy is sitting on the couch, staring back at me, just watching and waiting.

"Okay, we'll go," I tell her as calmly as I can.

Her squealing and bouncing around starts back up. "God, I'm so excited! I can't wait to see Mike! You think he remembers me?"

I snort and roll my eyes. "Of course he does. You guys only slept together like twenty times."

She smiles, and I see her eyes glaze over as she remembers it. "Maybe he'll want a trip down memory lane, you know?" Her smile only widens as she nods her head and wags her brows.

I shake my head. "Seriously, you'd sleep with him again?"

She shrugs. "Why not? We've already slept together, so it doesn't add to my body count. Plus, he's hot and famous!"

I roll my eyes as I lift my glass of wine and finish it off.

"You mean to tell me that if Ben wanted to hook up tonight, you wouldn't go for it?"

"Hell no! I'm not some random groupie, Lucy. Tonight, I'm going to make him miss me. He may have been able to forget about me on the road, but tonight, he's going to remember. All of it."

This only makes her cheer louder, and I laugh at her enthusiasm as I make my way toward my room to shower and get ready. All these years I've looked back and missed him, I felt sad that things ended the way they did, and honestly, I think a part of me is still in love with him—er, who he used to be. I don't know who he is anymore, and that makes me mad. How dare he do this to me, to us? Is being famous really that much better than being with the one you claimed to love? Then it hits me. He must not have loved me at all. If he did, he never would've done what he did. The fact that he'd played with me and faked his feelings for me while I was falling head over heels in love only angers me more.

I take my aggression out in the shower, washing my hair and shaving before climbing out to get ready. I blow-dry my hair, leaving it smooth and shiny. I curl it into perfect ringlets that hang down to my ass. I apply some makeup, going a little overboard with eyeshadow and liner. The smoky eye look makes my icy eyes pop. I contour my face and highlight my cheekbones, then apply some shimmery pink gloss to my lips. I look myself over and wonder who I'm even looking at. This isn't me. I don't do this. I don't wear this much makeup. But I am surprised by the outcome. I don't look like an innocent kindergarten teacher. I look... hot! I look like one of those girls on Instagram. My cheekbones look angular; my eyes pop almost unnaturally, and my lips are full, thick, and glistening. Now, I just have to find the perfect outfit.

I keep my towel around me as I move to my closet and flip on the light. The small space is crammed—I never get rid of clothing unless it's ripped or torn. I start at one end and work my way to the other. I push past all of my jeans, long skirts, and button-up tops. I need something that's going to make him notice me. I reach the end of the closet, and the only thing left is a black dress. I pull it out and look it over, remembering that I've only worn it one time to a party back in college. I pull it on and look at myself in the mirror. The dress is sleeveless, which is perfect for the warm weather. The top of the dress is fitted and is made of satin that's covered in a light sheen of glitter. At the waist, the dress turns to layers upon layers of a see-through fabric so that you can't actually see through the dress. It's soft and flows around my thighs, ending well above my knee. I pair the dress with a pair of black open-toed ankle boots that have cut outs to make them a little more rock and a little less classy.

I spin around in a circle and laugh as the dress twirls around me. The door opens and Lucy walks in. Her eyes are wide, and her mouth is hanging open. "Wow!"

I stop and turn to face her. "Too much?"

"Are you kidding? No way!" She walks over and circles once around me. "You're going to make him regret the last ten years of his life." She offers up a wicked smile, and her dark eyes shimmer.

I look over her black ripped jeans, killer high heels, and ripped-up tank top. "I think I should change. I look way overdressed compared to you." I spin to face my closet, but she catches my wrist and stops me.

"Don't you dare! This is perfect, Mia. Seriously." She moves us back in front of the mirror so I can see my whole body with her head peeking over my shoulder. "Look at you. He's going to lose his mind." That evil smile is back, and I can't help but let a little giggle slip.

The two of us load up in my car, and I drive us across town to Gordy's. The place is jammed. Every table is full, along with the bar, and people are gathered in groups around the pool tables and dartboard. I'm surprised to see that the stage isn't set up though.

"Why isn't the stage set?" I ask, leaning in and asking in Lucy's ear as she leads us to the bar to order drinks.

"Oh, there isn't enough room in here so they're performing out back. We'll grab some drinks and head out." She orders us two mixed drinks and starts a tab before leading us out the back door to the fenced-in area. A few years ago, a new law was passed so nobody could smoke inside the bar anymore, so Gordy built a beer garden. There's a stage, an outdoor bar, and tons and tons of picnic tables. The area in front of the stage is free, leaving plenty of room for dancing.

To my surprise, the outside area is just as crowded, with most people gathering around the stage. All the tables up front are also taken, so Lucy leads us to the back, and we have a seat. "Okay, talk to me. How are you feeling? Nervous? Anxious? Scared?"

I nod. "All those things. I mean, what if he sees me and doesn't care?" I lift my glass and take a long drink of my vodka and Red Bull.

She shakes her head. "That won't happen."

"How do you know?"

She shrugs. "I just do."

I let the subject drop. Maybe she was right the first time. Maybe he doesn't even have to see me. Maybe all I need is to let myself see him and hear him, so I can work all of him out of my system once and for all. Anything is worth a shot at this point. I suck down my drink faster than usual, but it helps with the anxiety and nervousness flooding my system. When my drink is gone, I stand to use to the bathroom and to hit the bar.

"Need a drink?"

"Please," she replies as I start to walk off.

I make my way back into the bar and hand off our glasses before using the restroom. On my way back out, I pick up the two fresh drinks. I make it back to the table just as the outside lights dim and the spotlight hits the stage. Suddenly, everyone is screaming and cheering. I look at Luce and she smiles, her eyes holding so much excitement as she stands to look at the stage. I can't move. I'm suddenly frozen. It's finally time to see him, and I don't know if I can do it.

Luce looks over, expecting to see me standing with her, but then she looks down and finds me. She nods her head upward. "Come on. Forget who he is and just have some fun."

I take a deep breath and stand up just in time to see the guys make their way onto the stage. Ben heads up front with his guitar hanging in front of him. His hand lands on the mic, and he smiles as he looks out over the crowd.

"How's everyone doing tonight?" he asks, and that voice hits me like a bullet straight to the heart. I feel the pain as it jolts through my entire body. I have to hold on to the edge of the table to keep from falling over.

"First off, let me start by saying thank you for coming out here. It really means a lot. I mean, some of you may not know this, but this is the town we were born and raised!" The crowd cheers louder, and I almost feel the need to plug my ears. Still, my eyes don't leave him. I know I shouldn't, but I'm burning his image into my brain. This is it. Probably the last time I'll ever see him. It needs to last a lifetime.

"We love the support we've received tonight and every night for the last ten years we've been on the road. If it weren't for this little town and this bar, our lives would be completely different. I have to admit, though, coming back here was hard. Like many of you, we have a lot of fond memories of this town, but we also have a lot of things that have been buried deep inside us—ghosts, if you will. And coming back here, well, it's making a lot of things resurface. But we do it all for you. We want to say thank you any way we can. So in memory of running away from this town and our own personal ghosts, here's our latest single, 'Ghost.'"

The crowd cheers and the music starts up. When his voice floods my ears as he sings the lyrics, goosebumps prickle my skin, and a cold chill runs up my spine.

FOUR

BEN

"We're here! Wake up!" Mike says, pulling the curtain to my bunk open and letting it fill with light.

I groan as I sit up and swing my feet to the side, setting them on the floor. With the bunk above me, I have to hunch over. I rest my elbows on my knees and hold my head in my hands. I rub my eyes and will myself to wake up. I stand up and stretch, walking to the front of the bus where the guys are sitting on the couch, looking out the windows. I join them and look out at the town I haven't seen in ten years.

We pass by the ice cream stand, and all I remember is taking Mia there every Friday night to hang out with our friends. I remember the way we'd sit at the tables and how I'd always pull her against me. How I liked to run my finger through her silky hair. How I'd lean in and smell her, her scent washing away every negative feeling inside of me.

We pass by the school, and I'm hit with memories of driving her to and from school, hanging out in the parking lot until the bell rang, and how more times than not, we were late because we were making out instead of paying attention to the time. Then we pull up at

Gordy's, and I know the minute we walk in, I'm going to be hit with more memories. The guys are talking back and forth about things they remember, but I'm too lost in thought to join their conversation.

I still don't know what I'm going to do if I see her. Will I act like I don't know her? Will I tell her how sorry I am to have hurt her? Or will I just want to pull her against me and kiss her like no time has passed. If I don't see her, how will that make me feel? Will I be happy, relieved, upset, angry?

The bus door opens and the guys stand up. "Come on," Mike says.

I wave him off. "Nah, you guys go on ahead. I'm going to shower and get ready for the show."

He frowns at me. "Dude, we have to go see Gordy and tell him thanks for hosting the show."

With a deep breath, I push myself up and step off the bus.

The day is sunny and warm with it being late May, and I take a deep breath, smelling the familiar scent of honeysuckle that grows in the trees surrounding the bar, a hint of grease from the fried food they serve, and stale alcohol from the dumpster. I walk into the darkened bar and look around, noticing that not much has changed at all. The stage, the wooden dance floor, the tables and chairs, it all looks the same and doesn't seem to have moved even an inch. There is a big flat-screen TV behind the bar now that didn't use to be there, and there is a framed poster that we signed hanging on the wall by the stage.

Gordy walks out with a wide smile. "There's my favorite band," he says, rushing toward us. He shakes each of our hands before pulling each of us in for a hug.

"How ya doing, Gordy?" I ask, smacking him on the back.

He nods. "Great, and you guys?"

Everyone replies with short, one-word answers.

"We can't wait to play on this stage again, Gordy," Quin tells him.

Gordy nods. "Oh, no. You're going to be playing on the new one out back. Come check it out." He leads us through the bar and out to the beer garden. Our crew is already getting busy setting up our equipment.

I whistle as I take in the whole new setup. "All this is new, right?"

He nods. "Yeah, the state decided it wanted to take smoking away from the drunks, so we built this on a few years ago." He looks between me and the guys. "I hope you're ready for tonight. It's going to be one hell of a show. We're sold out, but I'm sure that's nothing compared to what you're used to playing now. I had to hire extra security." He laughs.

"Well, we appreciate it," I reply.

"Anything to bring my boys home," he says with a fond smile.

I laugh. "I remember having to beg you to let us play here. Remember that?"

He joins in my laughter as he nods. "Yep, I thought for sure you were going to get my bar shut down, but I allowed it and haven't looked back since."

I wish I could say the same, but I clearly can't. The guys climb up on stage to direct the crew on how they want the setup, but I hang back and lean against a picnic table. "Hey, Gord?"

He looks over at me.

"She still come in here?"

It takes him a moment to remember, but acknowledgement washes over his face. "Not really. I mean, she was in a few weeks back, but that was the first and only time I've seen her."

"You think she'll show tonight?"

He shrugs. "I have a feeling if that Lucy has anything to do with it, she will."

And that right there is why I need a plan. Flying by the seat of my pants has never worked for me. Anytime I've done it, I've made a mistake. When I make a plan, I stick to it. But this is a little different. I don't know how she'll approach me or if she even will. Hell, I don't even know if she'll show up. But deep down, I pray that she does.

Even if she won't talk to me, I'll at least get to look into those deep blue eyes again.

I head back to the bus to shower and get ready for the show. I'm a nervous wreck and end up busting out the bottle of vodka kept in the freezer. I can't get wasted, not with a show to do, but I need something to take the edge off. I toss back a shot and replace the bottle back in its spot before sitting down and picking up my guitar. Strumming always helps to clear my head and to put things into perspective.

IT'S time to start the show, so I make my way from the bus to the back of the stage. I'm handed my guitar, and the lights go down. The crowd cheers. My heart starts to race, just like it does for every show, but nervousness washes over me just from thinking that Mia might be out there.

We make our way onto the stage, and the cheering from the crowd is almost deafening. I introduce us while making a little small talk as I search the crowd for her, but it's dark, and I can't see more than a few feet from the stage. I push the thought from my head and focus on the job I have to do. We open with our newest single, "Ghost," a song I wrote when I got to thinking about how Mia is basically a ghost to me now, nothing more than memories I can't escape. From there, we move into "Almost Human," "Take Me Back," and then the song I love and hate the most, "I Still Remember," a song I wrote about her about two years after I left. It's a song that I hoped she'd hear on the radio, a song that would let her know that I hadn't forgotten about her, that I was still in love with her and always would be no matter how far apart we were or how much time had passed. It's a slow song with a rock edge to it.

I'm singing the lyrics and looking out into the crowd where people are singing along with the words and swaying back and forth. Some people are holding up their phones and shining their flashlights, but a few old-school rockers are using their lighters instead. I study each of their faces, looking for her. Finally, my eyes stop roaming when I find her standing in the middle of the crowd. Her eyes are locked on mine, and they seem glossy and glazed over. She isn't singing, isn't swaying, isn't smiling. She's just watching, and goosebumps cover my body as I have to focus on singing the words I knew by heart only a few moments ago.

Looking at her now after all of these years feels surreal. I almost feel like I did the first time I saw her, like I'm not entirely sure she's really standing in front of me. This could all be a dream. Even though she's grown up, I'd still be able to point her out a mile away. Those eyes, there is no mistaking those eyes. Her face is slimmer than it used to be, her cheeks and jaws more angular now, but her lips are still thick and plump as they shimmer under the lights. Her tongue comes out and runs across her bottom lip, and then she pulls it into her mouth and bites down on it. I feel my body come alive in ways it hasn't in years. When the song ends, she turns like she's going to run, but I speak into the microphone without thinking.

"Wait!"

She stops dead in her tracks but doesn't turn.

"If you guys would do me a solid, would you let this beautiful lady here in the black dress come to the front of the stage?"

She turns and looks at me from over her shoulder, and the crowd parts. She waits there, switching her weight from foot to foot, like she's trying to decide whether she should do as I ask or take off running. She begins to turn, but then, at the last second, she shakes her head and runs in the opposite direction.

I take off my guitar and hand it over to Mike as I jump from the stage, chasing after her.

"Okay, well, there's that." Mike laughs into the microphone. "You have to excuse him. Remember those ghosts he was talking about? He's chasing after one right now." His voice echoes through the speakers, but I don't give a shit or stop as I run after her. I follow her back into the bar and out the door to the parking lot. She comes to a stop at a black Audi. She tries to open the door, but it's locked, and it doesn't appear like she has her keys.

I stop at the back of her car, frozen as I watch her.

She finally gives up trying to get inside and turns to face me.

"Mia?" I say her name, and it feels foreign leaving my lips after going this long without saying it.

She holds her hands in front of her at her waist, and her head is down as she looks at her black-painted fingernails.

"Mia," I say again, this time stronger.

Her head pops up, her blue eyes wide and glistening.

I step forward. "I can't believe it's really you," I think out loud as I take another step in her direction.

Her lips part, but no words come out.

"God, I've thought about this moment so much. I can't believe you're really here right now," I breathe out, closing the distance between us as I reach for her, but she steps back.

"Don't touch me, Ben." She shakes her head.

God, my name sounds like heaven leaving her lips, but I freeze.

"I can't do this. It's been too long."

She goes to turn, but I stop her.

"Wait," I say, reaching out and capturing her wrist. The moment my hand touches her soft skin, my nerve endings light on fire and explode, and heat makes its way from my hand, up my arm, and to my chest, consuming me.

"Don't run, please," I whisper, afraid of talking at a normal volume.

She turns around. "Why not?" Her brows knit together. "You did, right?" she throws back, and she may as well have swung on me. Her words hit me harder than any punch ever has.

"I'm sorry," I tell her weakly. I clear my throat and try again. "I'm sorry, Mia." This time, the words come out clearer. "Back then…"

"Don't," she interrupts. "Don't sit here and give me some long list of excuses. You can excuse being late. You can excuse missing a phone call. You can't excuse this. Whatever you have to say"—she shrugs—"it's too late. Too little, too late." She tugs her wrist out of my hold, and I release it in fear of holding on and hurting her. I stand there by her car, watching her walk away from me this time. I watch as her dress blows in the light breeze, watch as it sways back and forth from side to side as she walks. My dick hardens, wanting nothing more than to push that dress up and slide into her the way I always used to. Just remembering her heat has me sweating.

I lose sight of her as she walks back into the bar, but I have a show to finish. I go back inside and bump into Lucy. "Hey, don't let her leave," I tell her.

She smirks. "Well, hello to you, too, stranger." She crosses her arms over her chest.

I roll my eyes, just now remembering how big of a pain in the ass she is. "Just, please," I breathe out, "don't let her leave. I have to finish this show. I want to give her time to cool off. Please, do this one thing for me."

She looks up at the ceiling. "And what do I get if I do?"

"What do you want?" It's only now I find my bodyguard standing firm at my back. No wonder. People are coming up to me and asking for pictures and autographs.

"I want to talk to Mike after the show."

"Done," I agree.

She nods and turns for the bathroom where I'm guessing Mia went. I go in the opposite direction to the stage.

"There he is, ladies and gentlemen," Mike says into the mic.

I grab my guitar and put it back in place. "Sorry about that, guys," I say, strumming my guitar to lead into the next song. For the rest of the show, I have to remind myself not to rush. These people deserve more than a half-assed, rushed show, but the only thing I can think of is getting to see Mia again and finally talking to her.

It's funny how this is the way the night is going. Earlier, I wasn't convinced that I wouldn't run from her. Now, I'm chasing after her. See why I always make a plan? What good can come out of this? If nothing else, the pain of being rejected by Mia may be what I need to move on. Or better yet, maybe I can get her back. Is that even a possibility?

We sing ten more songs before we wrap up and say good night. We make our way off stage to the area behind it where I stop Mike. "Hey, so someone wants to talk to you."

He frowns. "Who?"

"Lucy," I say around a smirk.

He smiles wide. "Hell yeah! Looks like I'm getting laid tonight." He pumps his fist in the air.

I shake my head but lead the way through the private entrance into the bar. When we walk in, the crowd inside cheers. We make our way to the front where the stage is and start lining up to do pictures, but we don't offer autographs this time—there isn't time for it. Pictures are quick, but when you have five hundred of them to take, they take hours.

While we do our little meet and greet, I keep an eye on Lucy and Mia. They're sitting at the bar, talking and sipping their drinks. Mia looks a little buzzed, but that's fine by me. Hell, I'm a little buzzed too. Now that the show is over, we get our free drinks, and I'm not taking it easy. No, I need the liquid courage to do what I have to do next: make her forgive me.

FIVE
MIA

I got what I wanted, right? I got to see him, hear him. He even touched me and made my body burn for his. That's all I wanted. So why do I want so much more? After taking several minutes to cool off in the bathroom, I walk out to find Lucy waiting for me.

"You have my keys," I tell her.

She smiles. "I know, and it's a good thing or I'd be walking home right now."

I roll my eyes. "Let's go. I need out of here."

She grabs my elbow and stops me. "Let's just stay inside and have a drink first. You should think this over and cool off."

I really want to go, but I listen to her. I know I'm not thinking rationally right now, and I don't want to do something rash and regret this one chance I have. I let her lead me up to the bar, which is now almost completely empty since everyone is outside. We have a seat and she orders our drinks. I never should have let him see me. I just... I don't know. When I heard the song he was singing, somehow, I knew it was meant for me. His words got into my head and took over my body. One minute I was standing by Lucy at our table in the back, and the next thing I knew, I was standing directly in front of him. When his eyes locked on mine, I swear the world stopped turning, just like it did all those years ago.

But I got what I wanted. The look on his face said it all. He regrets the last ten years of his life. He wants me. I saw the way his eyes were smoldering when they landed on mine. He might not love me, but he wants me. Me. I don't know why that excites me. I shouldn't be willing to be used by him for one night and then get tossed aside. In fact, I'm not. Just the thought of him wanting me makes my body hum, but I will not allow myself to be used and treated like trash.

I get my drink, and I suck it down a little too quickly.

"Whoa," Lucy says, ordering me another. "Tell me what's going on in that head of yours."

And I do. It all comes rushing out without much thought. I confess everything I'm thinking, hoping she can make some sense of it since I can't seem to.

She laughs and shakes her head. "You're still in love with him, aren't you? Not like, caught up on him or wanting to prove something. You love him." Her eyes are wide.

I roll my head to crack my neck and straighten my back. "It doesn't matter, Luce."

"It does matter, Mia. I mean, what do you want to do? Do you want to face him again and tell him off? Do you want to kiss him and see if there are still sparks? Or spend the night with him in hopes of smothering those sparks? What?"

"I don't even know," I confess.

We talk and enjoy our drinks. I almost forget all about him, but then the bar grows full again and everyone is cheering. I look around and see them walk in with their security team. They go to the front of the stage and start taking pictures. I roll my eyes but feel my body warm up as I look him up and down.

He's taller than I remember, his muscles even more defined even though he's still on the slimmer side. He has a lot of new tattoos covering his arms, and I wonder where they lead. His dark hair is still a mess of sexy curls and waves, hiding his emerald-green eyes. His jaw is cocked, causing shadows to form under his sharp cheekbones in the bad lighting of the bar. Fuck, he's sexy as hell. How did he get better-looking with time? I look at his tattooed hand, and it causes a cold chill to wash over me from remembering all the times those hands were on me.

One night couldn't hurt, right? And maybe Lucy will be right. Maybe this will be the closure I've been needing. *No, remember your standards. This isn't some joke. This is your life, and you shouldn't allow him to screw it up more than he already has.*

Lucy leans in, pressing her shoulder against mine. "Look, I promised Ben that you'd hear him out."

My head jerks in her direction. "You what? Why would you do that?" Anger starts to boil inside of me.

"Because you're my best friend and I love you, Mia. Whether you see it or not, whether you want to or not, you need this. You need to put this all behind you so you can move on. Running from the problem obviously isn't helping. So, time to change strategies." She picks up her drink and takes a sip.

I turn my head around to look at him. He looks up just in time, and our eyes lock from across the room. My body burns from the inside out from something as simple as him looking at me. I bite down on my lower lip, and his jaw flexes. Every muscle in his body hardens like he's holding himself back. I break our contact and turn around to finish off my drink. When it's empty, I lean toward Lucy. "Don't wait around. I'll call a cab if I need it."

She smiles as I turn and head toward the back exit. I look over my shoulder at him, and he sees the look I'm giving him. He says something to his bandmates and comes after me. Outside, I wait by the door. Moments later, it opens and he comes rushing out of it.

"You wanna talk? Let's talk," I say, crossing my arms over my chest.

His jaw twitches as he nods, and then he takes my hand in his and pulls me toward the bus. I walk onto the bus and take everything in. This is where he's been the last ten years instead of by my side. One side of the bus has a long couch while the other holds a booth-style table. Behind the seating area is the kitchen with a small sink, fridge, and stove. There's a curtain so I can't see past the kitchen. I plop down on the couch and take a deep breath as I continue to look around.

"Can I get you something to drink?"

I snort. "Not unless it's alcohol," I joke, though I'm also completely serious.

He opens the freezer and pulls out a bottle of vodka. Then he opens the fridge and pulls out a can of Red Bull. He takes two plastic cups and mixes a small drink in both. He hands one over and comes to sit at my side. We both take a drink, and then the awkward silence sets in.

"Just say whatever you feel you need to say, Ben. I'm a big girl. I can take it."

He leans forward, resting his elbows on his knees as he hangs his head. "Would you believe me if I told you that every day for the last ten years, I've thought about you and regretted leaving you behind?"

A bitter-sounding laugh escapes, but I take control and cut it off. "No."

"Well, it's true." He looks up, and his green eyes meet mine.

"How can that be true? At any time, you could've called me, sent me an email, something. And you chose not to. That doesn't sound like regret to me."

He nods once. "I'm full of regrets, Mia. I didn't reach out to you because I didn't want to hurt you anymore. Back then, I knew the life you wanted. You wanted to go to college, become a teacher, settle down, and start a family. So if I would've reached out to you, that would have just been taking everything away from you that you wanted. That's why I stopped calling. I didn't want you to have to choose between being with me, a guy you'd have to give up your life for, and what you really wanted out of life. And even if we decided to make it work somehow, then what? I would've been gone on tour, and you'd be home alone, raising our kids by yourself, waiting around for my calls that wouldn't come before midnight. I've been in hell every day to give you want you want, Mia." He looks over at me, and I can see the honesty in his eyes. They're nearly glowing in the dimly lit bus, sparkling and glistening.

I tip back my cup and finish it off. "I've been in hell, too, Ben. Did you know that I haven't listened to the radio in nine years? I'm too afraid to hear your voice. I can't watch any type of music award show in fear of seeing your face. I've been running from you since the day I realized you left me behind."

"You haven't heard any of our music?" he asks, surprised.

I shake my head. "Not until tonight. When you sang that song, somehow, I knew it was meant for me. I don't even remember getting up and walking to the stage. One minute I was standing next to Lucy, and the next I was standing in front of you."

"That song was for you," he says, setting his cup on the table across from us. "All of them are." Without warning, he presses his lips to mine, and it's like an explosion going off. There's a big flash of light behind my eyelids, and the light is warm and all-consuming. It brings every fiber of my being to life in a way I've never felt before.

His warm, soft lips press against mine, and when his tongue slides into my mouth, he tastes of the mixed drink we just had. His calloused hand is rough on my skin as he holds my jaw, but it's perfect, scratching an itch I didn't realize I had.

My arms wrap around him, pulling him close, while my nails scratch up and down his back. Somehow, he ends up on his knees on the floor in front of me, between my legs. His hand leaves my face to travel up my thigh while his other hand holds strong at my hip, pulling me closer.

"Fuck, I've missed you," he breathes against my lips.

With the alcohol in my system, everything feels heavenly. His lips fall from mine to kiss across my jaw and to my neck and ear. His teeth scrape against my sensitive skin and nip, only teasing me further. A tightness begins to build in my stomach, and I know that I have to have him now. Damn the consequences. Right now, I can't think. I can't see past him. He's consuming me just like he's always done. I push his shirt up his chest, and he breaks the kiss long enough to pull it away. His mouth is back on mine in an instant.

Suddenly, he's standing up, and he's holding me against him. My legs tighten around his waist as he carries me farther back into the bus. We push past the curtain, and I open my eyes to find a bunk area. He turns so I can see the end of the bus where I expected to find a full-size bed, but there is only a closet area with mirrors and dressers. He sits on the edge of the lower bunk, then places his hand on my head as he lies back, shielding my head from coming in contact with the top bunk. Once we're nestled away in our dark little hole, he closes the curtain, shielding us in darkness.

His hands run up my thighs, pushing my dress out of the way as he kisses me. "Fuck, I've thought about nothing but ripping this dress off of you since I first saw you tonight." He lightly bites my lower lip. "I can't wait to be buried deep inside you again." His hands travel up my back, finding the zipper and pulling it down. As it lowers, the straps fall from my shoulders, revealing my breasts to him.

His hands leave me quickly, and then a small light turns on. It's mounted on the wall above our heads. It shines light down on the bunk, like one you'd need for reading, but it also gives him a perfect view of me. He licks his lips, then quickly moves them to my breasts. His hands are holding firm on my ass while his mouth ravishes my breasts, sucking them into his mouth and flicking his tongue against my nipples. I lace my fingers into his messy hair, tugging at the roots like I need them to hold myself down. If I don't, I may just float away with all this passion pumping through me.

His hands have managed to work my dress up over my ass. His fingers hook around my panties, and he drags them down. With me straddling him, they can't go far. He gets impatient and tugs them one time, hard. I hear the fabric rip as a burning sensation slashes across my skin. Moments later, they're gone and forgotten.

His hand moves around me, finding my wet center. He runs his finger through my slick folds before dipping inside and making me call out. When a heavy gasp leaves my lips, his mouth moves back up, locking on mine and absorbing every noise I make. He teases me with his fingers for a long moment before his hand falls away. I hear the sound of his zipper lowering, and seconds later, I feel his silky-smooth tip pressing against me. My body ignites in flames when I feel him guiding himself into me. With one roll of his hips, he's sliding into me, and we're both letting out a sound of relief.

"Fuuuuck," he says into my mouth as we both go still, savoring this moment as we finally come together. His hands squeeze my thighs as he lifts his hips, wanting to be deeper. "God, you feel better than I remember," he whispers as his hands start to lift me up his shaft. When only his tip is left inside, he pulls me back against him, and we both let out a moan. Goosebumps prickle my skin when I think about how he's finally back inside me. I was only sixteen when I gave him my virginity, and I haven't regretted it a day in my life. Now, it's like we're coming full circle. He was my first, and still to this day, I want him to be my last. Each moment he spends inside of me, it completely erases the other guys I've been with from my body and mind. He's plucking each one of them from my memory and blowing them away like a dandelion scattering in the breeze.

I rock my hips against him while his hands travel my body, his lips still moving with mine. I can feel my release building stronger and stronger, swirling around inside of me and ready to explode. With one last rock of my hips, I come undone around him. My hips move faster as I grind back and forth against him. Our kiss turns hard and rushed.

"Yes, come for me, Mia," he whispers as my orgasm washes over me. "Let me hear you." His eyes lock with mine in the softly lit bunk, and it's like getting struck by lightning. It only makes my release that much stronger.

As I ride out every last wave, I can't help but burn this image of him into my memory. The way his green eyes are smoldering. The way his lips are parted with his heavy breathing, the mess of his hair from my fingers running through it, how every muscle is flexed and tense.

After my release ends, he pulls my mouth back to his as he rolls us over carefully so neither of us fall out of the bunk. He settles between my legs again and guides himself back into me. His hands tangle into my hair as his mouth ravishes mine and his hips pump into me.

"God, I've missed feeling your hair between my fingers," he whispers, thrusting deeper. "I've missed these lips." He kisses me, his hips never slowing. "I've missed these eyes looking up at me. Fuck, I dream of these eyes." His thrusts become erratic. "And your voice... you have the voice of an angel, and just hearing you whimper beneath me is enough to make me come."

I dig my nails into his back and pull him down so his chest is pressing against mine and our lips can weld together. With one last kiss, I feel his release pump into me. He lets out a moan that makes my stomach tighten as his hips slow to a stop. He rests his head on my shoulder as we both calm our breathing. My heart is racing out of control, and I can feel his as it pounds against his chest.

Finally, he removes himself from me and settles at my side, pulling me against him as he wraps me up in his strong arms. I let out a sigh and breathe in his rich scent. Even after all these years, he still smells exactly the same. His bare chest is soft against my cheek, and I open my eyes to see the black ink that covers his entire upper body. His hand moves up my back to tangle in my hair. He combs through it gently. When a strand drops from his fingers, he repeats the process again. The need to sleep consumes me, but I don't want to give in. I finally have him back. I don't want to waste a minute of it sleeping.

"When do you leave?" I ask softly.

I feel his shoulder shrug. "I don't have to be back in California until next week to start recording."

"So... you can stay awhile?" I ask, holding my breath.

He rolls over to his side, forcing me onto my back as he looks down at me. "Oh yeah. I haven't had enough of you yet." His mouth meets mine, and my eyes flutter closed. Hopelessness washes over me, but so does happiness. I haven't been this happy in over ten years, and no matter how much I know this will hurt, I'm going to enjoy every last second of it.

SIX

BEN

I look out over the crowd and find her striking blue eyes watching me, and it makes my blood pump harder. I swear, I could pick those eyes out of a sea of people. I can feel the moment they land on me, making my body come alive and tingle. She could walk into a crowded room, not say a word, and I'd know she was here just from feeling her eyes on me. I'm only sixteen, and I know that I'm not supposed to feel this way yet. My mom says it's puppy love. My dad laughs and says it's just a crush and it will pass. But neither of them know the depth of this feeling I'm having. This love I have for her, it's not going to burn out and fizzle away over time. It's bone-deep. I can feel it in the pit of my stomach and the tips of my toes. She leaves me breathless, and that's okay because when I'm around her, she's the air I need to breathe.

I finish the last song and exit the stage even though the crowd is cheering and demanding more. But there is only one thing I want right now and it's her. I make my way across the grassy field we're playing in. She's standing with a group of people we go to school with, talking and laughing. I wrap my arms around her from behind, and she spins around to face me with a smile, knowing that I'm the one touching her.

I can't ever seem to take her by surprise. She must feel me the same way I feel her presence.

She hugs me close, pressing her cheek against my sweaty chest, but she doesn't complain. In fact, she never complains about how sweaty I am after a show the way girls have in the past.

She looks up at me, and her blue eyes land on mine, making an explosion go off in my body.

"Are you ready to go?"

She nods, a knowing look in her eyes. Lately, we've been getting closer and closer to crossing the finish line, and I think we both know that tonight, there's no stopping us.

I pull away but catch her hand in mine as I lead her across the grass and to my awaiting car. I open the driver's side door, and she climbs in and slings across the bench seat to ride in the middle like she always does. I put the key into the ignition, and the motor roars to life. I shift into reverse and back out. We start down a long gravel road, and I drive us to our secret spot. It's private property, but it's not gated off, the road swallowed up by dry grass and weeds. There's a big opening in the forest, and a pond sits in the center with the big bright moon shining overhead.

I park by the pond and shift into park, killing the engine. The silence of the night stretches on around us. I put my arm across the back of the seat, and she scoots closer to my side, resting her head against my shoulder.

"Did you have fun tonight?"

She nods. "You sounded good up there." She smiles. "You looked pretty good up there too."

A grin spreads across my lips. "Well, you looked pretty good from where I was standing too," I say, moving my lips to hers. She doesn't stop me. Instead, she pulls me in faster. My lips press against hers, and my body starts to tingle with need.

She turns in the seat so she's facing me, and then she lies back, pulling me down with her. I'm between her legs, and I know she can feel how excited I am. I slow the kiss and break away. "Are you sure?" *I ask, looking into her eyes.*

She nods. "I want this, Ben. I want you. Tonight. I'm tired of waiting."

With that, I kiss her hungrily, and our hands are in a hurry to strip each other of our clothing. I push her soft, cotton skirt up her legs and pull away. I look down to find her light-pink panties—the only thing standing in my way. I unbuckle my jeans and lift my hips to push them down. My aching dick springs free, and I look at her in time to see her eyes widen.

I tear open a condom and slide it on. With that done, I reach for her panties and start to lower them. Her eyes close and clamp shut to the point she has lines at the edges. When they're off, I toss them onto the floorboard and move back on top of her. I kiss her softly, feeling the way she's shaking beneath me. "Mia, are you sure? We can wait."

She shakes her head. "I don't want to wait."

I take myself in hand and position myself at her opening. "Open your eyes, Mia. Look at me."

She does, and I can see all the love and fear and nervousness they hold. "Stop me if I hurt you."

She nods and I push on past her barrier, claiming her as my own. She sucks in a loud breath as she stretches around me, and I think my eyes roll back in my head. My orgasm threatens to push past my hold, but I get myself under control.

"Are you okay?" *I ask, moving my hand up to cup her cheek.*

She nods, but a tear slides out of the corner of her eye. I wipe it away and lean in, kissing her as I begin to move again. She gasps when I can't go any further, so I pause before sliding out to start again.

"I love you, Ben," *she whispers against my lips.*

My heart starts to race. "I love you, too, Mia," *I breathe out, almost like a sigh of relief. I've been holding those words back, and finally saying them is like confessing all my sins.*

I wake in a panic, just like I always do when I dream of her. My heart is racing, and sweat is clinging to every inch of skin. My eyes dash around my bunk, like I'm trying to remind myself of where I am. Then my eyes land on her asleep at my side, and the memory of last night comes flooding back. I have her. She's still here. I squeeze her gently and breathe a sigh of relief.

She lets out a little whimper, and I press a kiss to the top of her head. Her hand comes up to land on my stomach.

"Are you awake?" she whispers.

"A dream woke me. Go back to sleep," I whisper back, only now hearing the guys' snores from the other bunks.

"I was scared it was all a dream." I feel her let out a long breath.

"Me too," I reply, running my hand through her hair again.

WE WAKE A FEW HOURS LATER, and the bus is completely quiet. The guys must already be up and out of the bus. "Good morning," I say, leaning over and pressing my mouth to hers.

"Good morning," she replies against my lips as she hitches her thigh over my hip and laces her fingers into my hair, deepening our kiss.

My hand finds her ass, and I pull her closer as my body comes to life.

"Alright, time to get up," Mike says, stomping his way back onto the bus.

Our kiss breaks off, and my head flops back against the pillow. "Go away!"

He laughs. "Nah, really. We gotta hit the road. I got a dog that misses me."

Mia looks over at me. "I thought you had a week?"

"I do, but the guys want to go home. I can either go with them, or I can stay and fly back later."

A small smile spreads across her face. "You can stay?"

I nod. "You know a place I can crash?" The corners of my mouth begin to lift up.

Her smile stretches wider. "I have an idea."

"Up! Don't make me drag you out of that bunk," Mike threatens.

I help Mia get her dress back in place, and she climbs out of the bunk. I pull on my boxers and stand up behind her. We both look up to find Mike.

He smiles wide as he looks us up and down. "Uh-huh. I figured it was you in there."

She tilts her head to the side. "How you doing, Mike?"

He rushes over and grabs her in a big hug. "A lot better now that I got to spend a little time with your girl."

She laughs and pushes him away. "Lucy is still here?"

"Nah, she took off last night... after we were... you know. Done."

She shrugs. "I didn't even hear anyone come in. I might have been out cold."

"No, we didn't want to bother you. Me and her, well..." He scratches his head. "We had a quickie in the bathroom." He motions toward the bar.

She shakes her head as she sits down on the bunk, pulling her shoes on. "I should have known. You two always were classy like that."

"Hey, you were the one riding a rock star on his tour bus. Now which of us is the classy one?" he teases.

"Mike," I threaten, but she just holds up her middle finger, making us all laugh.

Mike looks over at me. "So, what's the plan? You ready to hit the road?"

I pull my jeans up my hips. "Nah, I think I'm going to chill here for the week. I'll fly back."

Mike's eyes stretch wide. "Oh, okay," he says, surprised.

"Um, did Lucy take my car last night?"

Mike nods.

"It's fine. We'll just have the bus drop us off. Let me get my things and I'll be ready."

Mike and Mia go up to the front of the bus while I stay behind and toss some stuff into a bag.

I toss in some clothes and move into the bathroom where I grab the remaining items I'll need. I catch a glimpse of myself in the mirror and can't help but to notice that I'm wearing a small smile. My eyes seem more green and brighter. The dark circles under my eyes seem a little more faded. I did sleep pretty well last night. I wonder if that's because I was holding her against me all night. I have to admit, I feel happier today than I have in a long time. I feel lighter, like living is no longer a burden. Now, breathing isn't a curse. It's a want. I don't know how this could possibly end with us, but I do know that I'm not going to question it. I'm just going to enjoy it.

The bus stops at the address she gave the driver, and the two of us step off, hand in hand. I have my bag thrown over one shoulder and my guitar on the other as she leads the way up a sidewalk and to a door. She knocks.

"Sorry, I don't have my keys."

The door opens, and Lucy is standing on the other side. She's smiling until her eyes move over to me. Then the smile falls as her mouth drops open in surprise.

Mia walks past her and I do the same, but her eyes are wide, and her mouth is still hanging open as she turns to watch me walk past her.

I laugh. "What's up, Luce?"

"I'm behind. Someone catch me up," she says, closing the front door and looking at the two of us.

Mia looks up at me. "Ben, my room is the second door on the right. You can put your stuff in there, and I'll be in in a sec."

"Sure," I agree, moving past them and down the hall. Already, I can hear their whispers behind me.

I open the door and flip the switch. The room fills with light as I look around. There's a queen-size bed in the center of the room with a cream-colored bedspread, light-pink pillows, and bedside tables on either side. At the foot of the bed is a bench holding candles and knickknacks. Across the room is her dresser, and above it hangs a TV. On the far side of the room is a desk. I set my things down and move to the desk. I see a stack of graded papers and smile. She did it. She's a teacher.

There's a lamp on the desk, and on the other corner is a picture of her and Lucy when they were probably sixteen or seventeen. I see a large crowd of people behind them, so I'm guessing the picture was taken at one of our shows. A bulletin board hangs on the wall in front of the desk, and I look up to find a note that I wrote her.

Mia,

I can't stand to be without you. Every minute of the day, I'm thinking of you. I know I said I wanted this life, but now I'm left wondering why? I miss you more than words can explain. I miss running my fingers through your silky hair. I miss the smell of you on my pillows and on my sweatshirts you would always steal. I miss your laugh, your voice, your eyes. God, looking into your eyes could bring me to my knees. I just miss you. Please wait for me. I promise, I'll come back for you.

It was a letter I wrote after I'd only been gone a few months. I thought I was going to die without her. I know now that all that pain was just withdrawals. I was addicted to her then, and that addiction has never let up. Meeting her changed everything for me, physically and mentally. Being with her now is only letting that addiction take a stronger hold on me, but I don't care. I'd die for this week with her.

SEVEN

MIA

"What the hell?" Lucy whispers as Ben walks down the hallway.

"Shh, he'll hear you," I reply, turning to watch him walk into my room. I wait until I hear the door close, then turn back to address her. "Okay, now we can talk," I say, going into the kitchen for a drink.

"What the hell happened last night?" she asks, following along behind me.

"Well, we talked and kissed. Kissing turned into screwing, and here we are," I say, taking out two bottles of water.

"So does that mean that the two of you are back together?"

"No," I answer.

"Does it mean that you're going to get back together?"

"No," I say again.

"So what the hell?" She stomps her foot.

I roll my eyes. "It means that we've both been missing one another, and now that he's back and has a week off, we're going to enjoy it."

She nods. "And that's it?"

"Yep." I nod as I take the two bottles of water and head to my room.

When I open my door, I find him standing in front of my desk. I walk across the floor and hand him a bottle.

"So, you did it, huh?"

"Did what?" I ask, sitting on the edge of the bed and taking a drink of much-needed water. Drinking too much has caused me to feel tired and dehydrated today.

"Became a teacher." He smiles proudly.

"Oh." I smile and nod. "Yeah, I went to college, graduated, and got a job teaching kindergarten."

He comes to sit at my side. "That's great. How was it?"

I frown. "How was… college?"

He nods happily. "I want to hear about everything I missed. Tell me so it's like I was there with you."

I laugh. "Well, if you were there with me, I probably wouldn't have done the things I did."

"How so?"

I set the bottle of water on the bedside table and pull my legs up under me. "Well, college started out a bit rough, you know? I was heartbroken, but I had to move on because the world doesn't stop. So I went, but it didn't feel like I thought it would. I expected to be excited and have fun. But everywhere I looked, I was just reminded of your absence. I was sad, depressed, and lost."

Guilt washes over his face. "I'm sorry."

"I kind of rebelled there for a while. I went to parties, drank too much, dated too much…"

His eyes jump up to mine. "Dated too much?"

I nod. "I kept trying to replace you. Kept trying to find who could make me feel the way you did."

"And did you?" he asks, his eyes hidden away under his hair.

I shake my head. "I still haven't."

He leans in, pressing his lips to mine as his hand holds firm around the back of my neck, not letting me pull away. "Me neither," he says against my lips as he begins to lay me back.

I place my hand on his chest, pushing him back slightly. "Tell me about you. How did you fill the time? How many did you try to replace me with?"

He chuckles under his breath. "Not as many as you'd think."

"Really?" I ask, picturing him parading women through the bus.

He nods. "I didn't sleep with another woman until we'd been broken up for years. And then I only did it as an attempt to get over you. I knew I'd never find someone who could compare to you."

"So, you've only been with one other woman?"

"No," he answers, his eyes falling closed.

"How many?" I don't know why I have to know or if I even want to.

"Four."

My mouth drops open. "Only four?"

He nods. "How many for you?"

I feel my face heat, and I'm sure it's red. "Well, remember I said I rebelled?"

He nods.

"Well... I've been with eight others."

I expect his eyes to bug out with my number, but they don't. Instead, they fill with a darkness I can't explain. "I guess I have a lot of work to do to make you forget them, huh?"

I giggle. "You're the only one I care to remember."

He smiles, but it falls away when I lift my head and press my lips to his.

His hand finds my hip and he tugs me closer, but right now, there is only one thing I can think about, and for the first time, it isn't sex. It's a shower.

"Wanna take this to the shower?" I ask with a flirty smile.

"Hell yeah, I do," he replies, jumping up quicker than I thought possible. He catches my hand in his and pulls me up. My chest smashes against his as he picks me up and carries me to the bathroom.

I giggle the whole way at how playful he is as he sets me on my feet. His hands are already spinning me around and unzipping my dress. It falls to a heap at my feet, leaving me completely naked since I didn't wear a bra and my panties are lost in his bunk somewhere.

"That's better," he says with a smirk. He removes his shirt, revealing his strong chest and tattoo-covered abs.

I smile. "That's better."

He yanks me back against him and kisses me until we're both breathless. Finally, I pull away and rush toward the shower before he can distract me any further. The hot water rains from the showerhead down over my head, and I close my eyes as I smooth my hair back. When I open my eyes, I find him watching me, eyes burning.

"You're different than you used to be but the same in a lot of ways too."

He steps forward, erect and proud. "How am I different?" His hands grab my hips, pulling me chest against his.

"Well, you have more tattoos now."

He rolls his eyes, not accepting this answer.

"You seem more open about your feelings. You didn't use to."

"That's because I've had ten years of wishing you knew what you mean to me." His finger moves up under my chin, tilting my head back. "All I could do was write a song and hope you heard it. It's only now that I've found out you haven't heard any of them."

"Does that bother you?"

He shrugs. "Sort of. I mean, I told myself I was staying away not only so your dreams could come true, but so you'd be proud of me. I wanted to make something of myself for you. I finally did, and you're oblivious to it."

I place my hands on either side of his face and force his eyes to mine. "I am proud of you, Ben. Even with as much as I missed you, I never once regretted telling you to take your shot. You worked hard, and you achieved everything you set out to."

"Not yet I haven't," he says, closing the space between our lips.

I wrap my arms around his neck, and his hands move up and

down my back. I lace my fingers into his hair, tugging and pulling. His hand slips between us and moves against my center, massaging over my bundle of nerves and shooting fireworks through me with each flick. He slides two fingers inside of me, and I let out a moan that makes his cock twitch against me.

"Fuck, I'm never going to get enough of you," he says, pulling away and spinning me around.

My hands come out to land on the wall in front of me, stabilizing my dizziness, and the next thing I know, he's sliding into me from behind. I let out a loud moan, and he bites down on my shoulder. "I want to hear you. Show me how good only I can make you feel." He slams his hips against me again, and I call out even louder.

My release is already building just from knowing it's him manipulating my body. As he pounds into me from behind, his hand moves around to find my clit again. He presses his fingers against my bundle of nerves and slowly flicks back and forth, pushing me over the edge completely. Moments later, he's emptying himself into me with a loud animalistic growl.

———

"PIZZA'S HERE," I say, bringing the box of pizza into the bedroom and sliding it onto the bed before climbing up to join him. The TV is on, and we're watching a movie we've seen a thousand times: *Titanic*.

"I still love this movie," I confess as I take a slice of pizza. "For the longest time, I thought we were going to end up like them."

He looks over at me questionably. "Dead?"

I laugh. "No, that we wouldn't ever get our earthly happily ever after, but we'd get it spiritually. When we're dead, there won't be anything to keep us apart."

His eyes move from mine back to the TV, but he doesn't reply. Maybe he doesn't know how to yet. I mean, we haven't exactly talked about what we're doing here. Right now, all we know is that we have a week. I'm savoring every moment of having him here. But I know when it's time for him to go, it's going to leave that hole in my heart freshly reopened and bleeding. I try to push that thought away and stay in the here and now.

We eat our pizza, watch our movie, and climb into bed together. Like last night, he holds me in his strong arms. The sounds of his breathing and his heart beating bring me back to a happy memory.

"That was amazing," I say with my head on his chest as we lay across the front seat of his car.

He chuckles. "You have no idea."

I lift my head to study his face. "Did you mean it?"

"Mean what?" His eyes find mine.

"What you said earlier."

He thinks back and nods. "That I love you?"

I nod.

His hand moves up to cup my cheek. "I do love you, Mia, and I have for some time now."

I smile. "Good, 'cause I love you too."

He leans in and his lips capture mine. It's in this moment that I know that I'll belong to him forever. Even at sixteen, I know that this isn't just first love. This is it. This is real love. A love that will last a lifetime. There's no escaping it. No outrunning it. No matter where we end up in life, I will have him wrapped around my heart for the rest of my life.

In the morning, we decide to get out of the apartment and take a walk down memory lane, going to places we used to go and doing things we used to do. We stop at Becky's diner and have breakfast. We're so early that the place is full of older people and nobody even notices us.

He looks around the place with a smile. "I have to say, this is the first time I've ever been in here this early sober." He laughs.

I smile and nod. "Yeah, I remember coming here all the time after a night of watching you party." I never was a big drinker in high school. I'd go to parties and drink from a bottle of water that I brought while everyone else drank beer from a keg, Ben included. He'd start the night out on stage, but by the end, he was just as drunk as the rest of them. On those nights, I'd drive us home. But even when Ben was completely hammered, he was still the most caring guy I've ever known.

After breakfast, we drive over to the high school and park in the front parking lot in the same place we'd park every day. I shut off the car and look over at him. He's not looking at me. He's looking at the school and the yard, seeing our memories instead of what's actually there.

"I remember we were standing right there the first time I asked you out. You remember that?" he asks, pointing to an area on the sidewalk under a big oak tree.

I smile and nod. "Of course I do."

EIGHT

BEN

I'm leaning against my car as I watch the front doors of the school, waiting for her to come out. After meeting her at that party last night, I've been able to do nothing but think of her. I don't know why I feel such a strong connection to her. All I know is that I have to have her. She has to be mine.

She exits the school and starts down the sidewalk, her dark hair blowing behind her. My heart jumps to life, speeding like a freight train. I push myself up off the car and jog over to the sidewalk, coming to a stop directly in front of her. Her shocking blue eyes lock on mine, and the corners of her lips lift slightly. "Oh, hey," she says, tugging the strap of her bag up higher on her shoulder.

"Hey. You in a hurry, or do you have a sec?"

She nods and bites her bottom lip, the action making my muscles tighten. "I have a minute. What's up?"

"Well," I start but have suddenly forgot how to ask a girl out. "I was wondering if maybe... you would want to... go out with me sometime?"

Her eyes brighten and sparkle as the sun hits them. "Go out? Like on a date?"

I nod. Damn, she makes it sound so formal.

She shrugs. "Sure. Friday?"

I'm speechless. Did she just say yes? "Yeah, Friday is perfect. I can pick you up around... seven?"

Her smile widens. "Okay." She pulls a pen out of her bag and then takes my hand in hers. The moment she touches me, my skin breaks out in tingles. "Here's my number. Call me," she says, writing her number across the top of my hand.

She drops my hand and smiles one last time. "See ya." She walks past, leaving me to stand back and watch her go.

I look over at her, and she's staring off at the same spot I was. "You're even more beautiful now," I tell her and she rolls her eyes.

"Please, I've seen some of the women you've had on your arms."

I can't remember a single one of them. "They can't even begin to compare to you." I pick up her hand and kiss the back. "Come back with me."

Her eyes cut to mine. "Like to California?"

I nod. "You have the summer off, right? What else are you going to do? I can show you around; we can hit up some beaches; you can watch us record."

"I don't know, Ben," she says, unsure.

"What's not to know? I'm not ready to say goodbye. Are you?"

"Well, no, but—"

"No buts. This is the perfect time. And we'll get more time together."

"I'll think about it," she promises, reaching for the keys and starting the car.

The next place she takes us to is our pond. We've made love around this pond more times than I can count. She shuts the car off and looks over at me.

"Wow. I haven't been back here since that night." She knows the one I'm talking about.

"I've been back several times. I come out here, look out over the dark water, and it takes me back. I try to reimagine that night, but I never can. It always turns out exactly the same."

This isn't fair. I'm only eighteen. I shouldn't have to make this kind of decision yet. How am I supposed to choose between the only girl I've ever loved and the only dream I've ever had? She's told me time and time again to go, that she'll wait. But I don't want her to wait. I don't want to hold her back. She's a good girl, and she deserves someone to wait for her, not the other way around. Not to mention, it won't be long before the guys we go to school with will start sniffing around her more than they already do. Then in the fall, she'll go to college, and there will be a whole new set of guys sniffing around her.

My decision has to be made tomorrow. The guys have already agreed to sign with the label, and they ship out tomorrow. I was told that if I don't go, they still will. It won't be hard to replace me, but this is my band! I started it. These are the songs that I wrote. I'm sure they'll record new ones but still. I can't let them go without me, can I?

I park the car next to our pond, and the silence fills the air around us. She's sitting in the middle of the bench seat like always. She turns to look at me, and I'm not even sure what she sees in my eyes right now. Love, loss, fear, confusion? Without saying a word, she pulls my lips to hers. I kiss her like she's the air I need to breathe, like this may be our last kiss. For all I know, it could be.

"I love you," she says against my lips as she moves to straddle me.

"I love you too," I reply, my hands working her skirt up over her hips. We've gotten good at this car sex thing. Every time, she wears a skirt, making things a little easier. Plus, getting to look at her bare legs all night long is always a plus. Her soft thighs against my rough calloused hands feels better than heaven. Hard meets soft.

I think about going any amount of time without her, and my heart cracks. Then I think about her forgetting about me and moving on, and it shatters completely. I break our kiss and look into her eyes. "I'm not going. I can't." I shake my head.

She places her hands on either side of my face and forces me to look into her impossibly blue eyes. "You can, Ben. I know you. You're strong and determined. This is your dream. You can't let it pass you by."

"You're my dream," *I tell her.*

She smiles. "I've only become your dream here recently. This, the band, your music, it's always been your dream, and I won't let you give it up for me." *Her mouth is back on mine, but I shake my head anyway.*

"You're what I want," *I say against her lips.*

She pulls back. "I love you and you know I love you, but this is something you have to do for you. This isn't about me. If we're meant to be, things will work out. You just gotta have faith." *Her lips are back on mine again, but this time, I don't pull away because she reaches between us and frees me from my jeans. In moments, she's sliding down my dick and making me forget everything but her.*

"What do you wish was different about that moment?" I ask, pulling myself from that memory.

She shrugs. "That's the thing. I wouldn't change a thing because that moment was perfect the way it was. And that's with knowing that I would miss you for ten years. I would never take that away from you, Ben. Do I wish you would've stayed in contact with me, that I could have been backstage at some of your shows, that we had phone calls to get us through until we could see one another again? Yes. But you've explained your side of that."

I nod. "Come with me, Mia. Let me make up for lost time." It's the only thing I can think about. I'm nowhere near ready to leave, and even though we still have a few days together, I know this feeling will only get stronger. The feeling of holding on to her, loving her. I don't know how she feels about me anymore.

She used to love me, but it's been ten years. That could've changed. This thing we're doing here might be closure to her, not picking up where we left off.

She smiles, but it's not her usual, happy smile. "We still have a few days left. Let's just enjoy it and talk about it later."

It annoys me that she doesn't trust me like she used to. Before, she'd be down for anything I suggested. Now, she's holding back. I guess I can't blame her. I did break her heart and keep her waiting on me for ten years. Fuck, if I could take it all back, I would. I don't want this life, not without her. How do I get her to open up to me? How do I get us back to where we were? How do I make her fall back in love with me?

We spend the day going from one place to the next. After the pond, we grab ice cream from our favorite little stand. We visit a few places I played back in high school and a few the year after I graduated. We have dinner at our favorite Chinese restaurant before heading back to her apartment. By the end of the night, we've had a few drinks, and the trip down memory lane makes us feel like a couple of kids again. Neither of us mention the last ten years. Everything negative falls away, and we're left with nothing but the two of us and all of the love, passion, and yearning we hold for one another.

I chase her from the car up to the door. I catch her at the last second and pull her against me. She giggles but presses her lips to mine. I pick her up against me and open the door to carry her inside. My eyes are closed as I kiss her and try to remember the way through her apartment. I stumble and we fall into the wall, laughing.

"Ow, wrong way," she says, smiling and rubbing the back of her head.

"Sorry," I laugh, trying to figure out where we're at in her dark apartment.

Suddenly, the lights come on, and Lucy is standing at the end of the hallway I was trying to find. She has her arms crossed over her chest and a wide smile on her face as she stands there in her robe.

"What are you two doing?" she asks sweetly.

"Sorry for all the noise. Ben forgot the layout of the apartment. We're going to bed now." She grabs my wrist and tugs me toward the hallway.

"And keep it down in there tonight. I'm trying to get some too," Lucy calls after us.

As we're slipping into her bedroom, I see through the crack in her bedroom door and find Mike sitting in her bed, naked from the waist up.

I pull away from Mia and push open Lucy's door. Mike jumps when he sees me, then his wide smile spreads across his face.

"Hey, man! Fancy seeing you here." His smile is still in place.

I laugh and shake my head. "What the hell are you doing here? I thought you went back home?"

He nods. "Oh, well, I did, but then I just hopped a plane and came back. Lucy's great."

I close the door as Lucy is approaching, and she bangs on the door. "Hey! Let me in!"

I lock the door and step away from it. "So what? You and she are a thing now?"

"You and Mia a thing now?"

I shake my head. "What's that have to do with this?"

He shrugs. "I don't know. Just wondering."

I run my hands through my hair. "I swear, you better not ruin this for me."

His brows pull together. "How am I going to do that?"

"You're going to screw Lucy and leave in the middle of the night or something. She's going to get mad and complain to Mia. Then Mia is going to think I'm just like you. I'm trying for something here."

"Oh, so it's not serious... yet. Is that what you're saying?" One brow lifts as he waits for an answer.

I sigh. "Just... don't fuck this up. Be a gentleman for once."

That only makes him laugh as I let Lucy back in and head across the hall to Mia's room.

"What was that about?" she asks, walking out of the bathroom in a tiny silky nightgown.

I look her up and down. "Mike is over there."

Her eyes stretch wide as her brows raise. "In Lucy's room? I thought he went home."

I nod as I sit down to remove my shoes. "He did, then he flew back! I don't know what they're doing, but you might want to warn

Lucy that he's only in it for the sex. I'd hate to see her hurt in all this."

She waves her hand through the air as she makes her way over to me. "Don't worry about it. Lucy doesn't do relationships. She's only in it for the sex too." She giggles as she sits in my lap and wraps her arms around my neck. "Now, let's have sex." She smiles wide.

NINE
MIA

The week flies by too quickly with Ben here. We spend every minute of every day together, and I spend every night wrapped up in his arms. We chase after memories and make new ones. But tonight is our last night here together. I still haven't answered his question, and he hasn't asked again, but it's getting to the point where I have to make a decision. I know going across the country with him isn't anything major. It's not like I have work or anything, but if I go with him, it will only be putting off the inevitable. Eventually, we'll each go back to our real lives, and I'll be more broken than ever. Before, I missed the Ben I knew—the kid who was sweet and sexy but young and full of life, big hopes, and dreams. But now, I'll miss this Ben. The guy is sexy as hell but sweet at the same time, a man who is established and famous for working so hard at his dream. That's another thing.

If I go back to California with him, our little secret bubble is sure to pop. He's in the limelight a lot, and he'll be working and recording. Will being with him in California be like being with him here? I'm not meant to be some celebrity. I like my privacy. I like my life. Being with Ben would turn my life upside down, so the question is, how much do I want to be with him?

But most importantly, does he want to me with me? Forever, not just a week or two here and there. This is the kind of stuff we haven't talked about yet and the stuff I need to know before I can make my decision. Our last night, we plan a romantic dinner on my bedroom floor. I spread a blanket out across the hardwood and light some candles before turning the lights out. We eat some kind of fancy chicken with rice and vegetables and drink glass after glass of wine.

When dinner is cleaned up, he grabs his guitar and starts strumming while I lie beside him and listen to the sounds of his fingers moving across the strings. Just hearing it again causes goosebumps to prickle my skin. My eyes close as I listen to the sounds of him playing. Somewhere behind my lids, I get a vision of us as just a couple of kids doing this exact same thing. It makes my heart race and my body come to life. When he starts to sing, my eyes open and lock on his face in awe.

His voice is deep, thick, and raspy. The music he plays on stage is rock, but this is a slower, softer song. He sings of love and loss and memories and promises. My heart feels like it's being squeezed in my chest, and I know it's because it's not in my chest but in his hands. He sings the last of the song and moves to set the guitar back down. I sit up and turn to face him.

"What?" he asks, looking at me in the candlelight.

"I want to go with you to California tomorrow," I blurt out.

His eyes stretch wide and fill with excitement. "You do?"

I nod, not knowing if this is the right way or not. I know I don't have my questions answered, but that doesn't matter. If he needs more time to fall back in love with me, then that's what I'll give him. We'll figure the rest out from there.

"That's great," he says, pulling me into his lap. He kisses me and rolls us over so he's on top of me.

"Please tell me Mike isn't flying with us," I joke.

He laughs. "We can try to sneak off, but I doubt we'll get far. To be honest, I'm surprised that he made it here on his own."

I giggle. "Well, it is his home, so it's probably muscle memory at this point."

"We're going to have so much fun, Mia," he says, brushing hair away from my face as he looks longingly into my eyes.

"Ben," I whisper. "I love you" is on the tip of my tongue.

"Hmm?" he asks, leaning in to kiss my jaw.

"I..." I start, but the words won't come out. He nips my collarbone and I let out a gasp. "Take me to bed," I say instead.

He pulls away, blows out the candles, and picks me up, carrying me to bed where he strips off our clothes and covers my body with his.

"ARE you sure you're going to be alright while I'm gone?"

"Yes, Mia. I am an adult, you know," Lucy says as we're heading for the door.

"I know, but you know how I worry."

"Let's get going. Taxi is here," Mike says, walking through.

"You got my car key, right?"

"I got 'em," she says with a nod and a wave.

Ben is holding my hand, dragging me to the door.

"Call me anytime, okay? Day or night, call me!"

"I know, Mia. Go and have fun!" Lucy says, shutting the door between us.

I turn around and walk with Ben to the car. We all pile in, with me in the middle. I look from Ben to Mike and back. Suddenly, I feel like I'm seventeen again, squished between these two.

The flight feels long, but in reality, it isn't bad. My mind is just filled with questions that I desperately want to ask but that I also want to hold back as well. Do I really want the answers to these questions? What if he gives me answers I don't want?

I decide that I don't want to ruin the trip by asking anything too serious. I'll wait. I can hold it back. At the airport, Mike goes off in his own direction, and Ben, with his hat low and sunglasses on, pulls me through the airport and to a waiting limo.

"This is yours?" I ask, climbing inside.

He takes the spot next to me. "Well, it's not mine, but it was sent for us," he replies, removing his hat and glasses.

"It's beautiful here," I mumble, looking out the window at the bright sun and blue sky. The temperature is perfect, not too hot and not too cold.

"You're beautiful," he replies.

When I turn my head to look at him, he's got his head laid back as he looks in my direction. His eyes slowly move up my body, settling on my eyes. I feel my face heat up, and a nervous smile forms.

He lifts his hand and runs his fingers across my heated cheek. "I love it when you blush. It's my favorite shade of pink." He leans in and softly presses his lips to mine. The kiss doesn't last long, but the softness of it lingers on my skin.

After a long drive, we make it to Ben's house. It's in a gated community with expensive mansions all lined up. I wonder how many of his neighbors are celebrities, but I don't ask. I don't want to be a tourist. The limo pulls into a circle drive, and my eyes are too busy taking everything in to pay attention to much else. When the door opens, he climbs out and I follow. Standing up outside, I spin in a circle, looking at everything from the fountain in the center of the drive, to the perfectly potted plants along the house, to the big three-story house itself.

"This is where you live?" I ask as he reaches for my hand.

"Yeah, for about two months of the year. The rest of the time, I live on the bus." He leads me toward the front door. He stops and unlocks it. "I'm afraid we're going to be on our own for a couple days. The staff don't stay when I'm on tour, and usually the first couple days I'm back, I just sleep."

"Staff?" I ask, following him into the house.

The foyer blows me away. There is a large table in the center of the room with a bouquet of flowers. Stairs on either side of the room lead to the second floor. Straight back, I can see glass doors that lead to the patio and pool.

"The kitchen is to the right, and the living room is to the left. But I don't hang out down here much. It's a little too formal."

"So where do you hang out?"

"There's a theater upstairs where I watch TV. There is a recording studio if I get an idea. There's an office and a ton of bedrooms. But usually, I'm outside in the pool or hot tub. Come on, I'll show you around."

He takes my hand and walks me through the expensive kitchen full of top-of-the-line appliances, then the formal dining room with its big, long table—it reminds me of something you'd see on TV. The living room is rather formal with couches and chairs, but they all look stiff like they've never been sat in. There's a large fireplace and a huge TV. Upstairs, he shows me the theater. The screen takes up an entire wall, and there are rows and rows of comfy reclining chairs. He shows me the recording studio, but I don't know enough about them to know how fancy his is. Then he shows me his bedroom.

His bedroom is literally the size of my whole apartment. There's a giant king-size bed in the middle of the room. There is a sitting area with couches and a TV, and there is a walk-in closet and attached bathroom. I walk into the bathroom to find a deep bathtub with jets, a walk-in shower that's big enough to hold at least ten people, and a large built-in vanity with perfect lighting.

When I come out, I find him lying across the bed with his arms out at his sides. I climb up onto the bed and move to straddle him. "So, what do you want to do first?" I ask him with a smile.

The corners of his mouth turn up as he looks at me. His hands move to my hips, pulling me harder against him. "What do you want to do first?"

"That hot tub looks rather comfortable."

"Oh, it is," he says, sitting up. He stands with me in his arms and moves us to the bathroom where we both strip and sink into the tub. When it's completely full, he pushes the button and the jets turn on, massaging a sore spot on my back. I sink deeper into the water and rest my head against the side.

"So, what's the game plan? You said you have to record? Do you do that here?"

"No, we'll go to the studio tomorrow."

"How long does it usually take to record an album?"

He shrugs. "It depends. If we're serious, we can get it done rather quickly, but if we mess up or fuck off too much, it can take a lot longer. The bright side is that I won't have to go every day. They record vocals and music separately. So one day, I may just be playing the guitar. The next Mike will go in, then Quin. Then they'll put it all together, and I'll go back in to do the lyrics."

"So, in the meantime..."

"In the meantime, I'm all yours."

I smile as excitement pumps through me.

As we enjoy our Jacuzzi bath, he massages my feet and legs. Then he pulls me over to him. I rest my chest against his back, and he moves his lips to my shoulders while pressing soft kisses along my jaw and neck. By the end of our bath, I'm completely relaxed and turned on from his hands touching me the whole time. When we climb out and dry off, he pulls me against him and kisses me. The kiss is slow but grows in intensity until he picks me up against him. I wrap my arms around his neck as he sets me on the vanity in the bathroom. His hands push away my towel, and then he's sliding into me. With all the mirrors in the bathroom, I can see him from all angles, and damn, he's never looked so sexy. The visual adds to the pleasure, and it only takes minutes before we're both shattering around one another.

We're both too relaxed to do much of anything, so we curl up in the middle of his big bed for a nap. He pulls me close and keeps his arms wrapped tightly around me. I can hear his deep, even breathing only moments later. I smile to myself as I listen to the sounds of his breathing and the soft pitter-patter of his heart. I look around the room and try to imagine living here. What if we had stayed together all these years? Would this be our home? Would I be here while he's out touring, waiting for his next call? This isn't the plan we made growing up because we never thought it would be in the cards. I think back to that memory.

The sky is dark with a million brightly lit stars filling the sky around us. In a way, it almost feels like we're under a black blanket with the small holes letting in light from the outside world. Here, under this blanket, is the world we created. Our world.

The pond is silent. There's not a sound but a ripple here and a frog croaking there. There's no wind, just a calm night around us as we lie on the blanket that Ben spread out over the hood of his car, my head resting against his shoulder as he holds me close.

"Where do you think we'll end up?" I ask.

He chuckles. "Probably right here in this town. We'll buy a place here, something nice and roomy but not too big or overly done. Just something that can hold us and all our kids."

I lift my head to look at him. "All our kids?"

He smiles and nods. "Yeah, we're going to have a lot of kids."

"What do you mean by a lot? Like three?"

"Oh no. The way I can't keep my hands off you, we're going to have at least six or seven," he teases, making me laugh. "You'll be teaching. I'll get some kind of job that keeps me busy through the day and brings in some money, but on the weekends, I'll probably still be doing local shows with the band. We'll grow. The kids will grow. They'll eventually move out and leave us to act like kids again."

I smile. "But what if the band makes it big? Then what?"

"Then... I guess we'll be living on a tour bus for a while. You can do your college classes online. When you graduate, we'll pick where we want to live full-time. I'll take some time off until we're settled."

"Then what?" I ask, knowing the answer. Then he'll go back on tour and leave me behind because I'll have a normal full-time job. If we decide to have kids, I'll be raising them alone. He'll only get to be a

dad between tours. Or we could always get out own bus, the family bus just for the three of us, him, me, and our child. He could still live his dream, and I could be a mother and teach online. The only important thing to me is that we're together. I don't care where we end up.

When I wake up, the room is dark, but he's still asleep at my side. I get up and use the bathroom, and when I come back, he wakes as I crawl into bed.

"What's wrong?" he mumbles.

"I'm kind of hungry," I confess.

He stretches. "Me too. Let's go watch some TV and order some food."

We move into the theater. He gets on the phone, ordering enough food to feed an army. We watch episode after episode of some Netflix sci-fi show, and when the food arrives, he spreads it all out around us. We eat out of containers instead of making a plate. It really does feel like we're living in our own little world. We drink, we talk, we laugh and kiss and end up back in bed around two a.m. As I drift back off to sleep, I can't help but smile with how happy I am. Being here, with him, in his world, it's more than I ever could've dreamed of. If I died right now, I'd die happy. Although, I wouldn't mind sticking around a little longer and seeing where this takes us.

IN THE RECORDING STUDIO, I'm in one little room while he stands in another, the rooms only separated by glass. I sit on a long sofa next to Mike and Quin, and we all watch while Ben records his guitar parts for the next album. There is a man sitting at a big table full of buttons, switches, and knobs, and somewhere deep inside of me, I have the urge to get up and play with all the buttons, but I hold it back. After finding out what is paid to rent the studio, there's no way I'm costing them more time. It's too bad that the band doesn't think that way though. They're like a bunch of kids with the way they run around, laugh, and joke.

Ben seems to be the one who's really focusing and trying to get his work done, so the other two have made a game out of seeing who can make Ben fuck up first. This must be a regular game for them, though, because Ben is a pro and doesn't even look up from what he's doing.

Watching him in the studio is different than watching him on stage. On stage, he has to not only sing and play guitar but put on a show for the crowd. But here, there is nobody to put on a show for. This is just him, playing the guitar, living and breathing his life. When I watch the way his fingers move over the strings of the guitar, goosebumps prickle my skin, and a tingle rushes up my spine. I think about how talented those hands of his are. I watch more than just his hands though. I love the way his eyes close when he's really feeling the music. I watch the way his jaw flexes and relaxes when the moment requires concentration. I watch the way he wets his lips and the way his biceps flex. By the end of his session, I'm ready to push him into the first empty room I find and take advantage of him.

We don't make it back to his place until late evening. Then we eat, shower, make love, and go to sleep holding on to one another. The rest of the week passes in the same fashion. Each day, we go to the studio where he records the guitar and vocals. The magic of watching him perform never wears off, and each night, we come back home and repeat the same process as before. We spend every day and every night together.

Two weeks in and we still haven't talked about what we're doing or what the future will look like for us. I get the feeling that our time is coming to an end, and even though I've talked to Lucy on the phone nearly every day, I feel the need to go home.

So at dinner, I plan on bringing the subject up. He's planned some kind of romantic dinner on the balcony that overlooks the rolling hills and mountaintops. A table is set up with a tablecloth and candles in the center. There's wine and food, and soft music plays in the background. The weather is warm with a slight breeze, and everything seems so perfect, I don't want to ruin it, but I have to know.

I take a sip of my wine and take a deep breath. "Ben?"

His eyes move up to mine.

"I don't want to ruin the moment here, but I have to know." I work up the courage I need to get the words out. "What are we doing? Where is this going to take us?"

I see his Adam's apple bob in his throat when he swallows the food in his mouth. "Oh," he says, picking up his cloth napkin and wiping his face. "Are you asking me what I want?"

I nod. "I guess so, yeah."

TEN

BEN

I take a deep breath and sit up straight. "In my perfect world, Mia, you would stay with me. We could live here on my downtime, and then we'd pack up and go on tour. You'd teach remotely from the bus, and we'd never separate. In the years to come, we could slow down, only do smaller tours so we can focus on our family and living our lives, but I know that's very one-sided. You'd have to give up your whole life to join mine, and I know that's not fair. I've been trying to think of a solution that works for both of us, but I haven't been able to figure it out yet. I mean, either I have to give up my life or you do, and I'd never ask you to do that."

"So, you do want a future with me then?" Her lips turn up in the corners.

"Yes, of course I do. What did you think this was all about?"

She shrugs. "I wasn't sure, to be honest. We've never talked about it. I've been telling myself just to enjoy the time I have with you and worry about the heartbreak of leaving later."

"You seriously overestimate me if you think I can walk away from you twice," I say, reaching across the table and taking her hand in mine. "I don't know exactly how we can make this work, but I want to make it work. Whatever it takes. Even if you have to go back home and I have to go back on tour. I won't give up on us this time. I want this. I want you."

She smiles, and that pink starts to creep up on her cheeks again. "Long distance? You think we can handle that?"

I squeeze her hand softly. "As long as you're mine, I can do anything." I level my eyes on her. "I want our plan back. I want all the things we said we were going to do. I want to get married one day, have kids, grow old together. I want all of it. I've never stopped loving you, Mia."

Her eyes fill with tears. "I never stopped loving you either." A tear falls and rolls down her cheek. I stand up and fall to my knees before her, wiping her tear away as I pull her lips to mine. The kiss is soft, slow, and lingering. My hands cup her cheeks as I deepen the kiss, never getting enough of her. Her arms wrap around my neck as she pulls herself closer.

I pull back and look into her icy eyes, which seem to be drowning with need. "I'm done with dinner. You?"

She smiles, bites down on her lower lip, and nods as her cheeks flush pink. I stand as I hold her against me. Our lips meet once again, and I carry her into my bedroom where I lay her back across the bed. Her hands are already trying to push my clothing away. I rip my shirt over my head and sling it onto the floor before bringing my mouth back to her body. I kiss down her neck and to her chest. When her shirt stops me, I pull away and yank it up, tossing it onto the floor next to mine. My mouth finds the swell of her breasts as I unclasp her bra. It unsnaps and she works the straps down her arms. Her chest is now bare, and I kiss my way to her hard nipple. I flick my tongue against it first, teasing her. When she whimpers, I suck it into my mouth, and she moans loudly.

While my mouth torments her nipple, my hands get busy freeing her of her jeans. I pull away and yank them down her legs. Now that she's completely bare for me, I kiss down her stomach and to the junction between her legs. I run my tongue through her folds, spreading her wetness. She's always so ready for me, and it's a major turn-on, distracting me even when I know I can't take her right away. I sometimes find myself dazing off, wondering how easy it would be to slide into her.

I flick my tongue against her clit, and her moans fill the room. Fuck, I love the sound she makes. I feel my body harden with excitement. I slide one finger into her, then two. I curl them upward and drag the pad of my fingers against the spot that will have her seeing stars. While my hand and mouth work her over, her body begins to shake and quiver. She's fisting the bedsheet at her sides, and her back is arching upward. I keep going, her screams growing louder and louder the longer I pleasure her.

When her release washes over her, I don't ease up, not until her body is limp and her moans have quieted. I pull away, unfasten my jeans, and free myself. Her hooded eyes watch me as I guide myself into her. My cock entering her, brings her back to life. She's no longer limp and quiet. Now, she's curled around me, scratching her nails up and down my back while moaning into my mouth.

Fuck, I love this woman more than I ever thought possible. I don't know how I managed to stay away from her as long as I did, but I know now that I'm not strong enough to do it again. She's my rock. She's my heart and soul. Living without her was the reason I felt so hopeless and lost before. Now that I have her back, I'm never letting her go. She's mine. She's always been mine, and it'll take heaven and hell to keep me away.

―――

THE SUMMER PASSES TOO QUICKLY. We finish recording, and we do a few smaller shows around California, all of which Mia gets to be a part of. I perform on stage like never before, now that I have a reason to fight for it. Before, I was a robot, moving along and doing my job but without a reason to live. Since Mia's come back into my life, I have a reason to live, a reason to smile and be happy. Being on stage and knowing that she is watching from the dressing room makes every show that much better. And when the show ends, I don't run back to the bus to avoid the fans. I run to the dressing room to kiss my girl. The two of us walk hand in hand through the crowds to the bus. I sign autographs and take pictures, all the things I used to do when this started, all the things I quit doing when I lost my reason to live.

But now that the summer is over, Mia has to go back home to get ready to go back to work, and I have a major tour to prepare for to celebrate the release of the album. The tour will be six months long, and we'll hit every major city in the country. Tickets went on sale the day after our first single dropped, and we're nearly sold out already.

I'm excited to start this new tour, but at the same time, I know I'll hate having to be away from her. I've already secured her a backstage pass to a couple of local shows, but for the most part, I'll be on my own and counting down the days until I get to see her again.

"You're going to call me every night, right?" she asks as we ride to the airport in the back of the limo.

I smile and nod. "Yes, every single night. And I'll text you all day. By the time I get back, you're going to be sick of me," I promise her, leaning in for a kiss.

"Not possible," she says, pressing her lips to mine.

Her phone goes off, and she opens the message that Lucy sent. It's the picture of the tabloid stand at the grocery store. Almost every magazine has our pictures on it.

Lucy: *You're almost famous!*

Mia rolls her eyes and drops the phone into her purse. "Ugh, I'm sure my students's parents are going to be asking me about this tomorrow."

"Sorry, just comes with the territory."

"I know, but I wish we could have some kind of privacy. I mean, they snapped pictures of me asleep on a yacht that was a hundred yards from the shore."

I laugh. "It wasn't that far. But hey, at least there weren't any drones flying over the pool. They would've gotten some nasty shots there." I smile, thinking about all the time we spent in the pool this summer.

Her face flushes. "God, I didn't even think of that. I can see it now. Me completely naked and spread eagle on the raft with you giving me oral. Here we come, Pornhub," she jokes.

I shrug. "Doesn't sound like a bad idea. OnlyFans at least," I add on to the joke.

She doesn't think it's funny, though, and she smacks me across the chest while rolling her eyes and scoffing.

"I'm just teasing. This body of yours is only for me to see." I move back in, but the car comes to a stop.

"We've arrived, sir," the driver says.

It's finally the time we've both been dreading. Time to say goodbye.

I pull her against me and hug her close. "I promise this isn't the end," I whisper into her ear.

She nods against my chest. "I know," she whispers. When she pulls back, I see the tears building in her eyes.

I wipe them away with my thumbs. "Don't cry. If you cry, I'll never let you get out of this car. You'll just have to quit your job and tour with me like my own personal groupie," I joke.

She laughs but nods her head. "I'm sorry. I'm just going to miss you. I'm not ready for the summer to be over yet."

"I know. I'm not either," I say, slipping my hand behind her neck and bringing her lips to mine. I kiss her long and soft, wanting to burn every moment of this into my memory like last night wasn't enough. I don't think either of us slept for more than two hours at a time. We'd make love, fall asleep, and start all over.

The driver opens our door, and she pulls away. "I love you," I tell her.

"I love you too," she says, forcing a smile.

She climbs out and I climb out behind her. "Call me when you land."

She nods and leans in for one last quick kiss. When she pulls away, the driver is already there, handing Mia her bag. She takes it and starts walking toward the doors. Before stepping through, she turns back to me one last time, smiles, and waves.

I wave back and watch as she steps inside and disappears from view. With a sigh, I get back into the car, and we start the journey back to the house. During the ride, I pull out my phone and flip through the pictures we took over the summer. Being alone after three months feels weird. The loneliness sets in, feeling heavier than it ever did before.

I decide to make the announcement on Instagram and Twitter, making us official. I upload a few of my favorite photos we took and type: *I met you when I was sixteen and I've loved you ever since. #mylove #myworld #forever*

I hit post, and within seconds, it blows up. People like the status. Some say "aw" or "congrats," but some internet trolls also turn up saying horrible things, which I don't bother to read. Moments later, Mike calls.

"I saw your post," he says the moment I pick up.

I laugh. "Yeah, I think everyone did by now. What's up?"

"I was just calling to see what's up. I mean, Mia left today, didn't she?"

"Yep, I'm on my way home from the airport now."

"She's not going on tour with us?"

"No, she has to get back to work."

"Trying long distance, huh?"

"Yeah, but after this tour, I want a break."

"A break?" I know he's probably surprised. We've toured constantly for ten years, only taking a week or two off here and there. We'd tour America, take a week off, and go to Canada. Then we'd take two weeks off and go overseas. Then the process would start again, only stopping when we needed to record.

"Yeah, I'm fucking tired. Plus, I want other things in my life, you know?"

"Other things like...?"

"Like marrying Mia, starting a family, all of that. This rock star thing is great, but it's worthless if you don't have anyone to share it with, don't you think?"

"Yeah, I guess you're right. I mean, I wouldn't have said that at eighteen, but now that we've been living it for ten years, I would like a break too. So, you think Mia will give up her job and move to California?"

"Actually, and don't you dare say this to anybody, but I've been thinking about moving home. Buying some property and building a house. Then, when we're not touring, I'll live there, and Mia won't have to give up her life."

"Home? You want to go home?"

I shrug. "Yeah, kind of. What does California have? Nothing is holding me here."

"I guess home wouldn't be so bad."

"You're thinking of Lucy, aren't you?"

"No," he says, but I can hear the smile he's wearing.

"Mia says that Lucy isn't the relationship type, man. Better not get your hopes up."

"I'm not hoping for anything, but I think if I asked her to be only with me, she wouldn't have a problem with it. We have really good sex, man."

"Gross."

He laughs. "What? Too much?"

"Too much," I reply.

"What time are we shipping out tomorrow?"

"Ten a.m.," I remind him.

"What you doing today then?"

"Packing, I guess."

"Let's hang out. We can go to a sports bar. Get hammered to kick-start this tour right."

"I don't know," I say, not wanting to miss my call with Mia tonight.

"Come on. Don't be a pussy."

"We're going to be sleeping on a bus for the next six months, man. I just want to relax and catch up on some sleep."

"You've done that all summer," he points out.

"No, I've had a sex marathon all summer," I say around a smile.

He makes a gagging sound and then hangs up on me. I smile to myself as I slide the phone into my pocket just as we're pulling up to the house.

I walk inside and silence greets me. I drop my wallet and keys onto the entryway table and head upstairs to get started on packing. Upstairs, everywhere I look reminds me of her now. I think we've had sex in every room of this house. Well, not all the bedrooms and spare bathrooms, but the theater, the office, the studio, the pool, hot tub, bedroom, and bathroom have all been broken in. I walk into my room, and my eyes land on my empty bed. I get visions of her cuddled up under the black sheet, her dark hair fanned out across the pillows, a wild mess from my fingers always tangling in it.

I walk across the room and fall into bed. I pull the pillow around me, smelling her on the fabric. I drift into a deep sleep.

ELEVEN

MIA

The flight feels twice as long now that I'm by myself. I take advantage of the moment and sleep the whole way. Lucy is waiting for me, and when she sees me, she wraps me in a big hug.

"I can't believe you're finally home! I thought you might have stayed there forever, my famous friend."

I snort. "I'm not famous, my boyfriend is, and no way could I live there. It's too fast. Everyone is always going. I need my small, quiet town."

"Did you just call Ben your boyfriend?" she asks with a smile.

"What? You think I just shacked up an entire summer with a rock star and got no commitment?"

She laughs and shakes her head. "Come on. Let's get home so you can tell me how you spent your summer."

On the way home, Lucy orders a pizza for dinner, and it arrives only minutes after we do. I drop my things in my room and pour us each a glass of wine. She sets the pizza on the coffee table and looks at me like it's story time.

I take a bite of my pizza. "What?"

"Spill! What did you do all summer?"

I roll my eyes. "Well, I got to watch them record their upcoming album."

"That's awesome. What else?"

I shrug. "We had a lot of sex."

She rolls her eyes. "Of course you did. What else? Did you meet any famous people?"

"No, not really. We really didn't leave his house much. But oh my God, you should see his house. It's huge. We spent a lot of time in the pool and in the theater—and in his bedroom." I smile, thinking about all the times we had sex in each area.

She snorts and shakes her head. "So, boyfriend, huh? How'd that come about?"

"Well, we just talked about what it is we were doing, you know? That's when he said that he couldn't walk away from me twice and that he still wants everything I want—marriage and kids—and we agreed to do long distance for these six months he's on tour. After that, he's going to settle down so we can get on with our lives together."

"So what does that mean? You live here while he's on tour and when he's done, what? You go back there?"

"Well, no," I say, feeling my brows draw together. "I can't do that. I have a job."

"So, he's coming here?"

"I don't know. We didn't go into specifics. But I'm sure he will. He knows that I can't just up and leave." Now that I think about it, what is the plan? Is he going to move in here with Lucy and me? Or is he going to get his own place out here? If he does, will he sell the place in California or keep it for when he needs to go back?

My phone rings, pulling me out of my thoughts. I look at the screen and see Ben's face. "Hey, you."

"Hey, you just now getting off the plane? You didn't call."

"I'm sorry, I just walked into the apartment and was talking to Lucy. Everything okay?"

"Yeah, I was just worried. I just woke up from a nap. You wore me out last night."

I smile to myself. "Ditto."

"Ew, you're talking about something dirty. I can tell by that look on your face," Lucy says, and I smack her arm to shut her up.

"So, are you excited about starting the tour tomorrow?"

He snorts. "Yes and no. I'm glad that this will be my last one for a while, but I'm not looking forward to all the shitty parts. Sleeping on a bus again instead of next to you. Doing show after show after show. Always feeling tired. It's rough."

"At least this time, you can count down to seeing me again. We have what, two months until you'll be around here and we can meet up for the night?"

"Yep, two months."

"Sounds long."

"Yes, it does. But I guess you'll just have to send me pictures every day to make up for it."

"What kind of pictures are we talking?"

He laughs. "You know, one of you waking up, one of you taking a shower, and then of bedtime so I can pretend I'm doing everything with you."

His words make my body hum. I turn to face away from Lucy as I whisper into the phone, "We'll have to start having phone sex."

"Ewww! Come on. I'm trying to eat."

I giggle and so does Ben. "Sold," he agrees. "Alright, well, I'll let you catch up with Lucy. I gotta get packing."

"Okay, I'll call you tonight before bed."

"You better," he says.

"Love you."

"Love you, too, baby."

I hang up the phone and turn to face Lucy again. She's giving me a dirty look. "What? Don't act like you haven't done it. You probably have phone sex with Mike every night."

She rolls her eyes. "I do not."

"What's going on with you two anyway?" I ask.

"Nothing. We hook up after local shows. That's all it's ever been and all it ever will be."

"Why though? You like him, don't you?" I pick a piece of pepperoni off my pizza and pop it into my mouth.

"Well, yeah, but that's because the sex is really good." Her eyes stretch wide.

"Well, I think he likes you too. You two should make a go of it."

"Oh, please don't be one of those people."

"What people?"

"The people who get into a relationship and then suddenly everyone else has to be in one too. What Mike and I do works for us, and that's all that matters."

I roll my eyes. "But what happens when he gets married one day and isn't around for your random hookups anymore?"

"Then he'll be having the same boring sex with his wife every night while he's thinking of me, and I'll be out sleeping with whoever I want." She smiles like she's proud of her well-thought-out plan.

I shake my head. "There is seriously something wrong with you."

She shrugs but keeps eating her pizza like nothing was said.

Lucy and I finish our dinner, watch TV, and talk and laugh about how she spent her summer before calling it a night. I Facetime Ben as I go for a shower.

"Hi, beautiful," he says.

"Hi, I'm getting ready to take a shower and figured I'd let you watch. What do you think?"

He smiles his wicked grin. "Sounds great. I think I'll join you."

I see him walking through his bedroom and into the bathroom. I hear the shower turning on and then see him moving around like he's undressing from the waist down. His chest is already bare.

I prop the phone up on the bathroom counter and step back so he can watch as I take off my clothes. I pull off my top and then my bra. I look at the screen and notice that he's set his phone on the wire rack in the shower. I can see all the way down his naked body. His eyes are intently watching me.

I watch him as I unbutton and unzip my jeans. My hips move from side to side as I push them down. The lower my jeans go, the harder he gets.

"Looks like you got a bit of a problem there," I say, picking up the phone and taking it into the shower with me. I set it on the caddy that hangs from the showerhead.

"I do. So... about that phone sex?"

I smile as I let the water rush down my body, warming me. "I didn't bring my vibrator into the shower."

"Use your hand. Like this," he says, and I see him take himself in hand. Slowly, he starts pumping. Watching him jack off to me has my body humming and burning with need. As I watch him, my hand moves down my stomach to my clit. When I touch myself, his eyes grow wide with excitement, and he reaches for the phone.

"What are you doing?"

"Nothing, sorry," he says, his hand starting to work himself over. I watch as it moves faster and faster. His chest is heaving, and the veins are bulging out of his arm. My fingers move fast, and I can feel my release building. My eyes close as I push myself over the edge. A soft moan escapes as I ride out the waves. I open my eyes and see his hand moving faster than I thought possible. Just as I ride out the final wave of my release, he lets out a moan as he empties himself into the shower drain.

I smile at him. "That was sexy, watching you touch yourself while you watch me."

His chest is still heaving as he comes up to tap on the screen again.

"Why do you keep doing that?" I ask.

"Oh, I recorded the screen. That way I can watch it again and again on tour when I can't be with you." He smirks.

My mouth drops open. "I didn't know you could do that!"

He laughs. "Don't worry. I'll send you a video of me jacking off to your phone."

"What? No, no videos. What if someone gets their hands on your phone?"

He waves me off. "I'm super responsible, babe. Nobody touches this phone but me."

"Well, I hope not," I say, turning my back to him to dip my hair back in the water.

"So, was it any good?"

"What?" I ask, turning to look at the phone from over my shoulder.

"Getting off?"

I smile as I turn to face him and grab the shampoo. "It was nothing compared to you," I confess.

He smiles. "Yeah, I know the feeling."

I start massaging the shampoo into my hair as I watch him wash off. "Big day for both of us tomorrow," I say.

He nods. "Yep, but before you know it, we'll be back together. And I have something to give you." His eyes flicker with excitement, and he smiles.

"Why didn't you give it to me earlier when I was still with you?"

"Because I didn't have it then. Two months," he promises.

"Mail it to me," I try.

He scoffs. "What? No way. This is an in-person gift."

"Fine," I grumble and he laughs.

We both finish our showers and get out and dry off. I take the phone back to bed with me and lie down. "Get some sleep, baby. You'll need it for all those kids tomorrow."

I smile. "Okay, good night."

"Good night. Dream of me."

"I love you."

"I love you, too, Mia," he replies before hanging up the phone. I plug in the phone and set it on the bedside table before rolling over and trying to go to sleep. Behind my eyes, I only see him and the way we spent our summer—mostly naked and welded together. I look to the future to imagine how our story might end, and I drift into deep sleep with a smile on my face.

TWELVE
BEN

We've been on tour for one month. It's been a whole month since I've been able to touch or taste or kiss Mia. Every day, I feel like I'm going to explode until I hear her voice and see her beautiful face. We talk every morning before she goes to school. I usually go back to sleep afterward. Then we talk on her lunch break and before our show starts. Then I call her after when she's already in bed, but she always wakes up to take my call. These late-night calls don't get very far. She's too tired from being asleep, and I'm usually too tired from the show.

But today, we're having some kind of VIP meeting before the show so I can't call, which means that I'm going to have to wait until tomorrow to really talk to her about anything. She'll be too tired tonight, and I'll be too tired in the morning.

The guys and I leave the dressing room and head to the conference room where our manager's assistant is busy getting everything ready for the meet and greet.

"Hey, Steph," I say, walking past her as I go to grab a Red Bull from the table.

"Hey," she says with a smile. "What do you guys think? It look good?" She motions around the room.

The table is filled with drinks and snacks. There are band posters on the wall and balloons and streamers everywhere. It kind of looks like a kiddie party, but I don't want to hurt her feelings. "Yeah, it's great."

"Good, we're going to open the doors in ten minutes," she says, turning away to put the finishing touches on the snack table.

I have a seat on the couch and pull out my phone to send Mia a text.

Ben: *I miss you already.*

Mia: *Not as much as I miss you.*

I smile and slide the phone back into my pocket. The doors open, and people start filling the room. Fans, members of the press, and our security walk in.

I start to make the rounds, signing things and taking pictures. I try avoiding any weird conversations. Most of the girls ask about Mia, and I give them all the same response—"She couldn't make it tonight"—to which they stick their breasts out further and say, "That's too bad."

All the women want details of my personal life, whereas the men just want to tell me how much they love the music and what it's helped them through. I don't spend too much time with any one person. I work my way around the room and finally end up where I started. I look and find Quin and Mike doing the same thing, talking and signing things.

Steph comes up to my side, bumping her shoulder against mine. "Hang in there, champ. It's almost over," she says with a smile, and I look down at her and laugh. She knows me too well.

Eventually, everything wraps up, and we're allowed to go back to the privacy of our dressing room while they get the guests back to their original spots. Once back in the dressing room, I try calling Mia, but it goes to voicemail. I try a few more times, but eventually, I have to put my phone away and get on stage.

The show lasts about an hour and a half, and when I leave the stage, I pull out my phone to see that I have three missed calls from her. I immediately try calling her back, but it goes to voicemail. I notice that it's after eleven, so she's probably dead asleep. We pack up and get back on the bus. I try calling again in the shower before I climb into my bunk and then once more before drifting off to sleep. Apparently, this isn't a day I get to talk to my girl.

Sleep takes me and holds me under until midday. I wake up around noon and grab my phone, seeing a missed call from her again this morning and a text message.

Mia: *Sorry I missed all your calls. I had parent teacher meetings yesterday, and then I was so wiped that I couldn't keep my eyes open until you called last night. I love you and miss you. Hopefully, we get to talk later today.*

Even though I know she's in class, I text her back.

Ben: *Don't be sorry, just make up for it today. If I don't hear your voice soon, I'm going to explode. I love you, baby.*

I drop the phone and pull back the curtain on my bunk, ready to get up and start the day. The guys and I have breakfast, something Mike threw together: hash browns with scrambled eggs, fried potatoes, bacon pieces, and gravy all layered like a lasagna. Afterwards, none of us can move from the amount of food we ate, so we lounge around on the bus, all of us with our phones in our hands. I creep on Mia's Facebook and Instagram pages, noticing that her Insta followers have gone up into the thousands just from being linked to my account. Then Mike pulls me from my thoughts.

"Ugh, dude. You need to see this," he says, flipping his phone around for me to see the screen.

"What?" I ask, looking at the picture. It's a picture of Steph and me at last night's meet and greet. In the photo, she's looking up at me and I'm looking down at her. We're both wearing wide smiles because she was laughing at how miserable she knew I was. "What about it?" I ask, not seeing anything wrong.

"Read the headline." He scrolls so the headline is showing. It reads: Trouble in Paradise...Already?

I take the phone from his hand and read the article.

It hasn't been that long since Escaping the Darkness' front man, Ben Foster, professed his love on his Insta and Twitter accounts. Anyone who follows the band or Ben will know that this is a bold move for the socialite and guitarist. He's always been very hush-hush about his private life in the past, so that left many of us wondering, why now? We've done some digging into the heartthrob's love interest, Mia Weeks. Mia was born and raised in a small town in the Midwest where she still lives and works today. The kindergarten teacher stole our man's heart back in high school as the two were each other's first love. However, fame and fortune came between them until recently. The two rekindled their relationship when the band came back to town for their ten-year anniversary, putting on a homecoming show. The two have been inseparable since... until Escaping the Darkness' new tour started a month ago. Since then, the couple has not been spotted together. (Scroll further down for the images that were captured.) Now, with all of this being said, we are left to wonder: is this split just the couple parting ways for now due to work and the tour, or is this the beginning of the end? One might lean toward one more than the other, especially after this photo was taken during their meet and greet last night.

It shows the picture of me and Steph again.

Who is this woman, you ask? Well, it's not the woman Ben professed his love to only one short month ago. No, this is the assistant to the band's manager, Stephanie Kors. Now the real question isn't if they are still together. No, the question here is, which one of these women is Ben Foster really seeing behind closed doors? Pictures below show that it isn't Mia Weeks. At least, not lately.

I scroll further down to find pictures of Mia. She's back home, getting in and out of her car at her apartment, at the school she works at, and even the grocery store. She's not looking at the camera in any of the pictures, which leads me to believe that she didn't know the photos were even being taken.

I toss the phone back. "That's a bunch of bullshit," I say, feeling my anger rise.

"I know it is, but does Mia know? That's the important question."

I look at him for a moment, thinking it over. Surely, she knows, right? I mean, she never got to meet Steph because when we were recording, Dan was there himself. He only sends Steph when he can't make it. But Mia knows what she means to me, right? I'm sure she does. Regardless, I try calling her to explain, but the phone goes straight to voicemail like I knew it would with her being in class.

I let out a long breath, hoping and praying that she doesn't jump to conclusions. I pray that she thinks this through and can see through all the bullshit in that article. There's nothing concrete there. It's all just a bunch of insinuations and guesses, and none of it has any truth to it. Steph and I have never been anything more than friends, and we never will be.

My heart starts racing, and I start sweating from worrying if Mia will buy into this piece of shit article or not. Hours pass slowly as I wait for her call, but it never comes in. I call her at our usual time before my show, but it goes to voicemail, so I leave a message.

"Mia, please call me back. I don't know if you've seen the article or not, but none of it has any truth to it. She's our manager's assistant. Nothing is going on. Please don't let this ruin us. We're finally on the right path." I let out a long breath. "Okay, baby. I love you." I have no choice but to hang up so we can get on stage and get this one checked off too.

After the show, I go directly to my bunk and try calling her again. Once again, voicemail. I feel like crushing the damn phone in my hands. I have no missed calls from her and no texts. She must have seen it by now. If she hasn't, why isn't she answering the phone? What if something happened? What if she got into a car wreck or something? My heart starts to race as worry gnaws at my stomach. Surely, Lucy would call, right?

"Hey, Mike?"

"Yeah?" he asks from the bunk above me.

"Call Lucy and see if Mia is alright. She's not answering my calls."

"Oh, shit. You think she saw the article?"

"I fucking hope not. Just call her and check."

A few quiet minutes pass before I hear him say, "Hey, Luce. What's up?"

I wait.

"That's cool. Nah, I was just calling because Ben hasn't been able to get through to Mia. Is everything alright? So she did see the articles then, huh?"

Fuck. How can she believe that bullshit? Doesn't she see that it's all lies?

"Alright, I'll let him know. See ya," he says, hanging up the phone.

"So?" I ask, growing impatient.

"She saw the article. Lucy said she didn't want to believe it, but it did change her mood. She tried talking to her about it but said that Mia was suddenly aware of how much privacy you guys don't have, how cameras have been following her around, and how she's not sure she wants to live that way. She says she needs time to think."

Fuck, fuck, fuck. Goddammit! How can she let this come between us? I thought she loved me. She knows I love her. Why throw our future away for something as stupid as this shit? People write shit about me all the time. It doesn't make it true. Who cares if people see one moment in our lives? It's not like we have cameras living with us.

I can't sit around and wait for her to decide against me and never answer my calls again. I have to do something about this now. But what? What can I do as I'm driving across the country, nowhere near her, when she won't even pick up the damn phone?

THIRTEEN
MIA

My phone doesn't stop ringing, so I eventually turn it off to get a little peace and quiet. I haven't talked to Ben since yesterday afternoon. This morning, I woke up thinking that we'd be back on track and I'd get to hear his voice. That was before I got to school, and one of the nosiest teachers there brings this magazine up to me.

I look down at the cover to see Ben and another woman locking eyes, each wearing big smiles on their faces. Her arm is touching his, and her top is so low-cut, I can practically see her belly button. As easy as it would be to believe this lie, I don't. This could happen to anyone. Hell, I was talking to Mr. Frost today. Anyone with a camera could've caught the same image of us. Of course, I was dressed appropriately, but I was at a grade school, not a rock concert.

No, I don't believe what this article is implying, but it did plant a thought in my head I wish it wouldn't have. If I stay with Ben, my whole life will be plastered all over magazine covers and the internet for anyone to see. Being with Ben means being with the guy I've loved since I was sixteen, but it also means losing my privacy. Hell,

Ben isn't even around right now, and I still have cameras following me to my job and the store. I just want my normal life back.

But my normal life was lonely and empty. Now I have Ben. I have love and a future. Talk about the ultimate pros and cons list. I know I should call him back so he doesn't worry, but right now, I have a lot of thinking to do. I don't want to keep anything from him, so it's important that I be upfront with everything. And I will as soon as I make up my mind on how I want to spend my life.

I fall into a deep sleep and don't dream of anything, which is a nice break. I wake in the morning and roll onto my back. A wave of nauseousness hits me, and my mouth starts to water. I slap my hand over it as I race to the bathroom, falling down to my knees with just enough time to bend over and empty my stomach into the toilet.

I'm on the floor for a long moment, emptying everything I have. When I can no longer vomit, I stand up, flush the toilet, and move to the sink to brush my teeth. I put toothpaste on the brush and get started, trying to think of a reason for why I'd be sick. I didn't eat anything bad that I know of. In fact, Lucy cooked spaghetti last night, and she's not sick. Plus, how do you get sick on spaghetti? It's not like it can be undercooked—unless there was something wrong with the jar sauce she used. I guess I could be pregnant. I mean, Ben and I had unprotected sex all summer, but I'm on birth control. I'm a teacher, so even I know that it doesn't work one hundred percent of the time.

I walk into the living room and find Lucy moving about, getting ready for work.

"Hey," she greets me.

I can't move or speak. I'm suddenly scared to death. What if I am pregnant?

"What's wrong, honey?" She steps forward, looking worried.

"Do you still have a pregnancy test from that scare you had a few months ago?"

Her brows knit together. "Yeah, I think so. Why?"

I swallow down my fear. "I think I need one."

Her eyes stretch wide as acknowledgement washes over her, but she points toward her room and dashes off. She's back within minutes, handing it over.

I take it back to my bathroom and get busy. When I'm done, I set a timer for five minutes and back away. Someone knocks on the door, and I hear Lucy open it. Moments later, Ben is rushing into my room. I look up at him from my place on the bed. Our eyes meet as he crosses the room and drops down to his knees in front of me.

He takes my hands in his. "You know it isn't true. Tell me you know it isn't true."

I nod once. "I know it isn't true."

He lets out a long breath. "Then why haven't you been answering your phone?"

I shrug one shoulder, still too numb from shock to do much of anything else. "I just needed time to think."

"Then that's all you had to say, Mia. Fuck, you scared the shit out of me," he says, pulling me against him.

I wrap my arms around him and hold on for dear life. Right now, I need his strength.

"I know this life is hard, not having privacy and having your life up there for all to see, but I swear, it won't always be like this. Don't throw away what we have because of it. It will stop one day, I promise."

The timer on my phone goes off, and I stand and walk to the bathroom. I turn the timer off and look at the test on the counter.

Positive.

It's positive.

I turn to look at him. He's still on his knees by the bed, watching me. "What?" he asks, pulling his brows together.

I look back at the test. It's positive. I'm going to have a baby. We're going to have a baby. Our future is now, and I almost threw it all away. And for what? Because I don't want my picture taken? Who cares about everyone else? I only care about him and now, our baby.

He gets up and walks into the bathroom with me. He looks down at what I'm looking at, and I look up at him, watching the emotions change on his face. "You're..." he says, wiping his hands over his face. "You're pregnant?" His green eyes start to glisten.

I nod, wondering how he's going to take the news.

He doesn't say anything at all. Instead, he just pulls me against him and kisses me until neither of us can breathe. He picks me up against him and carries me to the bed. He lays me down and covers my body with his as our kisses become deeper and deeper.

"I can't believe this," he says, kissing down my neck. "We're going to have a baby."

"Are you happy?" I ask, cupping his face in my hands.

His eyes meet mine. "Are you kidding? Yes, of course I'm happy." He kisses me again, a kiss I can feel in my whole body.

I push him back. "Wait. What are you doing here? Shouldn't you be on tour?"

He laughs. "Yeah, I am. I have to catch a flight in a few hours and meet up with the guys in Vegas."

I wrap my arms around him, sad that he has to leave so soon. "But you have a couple hours, right?"

"Right," he agrees, pressing his lips back to mine.

I WALK him to the door. "Wait, didn't you say you had something for me?"

He smirks. "Yeah, but I was so anxious to get to you that I forgot to grab it. It'll have to wait until you come to the show next month."

I stick out my bottom lip and pout. He laughs but pulls me against him. He holds me close. "I wish I didn't have to go," he whispers into my hair, "especially now."

"Me too," I reply.

"One more month until I can hold you like this again. And promise me, if there is a problem or if you get freaked or anything, call me. Don't go silent on me again. You scared the shit out of me."

I smile. "I promise."

"Okay, come here." He leans in, kissing me softly but deeply, so deep that I'm sure I'll feel it in a month from now when he gets to do it again.

"HE'S IN THE DRESSING ROOM," Mike says. "He insisted on having his own since he knew you were coming."

I smile as I bring my hand up and knock on the door. Moments later, Ben is pulling it open. He sees me and smiles, immediately pulling me against him for a lip-crushing kiss. He pulls me into the room and shuts the door so we can be alone.

"I'm glad you made it," he says against my lips.

"Mmmm, me too." My hormones are going crazy, and I can't wait until he slides into me, but then he pulls away, taking my hand and leading me over to the couch where we both sit.

"So, tell me about the baby. What's the doctor saying?"

"The baby is due in May, which means I got pregnant in August, probably the last time we had sex before the tour. He can't tell if it's a boy or girl yet, and I told him I didn't want to know anyway. But the baby is healthy and everything is fine."

He's smiling the whole time I talk about the baby.

"Now, can we please get on to the lovemaking? I'm ready to explode." I move to climb onto him, but he stops me as he laughs.

"I'm sorry, but we'll have to wait until after. I don't have time right now. I have to be on stage in ten minutes."

"That's plenty of time," I argue, which only makes him laugh more.

"No, it's not," he says, pulling me against him. "When I slide into you, I want to be there all night long. There's no way I'll have enough of you after only ten minutes."

I pout. "But we don't have all night."

He nods. "We do. I got you a ticket to fly home the day after tomorrow. It's Friday night, so we have all weekend." He kisses me. "If that's okay with you, that is."

I smile wide and throw my arms around his neck. "Yes! Yes, that's okay." I kiss him back.

Someone knocks on the door, and I know that means that it's time for him to head to the stage. I break our kiss, and he offers up one more quick peck. "Don't forget to watch the show."

I smile. "What else do I have to do?" I say, getting comfortable on the couch and turning to the TV. I watch as the crowd goes wild when the lights dim. Then a big explosion fills the stage, and the guys come out, playing their opening song. The crowd gets loud as they scream and jump up and down. I can't help but smile at my man as he puts on the show everyone wants to see.

The show is amazing, but as good as it is, I'm counting down the minutes until I can have my boyfriend back. To my surprise, he stops the show on the last song and starts to talk to the crowd.

Ugh, why are you dragging this out?

I focus on him on the TV and listen to his words. "Guys, I'm sure you've all seen my girlfriend Mia, right?"

The crowd cheers loud.

"Alright, well, help me get her out here on stage! Come on, cheer louder," he says, egging them on.

Someone knocks on the door, and the redhead from the picture walks in. She smiles wide. "I know we haven't met, but I'm Steph. I'm the band manager's assistant."

I smile. "Hi, I'm Mia."

She nods. "I know. I've been directed to take you to the stage."

"What? Why? What is he doing?" I ask as she takes my wrist and starts leading me out of the room. I'm fitted with a mic.

She shakes her head. "I'm sorry, but I can't tell you. Remember to smile."

At the last second, I'm shoved gently on stage, and the crowd's cheers only grow louder.

"There she is," Ben says into his mic as he holds out his hand.

I take his hand, and he leads me to the center of the stage. "What are you doing?" I ask and then jump when I hear my voice echoing through the stadium.

He chuckles. "I just wanted to clear up some rumors." He looks at the crowd. "This is Mia, my girlfriend, and yes, we're expecting our first child." Everyone cheers and my face heats. "And yes, I am going to propose."

My head swings in his direction, but he's gone. My eyes fall down and land on his as he kneels in front of me with a box in his hand. He opens it, and the light hits the diamond, nearly blinding me.

"Mia, I've been in love with you since I was sixteen years old. I thought I lost you, but by some twist of fate, I got you back, and I'm never walking away from you again. I love you, Mia, and I can't wait to start this next chapter of life with you and our baby. Will you marry me?"

Suddenly, the crowd is deathly quiet. I look from him to all their watching eyes and back. "Of course I will," I breathe out.

The stadium erupts in loud cheers and screams as Ben slides the ring onto my finger. He stands and picks me up against him, kissing me until I'm breathless. The music starts up around us, and he pulls away. "Don't go anywhere," he says and swings his guitar around to the front again and starts strumming, singing, "I Still Remember," the song he wrote for me years ago that I'd never listened to until we met again.

My heart swells and fills with love for this man, the man who made me fall in love with him when I was only sixteen. The man who showed me what love was, what heartbreak felt like, and how it feels when that broken heart is finally mended. I watch with tears in my eyes as he sings and finishes the song. When he's done, he tells the crowd goodbye, and then he hands off his guitar and picks me up, carrying me off stage and back to his dressing room. His mouth is on mine as we enter the room, and he pushes my back against the door to close it. With me pinned between him and the door, his hands come between us. He pushes his way up my dress and rips my panties away. The next moment, he's freeing himself from his jeans and pushing into me, connecting us as one, just like the way we're meant to be.

I shatter on impact. My hormones are all over the place with this pregnancy, and I've needed his touch for so long that all he has to do is slide into me to make me break around him.

"Already?" he whispers, his hips not stopping.

I nod as I ride out every last wave. "I've needed you," I breathe out the moment my orgasm ends.

He chuckles but thrusts harder and deeper, filling me completely until we both come undone.

FOURTEEN
BEN

I'm on cloud nine. I'm engaged to the only woman I've ever loved, and she's carrying our first child. It may be a little late, but late is better than never. I can't get enough of her the whole weekend she's on the bus with us. In fact, I've grossed the guys out multiple times because I can't seem to keep my hands off her. It's even worse now that I know she's carrying my child. I just want to touch her in some way every minute I can. I run my fingers through her hair, kiss her neck, or rub her leg as she sits next to me on the couch. We ruin watching TV for the guys when things get a little out of hand and an innocent kiss turns into something more. They literally shoved us to the back of the bus where we were told not to come out until we could keep our hands to ourselves.

She seems to be better at holding back than I am, but sometimes, I look over at her and find her blushing with her bottom lip pulled between her teeth. When she does that, I end up pulling her back to my bunk where we hide out for a couple of hours at a time. But like everything else, our time together comes to an end.

I'm inside her the whole way to the airport until Mike has to threaten to pull me off her if I don't let her catch her flight. I finally pull away from her, and we get dressed. I put on my hat and sunglasses and walk her as far as I can into the airport. When I can go no farther, I pull her against me. "Only four more months," I tell her as she holds herself to me closely. I run my fingers through her hair, trying to remember the way it feels like silk as it falls back in place.

"I love you," I tell her, cupping her cheeks.

"I love you too," she says, leaning in to press her lips to mine again. I kiss her deeply, breathing her in and savoring this moment until I can do it again.

"Call me when you land so I'm not a nervous wreck."

She smiles and nods. "I will."

"Okay." I kiss her once more. "Love you."

"Love you too," she says, turning and walking away.

I stand there until she fades into the crowd, and then I turn and walk back to the bus. When I enter, Mike says, "About time!"

"Fuck off, man," I say, dropping onto the couch.

He laughs. "At least I'll be able to eat now. You guys and all your touchy-feely crap totally ruined my appetite."

"Well, you haven't lost a pound," I joke, smacking his stomach.

He rolls his eyes and holds up his middle finger.

I make my way to the back of the bus and lie in my bunk. I pull the pillow over my face and breathe her in. Fuck, how can I miss her already? She hasn't even been gone ten minutes, and already, I feel like a piece of my heart is missing. I pull out my phone and play the video she sent me of the baby's heartbeat. I listen and hear the steady beat, and it calms my heart. It feels like it keeps pace with the baby. I focus on the sound of the baby's heartbeat and then feel the steady rhythm of mine. It's not long before I'm fast asleep.

OVER THE NEXT TWO MONTHS, I live for our phone calls, text messages, and video chats. They're the only things keeping me going. I savor every one and don't miss any. If I'm asleep, I wake up. If I'm practicing, I take a break. Over the last two months, I don't miss a single phone call until we're finally close enough that Lucy and Mia both make it to the show. I refuse to let Mia drive herself all alone, so Mike talks Lucy into coming with, which is a plus for him too.

They don't make it in time for me to see her before the show starts, so I go out on stage, feeling annoyed and off. I don't put much into the show, and I hate myself for it, but I can't fake it. I wanted to see her. I was expecting to see her. I'm in the middle of a song when I catch a glimpse of her from the corner of my eye at the side of the stage. I stop and turn to face her directly. She smiles and waves. I drop the mic and run to the end of the stage, behind the curtain, so nobody can see. I pull her against me and kiss her like she's the air I've been starving for.

"You finally made it," I say against her lips.

She giggles and nods. "I made it."

I press my mouth to hers again and kiss her until I can't breathe. She pushes me away. "Go. You have a job to do."

I smile as I turn away and make my way back to the stage.

The show goes by much more smoothly after that. The energy I was missing is back, and the crowd picks up on it too. They're screaming, singing, and cheering. I sing my heart out and play my guitar so hard, I break a string and have to use my replacement. When the show is over, the crowd is nowhere near done. But I am.

I race back to my dressing room and find her waiting for me on the couch. I fall to my knees as I reach for her. "God, I missed you."

She smiles. "I missed you too," she says, reaching for me and directing my lips to hers. I climb up onto the couch and slide between her legs. "I love that you always wear a dress or a skirt."

She laughs. "You always did."

I push her dress up and find her slightly swollen stomach. If I wasn't used to her stomach being completely flat, I never would have noticed. I'm sure nobody else has. I freeze, placing my hand over the bump as our eyes meet.

"He's starting to show, huh?"

"You're beautiful," I whisper, lowering my head to press a kiss to our baby. Her hands lace into my hair, gently tugging as I litter her stomach with kisses. She pulls and pulls until I have no choice but to go where she's leading, and that just so happens to be her lips. I press mine against hers, and her hands get busy, pushing my jeans down my hips. I position myself at her entrance and slide in. Her warmth greets me, and I feel like I could explode already. I hold her hips, and I pull her into my thrusts as her nails dig into the flesh of my arms and back.

Her moans grow louder as her body grows tighter. I cover her mouth with mine to absorb her yells. Two more thrusts and I'm falling over the edge with her. I collapse against her, and she holds my head to her chest while we both work to calm our bodies.

"Two more months and we can do this every night," she pants.

I chuckle. "I don't know about you, but I'm really tired of waiting two months at a time."

She giggles. "Me too. Hopefully we won't ever have to say it again."

Someone knocks, and we both work quickly to get decent. I open the door to find Quin.

"What's up, man?"

"Can I chill in here? Mike and Lucy are going at it." He motions toward the other dressing room with his thumb.

Mia laughs but says, "Come on in, Quin."

He walks in and I shut the door. "You're lucky we're already done."

He laughs. "Yeah, I figured it wouldn't take you two long. I've been in the bunk next to you a time or two."

I smack him in the back of the head as I pass the couch and go to sit on Mia's other side. Quin takes over the TV while Mia and I talk.

"How's school going?"

She nods. "Good, when I'm not running to the bathroom to puke."

"I wish I could be there with you through all this." I place my hand on her stomach, hoping to feel the baby.

"You will be soon enough. And you'll be there for all the good parts. You get to skip the morning sickness and the food cravings."

I shake my head. "I want to be there for all of it, but I guess there's always the next one."

Her eyes stretch wide as she scoffs. "Don't you know you're not supposed to talk about the next one when I'm still pregnant with this one?"

TWO MONTHS CREEP BY, but it's finally the end of a grueling tour. I told Mia a little white lie and said I wouldn't be able to make it for another week, but the moment the tour ends, I hop a flight back home to California and pack up all my clothes. I hire an assistant to pack up the rest and to put it into a storage unit until I have a place to put it all. Then I hire a real estate company to put the house on the market. I catch a flight to her the next day.

When I arrive at her apartment, Lucy lets me in, but Mia is still at work, so I make her promise not to tell Mia when she gets home. Then I go to hide out in her bedroom. I put my bags away and take a shower. Then I lie in her bed and wait. I must have fallen asleep because I wake when I hear her scream.

I jump awake and sit up, looking for danger, but all I see is her flying toward me. I catch her in midair and pull her to me, rolling her under me as I kiss her long and hard. Her hands are touring my body, running through my hair and down my back to my bare ass.

"You're here," she says against my lips, trying to push her clothing away.

"I'm here. Slow down. I don't have anywhere to go."

"Phone sex isn't good enough when you're six months pregnant."

I laugh but get the point and give her what she needs. Afterward, we're lying in bed, holding on to one another. "I have a surprise for you."

"You do?" she asks, rolling over to face me.

I nod as I grab my phone and pull up the website. I show her the screen. "I'm selling my house."

She looks at the screen, and her eyes get wide. "You are?"

I nod.

"Well, where are you going to live?"

I flip to the other screen. "We're going to live here." I show it to her, and she takes the phone from my hands.

"Wait, I know this place." She looks at me and then back. "This isn't in California. This is here."

I nod, and she squeals and smiles. "We're staying here?"

I nod again. "If that's what you want."

"Yes, you know I do. I won't have to switch jobs. Our baby will get to grow up here, like we did!"

I smile as I pull her back down to me. "So you like it? The house and the plans that I sort of made without you?"

"I love it. I love it all and I love you." She pulls my mouth back to hers and steals the air from my lungs.

"So what are we going to name this little guy anyway?" I ask, snuggling closer.

Her hands move to her stomach. "Or girl," she corrects. "I think if it's a boy, we should name him after you."

I'm not big on the idea, but I'll let her have it.

"And if it's a girl, I'm thinking Skylar. What do you think?"

I smile. "I love it. How long until we find out?"

"Mmmm, about three months." She laughs and I roll my eyes.

"Great."

She places her hand on my jaw and turns my head until I'm looking at her. "We have all the time in the world now. Don't rush it." She presses her lips to mine, and for the first time in a long time, I don't rush. I don't look at the clock or wish I could jump into the future. Right now, the only thing on my mind is living in the present.

I plan on living the rest of my life that way. I've finally gotten her back, and we're right where we're supposed to be. Getting married, having a child, and living happily ever after. What more could I ask for?

I roll on top of her, and her warm center greets me. With one roll of my hips, I'm sliding into her. She holds me close and whispers her love to me in soft moans and whimpers. Goosebumps cover my skin when I think about how I'll never have to live without this again. Everything in the past is over, and the only thing we have is our future. A future I will fight to stay in right now with her, the only woman I've ever loved.

"I love you, Ben," she whispers as she rolls on top of me.

My hands find her hips and pull her down harder, making sure there is no space between us. "I love you, too, Mia. Forever and always," I whisper, rocking my hips upward. Her head falls back as a gasp escapes. Her nails dig into my chest, and I repeat the process until she's quivering on top of me. When she can no longer move, I roll us over and take my place on top.

"Don't stop," she whimpers.

"Never," I promise, and I mean that in every way possible. I'll never stop touching her or kissing her. I'll never stop loving her.

EPILOGUE

MIA-THREE MONTHS LATER...

"Ben!" I yell from the upstairs bathroom. I hear his heavy footsteps come running down the hall from the new recording studio he's building. He busts through the door so hard it slams back against the wall. "What? What's wrong?"

"I'm in labor," I cry, motioning toward the puddle I'm standing in.

"Ew, what's that?"

"Didn't you read any of the pregnancy books I gave you?"

He frowns. "Of course I did! Come on, let's get you to the hospital." He takes my hand and leads me to the bedroom. He digs around in the dresser, looking for some clothes. "Here, put these on."

"Ew, what's that?" I ask, looking at the orange sweatpants and green hoodie.

"What?" he asks.

"You want me to go in there looking like a swollen carrot?"

He rolls his eyes. "Seriously, you're in labor and worried about what you wear?"

"No, but not that. Give me those black pants and that cream-colored sweater there." I point to the items. He hands them over and then helps me to change out of my wet clothes. Our bags are already packed and are waiting by the door. I grab my purse and he takes my hands, helping me toward the stairs. We're about halfway down when a contraction hits, and I squeeze his fingers together as I fall to my butt on the step.

"*Ow!*" he squeals.

I cut my eyes to him and he shuts his mouth. After a few minutes, the contraction eases and he helps me up, slowly moving me toward the door. He grabs the bags at the door as he leads me outside.

"You have to call Lucy," I tell him, already out of breath.

"I will," he says, opening the passenger side door for me and helping me in.

He tosses in the bags before taking his seat behind the wheel. The trip to the hospital makes me feel like I'm in the Indy 500. I even hit my head against the window when he takes a sharp turn. The whole way to the hospital, I yell, either about the pain or the way he's driving. By the time we reach it, he doesn't have to help me out because I'm dying to get out of that death trap.

I'm taken to a room while Ben parks the car but he joins me moments later.

"Hey, you're in that rock band, aren't you? The famous one?" the nurse says with a flirty smile.

"I am," Ben says proudly.

"Hello! Over here. Baby coming out of my vagina here!" I'm waving my arms through the air and motioning to my lady bits.

"Oh, sorry. I was just starstruck there for a minute. I'm back," she says, flipping the basket up as she pulls on a glove. I look at Ben while she measures how far along I am, and Ben's eyes get wide.

"She's further than I've gotten in three weeks," he points out.

I roll my eyes. "Shut up."

He sits beside me and takes my hand. "I'm sorry. I guess now isn't the time for jokes, huh?"

I shake my head as another contraction hits.

"Bad news, folks. You're only about two centimeters dilated. Get comfy 'cause you're going to be here a while."

THE HOURS PASS SLOWLY as I wither away in pain while Ben sleeps off and on. I, on the other hand, only get to sleep a few minutes at a time. Every time a contraction hits, I'm jolted awake with the worst pain in the world. But I wouldn't take any of it back because all of this has led me to where I am now, holding my newborn baby boy. His eyes are blue. His hair is dark and curly. He has my nose and Ben's kissable lips. He has longer fingers, and when I place my hand in his palm, he squeezes it and doesn't let go.

"He's gorgeous," Ben says, looking down at the two of us. "You did an amazing job, baby." He presses a kiss to the top of my head. I lean my head back and look up at him. "He looks just like you. And look at these fingers. Perfect for playing guitar."

Ben smiles proudly, stretching out the baby's fingers to see just how long they really are. "We better get these hands insured. They're going to bring someone a lot of pleasure one day."

I gasp. "What's that supposed to mean?"

He frowns. "That he's going to be a great guitar player." But he smirks and it makes me wonder if that's really what he meant.

Lucy and Mike walk in together, soon followed by Quin. The nurse walks in and nearly screams.

"Oh my God! The whole band? The whole band is here? Can I get a picture?"

"Sure," Quin says, gathering everyone around me and the baby. I want to roll my eyes, but I smile for the picture despite how shitty I feel.

I hand Ben the baby, and he passes him around for everyone to see and hold. They all *ooh* and *ahh* at him while I catch a little nap. When I wake up, I find Ben holding the baby at my bedside. Seeing him hold our son makes my heart soar. I wonder how all those years of misery could have possibly brought us here. Either way, I don't question it. I'm happy to be where we're at, and there's no going back.

Ben looks up at me with a sleepy smile. "So, what are we going to name him?"

I smile as I look at the two of them. "Benny Weeks Foster."

Ben smiles. "Benny Weeks. That's cool. Already sounds like a rock star in the making."

I smile as I reach for him. He brings the baby and sits in bed with me. As I look down at this little baby, I realize all that matters to me is right here in one bed. All the pain of the past is gone, and all we have is the present and our bright future. I know everything will be perfect because I have the most precious baby in the world and the only man I've ever loved.

"I love you," I say, resting my head on Ben's shoulder.

"I love you. Forever," he says, pressing a kiss to the top of my head.

The End

HARPER AND ROWAN'S STORY

ONE
HARPER

The smell of cow shit and meth is the telltale sign that I've officially made it back home. I haven't stepped foot in this town in four long years, and if you're asking me, that's not nearly long enough. But college is over now, and I know that my dad could really use the help on the farm since he's getting older and his heath is declining. Really, it's the least I can do considering how much they sacrificed for me to get an Ivy League education. With my degree, I know I can easily land a job in the future. Right now though, I miss home and want to give back to my parents. Plus, free room and board in exchange for some manual labor? Sign me up!

I come to a halt at the stop sign in the center of town square. Flashbacks hit me of the little celebration that the town held for me here when I got accepted to Yale. There were Crock-Pot meals, a parade thrown by the high school band, and of course, we can't forget the bonfire. The bonfire wasn't planned though. That's what happened when Rowan Wilson set my float on fire. Just thinking about running into him again has my blood boiling and my heart quickening.

I push down the anxiety that bubbles up in my chest when I

think about him. Rowan Wilson was the high school quarterback in my senior class. He was good-looking, charming, and a royal dick to me and anyone else he considered beneath him. He made my senior year of high school complete hell. I guess I never crossed his radar before then. Landing in the same chemistry class senior year changed all that though. I think back to that day...

I walk into chem and take my seat at the head of the class like I usually do. I don't like to sit in the back. There are too many distractions back there, and I have to pass this class if I want any shot at all at Yale.

"Psst," I hear one of the jocks in the back whisper. "Who's the dork?"

I turn my head, knowing that he's talking about me. He doesn't stop his whispering though. No, instead, he shoots a smile my way. He wants me to know that he's noticed me, like it will have some kind of lasting effect on me or my panties. Sorry, bucko. Not happening.

I turn back in my seat when Mr. Moore walks into class. "Good morning, class. I hope we're all ready and excited to learn about chemistry."

"She's a dork, alright," another jock whispers. "But she is pretty cute."

I roll my eyes and shake my head.

"Cute? You call that cute?" The whispering continues. "I bet the only way that girl could look cute is with a bag over her head and my dick in her pu—"

"Mr. Wilson, is there something you'd like to share with the class?" Mr. Moore asks, narrowing his dark eyes on him.

"Ugh, no, sir?" Rowan says, but it sounds more like a question.

"I'd appreciate it if you could keep your commentary to yourself for the rest of the semester. I'm sure Ms. Mitchell would appreciate it as well."

I turn around to face Rowan with a grin. He glares at me, and if looks could kill, I'd be on the floor convulsing by now.

Yep, that fateful day did me in, and I wasn't able to escape Rowan no matter where I went or what I did. I've grown a lot since then, though, so if he thinks I'll be an easy target this go-round, he's got another thing coming.

I drive to the other side of the square and get on the road that will take me home. After a good mile of driving, I turn right into the long gravel driveway that will lead me to the house. The house is the same as I remember it. Nothing has changed. The two-story house with white siding, black shutters, and screened-in front porch sits on twelve acres of land. Off in the distance, I know I'll find the big red barn, the chicken coops, and private pond stocked with fish. Besides the constant smell of manure, it's the perfect place to live. It's out in the country, so it's always quiet, and there are no big cities around, so the sky is as dark as it can be, perfect for stargazing.

I park my car under the big oak tree just like I always used to and climb out. My old dog, Dozer, is already at my side to greet me. I bend down on one knee, petting her head and rubbing her ears. "Hey, girl. Did you miss me?" Her tail is wagging a mile a minute and she's licking me everywhere she can. "You must have missed me, huh?" I hug her close. "I missed you too."

A loud truck goes speeding down the old gravel road in front of the house, and she barks, taking off in a sprint to chase after it. "Okay, guess we're done catching up then, huh?" I say to myself since she's not around to hear.

I get up on my feet and move toward the house, deciding to get my things later. I have some catching up to do. I open the door and the house is silent. Paralyzing fear consumes me. What if Daddy had another heart attack? I jump when what sounds like a million people yell, "Surprise!"

I clutch my heart as a giggle bubbles out of my mouth.

"Welcome home, pumpkin," Daddy says, walking up to me and pulling me in for a hug.

"Thanks, Daddy. You didn't have to do all of this."

"I didn't. She did." He points at my best friend, Becky. "Bossy, that one is," he adds on as she comes up to me and pulls me in for a lung-crushing hug.

"Squeeee! I missed you, Harper."

"I... missed... you... too," I manage to croak out.

"Oh, too tight?" she asks, finally letting me go. "Sorry."

I suck in a big gulp of air now that I'm able to breathe.

As I look around the house, it seems like family members, friends, and townsfolk have come out of the woodwork. The entire house is filled with bodies. I don't know how there is any oxygen left in the room.

"Alright," Becky says. "Time to move the party outside per your father's request." She looks over at him. "See, I can follow the rules."

"Mm-hmm," he mumbles as he adjusts the waistband of his pants, which are already held up with suspenders.

Becky loops her arm around mine and leads me outside and around to the backyard. "So, spill."

"Spill what?" I ask, not surprised that she's already needing gossip.

"The tea! Spill the tea, sis. How many guys did you plow through in college?"

"Becky!" I shriek.

"What? I've been in the same relationship since freshmen year. I need to live through you. Now tell me about the men!"

I laugh. "Well, there were a few..."

"Good, good. Were they hot?"

I roll my eyes. "Oh, they were hot. And the best part was that they weren't from this town."

"God, stop teasing me, Harper. I can't take anymore," she jokes.

"Where is Tyler anyway?" I ask, looking around the now crowded backyard.

"You rang?" he asks, walking up with three red cups full of beer. He hands me one and then Becky one.

"Thanks, Ty. How you been doing? I'm surprised that you haven't put a ring on it yet," I tease, taking a sip of my foamy beer.

"Oh, I've been dropping hints up and down Main Street. But this one just doesn't seem to catch any of them," Becky says, causing us both to look at him.

He freezes with his hand in midair, raising the cup to his lips. "What?" he shouts, cupping his free hand behind his ear. Then he waves his hand. "I can't hear you. I'll be right over!" he says. "Sorry, ladies, but I'm being paged." He walks off.

"And that, ladies and gentlemen, is how you avoid an awkward subject," I say, grinning as I watch him walk away with no real place in mind.

"Yep," Becky agrees.

The grill is fired up and the country music is turned on. Before I know it, the sun is falling from the sky and the bonfire is lit. Becky and I are walking around the party lazily, taking everything in. "So, what have I missed around town lately?"

"Ummm, let me think. Oh, there was a knock-down, drag-out fight between Mrs. Frank and Mrs. Burke."

"What?" I nearly yell as my feet stop moving. "They're eighty years old!"

She laughs and nods. "Yeah, it was hilarious. Most of the town got chewed out by the city cop for watching and laughing instead of pulling them apart, but it was sooo worth it." She smiles.

I laugh. "What in the world did those two old ladies have to fight about?"

"Well, Mrs. Frank was pissed because Mrs. Burke mowed over her daisies. Mrs. Burke refused to pay to replace them."

"Why?" I ask, interrupting.

"Get this. Because they're basic flowers for basic whores. That's what she said!" She's jerking my arm up and down and laughing her ass off.

"No, she didn't," I argue.

"Swear to God. Ask anyone."

"There has to be more to this story."

"Didn't I mention that Mrs. Burke's husband has been talking long walks in the evening? Upon further investigation, he's only been walking next door to Mrs. Frank's house!" She's rolling in laughter once again.

My hand comes up to pinch the bridge of my nose. "Oh, what is wrong with this town?"

She shrugs. "I don't know, but I bet it's more entertaining than boring old Yale."

I laugh. "That it is."

Around ten, the party starts winding down, but I've been having so much fun catching up with Becky that I'm nowhere near ready to call it a night. The three of us agree to meet up at Walt's bar down the street, but I opt to drive myself so I can leave whenever I want instead of being at the mercy of those two crazies.

I watch them make their way down the driveway, then I turn for the barn. I didn't even finish one beer so I'm good to drive but a thought hits me. I toss my car keys back inside and grab the keys to the barn. I haven't gotten to ride on The Hulk in years. I open the barn and pull off the tarp, finding the old green ATV right where I knew it would be. The key is already in the ignition, so I climb on and turn her on. I line up the marks on the kill switch and push the button. It tries to fire, but it's been years, so the battery is drained. I flip the kickstart out and put my foot on it. Giving it my all, I kick it down and the four-wheeler roars to life. I give it gas with my thumb, letting it warm up. Hulk has always been cold-natured and won't go far if he isn't warmed up first.

After a few minutes of revving the engine, I shift into first gear with my foot and hit the gas. I drive out of the barn and down the drive. Dozer comes running after me just like she always used to. She follows me down the road and to the bar where I park in the gravel parking lot. She's panting and out of breath, but she ran pretty far for as old as she is. I turn off the four-wheeler and remove the key after wiggling it out since it was held in place with old, dried out mud. I tuck it away in my pocket and head for the doors.

TWO

ROWAN

"Twenty bucks says you can't chug that pitcher," my friend, Greg, says, pointing at the pitcher of beer in the center of our table.

"I want in on this," Steve says, throwing a twenty down.

"Me too," Bryan agrees, throwing down another twenty.

"Sixty bucks to chug some beer? Hell yeah!" I drop a twenty of my own onto the table as I grab the pitcher and bring it to my lips.

The guys start up their round of chanting. "Chug, chug, chug."

I start drinking from the pitcher as fast as I can, and I'm doing a pretty good job at sucking it back if I do say so myself. But I'm caught off guard when the door opens and in walks Harper Mitchell.

I choke on my beer and start coughing, spitting it everywhere. The guys start laughing as they wipe up the beer I sprayed at them. I set the pitcher on the table and wipe my mouth while the coughing continues.

"What the hell, man?" Steve asks.

"Sorry," I mumble, pushing up out of my seat with my eyes on her.

A lot has changed over the years. She's always been beautiful, but now, she's breathtaking. Her long dark hair hangs to her ass in soft curls, with strands of red and blond peppered through it. She's wearing a pair of cutoffs and a baggy white tank top with thin gray lines running across it horizontally. To top it all off, she's wearing her muddy, old cowboy boots. I nearly lose my mind when she turns to head to the bar, and I see her right bicep is covered in ink—a half sleeve done in black and white of what looks to be flowers.

I meet her at the bar, and when she sees me, she rolls her eyes and lets out a long drawn-out breath. "I've actually been having a pretty good night, so if you would do me a solid, wait until tomorrow to fuck with me, huh?"

I smirk. "Oh, come on, Harper. We had some fun times together, right?"

"If setting my parade float on fire is what you consider to be a fun time... No." She smiles up at the bartender, and my heart beats faster. "Can I get a beer?"

"Make it two," I say, tossing him some money for both. "Come on. You're still holding that against me? We both know that all they were going to do was burn it anyway. It would've sat in the middle of town square rotting for weeks before the job was even done. So really, I consider that a public service."

She scoffs. "And you couldn't wait for me to get off it first?"

My smirk widens, remembering her screams and panicked expression as she literally pushed people out of the way to get off that burning float. "So I jumped the gun a little. Sue me."

She turns to face me with a smile. "I didn't have to sue you. I made sure to get even with Tiffany." She's handed her beer and she flashes me a wink.

"That was you?"

"Who else in this town is smart enough to pull that off? Thanks for the beer." She taps her bottle off mine and spins around, making her way to her friend's table.

I can't do anything but watch her walk away while thinking about Tiffany.

The guys and I are lounging in the sun at our local swimming hole. It's nothing more than a pond the city poured a little bit of money into, surrounded with sand, and added a bathroom/changing room and a concession stand.

"So, which one are you picking?" Steve asks as we check out all the new seniors.

There's a girl that I haven't seen before walking along the beach. She has long blond hair, a tight body, and a red string bikini. I point in her direction. "I call that one."

"That's the new girl. Her name is Tiffany, I think. She's starting her senior year this fall. She's already eighteen though." Steve smiles.

"How do you know so much about her? You already hook up with her?" I ask, not wanting to touch her if she's been with him.

"No, I wish though. My granny is neighbors with her and her parents. You know my granny. She had to rush over and introduce herself the moment the moving van rolled in.

"I'll be back," I say, getting up and keeping her in my sights.

I walk over to her and give her the smile most girls can't refuse. "Hi. You new around here? I haven't noticed you before."

She nods and holds out her hand. "I'm Tiffany."

"Rowan," I reply, taking her soft hand.

She offers up a big, blinding smile. "Oh, you're Rowan. I've heard about you."

I smirk. "What'd you hear? All good I hope."

She bats her lashes and giggles. "I can't say. I've been sworn to secrecy."

I shrug it off. Hopefully, the girls from town haven't warned her about me already. "Want to grab a drink?"

"Sure," she agrees.

For the next five hours, I spend every minute with this girl. I pay attention when she talks; I laugh at her stupid jokes, and I buy her drink after drink and snack after snack. When eight o'clock rolls around, I've about given up on getting into her pants, so I say, "Well, I *need to get going. There's a party at a buddy's house. You want to come with?"* One final pick-up line.

"I'd love to, but I need to change first."

I nod. "I'll wait."

She grabs her bag and walks by me, heading to the bathroom/changing room. "Coming?" she asks, walking past.

"Not yet," I mumble to myself, getting up to chase after her.

She walks in and holds the door open. I'm damn near giddy, ready to get it on in the bathroom at the swimming hole.

I walk in and turn around, and by the time I'm facing her, she already has the door locked and her top off. Her tits are amazing—big, round, and perky. I move forward, grabbing her hips and moving my mouth to hers, but she gasps and pushes me back.

"What are you doing?" she asks.

I'm shocked. "Me? What are you doing?"

"I'm changing so we can go to the party."

"Then why did you ask me to join you?"

A knowing look crosses her face. "Because Harper told me you were gay and that I should befriend you in order to keep all the losers away."

I laugh. "Harper told you I was gay?" I point at my chest. "Do I seem gay to you?" I frown.

She's covering her chest with her arms as she shrugs. "I don't know. I mean, I just thought you were in the closet and playing straight. It made sense. You've hung out with me all day and haven't made a move. You laughed at my jokes and didn't hit on me. What was I supposed to think?"

I put my hands on my hips as my head dips forward, shaking slightly. Fucking Harper.

Yeah, it looks like I finally get to pay her back for that. And I intend on doing just that. I make my way outside for some fresh air and notice her green four-wheeler parked in the lot. I walk over to it, climb on, and go to turn on the key, but she's smarter than I thought and took it out.

I guess I could hot-wire it. I lean forward to check the wires when the door opens and loud music comes filtering out. I sit up, not wanting to get caught stealing the thing, and find Harper, making her way over.

She stops when she sees me on her ride. "What are you doing? Get off. I'm going home."

"Let's go for a ride," I insist.

"No way. I'm not going anywhere with you."

"Well, I'm not moving so you're going to have to take me with you."

She lets out a long breath, clearly annoyed. "Fine. Scoot back." She climbs onto the four-wheeler and I scoot back slightly. She turns the four-wheeler on and shifts into reverse. I bring my hands around her waist to hold on, and she stops.

"What are you doing? Why are you touching me?" She's holding her arms up, looking down at my hands on her stomach.

"Chill, Harp. I'm just holding on. I don't know if you still remember how to drive this thing."

I'm sure I get another eye roll, but she doesn't say anything as she shifts into first and we take off down the road.

THREE

HARPER

On the four-wheeler, I start driving in the direction of my house. If he wants a ride, I'm not going out of my way. There's plenty of property at my place to ride on. All I want to do is give him a quick ride so he'll leave me the hell alone. I smile to myself, knowing that he's going to have to walk back. I've had a long day that I've spent doing nothing but driving. All I want after today is a long bath to relax and a good night's sleep.

I turn into the drive and Rowan points off to the side. "Take that trail over there."

I stop. "Are you sure? The last time I went down that trail, there was a monster of a hole."

"Yeah, don't worry about it. We've all been filling it up. It's not bad now," he insists.

Even better. This trail just circles around and comes back out into the field. The shorter the ride, the better.

I turn to my right and cut across the field, entering the woods through the little gap in the trees. I downshift to second since trail riding is mostly just going slow and steady. The night is dark with the bright moon hanging over head. There are small gaps in the branches above our heads where the light is peeking through. Crickets are chirping, and all of it mixes together for a relaxing evening in the country. This is what I missed about home when I was away at college.

Up ahead, I see the mud hole in the trail and Rowan is right. It's not sopping wet and full of mushy mud. It seems rather dry and closed off. I inch forward slowly, and my tires sink a little in the mud. I keep going forward, but we're suddenly stopped. I take a deep breath and switch into four-wheel drive. Giving it gas, the engine revs, but the four-wheeler doesn't move.

Rowan is behind me, snickering.

I stop trying to get out of the mud hole and turn to face him. "You lied, didn't you?"

His smile is ear to ear. "Yep!"

"Seriously, we're keeping up with this shit?" I ask. I should've known better than to listen to him.

He shrugs. "Where we go from here is up to you. I was only getting you back for Tiffany."

"I used Tiffany to get back at you for my float," I argue.

"Well, I used your float to get back at you for my locker!"

I laugh. I completely forgot about stuffing his locker full of granny panties. "I only used the locker to get back at you for the football team!"

He scoffs. "Please, you liked that one. You got asked out on like twenty dates." He hops off the wheeler and starts walking away. Annoyed, I shift into reverse and hit the gas. The wheeler doesn't move, but the tires spin, slinging mud all up his back. He scrunches down when it covers him, and he turns back to look at me. "It looks like there will be no truce. See you tomorrow, Harper."

"Fuck you, Rowan. I bet Tiffany wouldn't have had fun with you anyway. Everyone in town knows about that li'l smokie you got in those boxers shorts!"

That gets him like I knew that it would. He stops and spins around, walking back the few steps he took. "That is not true!

Everyone knows that Stacy started that rumor when I called things off with her."

I snort. "Yeah, that's what I would say too."

He grabs at his jeans. "Want me to prove it, sweetheart? I'll be more than happy to show you what I'm packing."

I hold up my hand so I can't see anything beneath his waist. "No, Rowan. Gross!"

"Come on. I'll show you mine if you show me yours." He's smirking. He knows that I won't go for it. But maybe that's why I should. Element of surprise and all that.

I stand up, grabbing the bottom of my shirt. I pull it up, taking my bra up at the same time. My nipples harden with the soft breeze, but Rowan shuts the hell up, and his mouth drops open.

I lower my shirt, holding back my smirk. "Okay, your turn, li'l smokie. Let's see what you got."

His mouth opens and closes, but no words come out.

"What's the matter, Rowan? Is it so small that it just shrunk up inside you?"

"I... You... And then..." He shakes his head and rubs his hands over his face.

I let out an exasperated breath. "You going to help me get this four-wheeler unstuck or what?"

This time, he breathes out heavily. "Fine," he agrees, but I have a feeling it's only to get out of showing me what he's hiding away in his shorts.

He grabs ahold of his now muddy shirt and pulls it off, slapping it down across the four-wheeler. This time, I freeze as I take in his body. And boy, oh boy, has it changed since high school.

Rowan played football, so of course he's always been fit, but these last four years have treated him well. I guess working on his daddy's farm has toned muscles that I didn't even realize you could tone. He has two, four, six, eight abs. Eight abs! And they lead down to that sexy little *V* where his jeans cut off. His bulging pecs and wide shoulders are matched with hard, sculpted biceps. My, oh my...

He lets out a chuckle. "You going to help me, sweetheart, or we just going to stand here ogling one another?" He jumps down in the soppy mud and grabs ahold of the front rack.

I snap my mouth shut and take my seat. I shift into reverse and hit the gas. The motor revs loud and we wiggle a bit but don't move an inch. After several long minutes of him pushing and me trying to wiggle the four-wheeler from side to side, I let up on the gas, and we both just stop to catch our breath.

"Maybe if we both push," he says.

"Ugh, you want me to come down there in that mud?"

He shrugs. "It's either that, or you can go fire up that tractor and hope it doesn't wake your old man up. You'll be lucky if he doesn't come out with a shotgun."

Fuck. I know he's right. Daddy is sound asleep right now. If he hears the tractor fire up, he's going to think it's being stolen. And when Daddy thinks someone is stealing from his land, the shotgun is the first thing he grabs.

"Alright," I breathe out, jumping off the four-wheeler. I walk around it and step down into the mud. I sink up to my knees, and it quickly falls down into my boots.

"On the count of three, we'll push, and I'll reach over and give it gas at the same time. Got it?"

"I'm not an idiot. Let's go."

"Okay. One. Two. Three." We both start pushing and based on how loud the four-wheeler is getting, he's giving it gas. A lot of gas. Slowly but surely, the machine starts moving backward, and we're having to walk along with it. The suction of the mud holds my boot down, and I can't pull it free. I'm stuck.

Rowan gets the four-wheeler up on dry land and turns to look at me. "Fuck, that was really stuck."

"Yeah, so am I," I say, holding out my hand. "Pull me up."

He laughs. "Maybe this should be my payback. Leaving you out here all night for the coyotes."

"Don't you dare," I threaten.

"Fine," he says, rolling his eyes and stepping closer to grab my hand. The moment we touch, there's a tingling sensation that slowly starts making its way up my arm. My eyes jump to his to see if he feels it too. His eyes are wide with shock, but he quickly wipes the look away and pulls. He lifts me up, but the suction is still holding me down. He pulls harder, and this time, I pull against him while wiggling my foot to break the suction on my boot.

I guess he wasn't ready for me to pull against him, and he loses his balance and stumbles. The next thing I know, he's in the mud hole with me. Too bad for him, he isn't on his feet. He's practically swimming in it.

"Fuck. Are you kidding me?" he complains as he gets to his feet and pulls himself out of the hole.

Luckily for me, his fall broke the suction the mud had on my boot, and it's now free. I'm able to finally pull my foot free as I step onto solid ground.

He stands up, slinging mud everywhere. "You did that on purpose."

"I did not! I really was stuck," I argue.

"Then how come you were able to get out just fine now?"

"Your fall bumped my boot and released it from the suction. Don't be a baby. It's just a little mud. It's not like you haven't gotten worse over the years," I joke, referring to the time he thought he had contracted crabs only to find out later that I'd actually added itching powder to his boxer shorts while he was at football practice.

"Don't be a baby?" he repeats as he comes running at me.

I squeal and run around to the back of the four-wheeler, putting it between us. Every time he takes a step to the right, I step to the left, matching him step for step until we've made an entire circle around the machine.

"You're going to pay for that," he says, narrowing his eyes on me.

"You gotta catch me first."

"Oh, I'll catch you, and when I do, I'm throwing you in that mud hole. Hope you know how to swim," he teases.

The hole isn't nearly deep enough to call it a swim. More like wading through the goopy, soupy mud. I get the idea that if I can get him to chase me through the trees, I may be able to beat him back to get on the four-wheeler and take off, leaving him in my dust. So with a surge of bravery, I take off running through the trees. I'm running so hard that my lungs are working in double time, and my heart is pounding in my ears.

I can hear him running for me, yelling something with every step he takes. I make a big circle, and as I predicted, he's nowhere in sight. I jump on the four-wheeler and twist the key. Pushing the button, it fires up, and I work to shift into reverse, but he's right on my heels and wraps his arms around me, picking me up.

I yell and fight against him, trying my best to hold on to the handlebars. But they're slick with the mud that sprayed them. My grasp slips, and the next thing I know, I'm in his arms as he carries me back to the mud.

FOUR

ROWAN

For as small as she is, she sure can put up a fight. I have to force myself not to use my full strength in order not to hurt her. That's the last thing I want. This little rivalry between us has never been from hate. It's always been out of fun, and there's no sense in changing that now. Sure, she probably hates and has hated me for years, but it's actually quite the opposite for me. I guess I never outgrew that *boys are mean because they like you* phase.

Truth be told, I've always been afraid of telling her how I feel because I know the way she views me. I was nothing but a jock in high school that was a complete dick to her—at least in her eyes. She probably thinks that I couldn't have changed that much. But I have. Getting out of high school and working for a living has taught me some valuable lessons, like it doesn't fucking matter how many trophies you have on your shelf, if you aren't qualified for a job, you ain't getting it. And it doesn't matter who you know around here because everyone knows everyone. If you want something in this small town, you have to work for it and deserve it. Just as I'm about to drop her in the mud, I realize that if I want her, I have to work for her, and dropping her in the mud isn't the way to do it.

I freeze and so does she as she waits for the fate that's sure to come. "Say you're sorry," I demand, threatening to drop her in.

"What? No way!"

I lower her a bit more. "Say it."

"Fuck you," she says, digging her nails into the skin of my arm as she tries to hang on.

"Last chance, or you're going for a swim."

She takes a deep breath. "Fine. I'm sorry." Her tone isn't believable, but I lift her higher and set her on the ground.

"You're a horrible liar, by the way."

She grins. "Yeah, my daddy always said that I didn't have to worry about anyone telling on me, because I told on myself." She shrugs. "Anyway, let's get the hell out of here. I need a shower and my bed."

She climbs onto the four-wheeler, and I take my seat behind her. My hand comes around to land on her flat stomach, and this time, she doesn't argue. Maybe she's even learning to like it there. Now that's something to think about.

She backs up our ride until she can turn around, and then we start making our way back down the trail and to the barn, where she parks it and covers it with a tarp. "I'll have to power wash her tomorrow," she says, slipping the key into her pocket.

We make our way out of the barn, and she closes the doors behind us. Slowly, we start making our way around the house to the front door.

"Enjoy your walk," she says, stepping up onto the porch, but she turns to face me, and now we're eye to eye.

Her breath hitches in her throat. She wasn't expecting me to be here, so close. Close enough that I can smell her vanilla-scented perfume. I take a deep breath as our eyes lock. I can feel the current of electricity charging between us. Harper and I have never been this close before... well, unless we were yelling at one another.

My tongue comes out, wetting my lips that suddenly feel too dry. Her dark eyes fall down to my lips, and hers part like her breathing is picking up. I lean in slightly and she doesn't back away. Does she want my kiss? Either way, this is way too easy and can't be done this way. I want her to make me work for it. If I kissed her right now, tomorrow, she would excuse it as a lapse in judgment from being tired or drinking. When we finally do kiss, I want her to know that it's because she wanted it just as much as I did.

Instead of closing the distance, I smirk. "Well, good night," I say, spinning on my heel.

She lets out a long breath as if she'd been holding it, and her shoulders visibly fall. "Night, Rowan," she softly replies. Her tone is off, and it makes me wonder if she's feeling let down. If that's the case, maybe she really did want my kiss. Regardless, that doesn't change a thing.

I kick rocks as I walk down her drive, down the short road, and back to my truck, which I left at the bar. Instead of going inside, I climb behind the wheel and head in the direction of my house.

IN THE MORNING, the sun is shining bright and the heat of the summer has officially kicked in. I turn the air up in the house and plop down on the couch with my phone, wanting to see what everyone is doing today. I only know one thing for sure: I want to see her again. I've gone the last four years without seeing her or talking to her, but I thought of her every day. Now that's all I want to do. I don't know what's changed so much between us that makes me feel like she may be able to forget our troubled past, but I can feel it deep in the pit of my stomach. She wants me just as much as I want her. Maybe she always has, or maybe it's something new she's come to realize, but either way, I felt it the moment my hand touched hers.

I call Greg, and he answers on the fifth ring. "What's up, man? Where'd you go last night?"

I smile, remembering my romp in the woods with Harper. "Oh, I ran off with Harper. Took a ride on her daddy's four-wheeler."

"Bullshit! That girl isn't letting you anywhere near her," he argues in disbelief.

I don't try to win him over. I let the subject drop. "What's going on today? Anything going on in town?"

"Word is everyone is heading to the swimming hole. It's supposed to be a scorcher. Hell, it's only ten a.m. and in the nineties already. It'll be a good day to pack a cooler of beer and drink it on a float. You down?"

"Who all's going?"

"Everyone. I think I even heard Becky say that she was dragging Harper out of bed."

"Harper's going?" I ask.

"What is it with you and this chick, man? She's just a normal girl. She doesn't have the key to the universe's secrets in her twat or anything." He laughs.

I roll my eyes. Greg, nor anyone else for that matter, will ever understand what draws me to Harper. Fuck, I don't even understand it. All I know is that I've wanted her from the moment I saw her, and all the years haven't changed that. If anything, it's only made me want her more. "I'll meet you there," I say, hanging up the phone.

I take a quick shower, shave, and put on my swim trunks. I throw on a sleeveless shirt and slide my feet into some flip-flops. Next, I pack the cooler and load up in the truck, hitting the road. I stop by the diner to eat, knowing that if I'll be spending the day drinking with the guys, I'll need food in my stomach. I have a burger with fries and chat with a couple of girls who can't stop looking at me and smiling. I have to admit, it does make me feel a little better, knowing that I can still capture the attention of some women. Now, if it was only the woman I want, it would be a different story. I pay the bill and say goodbye, getting back in the truck and hoping that I'm not showing up too early.

By the time I get to the field where everyone parks their cars, it's completely full, and I know that I'm most definitely not too early. I park far in the back, then climb out and grab the cooler, lugging it through the field and into the trees. I follow along the trail that takes me to the water hole. At the end, the beach is before me, the sand completely covered in people. Some are sunbathing; some are chasing after their kids, while others are splashing and playing in the water, but Harper is standing at the concession stand. She's wearing a bright-red bikini, her long dark hair hanging nearly to her ass.

I freeze, unable to do anything other than watch her. She hasn't noticed me yet and I'm glad. Don't want her adding weirdo creep to her list of attributes of me. She's talking with an old boyfriend of hers. His name is Scott. He always acted so smug. He could see what nobody else could, and that was that I wanted Harper. He had her. I didn't. And he liked to rub it in my face.

Annoyed that we seem to be repeating the same old patterns, I pull my eyes away from her and go to find my friends on the beach. Finding them isn't hard, not with as loud as they are. They're lying on the beach, each with a cold beer in hand. They all have their sunglasses in place as they check out the ass of every woman that walks by.

I drop the cooler in the sand. "What's going on, guys?"

Greg looks up and holds up his beer. "What's up, buddy? Come to check out the ass with us?"

"You know it," I say around a smile. However, there's only one ass I want to check out, and as soon as she walks away from that loser, I plan on jumping on it.

I grab a beer from the cooler, pop the top, and take a long drink. I look out over the water, watching the kids play, the ladies tanning on their floats, and the soft ripples from so much movement in the water. The guys talk away at my sides, but I don't care enough to join in. All I can do is keep looking back to Harper every few minutes to find her still locked in conversation with that asshole. Fuck, when is she going to walk away from him? We started something last night. I know she knows it, and whatever it was that was started needs finishing.

"So, where'd you end up last night?" Bryan asks.

I look over at him with a grin. "I went for a ride with Harper. We got her four-wheeler buried, and I was too muddy to come back in the bar."

His brows draw together. "You? And Harper? Alone together and you're both still alive? Yeah, right. Come on, what'd you really do?"

"Why does nobody believe me?" I ask to nobody in particular.

"Uh, maybe because the last time the two of you were alone together, you were calling me from a locked bathroom to save you from her. Remember that?" Greg laughs, and the guys join in.

I can't hold back my own laughter at that either. That was after I set her float on fire and she came at me, angry as hell. She chased me into a bathroom, and I had to lock her out, calling Greg to get her away from me before she killed me.

"Yeah, but that was a long time ago," I say, looking over at her. "Things have changed."

FIVE
HARPER

I'm still slightly annoyed that Becky dragged me out of bed today. I was sleeping so good after all that driving from yesterday, the struggle in the mud wore me out basically leaving me dead to the world. But now that I'm finally here at our town's little swimming hole, I find myself having fun, just like I used to.

The day is hot, nearly pushing triple digits, and that doesn't include the humidity. The sun is high in the sky, beating down on our little town, baking the asphalt and frying the crops. This little pond is the only relief we can get.

I sit with Becky for the first hour until I decide to get up and grab a popsicle to help me cool off. As I'm waiting in line, my ex-boyfriend from high school, Scott, bumps into me.

"Hey, Harp. How ya doing?"

I smile up at him and give him a quick hug. "I'm great. How are you?"

He nods and smiles. "Good, everything's good. How was college?"

I laugh. "It was college."

"You home for the summer or...?" he asks.

I shrug. "I'm not sure. I graduated, so I came home with plans of helping my dad out with the land, but at some point, I'm going to have to find a job. I don't see myself being a farmer."

He nods, understanding. "You write, right?" His brows pull together.

"That's right."

"You should check out the newspaper here in town. It's mostly run by dinosaurs. I bet someone will be more than willing to retire."

I laugh. "I'll check it out." I step up to the window and order my popsicle, handing over my dollar.

I take the treat I'm handed and step out of line.

"So, what have you been up to? Did you graduate college?"

He waves his hand in front of his face after ordering a soda. "Nah, I didn't go. Dad needed help on the cattle ranch, so I've been working there ever since."

"Oh, well, that's nice of you."

He nods. "Yeah, I've been living in that small cabin on the far edge of the property. It's not the best, but it's good enough for me, you know?"

"Absolutely," I agree, looking out over the sand. My eyes happen to be pulled right to him. He's watching me, too, his jaw cocked and eyes narrowed on mine.

Scott comes up to stand at my side, seemingly taking in the same scene. "He's always had a thing for you, you know?"

I laugh. "Who? Rowan? No, he hates me. I mean, look at him glaring at me right now. If looks could kill..."

He shakes his head. "I thought you were smart."

I tear my eyes from Rowan's and look up at him.

"He's not glaring at you. He's checking you out!"

"No," I say, brushing him off.

He turns his body to face me now. "Harper, you remember all those fights he and I got into in high school?"

"Well, they weren't exactly fights, but yeah, I remember you two feuding a lot."

"It was over you. Always over you."

I'm speechless.

"He didn't like that I had you and he couldn't, especially since he was the big man on campus and I was nothing."

I look from him to Rowan. Was that the case? It did feel like something almost happened last night. But that could have just been my mind playing tricks on me. He almost seemed like he enjoyed teasing me. But I guess that's always been the case.

"Anyway, I gotta get back. I'll talk to you later, okay?"

I nod. "Okay, see ya," I say, still looking in Rowan's direction. Now that my eyes haven't shifted off of him, he's suddenly engrossed in what the guys are saying. Funny how that works. I could nearly feel his eyes burning into me before.

I eat my popsicle as I walk back over to Becky, who's sitting right in front of them but a little to the left. I take my place on the blanket and lie back, ready to catch some sun and get a tan.

"That took long enough," she says, smearing more sunscreen on her pasty skin, which is already turning pink and starting to freckle.

"I ran into Scott," I say, taking another bite of my treat.

"Scott? Your ex, Scott?"

"That's the one."

"Oh my God! What did he have to say? Did he ask you out?"

When she asks that question, I realize that the guys behind us get quiet, like they're also waiting for my answer. I sit up, holding myself up with one elbow as I turn to look back at them.

Rowan's blue eyes are on mine. "Well, did he?" Rowan asks.

"How's that any of your business?" I ask.

"It's not, but if you're going to talk loud enough for the whole beach to hear, don't leave us hanging now," he says with a smirk.

"No," I answer, looking directly at him, then turn to face Becky. "He did not ask me out." I shake my head at the same time a long breath leaves my lips, then I lie back down.

"What was that about?" Becky leans down and whispers.

I look up at her, annoyed. "Scott seems to think that Rowan has a thing for me," I whisper so he can't hear.

She looks back at him, and then her eyes flash to mine. "He's still looking at you." Her eyes flash away again and back. "And he's smiling."

"Quit looking at him," I order.

"I'm sorry. I can't help it." She looks again. "He's still looking, smile getting wider. Now he's laughing."

And I hear his booming laugh. Clearly, he knows we're talking about him.

"I'm going for a swim," I say, shaking my head and getting up to walk to the water.

The cool water splashes up onto my ankles when I step in, instantly cooling me down. I walk farther out until I can dive underneath. I swim around for a moment before breaking the surface. When I do, I look right in his direction, and he's watching me. I start my walk back, only now, my bathing suit is clinging to my wet body. I smooth my hair back, and his mouth drops open, his eyes glazing over. I can't hold back my smirk, and this causes him to quickly right his expression.

I fall back onto the blanket at Becky's side, and I hear the guys behind us.

"Damn, it's like girls gone wild around here."

"Shut the fuck up, man," Rowan says.

"Yeah, I don't remember her looking like that," another of the guys says.

"Quit fucking looking at her," Rowan whisper-yells.

I roll over onto my stomach and look at them. All of them are staring at me. "Take a picture. It'll last longer," I tell them.

"Hey, Harper," Greg says. "You wanna go out with me tonight?"

I've never seen Rowan's face more red.

I laugh. "No, I think I'm alright. Thanks though," I reply. I send him a smirk and a wink, and Rowan shakes his head.

I lay my head down now, letting my back get some sun to even out the tan I've already gotten today. I close my eyes and try to relax, but that's hard to do when I know his eyes are on me.

How would I feel about Rowan if we didn't have the past we do? If there wasn't ever any of the tricks or rivalry, would I be able to be with him? He's definitely hot enough, with his tempting muscles, flirty smile, and ocean-blue eyes. His dirty-blond hair is always disheveled in a messy but on purpose way, and his jaw is as sharp as glass, sometimes growing a light scruff across it. His lips are always plump and look soft. I would be lying if I said that I didn't look at him and see sex, but then he always has to go and open his mouth, ruining the fantasy.

If only there was some way to make him keep his mouth shut. Yeah, I'm definitely dreaming now. I push him from my thoughts and instead focus on relaxing. The sun is warm on my back, and I've managed to drown out all the noise from the other beachgoers, even the guys chitchatting next to me. There's a light breeze, and it cools off my already wet bathing suit, helping to ease the burn of the blazing heat on my back.

"Hey, Tyler, Becky, there's a party at my place tonight. You guys want to come?" I hear Greg ask them.

"Yeah, sure. We ain't got nothing going on," Tyler replies and I open my eyes. Clearly, taking a nap will be impossible.

Greg smirks at me. "You're invited, too, sexy." He shoots me a wink.

I laugh and nod along, my eyes moving over to Rowan to see his whole body tense as he finishes off one beer and moves for another.

Greg sees me watching Rowan, and he says, "He'll be there too. We all will be. You can have your pick." He looks at the guys. "What do you think? Ladies choice tonight?"

They all agree and cheer. I roll my eyes and move to sit up. I lean into Becky's shoulder. "So, we're really going to this party tonight?"

She pops a chip into her mouth. "You're going?" she asks, seemingly surprised.

I shrug. "I don't have anything better to do. There's no test to study for to get me out of it this time," I joke, thinking back on all the parties I'd missed in high school. Always the same excuse: I had to study.

"Yay!" Becky starts cheering and clapping her hands.

"Shhh," I say, grabbing them and pushing them apart. "Don't make it so obvious, would ya?"

"Why not?"

"I don't want Rowan to know that I'm going."

She nods. "Ohhh, playing hard to get, huh?"

I shake my head and roll my eyes.

"That's cool, but don't play it too long. He's a catch, even if it's only for one night."

I snort. "Yeah, right. All I'm going to catch from him is a case of the crabs," I say, not really meaning my words, more worried about keeping up with appearances that I hate him.

We spend the rest of the day at the beach, talking, hanging out, and drinking a beer or two. When the sun starts to set, everyone starts to gather their things to leave. I stand up and help Becky fold up the blanket.

"So, Harper, you're coming to the party, right?" Greg asks, and I can't help but feel like he's asking for Rowan. I guess this by the way his eyes flash from me, to him, and back.

I shrug. "I don't know. We'll see."

He smirks. "What else do you have to do?" He tilts his head to the side.

"Shower, wax my upper lip, muck the stalls, maybe water board myself. Anything other than being tortured by your homeboy there." I send Rowan an annoyed glance.

Greg walks up to me with a wide smile. One hand is waving back and forth while the other comes to rest on my shoulder. "I swear, he'll be on his best behavior."

I look over at Rowan and can see the annoyed look on his face, but it's not pointed in my direction. It's on Greg's hand that's resting on my shoulder. Is he mad that Greg is touching me? No, that can't be it. He's probably pissed because Greg is making a promise he knows he can't keep. He doesn't control Rowan. No one does.

SIX

ROWAN

I don't know what the fuck Greg is doing, but if he doesn't stop fucking with her, I'm going to kick his ass. He asked her out, knowing damn well that it would piss me off. Now, he's putting his hands on her and openly flirting. I don't know what he thinks he's doing, but it's only going to cause trouble for him later.

I grab my cooler and walk away, tearing my eyes off her face. She's still watching me, but her expression is hard to read. Is she enjoying the attention she's getting from Greg? Is she just happy to see how annoyed I am by it all? I shake my head and walk back to my truck, ready to get home and shower off so I can go to this party.

I make it to the party around eight, and while the house is already filling up, the one person I want here isn't here yet.

"So, is she coming?" I ask Greg.

"Who?" he asks, playing dumb.

"Don't be a smart-ass. You know who," I reply, leaning against the kitchen counter with a red cup in my hand.

He snorts. "Yes, she's coming. Alright? Just chill and be cool," he tells me, lifting a shot glass and tossing it back.

"What was your deal today? Were you trying to piss me off?"

He looks at me with his brows drawn together. "I don't know what you're talking about."

"Fuck if you don't. Talking to her, asking her out, flirting, and inviting her to the party." I list off all the reasons I wanted to punch him in the face today.

He laughs. "I was just trying to get you to step up, buddy. I don't know what your deal is with her. You've never been shy around girls before. Why this one?"

"I'm not being shy," I argue. "She fucking hates me."

He snorts as he wraps his bare arm around my shoulders. "She does not hate you, my friend. She's just as wrapped around you as you are her. No doubt."

I roll my eyes. "Highly doubtful, man."

"You'll see. She's playing hard to get. You up for the challenge?" He levels his eyes on me, but I don't answer. "If you're not, I am. She is hot as fuck, and I wouldn't mind testing her out for you."

I push him away, and his arm falls away. "Fuck off," I say, raising my cup and taking a drink. "Don't fucking touch her," I add on once I swallow.

This only makes him laugh harder. "That's what I thought. Grow some balls and stake your claim!"

Almost instantly, I look up and my eyes find hers. They fall down her body, taking in her short light-pink dress. The dress is tight up top, showing the curves of her tits and ribs. Then it flows out at her hips, ending well above her knee. I'm sure that if she bends over, I'd see her ass. She's paired the dress with a simple pair of flip-flops, and her long dark hair flows freely around her curvy body.

She's made more effort than she usually does. Tonight, her eyes are lined darkly; her cheekbones are more prominent, and her lips are glistening, begging for my kiss. I'm practically frozen as she makes her way to the island in the kitchen.

Greg smiles widely at her. "What's your poison?"

She smiles weakly at him. "Just a beer."

He looks over at me with a wink. "Head over to my man at the tap." He gestures to me.

Her shoulders fall when she sees that the only way she'll get a beer is if she comes to me. She rolls her eyes as she rounds the corner of the island back in the corner where I'm standing.

"Beer, please?" she asks, her tone off just from having to talk to me.

I set my beer down and grab a cup to fill up for her. "How ya been, Harp?"

"Just fine, Rowan. Can I have my beer, please?"

"I'll trade ya. Your beer for a kiss?" I flirt, knowing that it's not going to fly.

She scoffs. "Yeah, like I'm going to fall for that. I remember our last trade," she says. "You show me yours and I'll show you mine." She tries her best to mock my voice.

Fuck. That happened? Shit, I thought I'd dreamed that. My mouth drops open and I lean in. "That really happened?" I whisper.

She laughs and nods. "And you chickened out. Looks like you owe me one," she says, taking the cup from my hand and walking off.

Greg looks back at me, having heard the exchange. "Fuck, bro. Really?"

I shrug, lost in the memory I'd thought was a dream.

Hours pass, and she never comes back for another beer. I have my suspicions that she's sending someone else for them now so she doesn't have to deal with me. But I'm not that easy to avoid. After having a few beers myself, I go to search her out.

"You're on the tap," I tell Greg, passing him.

"That's my boy!" he shouts from behind me.

I laugh and shake my head as I leave the kitchen and step into the living room. I search the room quickly, but she's nowhere in sight, and neither is Becky or Tyler. I walk down the hallway. There's a long line for the bathroom, but she's not standing in it either. Finally, I slip out the sliding glass door and step out onto the patio. The pool is filled with way too many people, all of them splashing, drinking, or making out. The hot tub has another four people in it, and all the patio tables and lawn furniture are full too. I finally spot her in the back of the yard, talking with Becky, Tyler, and a couple other people we went to school with. She's standing up, gently swaying form side to side like she's enjoying the music, red cup in her hand. Her lips are turned up into a smile, and her eyes are glistening, no doubt from the alcohol running through her system.

I make my way over, not even sure what I'm going to say to her. When I approach, her eyes jump up and lock on mine. "Can we talk?" I ask, nodding in the opposite direction for some privacy.

"I'm fine here, thanks," she replies sweetly.

I cock my head to the side. "Come on, Harp. I won't bite... unless you like that kind of thing," I tack on with a smirk.

She rolls her eyes. "Fine. You have five minutes." She steps out of the group, then turns back to Becky. "If I'm not back in five minutes, send a search party."

"Oh, you'll be fine," Becky says, her smile wide. "I'd trade you places if I could." Her eyes flash over to Tyler, and he gives her a look that clearly says, *What the fuck*. But she just shrugs it off. They're a cool couple who doesn't seem to be overly jealous when the other gives or gets attention.

I lead Harper out the back gate and to the side of the house. There's a big streetlight on the corner lighting up the yard so we're not left in complete darkness. She spins around to face me. "So, what is it this time, Rowan? Did you slip something in my drink? Tape 'kick me' to my back? What?"

I laugh. "It's nothing like that," I breathe out, holding back my laugh.

"Then what?" she asks, acting annoyed.

"I gotta hold up my end of the deal, remember?" I put my cup in my mouth, biting down on the edge as my hands move to my jeans.

She stands back with a smug look on her face, thinking I won't do it.

I stop, remove the cup, and say, "You're just going to let me do it, aren't you?"

She smiles. "Hey, who am I to stop you?" She holds her hands out at her sides.

"You wanna see it," I challenge, "don't you?"

She just shrugs. "I mean, if you're too chicken..."

"Chicken?" I've been called a lot of things, but never have I been called a chicken. That's the deciding factor. I set my cup on the ground, my hands working to unbutton and unzip my jeans, secretly praying that he doesn't want to be shy and shrivel up on me at the worst possible time.

I reach into my boxers and grab ahold of it. "Are you sure?"

She raises an eyebrow in response.

I shrug. "Alright," I say, pulling upward.

"Wait! No! Stop," she says, holding her hand out so she can't see past it. "I didn't think you would really do it."

Instead of listening, I whip it out anyway. "Come on. Look."

Her fingers separate, and she peeks through them like a child watching a scary movie. She makes a squeaking sound and puts them back together.

"I owe you nothing, sweetheart," I reply, getting everything back in order. I bend down and grab my cup, taking a swig and walking back through the fence.

I'm sitting outside a little while later with the rest of the guys now that the keg is gone and the remaining party people have switched over to liquor. I'm not sure if this is a good thing or a bad thing. Everyone was trashed before the beer was gone, but now, they're just drinking the hard stuff. A lot of the party guests have left, but there is still more than a handful left lingering, Harper and her crew being one of the groups. She's at one end of the pool and I'm at the other. Even though there is plenty of space between us, my eyes are on her.

She tries not to pay any attention to me, but she fails miserably time and time again. There's nobody left in the house, only people going in and out for refills and bathroom trips. When she stands up to go inside, I follow in behind her.

I'm thinking she's probably just using the bathroom, so while I wait, I go to the kitchen to make a fresh drink. I'm surprised when I walk into the kitchen and find her behind the island, mixing one for herself. I come to a sudden stop.

Her eyes look up and lock on mine. They're darker than usual, a twinkle of sensuality in them. They're smoldering as her lips turn up in the corners.

"What can I get ya, Rowan?" she asks, pouring vodka into her cup.

I walk forward. "I guess whatever you're making."

She pours vodka into my cup and then grabs the Red Bull.

"I'll ask you one more time," she says, popping the top. "No going back. No second chances." She starts pouring the can into both cups, first hers, then mine. "What do you want?" Her eyes meet mine now, and I catch the hidden meaning there.

My mouth is suddenly dry, and my back is ramrod straight. I feel the challenge, and she's calling me out. I can't back away. Not now. Not after all the time I've waited.

"You," I answer honestly.

"It's about time you said it," she replies, walking around the island to stand before me. "And what are you going to do with me?" she asks, flirting as she reaches out and tucks her fingers into the waistband of my jeans, pulling me closer.

"Oh, you'll find out," I whisper. She's so close now that her breath is blowing against my dry lips. My tongue comes out, wetting them, and her eyes fall down to them.

When they lock back on mine, I lose all control and pull her flush against me as my lips move to hers.

Several things seem to happen simultaneously. Her arms wrap around my neck. Her legs wrap around my waist. As I kiss her, I push her back up against the fridge, my hands finding her ass beneath her dress.

Our kiss is hard and rushed, full of passion and need, years of longing finally overflowing and pouring out. Her hands find their way to my hair, threading through it and tugging at the roots. My hands squeeze her ass, feeling her skin bubbling up between each finger. Fuck, her lips are soft, her tongue sweet.

Suddenly, I find myself running through my choices. I could fuck her right here, against the fridge, but with as many people that are here, someone is bound to walk in on us, cutting things short—unless I pound one out real quick. But I don't want that. I've waited years for this. I'm taking my fucking time.

I could take her into one of the bedrooms, but Greg and the rest of the party would know the moment we didn't come back out those doors. Or I could ask her to come home with me. That way, we could lie and say she got sick, that I had to take her home. We wouldn't get caught, and I'd be able to bury myself in her all night long.

I pull back, looking into her eyes. "Come home with me," I whisper.

SEVEN
HARPER

What the fuck am I doing? I'm making out with Rowan fucking Wilson, the guy who made high school hell. The sexy as fuck guy that I've always loved to hate. The sexy as fuck guy I've always secretly wanted. But as it turns out, he's always secretly wanted me too.

"Come home with me," he says, pulling away from our kiss. It's a soft whisper, and it causes a shiver to race up my spine.

"What?" I ask, still in a daze from our kiss.

"We have about five minutes before someone walks through that door and catches us. Come home with me...unless you want to explain this."

I think it over. He's right. If I want this, we have to go now. But do I want this? It doesn't mean anything. We're both drunk and at a party. We've both wanted one another for years. Yes, I want this. Even if it's only for the experience alone.

"Let's go," I reply.

He drops me on my feet but keeps my hand in his, leading me out of the kitchen and to the front door. Moments later, we're in his truck and he's turning it over. It fires up loud, letting everyone know that he's leaving the party.

"Wait, should you be driving?" I ask knowing I've had enough that it wouldn't be safe.

"Trust me, I'm stone cold sober sweetheart. I wouldn't risk that with you."

I scoot over to the center seat, and his hand lands on my knee. The touch nearly scorches my skin, and I gasp and look over at him. Our eyes meet in the darkened cab, and something is exchanged, but I don't know what. I tear my eyes from his, and he goes back to watching the road.

Testing the waters, I place my hand on his thigh. It's hot and firm beneath my skin, even through his jeans. I know from that small peek earlier that if I move my hand an inch to the left, I'll feel how excited he really is. He isn't small by any means. I guess that li'l smokie was just an ugly rumor.

As he drives, his hand starts to make its way slowly up my thigh, and tingles break out, racing from my leg to my lower belly, pooling there like hot lava.

"Fuck it," I breathe out, giving in completely as I turn my upper body to kiss his neck. I place my right hand on his jaw, holding his head where I need it to kiss his neck and nibble his ear. He lets out a shaking breath and a soft groan of approval.

I feel his leg push against the gas harder, and the bumps become rougher, telling me that he's in as much of a hurry as I am. He makes a sharp turn and stomps the breaks, shifts into park, then grabs me, pulling me onto his lap where his lips find mine again.

With me straddling him, I can feel his excitement pressing against my core, and it causes a hot flood of need to wash over me. His hands are everywhere all at once—my outer thighs, my ass, moving up my hips and to my sides. They move up and down my back, then around to the front to massage my breasts. His lips fall from mine, kissing his way down my jaw and neck to the exposed area of my chest. He kisses the swell of my breasts, then tries to work his way between them, but there's no way he's getting there without removing my dress and bra.

He lets out a growl and shuts off the truck, opens his door, and holds me tight against him as he steps out. His mouth is back on mine as he walks through the small front yard and to the front door.

He manages to get it open quickly, and he steps inside the darkness. It's cool in here from having the air conditioner blasting, and it smells like his deep, rich scent. The moment we're inside, his hands find the zipper on the back of my dress, and he begins tugging it down as he walks us through the house.

He kicks open a door and it bangs off the wall, but then there's something soft beneath me. A bed. His body is pressing against mine in all the right ways. His weight feels good, just right. As we kiss, his hand travels up my skirt, finding my panties. With a quick jerk, I hear them rip. In their place is his hand, working its way between my folds, grazing my clit, and dipping inside. The moment I'm filled, I suck in a loud breath.

"Fuck," he says, removing himself from me.

He sits up on his knees and yanks his shirt over his head, exposing all those hard, rippling muscles. He's back to kissing me one moment later, his hands pulling at the straps on my dress.

I let him pull it off my arms, then he's reaching behind me to unclasp my bra. It pops open. He slowly breaks our kiss, watching as he pulls it away. He tosses it on the floor, and his eyes take me in slowly.

They start on mine, sinking down my face and settling on my chest. His eyes intently on my body, he begins to pull my dress the rest of the way down until it's off completely. I'm totally naked before him, lying sprawled out on the bed, watching his eyes look over every inch of my flesh.

"Fuck, you're perfect," he whispers, unfastening his jeans. He leans forward, capturing my hard nipple in his hot mouth. He sucks hard, then flicks his tongue against it before running circles around it.

My hands find his hair, holding him in place as my breathing picks up.

While his mouth is torturing my breast, his hand finds my clit again. His fingers slide into me while his thumb applies pressure to my clit. All the sensations are building up inside me, threatening to pour out at any second, but I can't let it. I don't want his hands and mouth. I want him. Inside me.

I reach between us with my free hand and capture his thick cock, working it up and down slowly. I feel the tip already wet with precum, and I work it over his shaft, spreading the wetness. I pull away even though I have a handful of his hair, and he reaches into the bedside table, pulling out a condom. He rips it open with his teeth and works to slide it on.

"Fuck, Harper. Please tell me you're sure," he nearly begs.

I offer up a smile. "I'm sure," I tell him, more than ready to feel him inside of me.

He positions himself at my entrance. "Good, 'cause I'm going to be inside you all night long." He pushes forward, filling me completely—almost overfilling me. I've only been with four guys in my lifetime, all of them in college, but none of them were this big. I feel as if I'm being stretched from the inside out. It's painful but teasing and pleasurable at the same time.

Once he's in, he doesn't move. His forehead falls down to mine. "Fuck, you're so fucking tight, I could explode right now."

"Don't do that. We have all night, remember?" I say, teasing him as I move my hips up and down.

His hands capture my hips, holding them in place as he pulls out slowly. He sends his hips flying my way again, thrusting into me hard and fast. I let out a moan that I had no intention of making. It sounds dirty, breathy, porn-like. Not me at all. That sound has his cock twitching inside of me.

His mouth smashes back to mine while his hips keep up their rhythm, forward, rolling upward, then back, only to repeat the process again and again. And each time he rolls them upward, I get pushed closer and closer to the edge of release.

My nails scratch down his strong, muscular back, and I bite his shoulder, maybe a little harder than I should, but he doesn't stop me. "I'm going to come," I pant out, which only makes him work harder, faster.

"Say my name," he whispers, nipping my ear and then biting my neck.

No way am I saying it. That would be the one thing that would bring me out of this heaven I've somehow found. His name ruins everything. It's not ruining this.

His hips slow, and my release begins to fade.

"Say my name, Harper." His hips are still moving but painfully slow now. "I want my name falling off those sexy as fuck lips when I make you come on my dick."

I don't want to, but that statement was too fucking hot. "Rowan," I call out, and his hips start back up at the pace I need. My breathing becomes labored, my muscles tightening, my release building once again. "Rowan," I moan out once again, and each time he hears it, he works harder, making my release climb to new heights.

My release rises too high, then breaks, raining down on me to the point of drowning. I can't breathe. I can't think. All I can do is ride out every last wave, his name falling from my lips again and again.

Once my body starts to soften around him, he pulls out of me completely and then flips me over, entering me from behind. If I thought he was large before, this position only makes him feel larger. With each thrust, it feels like I'm being split in two. His hands are squeezing my hips too hard, but I like it in a way I never thought I would. All my past lovers, they were always soft and slow. This is rough, fast, dirty. This is what people pay money to see on the internet.

As I'm bent over before him, his hand comes around my hip, finding my clit. He rubs it as he continues to move in and out of me.

"God, Harper. You feel better than I imagined. So fucking hot, tight." He bends down, nipping the skin that covers my shoulder blade.

His hands take my hips again, pulling me into his thrusts. All I can hear is the sound of our skin smacking together, the bed squealing in protest beneath us, and the sound of my heart pounding in my ears as my blood rushes my body. With my head on the pillow, my hands fist the sheet. Dropping my head down makes my ass poke out just the tiniest bit more, and he pounds deeper. It's only another couple of minutes before we're both falling over the edge of the cliff together.

EIGHT

ROWAN

We're both lying in my bed, side by side, with the blanket pulled up to our chests. There's an awkwardness between us now, and it's like neither of us realized what the fuck we were doing until now. Honestly, all I thought about was getting her into my bed. I didn't think about after. Apparently, neither did she.

We're both staring up at the ceiling as we work to regain control over our bodies. It seems like she's trying to figure out if she should get up and go home or if she should stay. I'd like her to stay, but that isn't up to me. I'd love to hold her against my chest all night and wake up in the morning to do it all over again because I already know once isn't enough. Not for me.

"Stop overthinking, Harper," I finally breathe out, running my hands over my face.

Her head whips in my direction. "How can I stop overthinking? I just fucked you. You, Rowan Wilson. I'm supposed to hate you."

I roll onto my side to face her. "Actually, I fucked you. But you seemed to have enjoyed it. I know I did."

She snorts, probably rolling her eyes, but it's too dark to see if she did. "Fine, I let you fuck me. That isn't any better. What are people going to say?"

"Who says we have to tell them?" I ask.

"They're going to know, Rowan. We both went into the house, and then they heard your truck start up and we were both gone. They're going to know."

"So we'll say you got sick and I took you home. Nobody has to know. This is our business. Nobody else's."

"So, you mean you won't go around telling everyone?"

"No, not if you don't want me to."

She rolls to her side, facing me now. I can feel her breath blowing against my face. "Why would you do that?"

I admit, the old Rowan would've gone around and told every fucking person who would listen. But I'm not that guy anymore, and I haven't been since high school. I grew up. And if she thinks I'm going to fuck this up by talking about it, she's out of her damn mind. "It's nobody's business but ours, Harper. Plus, I'd kind of like to do it again. I don't know about you, but once isn't nearly enough for me." I place my hand on her hip and pull her closer.

She lets out a giggle as her hand lands softly on my jaw. "Okay, our little secret then?"

"Our dirty little secret," I reply, pressing my mouth to hers.

And that's the last coherent words either of us say for the rest of the night. The rest of the night is filled with moans, whimpers, giggles, and screams of passion as I fuck her any damn way she'll let me. The bed, the shower, the kitchen table we happened to pass on the way back to the bedroom, the bedroom floor, up against the sliding glass door in my bedroom. All of it has remnants of us on it.

In the bright light of the morning, though, things come to an end. I wake with her putting her clothes on. "Where you going?" I ask, straining my eyes against the sunlight that's streaming through the glass door. I look over at it and see it all smudged up, her perfect ass print visible.

"I have to go home before Daddy starts to worry."

"Are you coming back?" I ask, sitting up, watching as she steps into her dress and pulls it back up her shoulders. She spins around for me to zip up.

She giggles. "No, probably not today. I have a ton of stuff to do. I need to unpack and do laundry. I promised Daddy that I'd help him with the land: feed the chickens and goats and run the horses."

I pull her zipper up and stand up behind her as I do. I'm still completely naked and more than excited to wake up to her. I know she can feel it pressing against her ass as I bend down and press a kiss to her neck. "I'll make it worth your while," I whisper in her ear.

She tilts her head to the side, enjoying the feeling of my lips on her skin. Her eyes flutter closed. "I know you will, but I can't. We've had our fun. Time to move on." She snaps out of the daze and walks away from me.

"Well, at least let me take you home." I bend down and grab my clothes off the floor from last night.

"Alright, but you can't drive up the driveway. Drop me at the road so I don't have to explain to my father that I spent the night riding your dick."

I chuckle. "You didn't ride shit, but I'm looking forward to that. Tonight?"

She laughs and rolls her eyes. "Come by tonight. After Daddy goes to sleep. You can meet me in the barn."

I smile wide now.

I take her home, dropping her off at the end of the drive like she made me promise to do, then head back home to get cleaned up for the day. Walking back into my house now that it's empty feels lonely. I wish she were still here. As I walk to the bathroom, I look around the house at all the places I was inside her. I pause in my bedroom door, looking at the glass door, remembering.

Fuck. She's better than I thought she'd be. I don't know how I'm going to manage getting out of this alive because now that I've had her, I want her forever. She's different than any other girl I've ever been with. With them, once was enough. Harper, though, I'll never have enough.

I shake my head at myself and go to shower. With as hot as it is already today, I dress in a pair of jean shorts and a t-shirt. Since it's Sunday, there isn't much going on in town. Everyone is either at church or preparing for the workweek. The guys and I meet up every Sunday at Walt's bar for lunch, some drinks, and a few games of pool. I head that way around noon.

"There he is," Greg says when I walk in. "What happened to you last night? You finally nail Harper?"

I shake my head as I plop down in a seat next to him. "Nah, she got sick and I took her home," I lie.

"Too bad," he says, "but maybe you scored some brownie points and you'll get her next time."

"Yeah, maybe," I agree.

"Who's turn to buy?" I ask.

"Mine," Greg says, tossing a menu down on the table. "Order up, boys."

We all place our orders and get a couple of appetizers for the table. We're drinking, talking, and laughing while we take turns throwing darts. The door opens and in walks Harper and Becky. Harper takes me in before ignoring me and going to the bar to order a large glass of Ginger Ale.

"Now's your chance," Greg says, walking past me to throw his dart.

I head over to the bar. "You feeling better?" I ask, loud enough for Becky to hear.

"Yeah, I guess. Just had to sleep it off. Thanks for the ride home last night. I'm actually surprised you didn't leave me in a dark field somewhere."

I shoot her a grin. "Any time. So... tonight?"

She frowns. "Tonight what?"

"Well, I gave you a ride. Don't you owe me a ride?" I smirk, hoping she catches the double meaning.

She snorts. "Not if my life depended on it."

Becky looks over at me. "Give it up, Rowan. If you haven't trapped her yet, you ain't going to."

"Nah, the game isn't over until it's over," I reply, turning to head back to my table.

"Shot down again?" Greg asks.

I just smile, looking over at her. "Yeah, but I think I'm weighing on her. She doesn't have it in her to keep fighting like this." I pick up my water and take a swig.

While we play darts, eat, and drink, I keep a watchful eye on her. The bar fills up, like it usually does once church is let out, and the place gets crowded. I happen to notice when Scott walks in, finds her, and takes a seat at her side. My jealously spikes instantly.

Someone turns on the juke box, and a few people start dancing. I watch as Scott holds out his hand. She shakes her head, telling him no, but he isn't backing down. Finally, she agrees, and he leads her to the dance floor.

My back straightens. If only he knew that I was inside her last night. It was my name falling from her lips. Maybe then he wouldn't fuck with her. I can see the look in his eyes. He's hoping to charm his way back into her life, but there's no room for him. I'm filling the void in her now.

I sit watching as he puts his hands on what's mine, one on her hip, the other in her hand. He spins her around on the dance floor until the song turns to one much softer. She tries to pull away, but he tugs her back. This time, he has both hands on her lower back. When his eyes catch mine, he smirks.

I know I shouldn't, but I can't help myself. If she's going to make me jealous, I'm going to make her feel the same way. Not only that, but I need an excuse to be close enough to hear what they're saying.

I grab a random waitress as she's walking by and tug her to the dance floor. I pull her against my chest, and we start dancing. She acts like she wants to get away, but I know she doesn't. Plus, she isn't pulling very hard, and then her thin resolve falls away and she gives in, a smile on her lips.

Harper's eyes flash to mine, and I offer up a smile. But at least now I'm close enough to hear what Scott is saying to her.

"Come on, Harp. It'll be like old times. Go out with me," he pleads.

"Scott, I don't think it's a good idea. I just got back into town, and I'm not wanting to settle here for long. I just want to keep my options open," she replies, her eyes still on me.

"You can keep your options open. I'm only asking for one date."

"One date will turn into two, and two will turn to three. You know the pattern. You used it to your advantage once before, remember? Plus, I'm kind of seeing someone."

He pulls back. "Who?"

She shakes her head. "You wouldn't know him," she lies. "I went to school with him."

"What's that saying? If you're in different zip codes, it doesn't count?"

She rolls her eyes. "That's not helping."

The song ends, and I release the waitress. Harper and I are eye to eye, and we both freeze, wanting more, but we both go our separate ways.

She watches me from across the room, and I watch her. Everyone else is completely oblivious.

NINE

HARPER

I know I have no claim to him, and I know that I was dancing with Scott, but seeing that waitress in his arms has my jealously sky high. I want nothing more than to rip her hands off for touching him. I try to talk myself down. What happened last night was nothing. He's not mine. We made no commitments. He didn't seem all that into her anyway, only dancing with her once he saw me and Scott. Maybe he was feeling jealous and that's why he did it.

Anyway, I shake my head, wanting to clear it of all thoughts, but my eyes keep going back to finding him watching me. There's so much space between us right now. I want nothing more than to close it, but doing so would only confuse everyone in the bar. There would be questions upon questions. Questions I don't have the answers to and don't want to answer to begin with. Rowan and I will have our time together later.

I try to focus on Becky and Tyler, who have now joined us. We all have a beer in front of us, but I haven't even touched mine. It's the middle of the day on a Sunday. While we're in a small country town with nothing to do but drink, I'm not in the mood. The only thing I can think about is Rowan and the things we did all night long, and how much I liked those things. It's a good thing we didn't do this in high school. I never would've been able to leave to go to college.

I catch him looking at me again, and I stand up, heading to the back where the bathrooms are located. There's a small hallway leading to the bathrooms and you can't see the doors unless you're standing right in front of the hallway. I slip into the women's bathroom, then turn and wait to see if he's followed me.

The door opens, and he pokes his head in, looking around.

"Get in here," I say, pulling him through and locking the door behind him. I push him up against the wall, moving my mouth to his. He kisses me, but his lips are taut, like he's smiling.

"What's so funny?" I ask against his lips.

"Someone's a little jealous, huh?" His hands move up to cup my face.

"I'm not jealous," I lie.

"I was," he whispers, pulling me back in for a kiss.

Hearing his admission makes the butterflies in my stomach take flight. My hands are on his sides, and I pull him closer. "Let's get out of here," I say, stepping back.

"Where do you want to go?" he asks, walking forward with me.

"My place. We'll take a ride, get away from all these eyes." I unlock the door and open it, allowing him to slide out. He walks out, and I wait a few minutes before I follow along behind him.

I stop by the table and tell Becky I'm leaving.

"Why?" she asks.

"I told you I still had work to do. I'll talk to you tomorrow," I promise.

"You want me to take you home?"

"I'll be fine. It's just down the road. Hang out and have fun." I wave goodbye, then make my way out the door and to Rowan's truck. He's already behind the wheel with the motor running.

"Isn't your dad going to think something is up?" he asks, climbing out of the truck at my house.

"My dad won't care," I reply, leading him to the barn. I don't feel the need to lie to him. Well, I don't feel the need to tell him the truth either. I mean, how would a father take the news that his daughter isn't in a relationship with a man, but she's just fucking him any time she has the chance? Yeah, that's not a conversation I want to have.

We saddle up two horses, and we each climb on. I lead him down the trail that weaves throughout the trees. The horses are trotting along at a slow pace, side by side, leaving plenty of room for the two of us to have a conversation, but I have no idea what to even talk about.

Neither of us say a word until we get to the clearing with the big pond in the middle. I hop off my horse to stretch my legs and take in the scene before me. He does the same, walking up behind me. His arms encircle me, pulling me to his chest. It feels weirdly normal, like this is something we do all the time.

"What are we doing, Rowan?" I breathe out.

"If you ask me, we're finally doing what we've always wanted."

I spin in his arms. "Is this wrong after everything we've been through?"

His hand moves up to cup my cheek. "Does it feel wrong?"

My eyes flutter closed with his hand on my face, his heat absorbing into my skin. I shake my head.

"Then how could it be wrong?" he asks, pressing his lips to mine.

He kisses me soft and slow, nothing like our kisses last night. "I've waited so long for you," he whispers against my lips. "This is a dream come true."

I pull away, laughing.

"What?" he asks, a laugh of his own bubbling out.

"You don't say shit like that."

"Shit like what?" he asks, still smirking.

"'This is a dream come true,'" I repeat.

"It's true though."

"You've already got me in bed, Rowan. No need in laying it on any thicker."

He shakes his head and rolls his eyes. "You're impossible."

We end up sitting on the bank, throwing rocks into the pond and watching the ripples. The sun is starting to descend in the sky, and the crickets are chirping. It's relaxing, especially the way I'm leaning back against him. I'm sitting between his knees with my back to his chest.

"Tell me about college," he says.

"What do you want to know?"

I feel him shrug. "How many guys tried to get in your pants."

I laugh. "All of them. Only four succeeded though."

"Who was your first?"

"His name is Gavin Parker."

"Not Scott?"

"Nope, never went all the way," I confess.

"That makes me feel better," he says, and I turn back in time to see his smirk. "I finally got what he couldn't."

"What about you? Who was your first?"

"You," he answers, and I turn back to look at him again.

"I was not your first. You were with a ton of girls in high school."

"Yeah, but in my head, they were all you." He leans forward, his breath blowing against my ear. "But you were a hundred times better than the lies I'd been tricking myself to believe."

I shake my head. "You are good. No wonder you broke so many hearts. You know exactly what to say all the time, don't you?"

"Nope, I just say what I'm thinking. Plus, I wasn't like this with any of them."

"What do you mean?"

"I mean, I wasn't the best guy back then," he confesses. "Back then, I thought it was all about numbers. I had to sleep with the most girls. That meant telling them what they wanted to hear and then not giving a shit about anything else after I got what I wanted."

"You really were an ass, huh?"

He chuckles. "Yeah, I really was."

I turn to face him, staying between his legs but putting my feet on either side of his hips. "Why aren't you that way with me? Or are you?" I ask, raising a brow.

He laughs. "I finally got what I want, and I'm not throwing it away," he says, leaning forward to capture my lips.

It's easy to lose myself in him. He's sexy as hell, good in bed, and knows all the right things to say. If I'm not careful, I'm going to end up like the countless other girls in this town who had him and lost him. I'm not stupid. I'm not falling for the lines he's throwing my way, but I will enjoy the time we have together. I'll have fun until it ends, then I'll move on with my life without looking back.

"It's getting dark. We should get the horses back."

He stands up and offers me his hand to pull me to my feet.

The two of us ride back and get the horses back in their stalls. When I turn around, he's leaning against the wooden workbench in the corner of the barn.

"So, is your daddy in bed for the night?"

I smile, knowing why he's asking that question. I nod. "He should be. Guess I owe you a ride, huh?"

His smirk widens to a full-blown smile. "I guess you do."

I take his hand and pull him up the wooden stairs. In the past, Daddy hired men to work the farm who didn't have a place to stay, so the upstairs has been converted into a small apartment. There's a full-size bed, a bathroom, and a small kitchen area with a microwave, fridge, sink, and a couple of small cabinets.

I drag him over to the bed and push him down. He falls onto his back, sideways on the bed, so his feet are still on the floor. Looking down at him, I pull my hair back into a ponytail, pull my shirt over my head, then fall down to my knees, between his.

His head pops up to see what I'm doing the minute I start unfastening his shorts. He doesn't argue when I free him from his boxers and slide him into my mouth. His hips lift upward, and he makes a hissing sound as he draws in a breath of air.

I work him up and down with my mouth, tip to base. I swirl my tongue around him, enjoying every labored breath and moan that leaves his lips.

"Oh, fuck, Harper," he breathes out, and I feel his muscles tense beneath me. But I don't stop. I want to push him to the edge. "Fuck, Harper. You have to stop." Again, I keep going, wanting more. "Harper, I'm going to fucking come." His whole body is hard now, rigid.

Finally, I pull away from him, and he lets out a relieved breath. I stand up and remove my shorts and panties. He sits up, grabbing my thighs, trying to pull me to him, but I can tell by the way that he's doing it that he's planning on putting me on bottom, and I owe him a ride.

I push his hands off me and then urge him back as I take my place on top of him.

"Fuck, I don't have a condom," he says, letting his head fall back against the bed.

"Then tell me when," I say, placing him at my entrance and sliding down his length. I stretch around him, and his hands move to squeeze my hips.

"Oh fuck," he breathes out. "You feel so much better with nothing between us." He gets up on his elbows to watch me.

I wrap my arms around his neck, letting my head fall back, and I take more and more of him, inch by inch. He gets impatient, though, and the next thing I know, his hands are on my hips, pulling me all the way down and making me cry out. Pain mixes with pleasure again in a delicious way.

As I ride him, his hand comes between us, rubbing circles around my needy clit. Each time I slide down him, I only get closer and closer to where I need to be. With his free hand, he reaches behind me and unclasps my bra. When it falls down my arms, he leans forward, sucking my hard nipple into his mouth. Now that every part of me is getting attention, my release builds higher.

"Oh, Rowan," I whisper, letting my body get tighter around him.

I thought before that saying his name would ruin this, but it doesn't. It makes it better. That love to hate thing we had before is only better now. Because now, I hate to love him.

"Harper," he whispers my name in response.

"You're so big. It feels too good. I'm going to explode," I say, not allowing myself to stop.

His hand tightens on my hip. "Come for me, Harper." His hips lift, and his hand works me over faster.

My release builds high and shatters, coming out of me in whimpers, moans, and breathless sighs. After I ride out every last wave, he rolls me over and pounds into me relentlessly, hard, fast, and never stopping, not until he finds his own release. Then he pulls out, takes himself in hand, and finishes on my stomach.

TEN

ROWAN

The moment I have control over my body again, I get up and grab a paper towel off the table. I clean up the mess I left on her stomach and then lie down beside her, pulling her to my chest. I press a kiss to her shoulder, and she takes a deep breath, slowly releasing it. She sounds completely content, lying here with me, in my arms.

"So, were you really jealous when I danced with that waitress?"

She giggles. "Yes. The only thing I could think about was ripping her hands off."

"You know I only did it so I would have a reason to hear what you and Scott were talking about, right?"

"So, I guess you heard him trying to talk me into going out on a date with him, huh?"

"Yep, and that only made me more jealous. Fuck that guy."

She laughs. "I said no."

"Why did you say no?"

She bites her lower lip. "Would you laugh if I said it was because of you?"

"No, that'd make me happy actually."

"Good. Then I guess you get how jealous I was seeing you with that waitress."

"I know how jealous I've been ever since you got back into town."

She laughs. "I thought you were getting annoyed at Greg at the beach the other day."

"Annoyed? I was ready to punch him in his throat, especially when he touched you. I knew you were going to be mine, and I don't want anyone's hands on what's mine." I kiss her shoulder where his hand was, reclaiming it with my touch.

We lie in bed together for another couple of hours, touching, kissing, teasing. Around midnight, I get up to go home, needing to work in the morning. I kiss her good night at her front door, then I watch her go in before I pull out of the drive. When I get home, I fall into bed, exhausted from the weekend and the hours I've spent inside her. Sleep finds me easy, but all night, all I do is dream of her.

I WAKE in the morning and shower and dress for work. I'm pulling out of the driveway at five on the dot, still tired as shit from lack of sleep, but farming starts before the sun rises, and there's more than enough shit to do.

It seems like working is the only thing that keeps her off my mind, and that's only if I actually have to think about what I'm doing. Plowing the fields, mucking the stalls, and feeding the animals keeps my hands busy, but nothing else. Every other moment, my thoughts are consumed by her.

I wish she wasn't so insistent on hiding away from the town. I would like to take her out to dinner, wine and dine her like I usually do with the women I'm seeing, but for now, she seems completely content with our hidden dates and stolen moments.

If she won't come out on a date with me, I'll bring the date to her. After work, I go home and shower, get dressed again, and then leave the house. I stop by the market and grab a bouquet of flowers, a bottle of wine, and enough stuff to have a picnic in the barn, our little hidden world.

I make the drive over to her house and knock on the door, holding everything at my side. She opens it with surprise written all over her face.

"What's this?" she asks, stepping out onto the porch with me.

"I knew you wouldn't go out on a date with me, so I brought the date to you. Barn?"

"I wish I would've known. I would have showered instead of wearing... well, this." She gestures down at herself. She's wearing nothing but some short cutoff shorts and a bikini top.

"Been to the water hole today?"

"No, I bush hogged the field. No better way to get a tan," she says, leading the way to the barn.

"Hmmm," I mumble, clenching my jaw.

"What?"

"I never thought bush hogging could be so sexy," I say around a smile.

She laughs and bumps her shoulder against mine.

In the barn, I spread the blanket out across the floor, and she opens the doors, letting in the light and giving us a perfect view of the sunset. I spread everything out on the blanket, then pour us both a glass of wine.

"Wine? Fancy," she says, picking up her glass and taking a sip. Then she wrinkles her nose and shakes her head. "It isn't very good."

I laugh and take a sip for myself. I force myself to swallow it. "Yeah, that's not very good."

She holds up her finger. "I got something better." She stands up and goes to the cabinet hanging above the sink. She drags a chair over to it, then stands up on it, reaching to the back of the cabinet and pulling out a bottle of Jack Daniel's. "I knew Daddy kept his stash here," she says, stepping down and bringing the bottle over.

She uncaps it, takes a sip, then passes the bottle with a hiss.

I laugh but take the bottle, taking a sip. "That's better." I breathe out the fire.

There's a creak from below, and we both freeze like we're a couple of teenagers who are sneaking into a liquor cabinet.

"Harper, who's truck is in the drive?" Her dad asks from down below.

She gets up and looks over the rail, down at him. "That's Rowan's."

I follow suit, moving over to the stairs and looking down at him. "Hi, Mr. Mitchell. How ya doing?"

"Well, I'll be… I haven't seen you since the day you decided to rip some donuts in my cornfield. How ya doing, son?"

I smile at the memory. "Very well, sir. And yourself?"

"Oh, I've had better days, but I've worse days too. It all evens out in the end."

I laugh. "That's right."

"Well, I'll leave you kids alone. What are you doing up there anyway?"

"Actually, we're on a date," I confess. "She won't go out with me, so I brought the date to her. Picnic in the barn. Sounds romantic, right?"

He chuckles. "If you say so. Good night."

"Night, Daddy," she says as we both get up to go back to our spot on the floor.

"Hey, when did you rip donuts in the cornfield?" she asks.

"It was a couple days after you left for college," I confess.

"Why'd you do that?"

"You left and I didn't know. I had to hear it through town gossip. I was angry."

She offers up a small smile. "Angry at me for leaving or angry because I didn't tell you goodbye?"

I shrug. "A little of both, I guess. It felt like I'd lost my chance. More like wasted it."

"Yet here I am…"

"Here you are," I repeat.

We sit and eat and talk before cleaning everything up and deciding, since we still have plenty of daylight left, to head out to the old pond to do some fishing. The two of us climb on the green four-wheeler, and she drives us through the trail that leads to the pond.

I pack the bottle of Jack with the fishing supplies, and as we fish, we take turns with the bottle, asking one another questions and taking a drink if we don't want to answer.

"What did you really think of me in high school?" I ask, the bottle sitting between us.

She rolls her eyes. "I thought that you were an asshole put on this planet to make me suffer... but a cute asshole, and I hated myself for thinking that." She giggles. "What did you think of me?"

I snort. "I wanted you the first time I saw you, but in high school, I was caught up in the whole popularity thing. I thought it was impossible for me, the quarterback, to get involved with a girl like you, someone who didn't give a shit about popularity, the smartest girl in our class. In fact, I couldn't even understand why I wanted you so badly."

"Why did you?" she asks.

"Besides the fact that you're beautiful?" I ask, looking over at her. "You were a challenge. I could've had any other girl in that school with a snap of my fingers. But not you. You made it fun. You matched me step for step the whole way." I reel my line in and toss it out again. "Now, my question." I quickly glance over at her. "Did you think about me while you were gone?"

She laughs. "Of course I did."

"Elaborate, please."

She shakes her head with annoyance. "For the longest time, I couldn't figure out why I kept thinking about you, wondering what you were doing now that I was gone, wondering who the lucky girl was that got to be with you on any given night. Then I started looking for guys who reminded me of you."

"Did you find any?"

"Four," she confesses and her cheeks turn red, "but none of them were exactly like you. None of them had all your qualities. One had the muscles, one had the attitude, one had hair similar to yours, and the last one... well, I don't know. He reminded me of you somehow. Maybe it was just the way he walked and talked."

"So every guy that reminded you of me, you slept with?"

"Something like that," she confirms.

"Sounds like we had more in common than I thought." She's only ever slept with four guys, and each one of them was some way to trick herself into thinking they were me. I've been with many girls, and every time, I'd always imagined that they were her. "We could have saved a lot of sexual partners if we'd just gotten together like we wanted to, you know?"

She giggles. "Yeah, but this way was more fun."

ELEVEN
HARPER

Something happens when I'm alone with Rowan that I never thought possible. I feel like a kid again. Time seems to stop completely, then it starts moving backward. I'm no longer in my twenties. I'm back in my teen years, but this time, it's better because I don't have tests to study for or a curfew to abide by. Being with Rowan is like rewinding the clock. When we're together, it's nothing but fun and laughter.

Somehow, the fishing poles get tossed aside, and we both strip down to our underwear and wade out into the water with the squishy mud between our toes. I splash him and he splashes me. He jumps at me, trying to catch me, but I fall back out of his grasp. I swim away, but he's bigger and stronger, and he latches on to my ankle, dragging me back against him. My legs wrap around his hips, and my arms circle his neck. His nose is touching mine as he looks deeply into my eyes. I can see the bright sunset in his pupils.

"You're beautiful, you know that?" he says, moving in for a soft kiss. His hands are splayed across my back as he holds me to him. He breaks the kiss and rests his forehead against mine. "Come home with me."

I smile, about to tell him no. We can't be so careless.

"I want you in my bed tonight, in my arms... all night long." His voice is barely above a whisper, and I can see the intensity in his eyes.

I can't tell him no.

WE WALK through his front door, and already, we're kissing and pulling away one another's clothes. He picks me up against him and carries me through the house. I open my eyes, expecting to find the bedroom, but to my surprise, we're in the bathroom. He sets me on my feet and pulls away to turn the shower on.

"I thought a shower first would be good. We both kind of stink from the pond water."

I smile and nod. We really do.

I yank off my clothes and leave them on the floor as I step into the shower. He steps in behind me. As I wet my hair to wash it, he gets the body wash and pours some into his hand. I expect him to start washing off, but instead, he slides his slick hands across my body, my stomach, my chest, around to my back, and down to my ass. I know it's an innocent act, but his hands always feel too good on my body. It lights a fire deep in my belly.

Suddenly, I can't get clean fast enough. I want the shower to be done. All I want is to feel him pressing against me, his lips on mine, his hands on my body. How I've gone this long without him is beyond me because each passing second we're not touching, I'm losing my mind.

After I rinse off and am clean, I switch spots with him in the shower so he can be beneath the flow of water. I start rubbing body wash over him, each ab muscle, his strong pecs, that V between his hipbones, then lower, stroking him. He grows bigger and harder in my hand. He reaches for me, pulling me against his chest where our lips smash together.

He rinses quickly while still kissing me. Then he reaches behind him and shuts off the water, picking me up and carrying me out of the bathroom, soaking wet and completely naked. We fall onto his bed, a mess of tangled limbs.

Each touch from him is like a fire being lit on my skin. It's a fire that burns hotter the longer it's left to smolder. It grows and races though my body, consuming me and burning me from the inside out, but it's a painless fire, just a heat that warms me.

After we make love, the rest of the night is spent simply holding one another, exchanging soft touches and kisses and letting the other person know that we're still here, awake. I drift in and out of sleep, always waking to the feeling of his lips on my body, my shoulder, back, or neck.

When the sun rises, I feel like I haven't slept at all, but I don't feel tired. I feel energized. He's back between my thighs, making me giggle and moan. There's a knock on his front door, and we both freeze.

"Who's that?" I ask, lifting the blanket so he can hear me.

"I don't know," he whispers from beneath it.

He crawls out the foot of the bed and grabs a pair of sweatpants from the chair in the corner, quickly pulling them on and shutting the door behind him. Moments later, I hear the sounds of two men talking: him and Greg?

"Where the fuck you been lately?" Greg asks.

"I've just been busy," Rowan tells him.

"Busy? With what? If I didn't know any better, I'd say you were seeing someone," Greg suspects.

"No, man. I'm just putting in some extra time at the farm, and when I'm not working, I'm usually sleeping."

"Extra time, huh? Why aren't you there now, then?"

"I overslept. Actually, I have to get going."

I hear footsteps and I panic. I quickly roll off the far edge of the bed and roll under it.

"Hey, where you going?" Rowan asks.

The door opens and both guys walk in.

"What the fuck, man?"

There's a long pause. "Sorry, I thought someone was in here."

"Even if there was, it's none of your business," Rowan tells him.

"Sorry, man. I just thought that maybe you finally landed Harper and was holding out on us."

"Don't you think if I got with her, I'd be screaming it from the rooftops?"

"So... who you fucking then?"

"Not that it's any of your business, but nobody. Why?"

"That glass door has a nice ass print on it. I'd say, size five?"

I glance at the glass door from under the bed. My ass print is still visible. Fuck, don't men ever clean?

"That's been there for months."

"No, it hasn't. I was just in here helping you move that dresser out a couple of weeks ago, and it wasn't there. Who was it?"

"Fuck off," Rowan says.

Greg takes this as a challenge though. "Alright. I see. Keep your secrets, but I'll figure them out. You know I will."

I hear their footsteps as they leave the bedroom, and I hear the click of the front door. Moments later, Rowan is back.

"Harper?"

"Under here," I say, sliding my naked ass across his carpet to get out from under the bed. "Ow, I think I got rug burn on my ass," I complain, standing up.

He laughs and shakes his head. "I'm sorry about that."

"He's nosy. He's going to ruin our fun," I tell him as I check out my ass.

"Nah, he'll get bored eventually and move on," he says. "But I guess I really do need to get to work. It'd be really bad to be fired by your own father."

I laugh. "Honestly, I'm surprised he isn't sick of your shit yet," I tease, grabbing my clothes off the floor and pulling them on.

"You ain't the only one," he agrees.

We get dressed for the day, and he takes me back to my place. I walk into the kitchen, freezing when I find Dad sitting at the table with a cup of coffee and his newspaper.

"You're getting in late... or really early," he says with a lift of his brow.

"Sorry. I didn't mean to make you worry." I head over to the coffee pot and pour a cup for myself.

"I wasn't worried. I knew who you were with."

I nod in acknowledgement.

He folds up his paper and levels his eyes on me as I sit down across the table from him. "Are you and Rowan dating now?"

I let out a long breath. "I don't know, Dad. We're just... hanging out, I guess. Getting to know one another. Spending time together." I shrug.

"He's a good guy, you know?"

I laugh. "Rowan? The guy that tore up your cornfield? The same guy that you caught riding a pig butt-ass naked? That same Rowan?"

He laughs at the memory. "Harper, I don't know if you know this or not, but us men, we're a bunch of dumbasses."

I laugh.

"Now, sure there's a smart man here and there, but as a group, we're all as dumb as the day is long. But when we find the one person who we love more than anything in the world, that's when we change and grow to become a man. I think that's what you are to him. You're the one."

My eyes nearly bug out of my skull. "What? Dad, no. It's not like that."

"Say what you want, but I call 'em as I see 'em. That boy is in love with you and has been since the first time he saw you."

"You mean when he set my float on fire, he was in love with me?"

He shrugs. "I told you, we're dumbasses!"

"And, not that I'm saying we're together, but if I were, you would approve?"

He nods. "I would. I've known that boy and his family my whole life. They're a good group. Sure, Rowan is still a boy right now, but that'll change. The moment you start to love him back, he will grow to be the man you need, just like I did with your mother."

Mom. Just mentioning her name makes my heart hurt.

"Thanks, Dad," I say, holding back my tears as I take my coffee up to my room. I wonder what Mom would think of me being with Rowan. Would she approve like Daddy does? Would she tell me to stop playing around with him and get serious?

I know in most families, the father is the hard-ass. But that was never the case in mine. From day one, Mom had to enforce the rules and dole out the punishments because she knew Daddy didn't have the heart to. While Daddy would let me do whatever I wanted, she was the one who would knock some sense into me when I needed it. So now I'm left wondering, should I be left alone to do what I want, or do I need the sense knocked into me when it comes to Rowan?

Unable to make up my mind, I decide to spend the day with Becky. It's been a few days since we've last hung out, thanks to all the time I'd spent under Rowan or on top of him.

I get cleaned up for the day and go by her house. I knock on the door, and she pulls it open, shading her eyes against the sun.

"Good morning, sunshine," I say with a bright smile.

Her hair is disheveled, her face lacking the makeup she usually wears, and she's still in her pj's. "Yeah, yeah," she says, waving me inside.

She flops down into the recliner in the living room, and I take a seat on the couch. I realize this is the first time I've been in her house. Before I left for college, she was still living with her mom. I take in all the photos she has hung on the wall. There are some of us growing up, but the majority of them are pictures of her and Tyler.

"Your place is cute," I say, looking around at her country-themed decor.

"Thanks. I made most of the decor in here."

"You always were crafty."

"So, what's up?"

"What's up?" I ask, confused.

"You don't usually come here, and you're not usually up this early. So... what's up?"

I shrug, not knowing how much I should tell her.

"So, it's about a guy, huh?" she guesses.

"Why do you say that?" I lean back against the couch, crossing and uncrossing my legs.

"You can talk about anything, Harper. So the fact that you feel like you need to beat around the bush tells me it's about a guy. Who is it? Scott? Someone from Yale?" She is wide-eyed now, excited to hear more.

"No, and the guy isn't important," I say, closing my eyes and rubbing my hand over my brows.

"What is important?"

"I don't even know anymore."

"Ughhhh," she groans. "Just tell me."

"I—"

"Tell me!"

"I can't."

"Tell me!"

"I've been fucking Rowan!" The words come pouring out of me, and she freezes, eyes locked on me.

"Rowan? Rowan Wilson? The guy you hate more than anyone else on the planet, Rowan?"

I don't speak. I can't. I just nod instead.

She busts out laughing. That surprises me.

"Hey, what's so funny?"

"I knew this would happen," she finally says as her laughing dies down.

I sit back, shaking my head and feeling annoyed.

TWELVE
ROWAN

I'm about done with work for the day. I've only got a few things left. I'm feeding the chickens when I hear the sound of crunching gravel. I turn in the direction of the drive and see Greg's truck making its way up, leaving a thick cloud of dust behind. He parks and gets out, walking over to lean against the other side of the fence.

"What's up?" I ask, squinting against the setting sun.

"I've been thinking a lot about this morning," he starts.

"Man, can't you give it a break?"

"I realized that whoever was over was probably hiding under the bed or in the closet."

"It's my house. Why would anyone have to hide?" I ask, still trying to throw him off our trail.

"Then I got to thinking, why hide?"

"Exactly."

"The only reason you'd have to hide is if you didn't want the town to know."

Fuck.

"And who's the one person in this town that would want to keep this little love affair private?"

Fuck. Shit.

"Harper!" he guesses with a wide smile. "It's Harper, isn't it? You've been nailing Harper!"

"Shhh, keep it down, man. I don't think the other side of town heard you."

He laughs. "I knew it." He's still laughing but suddenly shuts it off. "So, how was she? And first off, *wow*! How? When?"

I chuckle quietly to myself as I dump out the rest of the chicken feed and make my way out of the gate. I lean against the fence like he's doing. "The night of your party."

"I knew it. She wasn't sick, was she?"

I shake my head. "No. She was drunk, and she asked me what I wanted as she was making herself a drink."

"And what did you tell her?"

"I said I wanted her. Then she jumped on me. I pinned her up against your fridge, and we made out for a few minutes. Then I asked her to come home with me."

He smiles. "And? Is she as good as you imagined?"

I laugh. "Better, actually."

"That's my boy!" he says, shaking my shoulder. "So now you guys are just banging your brains out?"

Again, I laugh. "Yeah, something like that..." I say, staring off into the distance. "But it's more than that. For me anyway," I confess.

"Oh fuck. You telling me you got one taste and already you're wanting to propose?"

I shake my head. "Fuck off, man. Nobody knows, so if this gets out, I'm coming to you."

He shows me the palms of his hands. "I won't breathe a word of it to anyone... as long as you give me some gory details."

I laugh. "What kind of gory details do you want?" I ask, confused. What in the world could he ask me?

He shrugs. "I don't know. What's she look like naked?"

I reach over and shove him by his shoulder.

"That good, huh?" Then he looks up at the sky like he's imagining it. "Yeah, I bet she does look pretty good. I saw her in the bikini, and if I mentally take it off..."

I shove him again. "Don't mentally take it off!"

"Too late. I already got her top off, and damn, her tits are—"

I swing and land a solid punch to his arm.

"Ow," he says, rubbing the spot. "What's that for?"

"For mentally undressing my..."

"Your what?" he eggs me on.

"Know what, shut up!"

That only makes him laugh harder.

When we settle down, he pushes up off the fence. "Well, I gotta get out of here. I'll talk to you later."

I wave bye and get back to work, finishing up the few tasks I have left.

When I finish, I go home and take a shower after pulling out some fresh clothes for the evening. I grab my keys and load back up in the truck to go to her house. We didn't have any plans to meet up this evening, but staying away from her is harder than I thought it would be. I need to see her.

I pull into the drive and notice that her car is nowhere in sight. I wonder where she could be, then figure I'll just knock and see if her dad knows. I leave the truck running. Since she's not here, I won't be long. I knock on the front door. It's quiet, all but the sounds of my running truck. I try again, but still, nobody answers. I shrug it off and get back into the truck. I decide to go by the bar, thinking that maybe she's meeting up with Becky and Tyler, but her car isn't here either.

Anyway, I need dinner, and a beer wouldn't hurt while I wait. I head inside and sit at the bar. I order a beer while I check out the menu. I know it by heart, but I still don't know what I'm in the mood for.

"So, how's Bud doing?" I hear one of the old men down the bar ask.

That gets my attention, and I listen in a little more carefully.

"I'm not sure. I haven't heard anything other than he's been taken off in an ambulance."

My head pops up, and I turn to face them. "Bud? Bud Mitchell?"

One of the old men nods. "Yeah, he passed out today. His daughter found him in the yard, called the ambulance. They're thinking he's had another heart attack," he says.

"What hospital?" I ask, already digging in my wallet for some cash to cover the beer I haven't touched.

"Westco."

"Thanks," I say, sending a nod in their direction as I spin around for the door.

I hop into the truck and make the drive a town over. I park in the parking lot and run to the doors. Inside, I rush the information desk. "What room is Bud Mitchell in?"

"One second," she says, typing away. Only a few seconds pass, but it feels like minutes. "Room 203," she tells me.

"Thanks." I run for the elevators. The elevator seems to move at half the pace it usually does, but when the doors open, I step off, reading the sign on the wall that tells me which direction to go to find his room.

"Rowan?" Harper says my name, and I look to my right, finding her.

She rushes up to me and throws her arms around me.

"I'm so glad you're here," she breathes out.

"What happened?" I ask, pulling her back to study her face. She has streaks down her cheeks from crying and black smudges under her eyes from her mascara.

"I went to Becky's, and when I got home, he wasn't in the house. So I went out to look for him. I found him in the field, lying next to the tractor. I don't know if he fell off or if he got off and then collapsed. I called 9-1-1, and the ambulance showed up and brought him here, but they haven't told me anything yet. They're still running tests." Her tears start up again.

"Shhh," I say into her hair, holding her against my chest. "He'll be alright," I promise, praying that I'm right.

She nods, but it doesn't stop the tears. I move us over to the chairs that are pushed up against the wall in the hallway, and we both have a seat. "Why didn't you call me?" I ask, smoothing down her hair.

She shrugs. "I didn't know if I could. I mean, what we're doing hasn't really been defined yet and—"

"You can call me anytime... for anything," I tell her and she nods, resting her head against my shoulder.

"Do you need anything? Something to drink, eat?"

"I have everything I need," she whispers so low that I can barely hear her. Those words make my heart feel like it's in a vise, and I hold her a little closer.

Hours pass before we finally see a doctor. He walks up to her. "You're with Mr. Mitchell, correct?"

She nods. "Yes."

He opens the chart in his hands and skims over the notes. "It looks like your father has suffered another heart attack. He's being prepped for surgery now to put in a stent. He will have some diet and exercise changes to make, but I have no doubt that he'll make a full recovery."

She breathes out a sigh of relief. "Can I see him?"

"We only have a few moments before we take him back, so make it quick."

She nods and rushes inside, leaving me alone. "How long does the surgery take?" I ask.

"Usually just a couple of hours, but I'm afraid that visiting hours will be over by then. You two should go home and get some rest. Come back in the morning."

I nod as he walks away. It doesn't take long before a team of nurses are wheeling his bed out of the room. Harper follows them out and stands by my side.

Mr. Mitchell looks pale and tired, but he looks up at me with a small grin. "Take care of her."

"I will," I promise.

As they wheel him down the hallway, she latches on to my arm.

"The doctor said that visiting hours will be over by the time his surgery is done, so we should leave and come back in the morning."

She nods. "I don't want to leave him here."

I wrap my arm around her. "I know, but he'll be fine. Come on. Let's go get you some dinner. You have to be starving after being here all day."

THIRTEEN

HARPER

I don't want to leave, but Rowan is right. There isn't anything here for me to do now, not with Daddy back in surgery. I could wait, but they'd just end up kicking me out anyway, so I take his hand and let him lead me into the elevator and downstairs to his truck.

"Oh, I drove here," I suddenly say, remembering.

"Do you feel like you can drive home?" he asks, his eyes watching me like he's looking for any sign that I shouldn't drive.

"I'll be fine. Follow me home?"

He smiles and nods.

I get in my car and make the short drive home. I park under the tree I've been parking under since I turned sixteen. I climb out and look up at the big house that's suddenly so empty.

Rowan pulls up behind me, and he climbs out, coming over to my side. "What's wrong?" he asks, looking back and forth between me and the house.

"It's so empty now. I've never been here alone before."

He squeezes me a little tighter. "You're not alone now. Come on." He edges me forward and I let us in. Stepping inside feels weird, too quiet.

I lead him into the kitchen, pausing in the doorway. His coffee cup and paper are still sitting on the table, untouched. I'm sure if I walk over to the sink, I'll see his bowl from breakfast this morning. Everywhere I look are reminders of him and the fact that he's not here. I know the doctor said that he should recover fine, but that's this time. Next time, he might not recover, and I really will be left alone.

Tears sting my eyes, and Rowan quickly pulls me to his chest. "Everything is fine. Shhh, I'm here."

"I know," I cry. "Thank you for being here."

"I'll be here as long as you want me," he promises, but in my pain and tears, I can't think any deeper on that other than he will stay here until my father gets to come home.

I nod as I attempt trying to dry my eyes.

"You have to be hungry. Let me order us a pizza, and you can go take a long, hot shower. Try to relax. Okay?"

I nod and head for the stairs. I don't fight him even though I really don't feel hungry. I know I should eat since I haven't had anything other than a cup of coffee today, but all the worry has taken away my appetite. I pull off my clothes and step into the shower, keeping the water as hot as it will go in an attempt to wash this day off me. I know when I get out, everything will be the same, but maybe I can trick myself into playing house with him for one night. This is a glimpse into a possible future for us.

I stay in the shower for far too long, letting the water ease my tense muscles and wash my skin clean. When I get out, I go downstairs to find him at the door, accepting and paying for the food he ordered. I grab a couple of plates from the cabinet and take them into the living room so we can eat in front of the TV. I have hopes that food and entertainment will keep my mind off Daddy and how his surgery is going right now.

He sets the pizza on the table and opens the lid. I breathe the scent in deeply, suddenly feeling hungrier than I have all day. The aroma of the crust mixed with the smell of mushrooms, peppers, and melted cheese nearly has my mouth watering. Rowan places two slices on my plate. I'm sure he would've put more, but two slices are big enough to take up the whole plate.

"Thank you," I say, picking up the first piece and taking a bite. The heavenly taste is better than I thought it could be, and I find myself doing nothing but eating. I put away three slices before I realize that I'm far past full. Rowan finishes off the rest and takes the box to the trash.

He flops back down onto the couch at my side. "You want me to stay here tonight... so you're not alone?"

"Would you? I know it's a lot to ask and that you have work tomorrow but—"

"I've already told my father I can't come in tomorrow. I'll be by your side until your father is free to come home," he promises.

I smile at him. "Thank you." I curl up to his side, and he holds me close. The deep lull of his heart pulls at me. "You're different than I thought you'd be."

He chuckles once. "What's that mean?"

I shrug one shoulder. "You're just...more. More than I thought you'd ever be. I mean, I know we're just fucking around and not a real couple or anything, but you're really coming through for me more than I ever thought you would. Honestly, I thought you'd be done with me the minute you rolled off me," I joke, sort of.

"So you're saying I'm not the asshole you always thought I was?" he laughs and I giggle.

"No, you're far from an asshole," I reply, looking up into his eyes. He closes the distance between our lips and presses his mouth to mine for a soft, slow, building kiss.

The soft, innocent kiss turns passionate, and the next thing I know, I'm on his lap, straddling him. My arms are wrapped around his neck, and his hands are traveling my body. When I feel him harden, I pull back. "We can't do this here. Come on. Let me show you my room." I get up and grab the remote, turning off the TV.

He stands up with a wide grin. "I get to see Harper Mitchell's bedroom?"

I laugh and nod. "Yep, in all its glory."

I lead him up the stairs and to my bedroom. I flip the switch, and the room fills with soft light. I try to look around the room, seeing it from his perspective: the yellowed lace curtains, baby-blue walls, white trim, and old, faded hardwood floor. My full-size bed is in the center of the room with a table on either side, each littered with lamps, books, nail polish, and papers. At the foot is a chest for all the extra blankets and sheets. There's a chair in the corner, covered in clothing, and a dresser against the far wall. It's also littered in makeup, books, and papers.

He walks over to the shelf on the wall, and my face grows hot.

"Look at you, overachiever," he teases, looking at all the ribbons, medals, and awards I've gotten throughout my life.

"Yeah, yeah," I say, closing the distance between us. "We came up here for a reason, and it wasn't to look at old ribbons," I say, pulling him against me.

He chuckles. "Hold on. I'm not done." He pulls away and goes back to walking around my room, silently judging everything. "You have no idea how many times I pictured this room in my head."

"Yeah? Is it anything like you imagined?" I finally sit in the center of my bed.

He nods. "Pretty close. There are books everywhere, but I always thought there would be a desk, you know, one certain spot where you did all your homework and studying."

I nod. "I used to have one."

"What happened to it?"

I laugh. "Well, I brought my first college boyfriend home the first Thanksgiving I was away at school. Daddy wouldn't let him stay in my room so he snuck in later. We had sex on the desk because the bed was squeaking too much, and we ended up breaking the leg off the desk." I feel my face grow red just from telling the story.

"You've had sex in here?" he asks, clenching his jaw.

I nod. "Of course. Did you think I was a monk until this year?"

"No, I just hoped to be your first... in here. Like we could pretend we're still in high school and I'm sneaking into your window." He flashes me a grin.

"We can still do that."

He picks up a CD and knocks over a bottle of nail polish, which goes clattering against the floor.

"Shhhh, my dad will hear," I whisper and he chuckles, finally done walking about my room and coming to sit on the bed.

He kicks his shoes off, then reaches behind him, grabbing the back of his shirt and yanking it over his head.

I take a cue from him and move to sit on his lap, straddling him. Slowly, I move my mouth to his, and he kisses me softly.

His hands move up to cup my face, and he pulls back, but only an inch. "I'm going to fuck you like I've always imagined," he says, rolling us over and putting me beneath him. I let out a squeal from the sudden action, and he places his hand over my mouth with a smirk. "Shhh, we'll wake your dad up," he whispers.

He keeps his hand in place but moves his lips to my neck. As his lips descend my body, he removes his hand from my mouth and quickly unbuttons my shirt, kissing his way down my chest. He pulls the cups of my bra to the side, paying extra attention to my nipple, flicking his tongue against it, circling it, and then sucking it into his hot mouth. My hands fly to his hair, pulling as a soft moan escapes.

"Shhh," he says, kissing lower, across my ribs, down my stomach, and to the waistband of my jeans. He pulls back quickly, watching my eyes as his hands unbutton them and pull them down my hips. When he has them off, his kissing continues over my hips.

When his mouth lands on my clit, I nearly jump from the pleasure. His tongue runs between my folds, flicking against my clit and causing shockwaves to wash through me.

Even though I've been with four other men in my life, none of them have done this. He slides two fingers into me while his mouth continues to work me over. I'm no longer in control of my own body. I'm lost. My hands pull at his hair while my thighs clamp down around his head. My back arches and my eyes close. My lips part, and heavy breathing escapes them, along with soft moans of approval.

He keeps going, never stopping until I'm completely breathless and weak beneath him. When he pulls away, his lips are glistening with my arousal, and he's wearing that sexy smirk I can't deny. "It sounded like you enjoyed that."

"Well, you got one of my firsts," I breathe out, only now able to move my limbs again.

That only makes his smile widen as he frees himself from his jeans, positioning himself at my entrance. "I'm going to get plenty more," he says, pushing into me and making me see stars again.

IN THE MORNING, I'm in a hurry to get back to Dad at the hospital. I shower, dress, and start packing a bag for him. I get some fresh clothes for him to wear home from the hospital, and I also pack his bathroom necessities. Then I go into the office and start gathering his ID, social security card, and insurance information for the hospital paperwork. We went in such a rush yesterday, we didn't have any of the info they needed.

As I'm digging around in his desk drawer, something catches my eye. Actually, a lot of things catch my eye. Envelope upon envelope, all stamped in red. The red stamps read: IMPORTANT, URGENT, FINAL NOTICE.

What in the hell?

I pick up one of the envelopes and open it to see a letter from the bank. It looks like Daddy took out a loan on the house, and he's in the process of losing it. He's behind on the payments by almost twenty grand!

I shake my head. This can't be right. This house has been in the family for generations. It's been paid off longer than I've been alive. Why would he need this much money? I don't remember him talking to me about the farm not bringing in enough. But I guess he's never really talked to me about money and his finances. I always just assumed that we were doing okay. I've never noticed less food in the kitchen, and we've never had the power or water shut off.

I fold up the letter and slide it into my back pocket. I'm going to ask him about this and get to the bottom of it once and for all.

FOURTEEN
ROWAN

Harper is quiet on our way to the hospital. Actually, she's been quiet since she started packing a bag for her father. Maybe the heaviness of the situation is finally weighing on her again. I managed to keep it off her mind last night, but in the bright morning, it was there, waiting like we knew it would be.

I try several times to engage her in conversation, but she replies with simple one-word responses. After a while, I give up, deciding to just let her be. She'll get to see her dad and see that he's fine and everything will be better.

When we get to the hospital, she stops outside of his door. She looks up at me. "Would you mind if I went in alone? I just want to talk with him privately for a moment."

"Yeah, that's fine. I'll sit right here." I plop down in the chair outside of his room, the same chair I sat in yesterday.

She nods and goes inside. The door is open, but the hospital is busy and his TV is on. I am only able to hear their conversation if I listen really hard.

"How you feeling today, Daddy?" she asks, her voice muffled and sounding far away.

"Oh, I'm still alive, so that's good," her old man says, sounding weak and possibly in pain.

"Well, I brought some fresh clothes for you to wear home. I also brought in all your info to give to the hospital."

"Good. I was worried you wouldn't find it."

"Actually, while I was looking, I found something else too."

"Oh, that," he says.

"Yeah. What is this?"

"I'm just a little late on a few payments. It's nothing for you to worry about."

"Dad, that's a final notice. We're going to lose the farm. And why did you refinance it to begin with? Why did you need the money, and why didn't you tell me?"

"It's none of your concern," he tries to argue.

"Dad, this is my concern. You're laid up in a hospital bed. You could have died, and then all this would fall onto me. Tell me what's going on. Why did you take such a chance on our family property?"

There's a long pause as she waits for his response. "How many farmers do you know who are able to send their kids to Yale?"

I feel like someone has poured a bucket of ice water over my head, and I freeze.

"Are you saying that you borrowed against the house to pay for my college?"

"It was the only thing you wanted, and you worked so hard to get there. I didn't want you missing out because I didn't have enough money."

"Dad," she breathes out. "I could've taken out student loans or, I don't know, gone somewhere more affordable. You didn't have to do this."

"I know I didn't. But I made a choice. I thought that I'd have more than enough time to pay it off. But then I had that first heart attack, and it put me down for too long. I lost a lot of money. I've been playing catch-up ever since."

"I'm going to fix this, Dad. We're not losing the property," she promises him.

So that's why she's been so quiet today. They're about to lose their farm. Fuck. He's about to lose the only way he has to make money. He's about to lose his home, the property that's been in his family for generations. I can't let that happen.

I knock on the door and stick my head in. "Hey, are you wanting to stay here for a little while?" I ask Harper.

She nods. "I figured I'd stay the day... if that's okay?" She looks up at me, hopeful.

"That's fine. Something just came up, so I need to run and take care of it, but I'll be back this evening before visiting hours are over."

"Okay. Thank you for the ride."

"No problem," I tell her with a smile. I look over at Mr. Mitchell. "Get to feeling better."

I leave the hospital with one place in mind. My father's house.

When I pull into the drive, I find Dad out in the field on the tractor. I park my truck and climb out. He sees me, and he makes his way over as fast as a tractor can go, which isn't fast at all.

"Didn't think you were making it over today," he says as he shuts the beast down and starts climbing off. "How's Bud?"

"He got his stent put in last night," I tell him.

"Good. Hopefully it will do him some good," Dad says, squinting his eyes against the bright sun, which only makes the creases around them appear more prominent.

"Dad, I need a favor," I start.

He looks at me with concern. "What's going on, Row?"

"Well, I just found out that Bud is about to lose his farm. He put it up to take a loan out to pay for Harper's college. When he got sick, he wasn't able to make the payments."

"I hate to hear that," Dad says, "but what I can I do?"

"Well, I remembered you saying something to Pa about wishing we had more land to farm, that the price of beans would bring in more than enough money to cover the extra costs."

He nods, following along.

"Well, Bud has at least forty acres of land that he hasn't farmed in years. He won't be able to keep up with it or afford to pay someone else to. We could lease his land. You could get your extra beans planted, and it would give him some of the money he needs to catch up on payments."

"Yeah, I guess I could do that. But his daughter went to Yale. I don't think leasing forty acres will cover what he's needing to do."

He's right. "No, it won't, but every little bit helps."

I know that Bud won't want to go along with it if he knows that we're doing this for his benefit, so when I mention it to him, I plan on asking him if we can farm his land. It makes perfect sense because my family's land and his land are right up against each other. It's not like we'll have to haul the tractor across town to do it. We'd simply have to drive across an invisible line.

After I leave Dad's, I go by Becky and Tyler's house. I knock on the door, and Tyler answers with a surprised look on his face. "Hey, man. What's up?"

"Can I talk with you and Becky for a minute?"

"Yeah, sure. Come in," he says, opening the door wider.

He leads me into his small living room, and Becky is already on the couch, phone in hand. When she looks up and sees me, she turns it off, knowing that something is up. I've never been to their house before. In fact, we don't really talk or hang out all that much. We've always just ran in different circles, but Harper is pulling our circles together.

"What's going on?" Becky asks.

Tyler sits down next to her on the couch, leaving me the recliner. I sit down but stay leaned forward, resting my elbows on my knees. "I don't know if you guys have heard or not, but Harper's dad had another heart attack yesterday."

Becky gasps. "Oh no. Is he okay? Where's Harper?"

I hold up my hand, palm facing her. "Everything is okay, he's fine. He had to get surgery to have a stent put in, but the doctors are expecting him to fully recover. She's there with him now, but the thing is..." I wonder how I should word it, then just decide to come out with it. "They're losing the farm."

Again, she gasps.

"Harper found some paperwork when she was packing his things, and he confirmed it. He took a loan out against the property to pay for her college, and after he had his first heart attack, he fell behind on the payments. He's been trying to catch up, but it's too far gone now."

"What can we do?" Becky asks.

"Well, I've arranged for my dad to lease some land. I just have to spin it so it seems like he's helping us out and not the other way around. That money will cover a piece of what he owes, but we still need about ten or fifteen grand to catch him up on his payments."

"We don't have that kind of money," Tyler says.

"No, of course not. I wasn't meaning for us to pay it for him, but I'm thinking that maybe we could arrange something to raise the money for him?"

"Oh, that's a great idea!" Becky exclaims.

"Yeah?" I ask with the lift of my brow.

Her head is bobbing up and down. "Yes! We could have a silent auction, a rummage sale, a bake sale, a dinner. And we'll make it like one big town-wide party! We could have games for the kids, oh—" She stops, and her eyes get wide as she looks at me. "I have the best idea, and I bet it will bring in more money than all of the things I've listed off."

"Really? What?"

"Bachelor auction! Come on, Rowan! The ladies in town love you. I bet they'd pay top dollar. And not only you, but Greg and the rest of the guys too. You still in touch with any of your old football buddies?"

I think it over and nod. "Yeah, I'm still close with a few."

She starts bouncing up and down, cheering and giggling.

"But, guys, make sure nobody breathes a word of this to Harper or Bud. You know how they'll feel about being a charity case. Alright?"

"Our lips are sealed," Becky agrees.

I leave to head back to the hospital while Becky and Tyler start on the plans for the benefit. I almost feel high as I think about getting this down for them. We live in a small town, and we take care of our own. There's no way we won't have the town's full support, especially for Bud. He's loved everywhere he goes, and by extension, Harper too.

By the time I make it back to the hospital, visiting hours are nearly over. I walk back into his room and sit at her side. She looks over at me with a small but sad smile. Bud looks to be sound asleep.

"Now that you're here to sit with him, is it cool if I go grab something to eat? I'm starving, but I didn't want to leave him," she whispers.

"Yeah, of course. Go ahead. I'll be here waiting."

"Thank you." She leans over and gives me a quick kiss before leaving the room.

I space out, watching the silent TV.

"'Bout time she left," Bud says, nearly making me jump.

"Oh, hey. Sorry, did I wake you?"

He waves me off. "No. I pretended to be asleep. She wouldn't quit fussing over me, and it was driving me crazy."

I laugh. "She's just worried."

"I know it. She's a good girl."

"That she is," I agree.

"She'll make some lucky man a hell of a wife one of these days."

I just nod my head, not sure what to say.

"That man might just be you."

I let out a nervous laugh. "Well, it's a little early to be talking of all that, but I'm sure whoever ends up with her will be proud." Just saying that makes a pain form in my chest. I don't want to think of her ending up with anyone but me, but it's way too soon to already think we'll be together forever. Isn't it?

"You love her." His eyes hold firm on mine. He's sure.

I sit up, rubbing my now sweaty palms across the front of my pants. "I... uh. I'm not really sure what I feel just yet. It's still early."

"You love her. I've seen it for years. Even back in high school when the two of you were doing nothing but torturing one another, you loved her."

I smile. He's not wrong. I've always felt this connection, this pull to her, even before I could understand it myself. But that doesn't mean that I'm ready to confess my undying love to her already. If this relationship we've started up doesn't scare her off, that would for sure.

"Take care of her, will ya? She's my baby girl. I love that girl. She's my whole world, and I'd give up anything to make sure she's taken care of and happy. But you won't understand that until you have a daughter of your own."

This time, I can agree. "I will, sir. I promise. I'll never hurt her, and I'll always be here for her to fall back on. I won't let her fall."

"Thank you," he breathes out.

"On a different note, though, I was wondering..."

"Yes?" he asks.

"Well, it's just that my dad has been needing to expand his farmland, and I thought that since you had that back forty that you no longer use, could we lease it from you for a while? It would really help us out. I know you're not in the position to grant favors right now, but—"

"I've always been close with your dad. He can plant the land free of charge."

"No, we will pay you. It's the only way my dad would even consider doing it. You know how the old man is. He's stubborn and won't take nothing for free. We'll make it worth your while."

He lets out a laugh that ends with a cough. "Alright, he can pay, but I won't accept full price. We're as good as family. It's wrong to take money from family."

"Alright, you just get to feeling better, and we'll work something out when you feel up to it."

"Oh, you're up," Harper says, walking back in the room with a packaged sandwich and a bag of chips. "I don't know what you can eat, but if you're hungry…"

"No, I'm fine. I'm tired, though, so why don't you two kids take off? Let me rest, huh?"

"Oh, okay. If that's what you want." She seems confused.

"Go, Harper. Live your life. Have fun. You don't need to be stuck in a hospital all day. Go."

"But, Dad?"

"Go," he insists, using the strongest voice he can muster.

I take her hand. "Come on. Let's give him a break from entertaining, huh?"

She nods, goes in for a hug, and then follows after me.

FIFTEEN

HARPER

I don't want to leave Dad before I have to, but he insists, and it would be nice to enjoy the fresh air and sunshine. I'm too wound up though. After learning about the danger we're in from losing the farm, all I want to do is figure out a way to keep it. I don't have much as far as money goes, and I don't have anything worth any value. I'm sure there's some farm equipment we could sell, but I can't do that without putting us in a bad place, too, because we need that equipment to keep up with the land.

My mind is swirling in a million different directions.

"So, my dad is going to lease the back forty of your property to farm. I talked to your dad about it. But he's going to pay top dollar for the lease. Just don't let your dad know."

I offer up a confused smile. "Why would you do that? You know my dad would let you farm it for free."

"I know he would, but I had a feeling that with all these health problems he's having lately, that he could use the money. I'm sure he's going to have to pay some of it out of pocket, and that hospital bill won't be light."

Oh. He heard the conversation I had with Daddy earlier. "You know, don't you?"

"Know what?" he asks, but he's a horrible liar and I see right through it.

"You know that we're about to lose the property."

"Well... I may have overheard a little."

I can't do anything but laugh. I don't know why. Crying would make sense. Screaming would be understandable. But I laugh. The stress is most definitely getting to me.

"We'll figure this out. You're not going to lose anything."

I nod. "I don't see how. I mean, I could sell my car, but that isn't going to bring in enough. Any equipment I sell off will just be screwing ourselves over because then we wouldn't have what we need to farm the land anyway. I don't know what we're going to do." I hang my head.

He reaches over and places his hand on my thigh. "Don't worry about. Let me take care of everything. You just focus on helping your dad get better."

"Rowan, how are you going to come up with twenty grand? You don't have that kind of money, and I refuse to take it from you even if you manage to come up with it. This is our problem, not yours."

"Are you telling me that if you knew my family was about to lose everything they've worked their lives for, that you wouldn't help in any way you could?"

"You know I would," I reply.

He nods. "Alright. Then we're in agreement. Just focus on your father. I'll take care of the rest," he promises.

As sweet as his offer is, I have to think of something I can do myself. I can't just trust that he'll be able to come up with twenty grand. I need to look around and see what the options are.

Rowan talks me into stopping by Walt's on the way home for a few beers to help take the edge off. I don't think anything of it until we walk into the bar together and the whole place freezes as several pairs of eyes land on us.

Rowan and I both stop just inside the door and take the place in. I tap his arm. "What's happening? Why are they looking at us?"

The waitress walks over and places her hand on my shoulder. "Is everything alright, dear?"

I frown. "Of course. Why wouldn't it be?"

She leans closer. "Is he holding you hostage, trying to make you do something you don't want to do?"

I laugh. "What? No!"

She seems surprised but takes a step back. "Okay." She looks at everyone in the small bar. "It's okay, everyone. We've just entered the twilight zone." She makes her way back to the bar, and I turn back and look at Rowan.

He shakes his head. "Seriously, what's wrong with this town?"

I laugh and shake my head, throwing in a shrug because I'm just as confused as everyone else.

Rowan and I order a pitcher and find a table.

"Want to play a game of pool?"

"Sure," I agree, pouring beer into both our cups while he racks the table. I have a sip, then go to pick out my pool stick. I find one that's heavier and chalk it. Then I take my position at the end of the table and line up my shot to break. I pull my stick back and hear someone say, *"Damn!"*

I stand up and turn back to see Greg beside Rowan. I laugh and shake my head but ignore him as I line my shot up again.

I pull my stick back and push it forward quickly. The white ball travels down the table, knocking into the rest of the balls and scattering them in all directions.

I turn to face the two guys again.

Greg looks from me to Rowan and back. "I didn't believe the rumor and had to come check it out for myself," he says with a smirk.

"What rumor?" I ask. "We've been in here for all of four minutes. Surely, the news hasn't made it around town already."

He laughs. "You know how small this town is. Look, it's on Facebook." He pulls out his phone and shows me the screen.

Chester Black: *You'll never guess who just entered Walt's together!! Harper and Rowan, together without beating the shit out of each other. Come check it out if you don't believe me*, the post reads.

I turn and look in the corner where the seventy-six-year-old man always sits. "Really, Chester? Facebook?"

He lets out a long belly laugh.

"How do you even know how to work that smartphone, huh?"

"My great granddaughter is a wiz with these things. She taught me everything I know," he replies with a wide toothless grin.

I shake my head and laugh. I have to. What else could I do at this point? I turn back to see Rowan at the table. He comes to a stop beside me and Greg.

Greg looks between the two of us. "I don't believe it," he says.

"Believe what?" Rowan asks.

"That the two of you are like...together now. Tell me what's really going on, Harper. Did you lose a bet and this is your punishment or what?"

I laugh. "You know, Greg. You're probably onto something. I lost something, that's for sure. But I think it probably has more to do with losing my mind, not a bet."

Rowan smiles down at me, like he's proud of the burn I just delivered. "You saying you have to be crazy to like me, or that I've made you crazy and nobody else will have you?"

"I'll take her," Greg says, raising his hand midair.

Rowan holds his smile at me but reaches out and smacks Greg in the stomach with the back of his hand. Greg doesn't even see it coming, and now he's doubled over, laughing it off.

I shake my head at the boys' roughhousing and go to take my next shot.

Hours after arriving, after many games of pool and too many pitchers, we're finally heading out for the night, with Greg following behind us. We're all talking and laughing, but then we get to Rowan's truck, and Greg pauses like he's confused.

"You guys came here together?"

"Yeah, man. What'd you think?" Rowan asks, holding my door open for me.

Greg shakes his head. "Nah, I'm still not buying it. You guys are trying to pull one over on me."

"Greg, I swear. The feuding is done. We're seriously hanging out now," I tell him.

"Prove it," he says.

"Fuck off, man," Rowan says to put up a fight, but I take the horse by the reins.

I grab ahold of Rowan's shirt and pull him to me, his lips landing perfectly on mine. At first, his lips are taut, but they quickly give in, his lips softening and parting while his tongue comes out to taste me. I kiss him for a long minute, then pull back with a smile. I look over at Greg, and he's just standing there with his mouth hanging open.

"Man, I guess you guys will end up married soon, and I'll have to find a new best friend. Thanks a lot for stealing him, Harper!" He sounds like a child, but I'm sure he's completely serious. Greg is very childlike and immature after all.

I laugh. "I'll still let you borrow him, Greg. You just have to return him in the same condition he left in. No broken bones, no stitches or glue holding him together."

He waves me off. "That's no fun."

Rowan laughs but closes my door, saying goodbye to Greg as he walks around to get behind the wheel.

On the drive back to the house, he reaches over and takes my hand in his. "Sorry about him. He's a dumbass."

I laugh. "Yeah, but he's funny, and he actually took my mind off everything going on. But tomorrow, I have to get serious. I have to find a job or something. Find some way to make some money."

"I told you, let me handle that."

I smile at him. "Thank you, but even if you do find some magical way to get twenty grand, I'm still going to need to make up for lost income. It will take Daddy a while to get back up on his feet, and we'll need to eat and pay bills while he's recovering."

"Alright, well, check the newspaper here in town. Also, my dad is always looking for someone to manage his books for him. You can talk to him too."

I smile and squeeze his hand a little tighter. I never thought I'd be here where I am, but now, I suddenly can't picture it any other way.

SIXTEEN

ROWAN

When we make it back to her place, we waste no time in showering together and jumping into bed. She falls asleep within minutes, but I feel like I'm too amped up to sleep. There's so much that needs done around here and so much planning to do. I carefully remove my arm out from under her and go downstairs.

I sit at the kitchen table while a pot of coffee brews. I pour a cup and start making a list of everything we can do to make the money they need. Becky mentioned a lot of great ideas, so I focus on the food and entertainment aspects of the event we're planning. I have a couple of friends who are in bands, nothing big, but it will be live music that people can dance to, which is better than a DJ. I reach out to them and then send a message to the old football team. Some of them are still up at this late hour, and they reply instantly. They're more than stoked to help out for the cause. Even some that have moved away are planning to come home just for the benefit. Like I said, Bud is a well-loved man around here. There aren't many people he hasn't touched in some way.

Once I have the lineup for the auction, I look in what I can do around the farm. I pour my coffee into a thermos and head outside in the dark to take care of the animals. I feed and water the chicken, goats, horses, cattle, and pigs. That alone takes up several hours. There's more that needs done but nothing that doesn't require firing up some kind of machinery, and I can't do that without waking up Harper. I make a list of things to do in the morning and head back inside.

It's going on four a.m. when I finally fall asleep, but at least now I'm tired and can sleep. The sun comes far too early, and I'm back up two hours later. Now there's enough light that I can get the real work done.

I'm on the tractor at eight when I notice Harper standing on the back porch. I drive over to her and smile. "Good morning."

She hides her eyes away from the sun. "How long you been out here?"

I laugh. "Pretty much all night."

"You know you don't have to do this, right?"

"Who else is going to do it?" I throw back.

She shakes her head but smiles. She's happy I'm here. "I'm making breakfast. Can you take a break?"

I hop down and rush up the stairs, afraid that if I slow down, I'll fall over. I pull her against my sweaty chest, and she giggles. "I'll always take a break for you," I tell her, bringing her lips to mine.

I kiss her softly but don't take it any further. I still have a lot of work to do, and already, I feel like I've put in a solid day's work. I swat her on the ass as she turns to head inside.

I wash up while she gets busy making pancakes and bacon. The smell has my mouth watering, but my eyes keep falling closed as I sit at the table, waiting. I must doze off because I wake a little while later. She's running her fingers through my hair.

"Wake up. You need to eat after pulling an all-nighter." She kisses my forehead, and I can't help but smile at her softness.

"Damn, I haven't worked this hard in a long time."

She laughs as she carries her plate over to the table, sitting down across from me. "You work on a farm every day."

"True, but that's a farm that has twelve sets of hands. I've never had to do everything alone before. I don't know how your father keeps up with it at his age."

She gives me a weak smile. "Yeah, he's pretty amazing."

"So are you," I reply, sending her a smile.

We start eating, and the food tastes even better than it smells. I have to force myself to slow down. "How long is your dad going to be in the hospital?"

"They said about a week. He's already going stir-crazy but I know if he comes home, he'll jump right back into work and probably end up going right back, so I think it's best for him for the time being."

"You're probably right," I agree.

"What's this?" she asks, picking up the notebook I was writing in last night.

"Oh." I quickly grab it away from her. "That's a surprise."

She frowns. "What kind of surprise? It's not like the setting my float on fire type of surprise, is it?"

I roll my eyes. "Come on. You really think I'd do that again?"

She laughs. "I'd hope not. Once was bad enough."

"This is a good surprise. And don't go poking your nose around trying to ruin it either. Just relax and trust me."

"Trust you?" she says, tilting her head to the side. "The last time you said that, you got us buried in that mud hole."

I laugh. "I don't think I said trust me before that."

"I'm pretty sure you did," she argues.

She's always arguing. And I love it. She doesn't give in. She makes everything more fun, always keeping me on my toes.

We finish breakfast, and I drop her off at the hospital. I go and put in a few hours at work and then swing by Becky's. Her kitchen is full of shit. I can't even decipher it all. The table is full of papers and what looks to be homemade crafts. The floor is covered in totes full of random items.

"What is all of this?"

"They're donated items for the silent auction."

"You got this much stuff in one day?"

She smiles and nods. "Yeah, in a town this small, all you have to do is tell one person, and it spreads like wildfire. I called my friend Jenny who owns that little shop on Main, and she brought some stuff over. But she told people and people told people, and before I knew it, my whole kitchen was full. Also, Tyler and some of his friends are working on the games. So far, they've got the balloon dart game. They're setting up a goldfish game where you throw the ping pong balls. A local pet store is donating the fish. The Grigsbys are bringing over their ponies to have pony rides for the kids, and I thought we could have a petting zoo."

"Where are we going to do all of this at?"

"I thought the farm. There is plenty of land. Oh, also, Tyler suggested using a flatbed trailer as a stage for the band. I've also talked to Janett, and she's going to let us borrow some things for decorations."

"I got ahold of the guys. They're down to do the auction," I tell her, grabbing a cookie off the table and eating it.

"That's great! The older ladies in town will eat you boys up!"

I shiver. "Harper better bid on me."

"Oh, come on. Be a good sport," she says, looking down at her checklist. "So, it looks like we just have to figure out what we're serving and how much food tickets will be. Any ideas?"

I shrug. "What's something that's cheap to make that can feed a lot of people?"

She thinks about it for a moment. "I got it! We could do a chili cook off! It could be a contest, and then everyone in town can pay to eat, then we'll vote. Winner gets like a hundred bucks or something."

"But the amount of chili it would take to feed a whole town?"

"I could always see if the diner in town would cater and donate to a good cause?"

I point in her direction. "Good idea. Let's try the free way first."

She nods and writes a note to herself. "How long is Bud going to be in the hospital?"

"Harper said about a week. You think we can pull it together that fast?"

Her eyes widen. "A week! Any good benefit takes at least a month to put together."

"Well, we don't have a month. The bank is about to foreclose. We have a week."

"We're going to need more volunteers."

I'M NOT good at being sneaky, so it's a good thing that Harper is as preoccupied as she is with her dad and his recovery. She spends all day at the hospital and only leaves once visiting hours are over. By the time I get her home, she's hungry, in need of a shower, and then she's ready for bed. Since she isn't spending much time in town, the benefit is easy enough to throw together without her catching wind of it.

Today is finally the day that Bud is to be released from the hospital, and I've been working through the night to get everything set up in the field beside the house. I bush hogged the grass down yesterday, and the flatbed trailer is already in position. I wonder if she'll notice and ask about it, but she seems to not notice much of anything if it's not right in front of her face. I plan on taking her to the hospital and staying there until they release Bud. While we're gone, Becky, Tyler, and volunteers from town will be here, setting up.

I wish I could be here to help, but someone has to keep her away until it's time. We load up in the truck and head down the drive. I turn the music on and pray that she doesn't look to the left and see the trailer, but she seems to be focusing on something on her phone.

"What are you doing over there?" I ask.

"Filling out applications. I need to find a job. I have a meeting with the bank on Monday. Hopefully, they'll let me push back the foreclosure."

"I'm sure everything will work out," I tell her, placing my hand on hers.

I leave her alone as we drive to the hospital. She keeps her phone in her hand until we've parked. We head inside and find Bud in bed, eating his lunch.

"It's about time you got here. I've been ready to go all week."

Harper laughs. "Slow down, old man. Discharge papers still have to be drawn up. Relax, finish eating."

The two of us sit down in the chairs by his bed.

"Rowan, you didn't have to miss another day's work to come here," Bud says, looking guilty.

"It's fine. My dad is going to drop by the house later to write you a check and to sign the contract for leasing the land."

He nods. "You told him I wouldn't take full price, right?"

I nod. "I did," I lie. He must really not be thinking right. As far as he knows, he's about to lose the land, yet he's agreeing to let someone farm something that won't even be his? He must think he has more time than he does.

"What happens if the bank takes the land? Will that put your dad in a bad spot, or will the bank uphold his contract?" Harper asks, putting two and two together.

"I didn't even think about that," Bud says.

"Don't worry about it," I tell them. "We'll figure this all out."

As he eats and we wait for him to be discharged, I'm on my phone constantly with Becky, Tyler, and anyone else who has a question about where to put things. Becky sends me pictures of everything as it's coming together, and it all looks great. The flatbed trailer is parked in the field, and before it is a floating dance floor. In front of that are white tables and chairs. They've hammered in four posts around it all, and lights from the top so there will be plenty of light to see to eat and dance.

She sends me pictures of the silent auction tables, the tops covered in various items with sheets next to them to write in bids. Then she sends me a picture of the whole field, and it looks amazing, like a carnival. There are food booths and games, a petting zoo, and pony rides. I can't wait to see the look on Harper's face when we pull into the drive and she sees all this.

Hours pass, but we're finally able to take Bud home. I drive slow, wanting to give them the time they need to apply any finishing touches, and twenty minutes later, we're pulling into the drive.

"What in the world?" Bud asks, looking out across the field.

Harper looks up and gasps.

I park the truck, and everyone climbs out.

"What is all this?" she asks, looking over it all in amazement.

"This is how you're going to keep the farm. All of this was done by volunteers and donations. All the money brought in will be going to the bank to help you catch up on your payments, along with the money my dad pays for leasing the land," I add on.

She looks up at me with a wide smile, her eyes glowing with excitement. "You did it," she breathes out.

I shrug. "I did just what I had to do. Becky and Tyler have helped out a ton, so make sure you thank them too."

Bud walks up to me and holds out his hand. "Thank you, son."

Son. He's never called me son before.

"I can't tell you how much this means to me," he says, sounding like he's holding back tears.

"It's nothing. Really, I just had the idea. The town made it possible."

"How ya doing, Bud?" an old man asks as he walks over with his hand out.

Harper turns to me now. "I can't believe this," she whispers, taking my hand and pulling me toward the barn.

"It's nothing, Harp. Really."

Once we're inside, she spins around to face me. "Nothing? You call this nothing?" Her eyes are wide. "You saved my family, Rowan. You saved our home. This is far from nothing. This is... everything." I see tears welling up in her eyes, and I move toward her, cupping her cheeks in my hands as I lean down to press a kiss to her lips.

She kisses me softly, and I can't help but want to feel her pressed against me. It's been a long week, and I've never in my life been more tired, but being with her, it fills me with energy. She restores everything in me that I'm lacking.

"How can I help?" she asks when she pulls back.

"I don't know. Let's go see," I reply, taking her hand in mine and leading her back toward the door.

SEVENTEEN
HARPER

I can't believe he did all of this. All of it is because he loves me. I know this deep in my heart, but the words haven't been exchanged yet. I always felt like it was too soon to fall that quickly. But Rowan has always been like an anchor. An anchor that's tied around my heart. And well, when an anchor falls, it falls hard and fast, just like my love for him. I didn't even see it coming, it happened so fast. One moment I was standing in front of him, calling him every name in the book, and the next, I was on the ground with him wrapped around me.

I try to push my feelings to the back of my mind, at least for another day so I can focus on helping with setup. Before I know it, everything is done, and people are beginning to show up. The field to the left of the house is completely full, looking like a crowded carnival when our town is lucky enough to have one. There's face painting for the kids and novelty toy tables and booths set up with people selling their homemade items, such as jewelry, food, and decor. A percentage of all of it will be going directly to the cause.

Looking around, I can't help but feel overwhelmingly happy. This town, the place I was so desperate to escape a few years ago, it's perfect, and I couldn't ask for it to be any other way. I walk around alone, taking it all in and smiling. I smile at the kids as they ride ponies around in a circle. I giggle when I hear the toddlers laugh as a lamb licks the food from their hands. My heart expands and explodes when I catch a glimpse of Rowan helping a little girl onto the back of a horse.

His eyes meet mine, and he offers up a smirk and a wink that has the butterflies in my stomach taking flight. How did all this happen? How did I end up here? And why am I so lucky? Not only do I have a father who's still alive and breathing, but he was kind enough to risk everything on my education. I have a boyfriend—if that's what he is— that's broken his back this past week to make sure me, my father, and our land were taken care of. I have friends who pulled together to make all of this possible. I have to be the luckiest girl in the world.

The music starts up, and Rowan takes my hand, pulling me to the dance floor, while everyone sits at the tables to eat. He pulls me close, and my heart jumps in my chest.

"There's one more thing I need from you," he whispers.

I laugh. "What's that?"

"Well, we're having a bachelor auction, and I'm in it." He pulls back and looks in my eyes. "Please bid on me. Don't make me go home with an old lady."

I can't hold back my laughter.

"I'll pay for myself. There is no limit. Don't give up."

I nod.

"Promise?"

"I promise," I agree.

We finish our dance, and soon after is the live auction.

Becky takes her place on stage. "Okay, ladies! I have an awesome surprise for you," she says, walking back and forth in front of the crowd. "I know many of you have had your eyes on these men for a while now. So, for one night only, they can be on your arm. Get out the pocketbooks, ladies, and come check out the men!"

Women rush to the stage as the men take their places, lining up.

"First up, we have Tony Green. He's six four and can bench-press any one of you lucky ladies," Becky says, making me laugh. "Let's start the bid at fifty dollars."

Someone quickly bids fifty, and it gets bumped up to fifty-five. By the time the auction is closing on Tony, we've made seventy-five bucks. Tony walks off the stage and straight to the lady who's purchased him for the night.

"Alright, girls. It's time to buy Greg Murphy! I know ya'll have been watching this one, right?"

The crowd cheers.

"Let's start with fifty dollars."

I stand back, watching as the women duke it out back and forth until the price for Greg is up to one hundred and fifty dollars. Rowan is next, and the women are already hooting and hollering for him before the auction even starts.

Becky looks at me with a smile. "Ready for this?" she asks me.

I take a deep breath and nod.

"Let's start the bidding at fifty dollars."

I raise my hand and bid fifty, but I'm quickly outbid. I bid at seventy, one hundred, one twenty, one fifty, one seventy-five, and finally win when I jump all the way up to three hundred dollars. Nobody bids against me, and Rowan stands there, smiling, face red with embarrassment.

He walks off the stage and right up to me. "Three hundred bucks?" he asks, placing his hands on my hips.

I laugh. "You're worth it, right?"

He shakes his head. "I'm not so sure. Come on, let's go pay for myself."

"Hey, you said no limit," I remind him.

"Yeah, yeah," he says, walking up to the table and pulling out his wallet.

Everything starts to wind down after that. People are dancing while the food and carnival stuff starts to get cleaned up. Becky comes back on stage, stopping the music.

"Everyone, I just wanted to step up here and say thank you from the bottom of my heart. Harper and her dad have always been like family to me, and when Rowan came to me with this idea, I thought it was just crazy enough to work. And thanks to all of you, it did. We raised just enough money for Bud and Harper to keep their family land."

Everyone cheers, and I cover my mouth with my hand as tears fill my eyes.

"It's small towns like this that keep the world spinning," she says, wiping a tear of her own, "and just know that if any of you find yourself in a similar position, reach out, because you have a whole town of people here to fall back on."

I clap and cheer her on while the tears finally overfill my eyes and roll down my cheeks. Rowan pulls me against his chest.

"Thank you," I whisper, unable to find my voice through my tears.

"You don't have to thank me for anything," he reminds me, moving his hands up to cup either side of my face.

"I do," I reply. "I have to thank you for so much. If it wasn't for you, I'd probably be packing my whole life into a bag to go live in some cheap motel. Because of you, I have everything I could ever need, ever want."

"Almost," he says, and my head tilts to the side, wondering what he could mean by that. "I love you, Harper. I've loved you since that first day I saw you. One dirty look was all it took to have me wrapped around that finger of yours. I've always loved you, and I always will," he says, looking deeply into my eyes.

The tears form again. "I... I love you too," I reply.

He pulls me in for a long, slow kiss, a kiss that tickles my tummy and tingles in my toes. Our soft kiss turns to one of passion and need, and before I know it, he's carrying me up the barn stairs to the little bed in the corner. He lays me down, covering my body with his as his hands move slowly up the outside of my thighs.

"I promised your dad that I would always take care of you, and that's what I'm going to do," he whispers, pressing kisses to my lips, cheeks, and neck. "I love you, Harper. I love you."

I can't respond to him. I don't know how. There are no words in the English language that could tell him how much all this means to me. "Make love to me, Rowan," I tell him, pulling his lips back to mine.

Before I know it, we're both completely bare, and he's sliding into me, owning every part of my mind, body, and soul. I'm no longer scared of the feelings I'm having toward him. I no longer think that we're just messing around. Over these last two weeks, things got serious and rushed, but I know that when it comes to Rowan and me, there is no other way. We hated each other instantly, we threw caution to the wind in an attempt to annoy the other, and we fell in love just as quickly and carelessly. This is just the way he and I work, at our own pace but side by side. I don't know what kind of life I will have with him here in our hometown, but I don't care, because I know that we'll have it all. Everything that really matters anyway.

As he pushes into me, he holds me close and whispers again how much he loves me. My release rises and shatters, pulling me under the dark water that is our love. It's so thick and hot that I can't breathe, but it's painless and passionate, captivating, holding me hostage for the rest of our lives.

EPILOGUE
ROWAN

"It's time?" I ask, feeling my brows raise on their own. "Are you serious? We're supposed to be getting married in twenty minutes. You're not due for another three weeks!"

She grabs her large, swollen stomach. "I don't care. The baby is coming now. We'll just have to push back the wedding. They'll understand, right?"

I laugh. "The whole town is waiting for us in the town square. Can't you just, I don't know, cross your legs and keep her in there a little longer? Long enough to say I do and kiss me?"

She frowns as I lead her down the front steps. "Right now, I wouldn't get your lips anywhere near my face. I may bite them off. Take me to the hospital. Now, Rowan!"

"Alright, alright," I agree, loading her into our brand-new SUV. The truck and her crappy car weren't nearly in good enough condition to trust them with a newborn baby.

I hop behind the wheel and start the engine. Her dad makes his way out to the front porch. "Good luck," he says with a smile and a wave.

I wave back but quickly pull out onto the road. We're at the hospital only moments later, and I'm rushing her inside. She's quickly put in a wheelchair and pushed to a room. I follow along the whole way, feeling my anxiety rise.

I'd never given much thought to settling down and getting married or having children. Hell, when Harper and I got together, I was still a child myself. But now, here we are, three years later. Our wedding day was supposed to be today, but our daughter will be born instead. Sure, I was looking forward to having that ring on her finger and having her last name match mine, but it can wait. This is far more important.

My phone rings as the nurse is helping her into bed and finding her a gown.

"Hello?" I answer.

"Mr. Wilson?"

"Yes?"

"The concrete truck has just pulled off. I said I'd call and let you know."

Fuck. I forgot all about that. "My fiancée is in labor and we're at the hospital, but my father-in-law is there and the spot is clearly marked."

"Alright, good luck and have a great day, sir." He hangs up.

"Who was that?" Harper asks.

"The concrete truck just left to go pour our foundation," I tell her.

"Do you need to go back?"

"Are you serious? Hell no. I'm not leaving you. Your dad will handle it," I say, pulling up a chair and taking her hand in mine.

These last three years has been a bit of a rush to get her farm paid off. We're now building our own place on the land, not too far from her father's. We thought it would be the best route to go, considering that my father's land sits right next to it. And since I'm an only child, it will automatically go to me. She and I together will have the largest piece of land owned by a single household in all of town. I sold my last place and used the money to pay off the bank for her father. The rest went to starting construction on the new place. These last few months have been a little hard, living with her father, but soon enough, we'll have our own place that we've built and designed together. Our first home.

She squeezes my hand and brings me out of my thoughts.

"Just breathe," I tell her.

She nods, but her face is turning bright red with the contraction. I coach her through them, just like I've learned to do from all those birthing classes she made me attend. After a few minutes, the contraction ends, and she's able to rest a moment.

"You know, we still haven't thought of a name for this little girl yet."

She wrinkles her nose. "Actually, I was thinking about Abby, after my mom. And Danielle after your mom. Abby Danielle Wilson? What do you think?"

I smile. "I love it. And I think my mom will too." I kiss her hand just as another contraction starts.

The doctor comes in and finds that she's much further along than we thought. It's already time to start pushing. He flips the blanket up, and I opt to stick close to her head, not wanting to pass out and leave her alone. My girl is tough and she gives it her all. After two hours worth of pushing, our baby's cry makes its way to my ears.

"You have a daughter," the doctor says as Harper falls back against the bed.

"Abby is here," I tell her, pressing a kiss to her forehead.

She smiles and tries to lift her head to see, but she's weak.

"Just relax. She's fine. She's beautiful," I say, my eyes watching as they move her around to check her out. Tears fill them quickly, but I will them away. The moment they put that little girl in her arms, I can't will them anywhere. I feel happy, excited, and overjoyed that I have my whole world in this one room.

I stare down at my soon-to-be wife and my little girl in awe. She's gorgeous with light-brown hair, blue eyes, and pink skin. She's tiny, weighing in at only at six pounds, and she's short, only seventeen and a half inches long, but I think her legs are the longest part of her. "She looks just like you," I tell Harper, reaching out to put my finger in the baby's tiny hand. She squeezes it, and my heart cracks open again.

"Thank you," I whisper.

"For what?" Harper asks.

"For everything. For dismissing our past and loving me in spite of it all. For falling in love with me. For agreeing to marry me and for giving me my daughter. I don't know where I'd be right now if it weren't for you coming back into town."

She reaches up and cups my jaw, and her watery eyes land on mine. "Thank you for making me run that stupid four-wheeler into that stupid mud hole."

I laugh. "You think that's what started it all?"

She nods. "You pulled your shirt off, and I couldn't remember why I hated you."

I laugh and shake my head. "You lifted your shirt up, and I couldn't remember why we weren't already together."

She rolls her eyes. "You have a strange fascination with my breasts, you know?"

I laugh. "Yeah, but I have a feeling they're going to be taken away from me for a while." I look down at the baby and shake her hand slightly. "It's okay, but don't break them, and return them when you're done," I joke, and Harper giggles and rolls her eyes again.

"There is seriously something wrong with you."

I smile. "Yeah, but you like it."

We spend the next few days in the hospital, getting everyone checked out. Harper lost more blood than the doctor liked, so we were given extra attention until she no longer felt dizzy when she stood up. The baby's health screens all look great even being a few weeks early and we're finally given the green light to take her home. I help Harper in the shower to get ready to leave and then I brush out her hair and help her into some clothes. I pack all our things and put Abby into the car seat.

"Well," I say, "I guess this is it, huh? They're really going to let us just walk out of here with a human being?"

She laughs but folds up a baby blanket and shoves it into the diaper bag. "Yep, I guess so."

Abby starts to cry, which only makes us laugh.

"See, even she's scared," I say as we both walk over to her seat and stare down at her, trying to figure out what she's crying about.

Harper picks her up, and the smell hits us. Suddenly, we know. "I promise we'll take really good care of you," Harper tells her as she lays her down to change her diaper. "We'll love you no matter how much you cry or poop."

I laugh but have a seat, in no rush to leave.

After Harper changes Abby's diaper, it's time to eat again. Harper gets back in bed, and the baby attaches herself to one of my favorite toys. "This is how our life is going to be from now on," she says with a smile.

"Only for a little while," I remind her. "Plus, we have a wedding to get to."

"Oh yeah. When are we going to reschedule it?"

I smirk. "They're already there, waiting on us."

"Really? I'm getting married in my sweatpants and with pads in my bra?"

I laugh. "Yep, but I think we'll have to wait a while to consummate the marriage."

She lifts the baby up and burps her. Finally, we're ready to go.

I put Abby back into her little seat and pick her up. I hold out my free hand to Harper. "Come home with me?" I say the words that first got us into this.

She smiles but puts her hand in mine. "What will the town think?" she asks in her breathy tone, causing us both to laugh as we leave our hospital room behind.

On the way home, we roll up to the town square, and just like I thought, everyone is crowded around. The decorations look a little haggard from hanging for a few days, but everything is perfect in my eyes. I have my daughter and the only woman I've ever loved. Today, we get to start our new lives.

Becky takes the baby seat and holds it, fawning over the baby as we stand before the preacher and the whole town.

"Do you take this woman to be your lawfully wedded wife for as long as you both shall live?"

"I do," I agree almost a little too excitedly.

"And do you take this man to be your lawfully wedded husband for as long as you both shall live?"

She smiles with her eyes locked on mine. "I do."

"You may kiss your bride," he tells me, and I waste no time in pulling her against me and kissing her until we're both completely fucking breathless.

The town around us breaks into loud cheers and applause, and I pull away, taking her hand in mine as I lead us back down the aisle, taking the baby as we go, back to the SUV.

She laughs as we climb back in.

"What?" I ask.

"That was one hell of a shotgun wedding if I've ever seen one."

I can't hold back my laugh.

"Let's go home," she says, her smile still in place.

KAYLEE AND LANDON'S STORY

ONE
KAYLEE

My phone rings from my bedside table. I roll over with a groan and grab it, yanking it from the charger and smashing my finger against the screen to answer it.

"Hello?" I ask angrily. The annoyance is clear in my voice.

"Don't tell me you're still in bed. It's going on seven thirty," my annoying twin brother, Kyle, says in his overly cheery morning person voice.

"No, I'm not in bed," I lie. "I'm just trying to get ready for work."

"Riiiight," he says, not buying a word of it. "Anyway, Mom's birthday dinner tonight. You going to be able to make it?"

"Of course," I breathe out, attempting to wipe the sleep from my eyes.

"It's at six. Pearson's Steak House."

"I know, Kyle. Geez, I'm not a child anymore."

He scoffs. "Okay, talk to you later."

"Wait!" I yell.

"What?"

"What time did you say again?"

I can practically hear his eyes roll. "Six, Kaylee."

I smile. "Love you."

"Uh-huh," he says, hanging up.

I drop the phone and roll back over. My brother is older by three whole minutes, and he's taken that seriously our whole lives. Being raised by a single mother was hard. Not only did my three-minute-older brother think he was the boss of me, but he was also the man of the house. If Mom asked me to do something and I didn't do it, he would torture me until I did. If I wanted to tell Mom I was going to a study group and hit up a party instead, he showed up and dragged me out. If I liked a guy and he didn't approve, he'd chase them off. My whole life has been controlled by him, and that hasn't changed now that we've grown up and have gone our own ways.

The alarm that I have set to wake me up at seven thirty starts going off. So much for going back to sleep. With a sigh, I shut up the annoying noise and go to shower. An hour later, my blond hair is curled to perfection, my makeup is done flawlessly, and I'm dressed in fitted slacks and a dress shirt for work. I slide my feet into my favorite heels and gather up my things.

My office is only a few blocks away, and I walk every morning to get my steps in. Plus, walking makes it easier to stop and grab a cup of coffee on the way. I dip into my local Starbucks and order a coffee and a pastry. I'm handed the items, and I hit the sidewalk with only one more block to go. When I make it to the door, my eyes graze over the words on the glass, *Kaylee Cash Designs*, as I unlock the door.

Walking in, I disarm the alarm and set my things down as I turn on the lights. The room brightens, and I take a few moments to straighten up the front waiting area. My assistant's desk is a mess, and she knows it drives me crazy. This is the front of my office, the first thing people see when they come in. Everything needs to be perfect.

I open her top desk drawer and swipe the items on top into the drawer before closing it. Then I fluff the pillows on the couches and make a mental note to have her dust the tabletops and picture frames. I grab my things and head to my own office. My office is set up perfectly. In the corner, there's my drawing and light-up table.

My desk is in the center for consultations, and along the far wall, I have fabric and paint samples. Each drawer in the table holds a different sample book for walls, floors, and fabrics for window treatments.

I'm extremely proud of myself for opening and running my own successful interior design business. Just don't ask my brother what he thinks. He says that I'm just a little girl who likes to play makeover. While I was in design school, he was going to college to become an architect. He's now one of the best here in Chicago, and he's about to start on his next building. He's proud enough of himself for the both of us. If the difference between us isn't clear yet, let me spell it out. In school, he got straight A's, was the president of our class, and he did every extracurricular activity offered. He was never late for school, and he always arrived home before curfew. I, on the other hand, was a solid B student. I was voted most likely to end up in jail—long way from class president—and I also didn't do anything more than what was required to graduate. I was late to nearly every class, and I don't think I was ever home on time, missing curfew every weekend. He's a morning person while I work better at night. He makes millions while I... do alright for myself, but nothing compared to him. He's very formal and goes to elegant parties that require you to wipe out four hours of your time for dinner, and I'm more of a *do shots and dance on the bar* kind of person. Well, I guess he does have a reason to worry about me.

I shrug it off as I sit behind my desk and turn the computer on. I sip my coffee and pick at my pastry as I go through my daily emails. I have an appointment at four this afternoon, and in the meantime, I'm putting together a presentation for a local hotel brand here in the city that's looking to update all their guest rooms.

I hear the front door open, and Andrea, my assistant, says, "It's just me. Aw, man. You cleaned my desk again?"

I smile as I stand with my coffee and move out to the front. "How many times do I have to tell you that this is the first thing clients see? It needs to be neat and orderly."

"I was going to do it when I came in," she points out, taking off her coat and hanging it on the back of her chair.

"Yeah, yeah, story of your life," I tease.

She rolls her eyes. "Your brother has called me at least ten times in the last two days to confirm you're going to your mother's birthday dinner. Please tell me you haven't forgotten."

I shake my head—typical Kyle. "Yes, I'm going, but I need you to run out and find her a gift."

She smiles and claps her hands silently. "Shopping on the clock? Yes, ma'am." She grabs her jacket and pulls it back on. "Any ideas?"

I shrug. "No home décor. She has enough of that shit. Nothing cheap like a candle. Nothing boring like flowers. Go for the classics: designer scarfs, broaches, and cashmere."

She nods. "Got it." She shuffles back out the door.

With her gone, I turn back for my office to get started on my work for the day.

I'M LOST in my new design when Andrea pops her head into my office. "I know you don't like being interrupted, but dinner is in twenty minutes. If you're late, I'm never going to hear the end of it."

I look at my watch. Shit. I drop my pencil and rush around to gather my things. I pull on my coat and grab my purse. "Shut everything down for me, would ya?" I ask, rushing past her.

"Sure."

I'm darting for the door when she calls out.

"Wait!"

I spin around.

"The present!" She rushes over to her desk, opens the bottom drawer, and pulls out a box that's wrapped beautifully.

"Thanks," I say, grabbing it and heading for the door. I flag down a taxi, and when one pulls over, I climb into the back. I rattle off the restaurant's address and pull out my mirror to check my makeup. I know my brother and my mom will be dressed perfectly. I'll never hear the end of it if my lipstick is faded or my eyeliner is smudged. I know I'm probably going to get chewed out for the clothes I'm wearing anyway. Clearly, I should've worn an evening gown.

When the taxi pulls up to the restaurant, I pass him some cash and climb out. The air is cool around me, and it helps to extinguish my burning skin from my rising blood pressure. I walk into the restaurant and am greeted immediately.

"I'm joining the Cash party," I say, slipping out of my coat.

The man nods. "Right this way." He leads me in their direction. Of course my brother and mom are already here. I check my watch and I'm five minutes early, but to them, I'm the last one to arrive, so I must be late. My mom and brother are cut from the same cloth. I take more after my father, whom I never got to meet. All I know about him is what my mother has told me: he was irresponsible, a drunk, and didn't make enough money. She may as well be describing me.

Kyle stands up and pulls out a chair for me.

"Thank you," I say as I sit down.

He slides the chair forward as he bends down to whisper in my ear. "My God, Kaylee. You couldn't have changed first?"

My eyes cut in his direction. "I came straight from work. Hi, Mom. Happy birthday." I force the annoyance I'm feeling toward my brother to the back of my mind while I try focusing on my mom.

"Thank you, dear. How is work going?"

I smile wide. "Everything is great. I just landed a huge deal with a local hotel here in town. I get to redesign all their guest rooms."

"That's wonderful, Kay," Mom says.

"Yes, congratulations, Lee Lee," my stupid brother says, using his nickname for me. "I guess I should tell you all my good news." He waits to add a dramatic flair. "You're looking at the new head architect for The Mason's Group." He beams and my mother swoons.

The Mason's Group is a large architectural firm that designs most of the lavish, up-to-date buildings in the country. The company Kyle had been working for only works locally. The Mason's Group will take him worldwide. He's had his sights set on it for years now.

I smile and say, "Congratulations." I mean it, but I'm so sick of competing with my overly confident brother. Nothing I do is ever good enough to stand against his achievements. You'd think at this point I'd stop trying, but it's been the theme of our relationship our whole life, so why stop now?

It annoys me that Mom is so willing to cheer him on and celebrate with him for every little thing he accomplishes. It makes my stomach turn, and I pick up my glass of water and take a sip to wash down the acid in my mouth. It's no wonder we have the relationship we do. Everything I do, I've done to annoy him. I have to admit, causing him grief has always been a fun pastime.

A round of drinks is brought over to celebrate *our* achievements, and we toast to a bigger and brighter future since nothing is ever enough for this family. Even in my head, I sound bitter. I push the negative thoughts away and instead focus on my mom and her birthday dinner.

"Oh, I got you a gift," I say, bending down and pulling the box out of my purse.

"Oh, you shouldn't have. What is it?" she asks, taking the box.

I force a smile. "Open it and see." I pick up my wineglass and take a sip, just as curious as she is. I can't believe I forgot to ask Andrea what she picked out.

Mom opens the box and pulls out a cream-and-gold-colored scarf. The Gucci price tag is still attached, and when she glances at it, she smiles. "Oh, it's beautiful, Kaylee. You shouldn't have spent so much."

When I catch sight of the tag, my eyes nearly bug out of my head. No shit. I'm going to be paying that off until her next birthday! I know I told Andrea designer, but she couldn't have gone with a cheaper designer like Michael Kors or something? Hell, Coach would've been cheaper than that overpriced square of material.

Mom rubs the scarf against her cheek to check its softness, and she smiles before placing it back in the box. I look at Kyle, and his eyes narrow on me. I must have one-upped his gift.

"I also have a gift, Mom," he says, pulling an envelope out of his breast pocket.

He hands it over, and she makes such a fuss about the gifts, but she smiles when she opens it.

"A gift certificate to the best spa in the city," Kyle says. "You can go and get pampered all day long." He beams his bright smile her way.

"Thank you, Kyle. This is the best birthday ever."

The waiter makes his way over, and we all order. About time we get on with this dinner.

The dinner lasts two hours. It's after eight when we're all finally walking out.

"You need a ride home, Lee?" Kyle asks.

You kidding me? After this night, I'm going to a bar somewhere. "No, I'm good. Thanks though."

"You sure? It's a long walk back to your place, and I'm heading in that direction anyway. May as well save you some cab fare."

I wave him off. "I'm meeting a few friends for drinks. Thanks. Talk to you tomorrow." I wave and turn quickly, walking away before he can stop me again.

TWO

LANDON

"Make it a double," I tell the bartender as he picks up my glass and carries it away. I turn my attention back to my buddy Craig.

He lifts his glass and takes a sip of beer. He shakes his head. "I don't know how you can drink that stuff. I have three beers and I'm tapping out."

I laugh. "Years of practice."

A fresh drink is placed in front of me, and I raise the glass to take a sip. With the glass tipped back, my eyes land on the door and the blonde that just walked through it. I set the glass down as I force my eyes to focus on her face. "Kaylee?" I whisper to myself.

"Who's Kaylee?" Craig asks, looking down the bar.

I smile. "She's the sister of someone I used to be friends with."

"The blonde?" he asks and I nod. "She's fucking hot. You ever get it on with her?"

I laugh. "A few times back in high school. It was always on the down-low though. If her brother found out I was fucking his sister, he would've torn my balls off. He's the overprotective type, if you know what I mean."

"Yeah, and I mean, who would like their friend fucking their little sister?" He's being a smart-ass.

"I'll be back," I tell him, taking my drink with me as I walk down the bar.

"This seat taken?" I ask, and she looks over her shoulder at me.

Her eyes stretch wide as a smile spreads across her face. "Landon, oh my God. Is it really you?" she asks, standing and wrapping her arms around my neck.

I place my hand on her lower back and squeeze her tightly. Her scent wafts up my nose, and it brings back a flood of memories.

"What are you doing here?" she asks, pulling away and taking her seat.

I sit on the stool next to her. "I work at the bank across the street. A coworker and I just stopped in for a drink."

"I had no idea you were back in the city. The last time I saw you was..." She has to think about it. "I guess before you left for college. It's been what? Ten years?"

I laugh and nod. "Yeah, ten years."

"So what have you been up to?"

"Well, I went to college and got a degree in business management and accounting. After graduation, I landed a job at an investment bank in North Carolina, and then I just moved back here about a year ago when I was offered the bank management position here." I motion over my shoulder. "The job pays more since it's not entry-level, and I missed home. The move made sense."

She playfully smacks my arm. "You've been here for a year? Why didn't you look me up?"

I shrug as I take a drink. "Kyle and I didn't end our friendship on good terms. I just assumed you were on his side."

She rolls her big brown eyes. "Me? On his side?" She laughs. "I've never been on his side; you know that."

I smile as I take her in. "So what have you been up to?" Her blond hair is longer than she used to keep it. Before, it was always just to her shoulders. Now, it falls halfway down her back. It's curled too.

It looks silky, and all I can remember is the way I used to tangle my fingers into it. Her chest is bigger—that's always a plus—and her waist is narrow compared to her hips. The girl is like walking sex. She's always been hot, but damn, she's only gotten better with age.

"Well, I went to design school, and after I graduated, I worked as an assistant and then an apprentice for a few local designers, but I gave up on that and opened my own design studio. You're looking at the owner of Kaylee Cash Designs." She smiles proudly, and I can't help but return it.

"That's great!" I hold up my glass, and she knocks hers off of it. "So, how's the family?"

She nods as she sets her glass back down. "My mom is good. I just left her birthday dinner, and Kyle, well, he's just on top of the world right now. He just landed his dream job with The Mason's Group."

I remember him talking about wanting to work there even when we were in high school. "Wow, that's amazing. Good for him."

"Yeah, yeah. Big surprise. He always gets what he wants."

I laugh. Those two have always been very competitive. "Well, it was good running into you. You've really grown up."

Her eyes run up and down my body. "You too. Hey, let's do a shot to celebrate."

"What are we celebrating?"

She shrugs. "To being awesome." She smiles and waves the bartender down, ordering two shots of Fireball.

"Geez, what are you doing? We're not at a frat party," I say, taking the shot. I'm not looking forward to putting it into my mouth.

She laughs. "What? Cheap and effective." She shrugs. "To being awesome." She clinks her glass of mine and throws the shot back like a pro. I shiver at the thought, but I put the glass to my lips and tip it back, spilling the sticky sweet liquid into my mouth. My stomach turns, wanting to reject it, but I force it down and slam the shot glass back onto the bar.

"Whoo," she says, watching me with glistening eyes.

I shake my head. "That's the worst fucking thing I've ever drank."

She tilts her head to the side. "Really? Is it?" She scrunches up her nose.

I laugh. "Fuck off, I forgot all about that night." The incident she's referring to happened back in high school. The two of us crashed at a party and woke up still drunk the next morning. I grabbed a bottle of Gatorade and took a swig, only to discover that it wasn't Gatorade but piss. Someone had pissed in a Gatorade bottle and left it sitting around.

"To be fair, I didn't swallow the piss."

She giggles. "You had pee in your mouth."

"Better than what you had in your mouth," I point out.

She frowns. "Which time?" she jokes.

I laugh and shake my head. "Well, you've grown up a lot, but you haven't changed much."

She moves her head from side to side. "A blessing and a curse."

"You and your brother still see each other a lot or is he too busy now?" I ask as I watch her full chest rise and fall. I wet my lips, remembering all the good times we had behind his back.

"You could say that. I mean, I hate him most of the time, but we talk every single day. He's my big brother, so I don't really have any other choice but to love him."

"That's a shame," I tease and she laughs.

"I know."

Hours pass, and the conversation eases along smoothly. Kaylee and I sit and talk about the old times and catch up on what's been going on with us the last ten years we haven't seen one another. We talk about college, old boyfriends and girlfriends, and everything in between. I forget all about Craig, but he seems to understand when he comes over to say goodbye.

I forgot how much fun the two of us used to have together. It's fun drinking, laughing, and catching up. It almost feels like the last ten years didn't even happen. It feels like this is the way we've always been.

Then she grabs my hand. "Let's dance," she insists, slipping out of her chair.

"What? No. I don't dance," I tell her, holding her back.

She rolls her eyes and scoffs. "That what you've always said, yet you always dance with me. Come on. For old time's sake." She bats those lashes and smiles, and I'm like putty in her hands. I let her pull me out to the dance floor where she wraps herself around me. My hands hold firm on her hips as her body moves against mine.

When she spins around and sticks her ass against my groin, my hands squeeze her hips, wanting to slow them. With each wiggle, I get harder and harder. I place my lips at her ear and whisper, "Keep this up, and we really will be going back to our past ways."

She looks over her shoulder with a smile. "Show me how much you've grown, Landon."

I spin her back around, and her chest smashes against mine. My right hand stays on the small of her back while my left cups her jaw as I pull her lips to mine. They're soft and sweet from the cocktail she's been drinking. When my tongue slips past her lips, she lets out a soft moan into my mouth, and that sound is the last piece of the puzzle. I'm gone, completely lost in her the way I was growing up. Logical thinking has been thrown out the window. Now, the only thing I'm thinking is if I should take her to the bathroom or the back alley.

She pulls back, and her dark eyes meet mine. "Come back to my place," she whispers, and I can't do anything but nod.

She spins around and pulls me back to the bar where she drops some cash for the bartender and grabs her coat. I finish off my drink and follow her out the door. She steps up to the curb and flags down a taxi. One quickly pulls over and we both climb inside. She rattles off her address, and as soon as we're moving, her mouth is back on mine as my hands tour her hard body.

By the time we make it to her place, I couldn't talk myself out of this even if I wanted to. I toss the cab driver some cash, and we both get out. She leads me up to her apartment, and the moment we're inside, I'm pulling her against me. I shove her back against the wall as I move my lips to hers. She pushes my jacket off my shoulders, and I let it fall onto the floor. Next, she loosens my tie and starts unbuttoning my shirt. I unbutton the cuffs and shake the shirt off my arms as I break the kiss to pull my tie off.

With me only in my pants and undershirt, I work on removing her coat and unbuttoning her shirt. I push the fabric away and find her black lace bra underneath. I smile as I kiss my way down her neck and to the swell of her breasts. Her hands move to my hair, fingers lacing through it as she pulls and tugs.

I pick her up against me, and her legs lock around my hips. "Where's your room?" I ask around my labored breathing.

"Down the hall and to the right," she breathes out, bringing her lips back to mine.

I carry her through the apartment and find the bedroom. We crash onto the bed, tangled up with one another. As I kiss down her neck again, I unsnap her bra and pull it from her arms. The quick action has her breasts jiggling inches from my face, and I can't stop myself from sucking one hard nipple into my mouth and flicking my tongue against it. Her back arches up as a moan escapes.

As I work my way down her body, my hands clear the path for my mouth. I'm on my knees between her parted legs when I pull off her pants. There's only a pair of thin lace panties standing between me and what I want. I look into her dark eyes as I run my finger beneath the band. She grins and lifts her hips for me. Slowly, I pull them down her hips, thighs, and off her feet. She spreads her legs for me, showing me the glistening pink I'm dying to taste.

I wet my lips as I lower them to her. Running my tongue between her folds, her body jerks as a whimper slips past her lips. Fuck, I remembered she was sweet, but not this sweet. She's like a ripe fruit ready for the taking, and I'm going to eat her up. I flick my tongue back and forth across her clit as she wiggles beneath me and moans my name. I don't know what it is about Kaylee, but I've never been able to get enough. I prayed for her virginity as a teen, and then when

I got it, I made sure to ruin any other man for her, not stopping until she was pleasured time and time again. There was a reason she was always running back to me. It's the same reason that made her ask me to come home with her tonight.

When she shatters around me, I keep sucking her clit until she's quivering. Finally, she laces her fingers into my hair and pulls me away. "You've got good oral skills. Now show me what else you can do." She smashes her mouth against mine as her hands work on my belt. I love the way she sucks the taste of herself off my tongue. I'm seeing stars and haven't even slid into her yet.

I kick my shoes and pants off my feet before positioning myself at her entrance. I pause and she groans, getting impatient.

"Do you have a condom?" I ask around my labored breaths.

"I'm on birth control. Just fuck me already," she begs.

I shove into her in one swift movement, and she lets out a relieved moan. My eyes flutter closed with the sensation of having her wrapped so tightly around me. Fuck, she's got something no other woman has, and I don't even know what it is. All I know is that no other woman has felt this amazing.

Her nails dig into my lower back as her hips start to wiggle beneath me, begging me to move. It takes me a moment to gather my composure, but then I get it together enough to pull out. When only the tip is left inside her, I shove forward again, harder than before.

"Yes," she cries into my mouth.

The fact that she's still just as forbidden as before only makes me want her more. She's mine and has always been mine. It's time I remind her of how well I can manipulate her body and make her bend to my will. I move in and out of her as I roll my hips and brush against that spot that will have her crying my name. I feel her tighten around me, and I keep up with my torture. It's like a dam bursts open when I make her come. Her muscles quiver around me as she rides out every last wave of pleasure I provide. When her body is limp and her cries have quieted, I remove myself from her and flip her over onto her stomach. I smack her ass and she moans.

I grab her hips and pull them up into the air until her knees are beneath her. I take myself in hand and guide my aching dick into her hot core. I push in gently and slowly until I meet the halfway mark, then I thrust the rest in deeply. She calls out, her scream muffled by her pillow. I pull out only to shove back in, repeating the same steps over and over. I can feel my release rising, so I reach around and massage her clit with my fingers, wanting her to come undone one last time. It doesn't take long until her muscles are clamping down around my dick, milking me for everything I have. With one final thrust, I spill myself into her as she orgasms with me.

THREE
KAYLEE

My eyes flutter open in the morning as the urge to relieve myself makes itself known. I throw back the blankets and push out of bed, my bare feet slapping against the hardwood floor as I make my way to the bathroom. I close the door behind me and go pee. I wash my hands and splash some water on my face. My eyes are bloodshot from not getting an adequate amount of sleep. My mouth tastes like a can of stale Red Bull. I grab my toothbrush and rinse the awful taste from my tongue. I open the bathroom door, and my eyes land on my bed and the man who's still in it.

Well, shit. What do I do now? Do I crawl back into bed with him? That seems weird. Maybe I should go make some coffee and let him wake up whenever he wakes up. But I don't want coffee. It's Saturday. I want a couple more hours of sleep. I tiptoe over to the bed and slide back under the blankets. The warm, soft bed welcomes me back with open arms, hugging and squeezing me close. A smile forms. I'm happy I get to go back to sleep, but then Landon rolls over, his big arm wrapping around me and pulling me closer. He nuzzles his face into my hair and breathes me in deeply.

I keep my eyes closed, trying to pretend to be asleep. I'm not sure why. Landon and I have slept together many times, so there shouldn't be any awkwardness, but something feels different this time. My eyes open when he presses his lips to my bare shoulder, then his hands start gliding up and down my back, going further down with each lap, finally landing on my ass with a firm squeeze.

I smile as I roll over to face him. "Didn't get enough last night, huh?"

He smirks. "Did you?"

My nose scrunches up as I shake my head. "I'll never get enough," I tell him as I lean in to capture his lips. He lifts his upper body so that his chest is pressing against mine as he hovers over me. My body starts to tingle and come back alive, but the sound of my front door slamming shuts everything down.

"Lee Lee, don't tell me you're still in bed!" Kyle says, too loud to be outside of the apartment.

We quickly pull apart.

"Your brother has a key to your apartment?" he whisper-yells.

"Just stay here. I'll go out there and get him to leave," I say, pulling on a long sweater that's big enough to cover everything. I open the bedroom door and slip out to find Kyle in the kitchen, moving about to make coffee.

"Hey, what are you doing here?" I ask, standing on the other side of the island from him.

He sets two cups down. "Making coffee."

"Do you not have coffee at your place?" I ask, lifting one brow.

"No, I do," he says, confused. "I thought that we could hit up those antique stores or whatever you've been begging me to do with you."

I tilt my head and give him a look that says, *Seriously?* "Kyle, I've been asking you for months to go with me to find a gift for Mom. It's too late now."

"Oh," he says, looking defeated. He shrugs. "So, let's do something else."

I shake my head, about to explain, but a banging from the other room fills the kitchen.

His eyes pop up to the wall that separates my bedroom from the kitchen. "What was that?"

"Nothing," I say.

He steps around the island, heading for the bedroom. "Is someone in there?"

I jump in front of him and let out a long breath. "Yes, I met someone last night and brought him home. Now, if you don't leave in five seconds, you're going to know what your sister sounds like when she orgas—"

"La la la la la," he says, sticking his fingers in his ears as he turns around.

I want to laugh, but that was too close.

He pulls open the front door and steps through. "Call me later," he says, fingers still in his ears as he rushes down the hallway.

I breathe a sigh of relief as I close and lock the door, this time putting the chain in place. I head back to the bedroom to find Landon sitting on the edge of the bed, pulling his shoes on.

"He's gone. You don't have to leave," I tell him, flopping back onto the bed.

"Nah, I need to get going anyway. It's getting late." He stands up and tucks in his undershirt. "I guess the rest of my clothes are out there." He motions toward the entryway.

I nod and stand up, leading him out of the bedroom and down the hall, back to the front door where both our clothes are lying on the floor.

I bend over and grab his white dress shirt, tie, and jacket. I turn around to find him standing there, staring at me with darkening eyes. "I had a good time last night."

He wets his lips and flexes his jaw. "So did I." He takes the items I'm handing him.

I bite my lower lip, unsure of how to do this. Before, we were just a couple of teenagers, and we'd have to rush home before anyone discovered we were gone. There wasn't a lot of time for the morning after. But now, we're adults, and there is no rush to get home. There's nobody waiting to bust us. For the first time in our lives, there's nobody to worry about but him and myself.

When I look at him from beneath my lashes, he says, "Fuck it," tossing his clothes down and pulling me back against him. The rest of the weekend is spent holed up in my apartment, making love, snacking in bed, and sleeping, again and again and again.

"HEY, ANDREA. ANY MESSAGES FOR ME?" I ask as I walk back into the office on Monday morning after a meeting with a client at the nearby coffee shop.

"Actually, your brother called," she says, following me into my office.

I set my things down and turn to find her leaning against my doorframe.

"You two have a weirdly close relationship," she points out, wrinkling her nose.

I laugh. "Yeah, thin line between love and hate. Anyway, what did he want?"

She lifts up the paper in her hand and reads it off. "He says, today is his last day in his current office and he has to pack everything up. He wants to know if you want to come by and pick through things to keep for yourself so he doesn't have to pack them up and carry them down twenty-four flights of stairs."

"AKA will you help me pack my office and move?"

She laughs. "Pretty much."

"How's my schedule looking for today?"

"You're free."

"Alright. Shoot him a text and let him know that I'll be stopping by after lunch."

"Will do," she says, spinning around and leaving me alone.

I take a seat behind my desk and look at my upcoming week. I place a few orders for the items I'll need to get started on the guest room makeover for the hotel and return a couple of emails to book appointments. At noon, I shut my office down and step out front. "I'm out of here for the day. Can you hang around until closing time to monitor the phones?"

"Sure can," she agrees.

"Thanks, babe. You're the best. But please, clean off that desk!" I roll my eyes but smile, and she laughs but nods along.

Leaving the office, I swing by my place and change into more comfortable clothes. Instead of dress pants, a button-up shirt, and heels, I change into a pair of jeans, a cute T-shirt, and my favorite tennis shoes. I pull my hair up into a ponytail and pull on my jean jacket. Instead of wasting money to go out for lunch, I stop in my kitchen and pull out the leftover salad I didn't finish yesterday. I toss it onto the island and grab a fork. As I'm pulling out the barstool, my phone chimes.

Landon: *So glad we exchanged numbers. I wanted to wait the three-day rule, but I suck as an adult and fuck everything up. Anyway, what's up?*

I laugh as I take a bite of my salad. I reply as I chew.

Kaylee: *We're friends. Friends don't follow the three-day rule! I just skipped out of work to go help Kyle pack up his office.*

Landon: *What are you doing later? *smiley face.*

Kaylee: *You *winky face.*

Landon: *That's my girl. I'm all for rolling around in the sack with you, but if it's anything like last time, I'm going to need some substance. Dinner first?*

I laugh and shake my head.

Kaylee: *Ohhhh, you're going to wine and dine me before fucking my brains out? Yes, sir!*

Landon: *I'm nothing if not a gentleman. 7 o'clock. I'll pick you up.*

Kaylee: *It's a date.*

Wait? Was that the wrong term?
Landon: *A date, huh?*
Quick! Think of something.
Kaylee: *A booty call date, duh. Gotta go!*
Phew, nicely recovered. I think...

"YOU KNOW you don't have to speak in code to my assistant, right? If you want help, just ask," I say, taking a book that's so big it shouldn't even be called a book and putting it into an empty box.

He laughs. "You caught that, did you?"

I lift one eyebrow. "Catch it? Yeah, I caught it. My assistant caught it. Everyone caught it," I tease.

He just chuckles quietly as he takes down a glass vase and wraps it in paper.

"Hey, you know who I ran into the other night?" I ask, testing the waters.

"Who?" He glances over his shoulder at me.

"Landon. Can you believe it? He's back in the city now."

A grunt is the only response I get.

I sigh. "What is it with you two? You used to be best friends."

"'Used to be' is the key phrase in that sentence."

I shake my head. "Well, what happened? Don't you think enough time has passed that you should... I don't know, let it go and move on?"

"I have moved on, but you know me better than anyone. I don't let anything go."

"Are you going to answer my question?"

"What question?"

"What happened to drive a wedge between you two?"

"I don't want to talk about it, Lee."

I roll my eyes. "Come on. Tell me."

"Why's it so important to you?"

"Why?" I repeat his question, trying to think up a reasonable answer. "Because you guys used to be so close. I mean, he was practically part of the family. He was there every Thanksgiving. Every Christmas dinner. Every weekend, I basically had to fight him to get into the bathroom. Seeing him again, it just made me realize how much I've missed him being around. I mean, he's practically another brother to me."

Kyle scoffs and rolls his eyes. "It's stupid, alright."

"Well, if it's stupid, why you still holding a grudge?"

"Because he fucked me over once. I'm not trusting him not to do it again. We're better off not anywhere near one another. Can we please just drop it?"

"Fine," I agree.

FOUR

LANDON

This is fucking crazy. It's Kaylee. It's fucking Kaylee, for crying out loud—the girl whose virginity I took, even after I promised her brother, my best friend, I would never touch her. She's the girl I used to hold under the blanket when I'd fart. The girl who made every one of my high school girlfriends jealous. She's like my sister—well, she should feel like my sister. But the things we do, there's no way I could look at her that way.

I admit, sleeping with her back in the day was fun and all in the name of being a stupid teenager. Sleeping with her now, though, is a different story. I expected it to feel the same as it did back then, but it didn't. It felt like more. It felt perfect and monumental. It felt like I'd finally come home after a long journey. Everything made sense again. Now, nothing makes sense. I mean, I shouldn't be asking her for round two. I shouldn't be taking her out to dinner. But I am and I don't know why.

I haven't been able to stop thinking about her. All day, she's plagued my mind. Just when I thought I had myself distracted, she'd pop right back in. Thinking over how we spent our weekend, my body gets excited, and when that happens, thinking with my brain is a little harder.

Fuck it. I'm an adult, and if I want to spend time with her and she wants to spend time with me, there shouldn't be anything stopping us. My friendship with her brother ended long ago. And when the friendship ended, any promises we made are void. That's what I'm telling myself anyway.

Work drags by once Kaylee agrees to meet up with me tonight. I can't keep my eyes off the clock. I just want to count down the hours, minutes, seconds until I can be with her again. This not only makes me anxious but angry. Why the fuck do I want her so damn bad? She's no longer forbidden, so it can't be that. Maybe it's because we've gone so long without seeing one another. I'm sure the new will wear off eventually, and then things will go back to the way they're supposed to be.

It nearly kills me to wait until seven, but it finally rolls around, and I'm knocking on her door. After waiting for several minutes, she pulls it open as she's hopping on one foot, trying to put a black high heel on the other.

"Sorry, running late. Come in." She waves me forward. With a smile, I follow her into the living room, watching her ass sway from side to side in those tight skinny jeans. The heels make her legs look longer and more shapely even though she already has a great shape. She's wearing a small T-shirt, and she pulls her jean jacket on over it. She pulls her hair out of the back, and it falls down around her in soft curls. Fuck, she's breathtaking. "Ready." She beams.

I laugh. "You look great."

She smiles as one arched brow lifts. "Thanks. I just threw on the shoes, pulled down my hair, and bing, bang, boom." She grabs her purse off the table by the door and locks her apartment behind us. I lead the way to the elevator where we stand, waiting for it to arrive.

"How was your day?" she asks, digging around in her purse. Why does she look so cool and relaxed? I feel wound tight, nowhere near as carefree as she is.

"Long. Boring. Yours?"

She pulls a tube of lipstick out of her purse and applies it to her lips perfectly without even needing a mirror. "Same. I spent most of the day packing up Kyle's office."

I nod. The elevator door opens, and I motion for her to step inside ahead of me. She does and I join her, pushing the button to go down to the ground level.

"I asked him about you."

"Yeah, and what did he have to say?"

She shrugs. "Not much. He refused to tell me what tore you two apart." She smiles and bats her lashes. "I was hoping that maybe you'd tell me."

I laugh. "Were you now?"

She nods.

I chuckle and shake my head. "It's nowhere near as scandalous as you think."

"I'll decide for myself."

"I took out a girl who he liked," I confess.

Her mouth drops open. "No."

I nod. "Yep."

"All of this is over some girl neither of you have seen in years?"

"Right again."

She shakes her head and lets out a long, drawn-out breath. "I don't get it. There has to be more to the story."

"No, there's really not. There was this girl in our homeroom class, and I had my eye on her, but then he told me one day that he really liked her and that he was too afraid to ask her out. So I decided I'd back off and give him the space to do it on his own terms. Well, I waited. And waited. And waited. I waited all damn year to be exact. He never made his move. So, at our graduation party, I hooked up with her. He found out, lost his shit, and the rest is history."

The elevator door opens, and we both step out into the lobby. As we're walking across the floor to the door, she says, "It just doesn't make sense. Why let all those years of friendship go over some stupid girl?"

I shrug. It probably had more to do with our argument than the actual girl, but I don't add that on. "Water under the bridge," I say, opening the door and letting her walk out ahead of me.

She doesn't reply as I lead her to my car, which is parked on the street. I unlock the doors using the key fob and open the passenger side door for her. She slides into the seat, and I close it behind her. As I walk around the vehicle, I take a deep breath and hope the subject of our conversation changes on the ride to the restaurant. Dredging up old memories is useless. Kyle and I are no longer friends, and that helps me out with this thing I'm doing with her. If we were still friends, I'd have a whole lot more guilt about fucking her six ways to Sunday.

At the restaurant, we're seated in a far back corner, far enough away that we can talk and laugh and not disturb anyone around us. I order a glass of bourbon, and she sticks with a classic glass of wine. We take our time going over the menu and making our selections, and then we're left alone to wait as our food cooks.

"So, what made you want to get into interior design?" I ask, not wanting to leave a silence for her to fill with more talk of her brother.

She smiles. "My brother says that I'm just a kid who still likes to play makeover."

More with her brother? "What do you say?"

She seems surprised, like nobody has ever asked her that before. "I just... I like to take something plain and boring and make it sparkle and shine. I know it's stupid, but it's like I'm doing my part to make the world a better, prettier place. Besides, a room can really set you at ease or make you feel like you're home." She shrugs and her cheeks flush pink.

"That's not stupid," I tell her.

"No?"

"No. I mean, what the fuck am I doing?"

She laughs. "That does seem like a weird job for you. I always thought you'd be bartending on some secret beach, surrounding yourself with half-naked women and having the time of your life."

I smile as I pick up my glass and take a drink. "That's not far off what I originally wanted to do. But my dad talked me straight. He reminded me that I wouldn't be young and good-looking forever." I laugh, remembering the speech. "He said I better secure my future with a real job and prepare for when that time comes."

She smiles. "I don't know. You look a lot like your dad, and the last time I saw him, he was still pretty hot."

I laugh louder. "I'll tell him you said so. It'll make his year."

"Well, to be fair, I was a senior in high school the last time I saw him."

"Well, ten years can change a lot."

She nods as she runs her fingers up and down the stem of her wineglass. The action teases me, and I wish they were running up and down something on me instead.

"So, who was she?"

"What?"

"The girl you two were fighting over?"

Fuck. She's not going to let this go, is she?

I pick up my glass. "You wouldn't know her," I say, swallowing the rest of the liquid in the glass.

Her brows draw together. "What do you mean I wouldn't know her? We were all in the same class."

I roll my eyes and wave over the waiter, needing a refill. "It was... Lauren Beck," I confess, quietly while hoping she didn't hear me.

Her eyes double in size. "Lauren Beck? My old best friend?"

I swallow and nod.

"You had sex with my best friend?"

"It was a long time ago, Kaylee."

She frowns. "Why didn't you tell me? Why didn't she tell me?"

"I didn't tell you because I didn't want you getting mad at me. I mean, we weren't a thing or anything, but I didn't want it to seem like I was rubbing it in your face."

She rolls her eyes as she picks up her wineglass and finishes it off. "She always wanted everything I had. I'm not surprised she had to take you too."

I reach across the table. "See, this is why neither of us wanted to tell you."

"Do you think that Kyle never asked her out because she was my friend and he didn't want to be sleeping with my friend behind my back?"

"Huh, I never thought of it like that before." Fuck, that makes me feel twice as bad now, considering I had been banging his sister behind his back at the time. It doesn't make me feel bad enough to stop though. No, I don't think anything could do that. Kaylee worked herself under my skin years ago. She's been living there ever since—itching, festering, and multiplying. Getting her back now, well, it's like I finally scratched that itch, and now the rash is spreading, consuming my whole body.

"Can we please drop this conversation? It's all in the past."

The waiter brings our fresh water, with another following behind him with our meals. The food is placed on the table in front of us, and neither of us wastes time digging in. I try sparking new conversations as we eat, but the most I get out of her are simple, one-word replies. She never volunteers information and always leaves me searching for the next topic to discuss.

When we're both done, I pay the check and lead the way back to the car. She takes her seat and keeps her hands in her lap as she stares out the passenger side window. I was planning on bringing her back to my place, somewhere where we wouldn't be caught by her brother again, but the sudden silent treatment has me driving back in the direction of her apartment.

"Did I say something to upset you?" I ask as we approach her building.

She glances at me. "What? No."

I pull in front of the building, shift into park, and then kill the engine. "It's just that you've gotten quiet on me. I know when you do that, you're mad or upset or lost in your thoughts."

She unbuckles her seat belt and opens the door. "Everything is fine. Thank you for dinner." She climbs out, slamming the door behind her.

I get out and chase her around the car. She's already heading into the building, and I barely catch the door. I follow her to the elevator. "Are you sure nothing is wrong?"

"Completely," she says, refusing to look at me.

"So you're not mad that I slept with your friend over ten years ago?" I ask as the door opens. She steps inside and I follow.

"Nope. I mean, it was ten years ago. We weren't a couple then, and we're not a couple now, so whoever you sleep with shouldn't upset me, right?" She jabs the button to her floor a little too hard.

"Kaylee," I breathe out.

"No, no," she says, shaking her head. "I don't care that you were sleeping with me and then went and slept with my best friend. Why would that upset me?"

"Maybe because you and I hadn't slept together in six months because you were dating what's-his-name? Chase?" The doors open, and she steps off with me following along behind her. "You know that if we were still messing around then, I never would've slept with anyone else. It's not like I cheated on you."

"You kind of did though," she says, stopping at her front door and digging through her purse for her keys.

"No, I did not," I argue.

"You slept with my best friend, Landon."

"Well, you were sleeping with your brother's best friend. How's that any different?"

Now that I'm throwing accusations around as well, her eyes widen with anger. "It's different."

"No, it's really not."

She shakes her head as she unlocks her door. "God, you're as big of a pain in the ass now as you've always been."

"And you're still just a spoiled brat who has a tantrum when she doesn't get her way," I throw back. That is what she's doing right now, and she knows it.

She turns and levels her eyes on me. "Take it back."

"No." I square my shoulders. "You take it back."

She acts like I've slapped her. "Take what back?"

"You said I cheated on you, and we both know that there was nothing to cheat on."

She rolls her eyes and scoffs. "I'm not the problem here. You're the problem here. You're the *oh, every girl is always bending over backward to be with me, might as well try them all out* type of guy, right?"

I laugh. "What the fuck, Kaylee? Are you mad because I screwed your friend or because I wasn't screwing you?"

She gasps. "Fuck you, Landon." Her hand moves up to slap me, but I catch it. We're nose to nose now, her eyes boring into mine. She's angry and her eyes are heated. I can see the fire dancing within them. Fuck, why is she so goddamn stubborn? Why the fuck do I want her so badly? I lose myself in her eyes, and the next thing I know, my mouth is smashing against hers. She doesn't push me away. No, she's never been able to do that. Instead, she laces her fingers into my hair and pulls me closer.

My hand lands on the small of her back as I pull her flush against me. Her tits press against my chest, and they feel soft as they tease me. Without asking what she wants—because I know she wants me, always has and always will—I pick her up against me, and her legs wrap around my hips. I carry her into the apartment and kick the door closed. I turn us around and hold her against the door while I do my best to lock it. When the door is secure, my hands are back on her, pushing her shirt up her stomach. Her hands fall to my chest where she starts unbuttoning my shirt.

"You're going to fucking kill me one of these days," I say against her lips.

She lets out a giggle as she wraps her arm around my neck, pulling me in till our lips collide.

FIVE
KAYLEE

"Was she better than me?" I ask as I'm lying with my head on his bare chest.

"What? Who?" he asks, surprised by my question.

"You know who," I reply, needing to know. I don't know why it's bothering me so much. Like he said earlier, we weren't sleeping together at the time. We weren't a couple and didn't have any kind of rules in place to keep things like that from happening. But knowing he screwed my old best friend, and that I'm just now finding out about it, it's eating at me.

"No, of course not," he finally tells me.

"Are you just saying that to make me feel better?" I ask, being a total girl. I don't like it. It doesn't suit me well. It's like having a wardrobe of all black clothing and then trying to pull off a baby pink dress. It just feels awkward.

"Not at all, Kaylee. That girl was nothing special. In fact, I treated her rather badly. I talked her into my bed, I fucked her until I got off, and then I asked her to leave."

"You did not." I laugh.

"I swear. It was a shitty thing to do, but it was what she deserved at the time."

"Why's that?"

He doesn't reply right away, and I know he's holding something back.

"Tell me."

"Are you going to get all pissy with me again?"

I laugh. "No, I'm under control."

"Because she was fucking your boyfriend behind your back."

I gasp. "What? How do you know that?"

He shrugs. "Kyle and I, we caught them. There was this party that summer, and Kyle thought that you'd snuck off to go to it to be with him. He didn't like him much, and it turned out to be for good reason, but he forced me to go with him. He was going to bust in on you two and drag you out of there. I was the muscle. He knew that if Chase wanted to fight him, he wouldn't stand a chance, and I wouldn't let someone beat the shit out of my best friend. So we went to this party. We asked around about him and found out he was in one of the rooms. So we went to every single room until we found him. But we were surprised to see that you weren't the one under him."

"So, let me get this straight. He's pissed because you screwed the girl he liked, but you only did it to get back at her for fucking me over?"

He chuckles. "Not exactly."

"Then why?"

He takes a deep breath. "At first, everything was fine, but then he started to wonder why I cared so much. I think he knew that I had a thing for you. So, he picked a fight with me in order to keep me away from you. That's my theory anyway. The real reason, you'll have to ask him."

That can't be it, can it? Kyle never mentioned anything to me about Landon. There was never a moment where he sat me down and was like, *listen, you can't date my best friend*. It was always just agreed upon in our weird little twin way we have. We've always seemed to know what the other was thinking. I could look in his eyes and know exactly what he was trying to wordlessly convey to me. The same goes for him. I believe he didn't move forward with his feelings for Lauren out of respect for me, but did he have a feeling something was going on between Landon and me? If he did, why didn't he say anything?

"Thank you," I say into the darkness as Landon holds me to his chest.

"For what?" he asks, turning his head my way to better hear me.

"For... I don't know, standing up for me and defending my honor and all that."

The side of his face is resting against the top of my head, and I feel his cheek pull up in his lopsided grin. "Anytime."

The two of us stay in bed a little longer before pulling apart. I show him to the door, thank him for dinner, and watch him walk down the hallway. When he's no longer in view, I close and lock the door. I swing into the kitchen, make myself a cup of hot tea, and take it back to bed with me. I crawl beneath the covers and turn the lamp on beside the bed as I pick up my phone. I turn the TV on for background noise as I scroll through meaningless posts on Facebook and sip my tea. The warmth of the tea and my bed, mixed with the exhaustion of the late hour, helps to relax me.

But even though I'm tired, I'm not too tired to look up my old best friend, Lauren Beck. I find her page easily enough under the name Lauren Beck Ingrum. Her profile picture is of her, a man who I'm assuming is her husband, and a little baby boy. The photo is taken from above with all of them looking up with big, proud smiles. Her bleached blond hair is now back to its natural brown color. Her face is more rounded, but that makes sense given she's just had a baby. I click on her profile and go to her page only to realize that it's private and I can't see anything. I could send her a friend request, but what good would that do? She's obviously moved on, and to be honest, so should I.

I'm about to put the phone down and attempt sleep when I type in one last name. Chase Benton. His page pops up easily as well, and his isn't private. I'm able to see everything, including photos of him in random poses—one by an expensive car, one of him holding up dozens of hundred-dollar bills, and one where he's just leaned back, body decorated in gold chains and diamonds. It's clear to see that I didn't miss out on anything there.

I'm also allowed to see his friends list, and lo and behold, he's friends with Lauren Beck Ingrum. I roll my eyes but decide to scroll through his posts. An hour later, I look up to find that I've lost myself on his page, studying every pic, every song lyric, and every tagged post. I've accomplished nothing here, and I feel like a stalker. I swipe everything away and settle in bed. Turning the light out, I leave the TV on for some light and background noise as I fall into a deep sleep.

"Where were you last night? You missed an awesome party," Lauren says over the phone.

I fling myself onto my bed and groan. "Grounded after that last party I snuck out to go to."

She laughs. "Well, you didn't miss much. Andy got hammered again and fell into the fire."

"That's a pretty normal occurrence now, isn't it?"

"Yeah, here lately it is. Camilla got hammered, and Chuck found her making out with another guy on the dance floor, so you can probably imagine how that turned out."

"An explosive yet entertaining fight?" I guess out loud.

"Exactly. And... I hooked up with someone," she admits, not sounding all that pleased with herself.

"What? Who?" I ask, wanting all the juicy details.

"Ugh, it doesn't matter. All I'm saying is that the guy was a grade-A jackass. He flirted with me all night; we started dancing and kissing, then he took me upstairs. It lasted a whole ten minutes. I didn't even get off, then he just got up and left."

My mouth drops open. "Damn. What an asshole."

"I know, right? I mean, who does that?"

"He didn't say anything?"

I can practically hear her eyes rolling, even over the phone. "I don't know. He said, 'Thanks for being such a whore and making this easy on me.'"

I gasp. "Who does that kind of thing?" I get a beep, and I pull the phone away to read Landon's name on the screen. "Hey, let me call you back. Landon is calling."

"Ugh, seriously, Kay? I'm your best friend, and I'm obviously upset here."

"I know, but I'll call you back. I'm sure it won't take long. He's my best friend, too, you know?"

"No, he's your brother's best friend. You don't leave your friends hanging for a guy! Hoes before bros!"

I roll my eyes. "Stop being dramatic. I'll call you back." I hang up the call and switch lines. "Hey, Landon. What's up?"

"Shit. Where you at?"

"Home. Grounded again. Why?"

"I... I was just wondering. I didn't see you at the party last night and wanted to make sure you were covered."

"Covered?"

"Yeah, like home safe and not lying trapped under some frat boy somewhere."

I laugh. "How many frat boys come to high school parties?"

"Shut up. You know what I mean."

"So, how was the party anyway? Lauren gave me a quick rundown. Sounded like a mess."

"You talked to Lauren?"

"Yeah, she ran me through the important events. Did you see who she was with last night? She said she hooked up with a total asshole but wouldn't tell me who."

"Oh, no, I don't remember seeing her," he says, but his tone is off. Since when does Landon worry about covering for Lauren?

"Oh," I say into the phone.

"Listen, I gotta go. I just wanted to make sure you were okay."

I smile. He can be sweet when he wants to be. "I'm fine, but thanks." *I go to pull the phone away from my ear to hang up, but I hear him call my name.* "Yeah?"

"You and that Chase guy still dating?"

I frown. "Yeah, why?"

"It's nothing," *he says, hanging up.*

My eyes open, and it's like my subconscious was busy all night piecing together all the information I received the night before. Lauren slept with Landon that night. And only a few hours after that call, my boyfriend called and broke up with me. It makes me wonder now if Landon had anything to do with it. If he'd cheated on me, surely, he would have wanted the relationship to end, right?

I take a deep breath. There is still plenty of stuff to figure out, not to mention uncovering the reason that Kyle is so hell-bent on being enemies with Landon in the first place. But for now, I have another day of work to get to. I throw the blankets off my legs and swing them out of bed. I sit up with a groan, my eyes landing on the clock to see that it's only seven twenty-five. Five minutes before my alarm is set to go off.

I go for a shower and then quickly get ready for work. I walk out of my bedroom to find my brother in my kitchen, making coffee and packing my lunch.

"What are you doing?" I ask, tired of him just popping in whenever he wants.

"Good morning to you too, sis." He's wearing a super annoying smile. "I ran into Aunt Katie last night at Mom's, and she just happened to have her famous chicken and dumplings. She invited me to take some home for myself, so I figured I'd split them with you so you would have a good lunch."

"God, I love you," I say, moving closer to him so I can see exactly what he's packing into my lunch. There is a bento box full of chicken and dumplings, mashed potatoes, stuffing, a roll, and a small side salad. My mouth waters just from looking at it. At least I have something to look forward to now.

He places the box, a bottle of water, and silverware into my lunch sack and slides it over to me. Then he pulls out two thermoses and fills them both with coffee. He hands me one, and I top it off with the desired amount of cream and sugar. But looking at the clock, I still have a few minutes before I have to leave, so I sit at the barstool and think about how I'm going to attempt going about bringing him and Landon back together.

"So, I ran into Landon again last night."

He frowns. "Again? Where the hell do you keep running into him?"

My place, I think but instead say, "There's this little bar I go to after work sometimes. It's not far out of the way. And he just happens to work at the bank across the street. Anyway, we've been running into one another and hanging out, sharing a few drinks, and talking about old times."

Kyle shakes his head. "You should really just leave it alone, Lee."

"I don't want to leave it alone, Kyle. I want to fix it."

"Nothing needs to be fixed. It's been over ten years since I've seen him, and I'm not upset by that in the slightest. Nothing to fix. Really." He puts the lid on his thermos, and I know he's preparing to leave, not only because he has a new job to get to but because the topic of our discussion isn't to his liking. I have to be fast.

"He told me about Lauren and Chase," I blurt out.

His jaw twitches. "He really shouldn't be dredging up the past. No good will come of it."

"Is it true? Did you two catch him cheating on me with my best friend?"

His eyes level on me. "Lee," he breathes out, pinching the bridge of his nose.

"Kyle, just tell me. I'm a big girl. I can handle it."

"Yes, okay? Yes, we went to the party, thinking we were going to catch you sneaking out, but we found them instead. Okay? Are you happy?"

"And then Landon screwed Lauren to get back at her for fucking me over?"

He nods.

"And you got mad at him for it? Because you liked her, right?"

His brows pull together, and his eyes abruptly leave mine. "Yeah, something like that. I gotta go." He takes his coffee, lunch, and briefcase and heads for the door, leaving me alone.

SIX

LANDON

I'm sitting at my desk, going over loan documents and inputting numbers into the computer when my phones chimes at my side. I pick it up and see Kaylee's name on the screen. I smile to myself as I swipe the screen to unlock it and read the message.

Kaylee: *My brother stopped by today. I asked him about all that. He agreed to everything but got weird when I asked him if he got mad because he wanted Lauren for himself. I think you may be onto something.*

Landon: *I don't know why you keep insisting on picking the scab, Kaylee.*

Kaylee: *If you just found out that things from your past were kept from you, don't you think you would too?*

Landon: *Well, when you put it like that...*

Kaylee: *Exactly. I'm not letting this go until I get to the bottom of it.*

I smile.

Landon: *Well, you've already got to the bottom of it on my side of things. Does that mean you're letting me go?*

Kaylee: *Not unless you want me to.*

Landon: *As far as I'm concerned, we're both adults who are enjoying our time together. Nothing wrong with that. In fact, I wouldn't argue against spending even more time with you.*

Kaylee: *Is that so? Well, I might just have to pop in on you sometime and surprise you.*

Landon: *How are you going to do that when you don't know where I live?*

I hold the phone, waiting for a response, but it never comes, and I'm forced to get back to work. Thirty minutes later, my door opens and Kaylee walks in.

"What are you doing?" I ask, pushing away from my desk.

She rushes around it. "Surprising you. And since I don't know where you live, this will have to do." She pushes me back into my chair just as I'm rising up out of it. Then she drops down to her knees, her hands working on my belt.

"What are you doing?"

"Shhh, you're ruining the surprise," she says, pulling my chair back up to the desk while she shimmies under it. She unzips my pants, then her warm hand is wrapped around my length. She works it up and down once, twice, then three times. Already, I'm coming to life. I jump when I feel her hot mouth wrap around me.

"Geez. Fuck, Kaylee," I breathe out as she pushes me to the back of her throat.

She doesn't reply as I lean my head back against my chair, my eyes falling closed as I enjoy the pleasure she's providing.

My door busts open. I sit up quickly, surprised when I find Kyle standing in front of my desk.

"Kyle, what are you doing here?" My hands desperately try to push Kaylee away, but she's not stopping.

"Listen, I don't know what you're doing with all these casual run-ins with my sister, but stay away from her. Got it? I didn't want you messing with her then, and I don't want you messing with her now."

My eyes go wide with his accusations. "What the fuck are you talking about? I've run into her what, two or three times? Nothing is going on," I lie.

"Good. Keep it that way. And while you're at it, find another bar to drink at after work. That one is hers."

I laugh. "What the fuck, man? You don't get to walk into my office, tell me who I can and cannot see, and order me to drink somewhere else. How the fuck did you even know I worked here?" Oh fuck, Kaylee's mouth is magical, and the fact that my dick is in her mouth while her brother is right in front of us demanding that I stay away just makes me want to fuck her that much more.

"Kaylee told me you work at a bank across the street from a bar that isn't too far from her office. It didn't take a genius. Just keep your word. Just because we're not friends anymore doesn't make her free game." He turns and leaves, slamming my office door loudly.

"Fuck," I mumble, scooting my chair back enough to see her head bobbing up and down. "Just FYI, when you're sucking my dick and someone comes in, for the love of God, stop! I almost came three times while he was in here."

She pulls back, giggling and smiling.

I shake my head. "What the fuck am I going to do with you?" My hands cup her cheeks, and I pull her mouth up to mine. Now, how to fix this little problem I have since Kyle had to storm in here and ruin my personal private time?

"Go lock the door," I tell her, pulling back.

She walks around my desk and over to the door, locking it.

"Now, come back here."

Her cheeks flush pink, but she does as I say. She comes to a stop in front of me. I slide my hands up her gray knee-length skirt and hook my fingers around her panties, yanking them down. They fall around her feet.

I push my pants down further, not wanting her to hurt herself on my belt buckle, then I pull her back to me. As we kiss, I push her skirt up her thighs until I have it over her hips. I place my hands on her ass, picking her up and setting her onto my lap. Slipping a hand between us, I guide myself into her. She sucks in a loud breath the moment we're connected, and her head falls back. I nip her throat with my teeth as I lift her up slightly and let her fall back. The motion is slow, but deliberate, and it only takes the two of us minutes before we're shattering around one another.

AFTER WORK, I'm sitting at my usual bar and my buddy, Craig, walks in. He claims the barstool next to mine. He slouches down, tosses down his money, and flags down the bartender, ordering a beer.

"Have a rough day?" I ask, tipping back my glass of bourbon.

He nods. "I swear, if I have to listen to one more excuse about why someone is late with their payment, I'm going to snap."

I laugh. Craig works in the loans department, and he has the unfortunate job of calling up people who are late with their payments. Not the best job. You either get a long list of excuses or you get angry people who just cuss you up one side and down the other. Either way, every day is rough for him.

"So, what happened the other night with blondie?"

I smile and take a deep breath. "I've kind of been seeing her ever since," I admit.

"Score!" he cheers me on. "At least one of us has a way to forget about our shitty jobs."

I nod. "Yeah, but there's been a complication."

He frowns. "What kind of complication?"

I give him the brief rundown of how Kaylee and I have snuck around behind her brother's back since we were a couple of stupid teenagers, how we've started doing it again since I'm no longer friends with her brother, and how he came into my office uninvited today to tell me to find a new bar.

He whistles as he picks up his beer and takes a swig. "That sucks, man."

I nod. "So what do you think I should do? Should I keep doing what I'm doing? Should I confront her brother and tell him how it is?"

He shrugs. "That's a tough one. I mean, I don't think I would go outing you two to her brother. That's her family, man. Not yours. You may think you're doing the right thing, but she's the one that will take the heat, you know?"

I nod. He's right. But can I keep doing what I'm doing, even after he came to my office today?

"You could, I don't know, call things off with her if it bothers you that much," he suggests.

I want to laugh. "You saw her that night, right?"

He nods. "Oh, yeah. She's nice to look at," he says around a smile.

I nod. "Right, so add that to the best sex of your life. Could you walk away from that?"

He laughs, causing little wrinkles to form around his eyes. "Nah, I don't think I could."

My phone chimes on the bar, and I pick it up to read the message.

Kaylee: *Working late tonight so I won't make it to the bar. If you get bored there without me, you could always bring me a drink to the office. *winky face.*

I raise my hand, and when the bartender makes his way over, I cash out. "Gotta go," I tell Craig.

"Booty call hitting you up?" he asks, amused.

"Something like that." I get up and pull my coat on while patting him on the back. Then I make my way outside and around the corner. I pick up a six-pack and find her office a block away. The sign on the window says Closed, but when I try the door, it's unlocked.

"Hello?" I say, trying to see through the dark room Another door opens, and the front of the dark office floods with light as Kaylee comes out.

She smiles. "Hey, you made it."

"And I brought beer," I say, holding up the six-pack.

"My man." She motions me forward into her office.

"Shouldn't you lock that door? I mean, anyone can just walk in."

"Good idea." She rushes to the door, locks it, and then comes back to join me in her office.

I set the six-pack down on her desk and open a bottle, handing it to her before grabbing one for myself. "So, what are you working on?"

"Um." She tips the bottle up and takes a swig. "I just landed a big job for a local hotel here in town. I'm going to be updating all their guest rooms. What do you think of this?" she asks, motioning me over to some kind of light-up table. I look down and find a series of drawings and fabric samples.

"Do you like the colors?"

"Sure."

She rolls her eyes. "I was going for more of a classy vibe. I hate those hotel rooms that nearly make you go blind when you walk in. You know the bright-colored blankets with their funky designs. The matching drapes. The weird-ass carpet. Ugh. I thought this would appeal to more people just being clean and classy. The carpet is stain-resistant, but with it being a brownish color, it will hide a lot of the foot traffic. Crisp white sheets so guests feel secure about sleeping on clean linens. And then a khaki-colored duvet to pull it together. Keeping the room neutral like this will also leave plenty of room to brighten the place up with any color throw pillows. Of course, the hotel has their own furniture supplier that allows them to get items discounted, so any furniture I choose has to come from them and not my usual antique sweep, but hey, it's a job, right?"

The whole time she's been rambling on, I haven't listened to a word she said. It's all a mess of throw pillows, duvets, and drapes. But what I see is what is draws me in. There is passion in her eyes as she talks about this job. There's excitement and wonder. Her eyes are lit up and sparkling. Her body is turned toward her work, but her back is straight because she's confident in her selection. Somehow, the little girl I grew up with, the one who blossomed into a teenage girl next to me, is now a full-grown adult who is sure of herself and her talents. It's a major turn-on to listen to her talk about shit I wouldn't care about otherwise.

I put my beer down and move toward her. "Did you know that listening to you talk design is a major turn-on?"

She smiles. "It is? Hmmm, maybe I should do it some more. Bolster," she says, wrapping her arms around my neck. "Alcove," she whispers as I run the tip of my nose up her neck. "Credenza."

Hearing her say all these words that I don't understand, I'm filled with the overwhelming need to kiss her. I press my lips to hers and don't hold back.

SEVEN
KAYLEE

"Will you please talk to him, Mom?" I ask as the two of us have lunch at her favorite Italian restaurant.

"I will try, but I don't see a point," she says, picking up her hot tea and taking a sip. "You know your brother. When his mind is made up, it's made up and there is no changing it."

I roll my eyes. "Don't you think this has all gotten a little out of hand? I mean, don't you miss Landon?"

"Of course I do. He was like one of my children."

"Okay, then you don't think that Kyle is being a little bit of an ass about this?" For lack of a better word.

"That's not for me to say, Kaylee. Who knows what really happened between those two."

"Okay, fine. You're right. Nobody but those two know for sure. But he shouldn't be breaking into Landon's office to tell him to stay away from me. We're adults and not doing anything wrong. I get to choose who I hang out with. Not Kyle."

She points at me. "That is something I agree on. I will talk to him."

"Talk to who?" Kyle asks, walking in and pressing a kiss to the top of Mom's head as he sits across from me.

"You," I say, looking directly at him.

"Me?" he questions, looking surprised. "What did I do?"

"Um, I don't know. Maybe bang down Landon's office door to tell him to stay away from me and to find a new bar because the one he goes to just happens to be mine?"

He rolls his eyes. "Is that what he said?" he asks, waving his hand through the air and dismissing me completely. "He's being dramatic, as usual. I didn't bust into his office. I simply tracked him down and went to talk to him. That's all."

"So you didn't tell him to stay away from me?" I ask, knowing damn well I can't call him out completely, not without giving away my own secret.

"I may have mentioned it," he says, pushing his salad around on his plate.

"Why?"

He lets out an annoyed breath. "Seriously? The guy is a total asshole. I know for a fact. He fucked me over once, and he'll do it to you, too, if you let him. I'm only trying to protect you."

"Protect me from what exactly, Kyle?"

"Alright, enough you two," Mom says. "You're getting too loud and causing a scene." She smooths down her hair and smiles at a woman who's looking our way.

I roll my eyes, let out a long breath, and sit back in my chair as I cross my arms.

"Now, I invited my two children here for a nice lunch. Whatever fight you two are having will have to be discussed and figured out at a later time. Got that?" she asks, her eyes moving from me to Kyle and back.

"Yes, ma'am," we both say at the same time.

Lunch is awkward after that. Kyle and I listen to Mom talk about her book club, the surprise direction her favorite show has taken, and how this man from church is sending her stalker vibes and staring at her from down the pew. Kyle and I takes turns *hmm*-ing, but neither of us offer much. Mom seems happy, and after lunch, she gets up to leave, leaving the two of us alone at the table.

"Seriously, what is your problem with him?" I ask, leaning in and whispering across the table.

He leans in the same way. "I don't see why you care so much, Kaylee."

"You don't see why I care so much? He's a good guy and he's your best friend."

"No," he whispers, pointing at me. "He's not and hasn't been for ten years. Move on and get over it."

"What if I don't want to get over it?" I whisper back. "Look, if you don't want to be around him, fine. But you don't control who I hang out with. You have no say." I get up.

He gets up and comes chasing after me, whispering, "I do have a say, Kaylee! You're my little sister, and all I'm doing is trying to protect you."

We step out of the restaurant and onto the sidewalk where we can talk at a normal volume. "I'm not a child anymore, Kyle. I can protect myself."

"He's irresponsible. He takes what he wants when he wants and doesn't give a shit about anything else. This is the kind of person you want as a 'friend'?" He uses air quotes, and he knows I hate it when he does that.

"Don't say it like that," I say, wrinkling up my face.

"Like what?"

"Like you're implying we're more than friends."

"Well, are you?"

My eyes stretch wide. "No! Of course not," I lie, "but even if we were, then what?"

His mouth drops open as his back straightens. "Don't fucking go there. I didn't bend over backwards all these years to protect you from him just to have you starting up shit with him now."

I want to laugh. "Hell of a job you've been doing," I say, turning to leave.

"What's that mean?" he asks, chasing after me.

"Nothing." I shake my head and keep going. He doesn't bother to follow me. Once again, because he doesn't like the direction this conversation is going, he'd rather ignore what just went down.

I walk back to the office, and when I walk in, Andrea says, "Hey, welcome back." She gives me a warm smile.

"Mm-hmm," I mumble, walking straight to my office.

I'm setting my stuff down and plopping into my desk chair as she comes walking in.

"Want to talk about it?"

"My brother just drives me so crazy!"

She rolls her eyes. "I swear, you two get along one day and are at each other's throats the next. I can't keep up," she says, sitting across from me. "What did he do now?"

I tell her the whole story about growing up and always having a crush on my brother's best friend and about how once we were teenagers, we started sleeping together. I tell her about running into him and how we started things back up.

"Oh, so you want your brother to become friends with him again for what exactly?"

"So that when things get serious with us, he will take it a little easier."

She frowns. "Have you and this guy even talked about the next steps yet? I mean, what if he's just looking for a good time and doesn't see himself having a future with you?"

"I guess I never thought of that." I think it over. "It just... It feels like that's where we're headed, you know? Like this whole thing with us, it feels like it happened for a reason."

"So, you like... like this guy, huh?"

I smile as I picture his face.

"You have a picture?"

I giggle as I pick up my phone and pull up his Facebook page. I click on his profile picture and flip the phone around. In this picture, he's sitting beside a pool on a sunny day. He's wearing only swim shorts, with water rolling over his chest. His dark hair is pushed back, and the sun is lighting up his blue eyes.

Her mouth drops open as her eyes take him in. "Marry him. Give him children. Hell, give him anything he wants," she says with a wide smile.

"I know, right?" I look back at the picture and notice the drink he's holding in his hand. Then I think of the ways those hands have touched me, and my blood burns.

Landon is easily the hottest guy I've ever been with. On top of his good looks, he's charming, demanding, funny, and an overall good guy. Why doesn't Kyle see that? Why is he so concerned about Landon staying away from me? I mean, I've dated much worse.

"So, what do you think I should do?"

"I already told you. Marry that man!"

I laugh. "But what about my brother?"

She shrugs. "He'll get over it... one day. You guys shared a womb, he can't hate you forever."

Yeah, that's what I'm afraid of. One day. How long will that take? Are family lunches a thing of the past if I keep up this secret life I have? Will holidays be canceled because we can't be in the same room together without fighting and arguing and driving my mom crazy? Is Landon really worth all the hassle?

I look back at his picture.

Yes. Yes, he is.

"THERE SHE IS," Landon says as I meet him on the sidewalk outside of Pub and Son's Bar and Grill. He's holding his arms out at his sides, ready to welcome me with a hug.

I walk into his outstretched arms, and he squeezes me gently.

"Hey," I say with a smile, looking up at him.

"Hi, gorgeous," he replies, his hands moving up to cup my cheeks as he brings his lips down to mine. The kiss is soft and sweet but holds plenty of naughty promises for later. "Hungry?" he asks, opening the door.

"Famished," I tell him, walking in before him.

"Good. Let's get my girl fed so I can take you back to my place and have my way with you."

EIGHT

LANDON

After dinner, I take her to my place. It's nothing crazy, just a two-bedroom apartment with a living room, two bathrooms, a chef's kitchen, and a formal dining room. We ride the elevator up, and I lead her down the hall. I unlock the door and push it open, allowing her to walk in first. She steps in and walks to the center of the living room, spinning around in a circle to take it all in.

"Wow," she says while I stand off to the side, removing my coat to hang it on the wall by the door.

"It's nothing special."

Her eyes widen. "Nothing special? This is like my stupid brother's apartment. What is it with you two? Can't get women with a normal apartment so you have to go all out?" She shrugs out of her coat.

I laugh. "I've never had trouble getting women, and once I bring them home, it's hard to get them to leave. So this isn't something I do much."

She tosses her coat over the back of the couch with a smirk. "I bet that's what you tell all the girls," she says, walking closer.

I take her in, from the top of her blond head to the tips of her pink-painted toes that I can see through her open-toed shoes. "Caught me," I joke as she wraps her arms around my waist. "Why don't you get comfortable and I'll go find us some champagne and some strawberries?"

She throws her head back and laughs. "Oh, you're too good. Seriously, you do this with every girl?"

I smirk. "The rug in front of the fireplace is very comfy. Try it out," I suggest, walking into the kitchen. I'm a big smoothie guy so I know I have plenty of fresh strawberries in the fridge. I'm not so sure about the champagne though. I search through the fridge and wine cooler but come up empty. I grab a bottle of white wine instead. I pour two glasses and wash and plate the strawberries. When I walk back into the living room, she's sitting on the rug, slipping out of her shoes. I hand her the wine and set the plate down before hitting the button that sets the fire blazing. I sit at her side and pick up my glass. "Ran short on champagne, so wine will have to do."

She smiles. "Too many dates this week, huh?"

"Yeah, Mandy was an alcoholic. I couldn't keep any bottle away from her," I joke. As much time as I've been spending with her, she should know there is no time for any other women.

She laughs and playfully smacks my arm. "So this is your thing, huh? You take women to some fancy restaurant and woo them, then bring them back to your nice apartment, offer them a romantic fire, strawberries, and alcohol?"

I shrug. "It's not bad, right?"

She agrees with a nod as she sips her wine.

"So, what's your thing?"

"My thing?"

"Yeah, what do you do that lets the guy know that you like them?"

"Oh, let's see," she says thinking. "Well, there's different scenarios. Like, if we're in a club and start dancing..." She stands and motions for me to stand with her. I do and she turns her back to me. "Now, dance."

I place my hand on her hip as I move from side to side. It's not close enough, though, so she steps back until my groin is pressed against her ass. After a moment, my dick twitches with excitement, and she looks over her shoulder with a sexy little smile.

Her eyes are downcast, but they move up slowly, locking on mine from beneath her thick lashes. "So uh, your place or mine?" she asks, spinning around and wrapping her arms around my neck. Her eyes are back on mine, and the corners of her mouth tip upward.

"That's pretty good," I say, laughing. I step back and take a seat. "It works all the time?"

"Every time I've done it," she says, sitting back down. "Of course, if it's just some cute guy in the coffee shop and I want his number, I'll just accidentally bump into him from behind. Then I'll spin around, acting all embarrassed and apologize. If the guys makes conversation, I know he's interested. If he accepts my apology and takes off, I know he's not." She picks up a strawberry and takes a bite.

"And what do you do if you've already lured the guy to your house?"

"Oh, that one is simple," she says, putting the strawberry down. "It goes something like this." She moves in and presses her lips to mine. It's a soft kiss, slow, simmering. She's holding back just slightly, just enough to make me want more.

My hand moves up, tangling into her hair as I pull her closer. The closer she gets, the deeper our kiss gets. The deeper our kiss gets, the more I pull her toward me until she's on my lap, straddling me. I roll until I have her trapped beneath me. I pull back enough to move my lips to her neck and she whispers, "Works every time."

I smile as I scrape my teeth against that sensitive spot on her neck, and her eyes flutter closed as her lips part and her breathing picks up. From there, we slowly strip off one another's clothes until there's nothing left. I sink into her slowly, causing us both to let out a relieved moan. The rest of the night, we don't part.

MY ALARM WAKES me in the morning, and I roll over to find her in my bed. I shut off the alarm. Her back is to me, so I wrap my arm around her waist and kiss her shoulder. She stretches as she backs up against me.

"What time is it?"

"Six," I answer, kissing across her back and up to her neck. "I have to get ready for work."

She nods once. "Yeah, I should probably get home."

"Want to take a shower with me and I'll drop you off on my way to the office?"

She agrees, and we both get up and head to the bathroom. The toilet is in its own little room, so she goes in there while I turn on the water to get it warmed up. When she comes out, I go in to relieve myself. When I step out, she's already in the shower. Watching her through the fogged-up glass has my body coming alive again. Fuck, when I'm around her, I feel like a teenager again. I have absolutely no control over my body around her. It's funny how different she is compared to the other women I've been with. I never let any of them have this much power over me. I've never had a craving for them, not like I do her. I wonder why things are so different with her, but I don't give myself time to think it through as I'm climbing into the shower with her and pulling her against me.

After our round in the shower, we both get dressed and gather our things to head out. She climbs into the passenger seat of the car, and I drive her home before going to work myself. When I get to work, instead of going straight inside the bank, I head to the Starbucks next door. I order a coffee and some kind of breakfast sandwich and take them both back to my desk. While I eat, I go through emails and return a few. When I'm done eating, I wad the paper up and toss it into the trash. That's when my door opens and Reese Silverstone walks in. She's wearing one of her famous skirt and jacket combos today. Her outfit's all black and the jacket is open, showing off her yellow blouse and narrow waist. Her dark hair is shoulder-length and curled in a messy sort of way. Her legs look long in that skirt, and the heels are sky high, giving them a shapely appearance.

Reese and I have a long-running arrangement for hooking up when we're both single. Recently, she's been in a relationship with the boss's son, but if she's coming in here, something must have happened.

She rounds my desk and sits her ass on the edge, facing me.

"Good morning."

She smiles. "Good morning."

"What's brought you into my office?" I ask, leaning back in my chair.

She smiles and tilts her head to study me. "I have a feeling you already know."

"Boss's son not working out?"

She rolls her eyes and scoffs. "Not in the slightest. What do you say we have a private meeting for old time's sake?" She offers up a sexy smile as she bats her lashes.

"I'd love to, but you seem to have caught me at a bad time."

Her brows pull together slightly, but then she realizes that she's supposed to remain emotionless, and she wipes it away. "Are you referring to your workload, or have you met someone since the last time we talked?"

I nod my head. "There is a woman I've been seeing."

She straightens her back. "Is it serious?"

"I'm not sure yet." I look up at her. "I'd like it to be, but it's still too early to tell."

She cocks one eyebrow. "Oh, so the great and legendary Landon Styles has been brought to his knees by a woman... finally?"

I laugh and shrug. "We'll see."

She pushes away from my desk as she heads for the door. "I want to meet this woman. If she's managed to get you to commit, she must be as legendary as you are," she says, walking out of my office and leaving me alone.

It doesn't occur to me until later when Craig is asking me to go on a double date with him and a girl he met—her sister's in town and needs a date too—that Kaylee and I haven't had the talk yet. I've been turning women away without knowing if she's doing the same thing with men. Is she still seeing other people, thinking that she and I are just messing around like we did in high school? That thought makes acid bubble in my stomach. I don't like to think of her with other men. The acid boils over and comes scorching up my throat. I have to grab a Tums from inside my desk drawer and pop it into my mouth to extinguish the burn.

I sit back in my chair, wondering how to go about bringing up this subject. It's important not to force her into anything, but it is something that we both need to know and agree to. I guess if she still sees me as just someone to screw, there's a chance that she doesn't see me being in the picture for very long. However, when I picture my future, she's right by my side. I don't know how that can work with her brother, but it's something I'm willing to try. Maybe I do need to address him, tell him I'm sorry for any wrongdoings he thinks I've done, and try to smooth things over. If I can get him on my side, maybe my future with Kaylee won't be so hard to achieve at all—or it could make things harder, just like it did in high school.

But there's one very big difference this time around.

We're not in high school anymore. We're both adults who know what we want. We're allowed to make our own choices. And if I want her and she wants me, Kyle isn't enough to stop it. Not on my side of things anyway. Her? He might just be. They've always been very close while still having all the usual fights and competitions that a brother and sister do. Everyone around them thinks they hate each other, but they share a bond like nobody else, and it's just the way they do things. It doesn't matter how pissed off Kyle is at his sister. He will always run to her in her time of need. But now, I want to be that for her, and he has to willingly give up his role as knight in shining armor. After playing that role his whole life, it won't be all that easy to give up, especially when he's still trying to save her from someone like me.

I pick up my phone and send Kaylee a text.

Landon: *What's your brother's contact info?*

She texts back almost immediately.

Kaylee: *Why?*

Landon: *I think it's time we put all of this shit behind us.*

My phone chimes moments later with the info. Name, address, cell phone, house phone, office phone, and address. I take a deep breath and push myself away from my desk. This conversation isn't one to be had over the phone. It's a face-to-face kind of deal.

NINE
KAYLEE

I'm stunned when I see Landon's message. I can't believe he's willing to talk to my brother again. It just goes to show you how much more grown-up he is than Kyle. A part of me wonders why he's feeling the need to bring this little of fight of theirs to an end after all these years. I can't help but feel like it has something to do with me, and I pray that he doesn't bring me into their conversation. Not yet.

I know my brother, and getting news of Landon and me being together will sit better if he hears it coming from me. An outside source will only anger him more and make him wonder why I couldn't tell him myself. But I guess I could be wrong about why Landon is wanting to fix his relationship with my brother. It may have nothing to do with me—or it could just be that being around me has made him miss his old best friend.

We still haven't had the talk yet. On one hand, that seems normal. We haven't been seeing one another for very long, but at the same time, I know what I want already. Shouldn't he? Landon has always held a spot in my heart. He's been a friend, a protector, a lover. But recently, he feels like so much more. I can't help but wonder if this thing we're doing is one-sided. Is he thinking that we're just doing what we've always done? Hook up until someone better comes along, then we call it off?

These last ten years, I've been with my fair share of men, and none of them have compared to what Landon and I have now. None of them have been able to make me laugh with just a look. None of them have been able to take away every negative emotion with just one sentence. None of them have held me in their bed while I thought about how badly I wish I could stop time to lie there for eternity. None of them but Landon. That has to mean something. I know it does.

But does it mean that I'm in love with him? I love him, I know that much. I always have. He's been in my life too long not to. But there is a very big difference in being in love with someone and loving someone. I guess I need to look inside myself and figure this thing out. But first, we need to figure out what it is we're doing in the first place. I'd hate to be falling in love if he's just looking for a good time a couple nights a week.

Andrea walks into my office. "Hey, the contractor you hired for the hotel is on the phone."

"Okay, thanks," I say, rushing to my desk and picking up the call.

We go over everything one thing at a time before he starts on the job tomorrow. I confirm carpeting for the rooms, tile for the bathrooms, and the vanities and wallpaper selections with a series of identification numbers. Once our numbers match, the call ends, and I'm filled with excitement. The hotel has three hundred and six guest rooms, and the contractor can only do one floor at a time. Once one floor is finished, I go in with design. Then we move on to the next floor so the finished rooms can start to be rented out.

This is my first hotel. So far, I've always done private work in homes or apartments. This is my first business, and I'm hoping it opens me up to a whole new clientele. When I'm able to get my excitement to simmer down, I go back to the sketch I'm working on for a meeting this afternoon. I'm so busy that the day flies by, and

Landon and my brother's meeting is the last thing on my mind—that is, until my day is over and it's time to go home.

I get to the apartment and strip out of my work clothes first thing. I start a load of laundry and move to the kitchen to find some dinner. My head is full of questions about how their impromptu meeting went, but I resist the urge to call. I have a feeling that Landon will call or come by when they're finished.

My kitchen is completely empty, so I end up having to run out to grab some food. I pull on a pair of boots with my leggings and oversized sweatshirt and grab my purse. I walk a few blocks down to my favorite bar and grill and stop at the bar to grab a menu. I look it over, settling on a burger, fries, and a side salad. I place my order with the bartender, and he takes it back to the kitchen. While I wait for it to cook, I order a beer.

Now that I have nothing keeping my attention, I start looking around the bar for any friendly faces. In the back corner, sitting in a booth, are Kyle and Landon. They're talking and laughing over their drinks, and I smile as I watch them. It's like I've been shot back ten years in the past, and we're not all pushing thirty but pushing for our independence. I take my beer as I stand and walk over.

"Well, well, well. Look what we have here," I say, slipping into the booth next to Kyle. The mental tug of war it took to decide where to sit is nearly too much. Hopefully, this isn't a thing too much longer. Until I know for sure that everything is out in the open, Landon is just a friend who I've recently been in touch with again.

"What's going on, guys?" I ask, looking from Kyle to Landon and back.

"Oh, we're just enjoying a few drinks and catching up," Kyle says.

"Catching up, huh?" I flash Landon a smirk. "What brought all this on?"

"Landon came by today, and I threatened to throw him off my balcony," Kyle says.

Landon jumps in. "But then he realized that he couldn't so I made him hear me out," he finishes, making Kyle laugh.

"Good. So everything is fixed now?" I ask, taking a sip of my beer.

The two guys nod. "Everything is fine, and now I have someone to join pool league with me," Kyle says.

"Hey! I thought I was joining with you?"

He snorts and rolls his eyes. "Someone good."

"Someone good," I mock, making Landon laugh.

A waiter brings my food over, and I finish off my beer and stand up. "Well, I guess I'm going to go home and eat. Call me," I say to nobody, or both of them, but I'm learning more toward one than the other. No offense, Kyle.

When I get home, I take my food to the couch to eat while I watch TV. The food is good and the show keeps my attention, but in the back of my mind, I can't stop wondering what was said that finally got those two back together.

After dinner, I take a shower and get ready for bed. I'm in the kitchen fixing a cup of tea in my pajamas when someone knocks on my door. I drop everything I'm doing and run to answer it. I'm not sure which one of them is behind it, but I know it's one of them. I pull the door open and find Landon leaning against the doorframe with a smile and bloodshot eyes.

"There's my girl," he says, his hands grabbing my hips as he pulls me toward him for a kiss. We kiss for only a moment before I'm stepping back and pulling him inside.

"What happened? I'm dying to know." I lock the door behind us and go into the kitchen. I lean against the counter and pick up my cup, taking a sip before setting it back down. He walks into the kitchen, looking a little wobbly, but his smirk is still in place.

"Are you drunk?" I ask, crossing my arms over my chest as I try my best to hold back my smile.

"Maybe," he says, making his way over to me as he tugs off his jacket. He tosses it onto the island just as he pulls me against him. He kisses me softly, and I can taste the bourbon on his lips. He breathes me in. "Fuck, I've missed you." His hands find my ass, and he squeezes me as his mouth moves down to my neck. "I missed having the taste of you on my lips today."

My eyes flutter closed as he kisses and nibbles my neck and ear. "And this hair." His hands move up to tangle in the wet mess. "I've missed the feeling of it wrapped around my fingers." He nips at my lip forcefully. It's not painful, but it's just enough to let me know how serious he is, and it makes my muscles tighten in excitement. "And these legs." His hands drop down to my thighs, slowly working their way up to my hips. "I've dreamed of having them wrapped around my hips all fucking day." His hands land on my ass, and he picks me up, pulling me against him. My legs automatically wrap around his hips while my arms snake around his neck. "You have no idea how badly I crave you, Kaylee," he whispers, bringing his lips back to mine.

Five minutes ago, the only thing I could think of was how Landon and Kyle are now getting along, but it's the furthest thing from my mind now. Now all I can think about is how long I have to wait until he's sliding back inside me, claiming me, owning me.

"Take me to bed, Landon," I whisper against his lips, and he doesn't say a word as he spins us around and carries me to my room.

NOT MUCH TALKING was done last night. Well, not the talking we needed to figure out where things are heading with us or how he managed to get Kyle to forgive him. There was plenty of talking, though, and all of it is still fresh in my mind and making goosebumps prickle my skin as I remember it in my shower the following morning.

While I'm washing my hair, Landon is standing at the sink, brushing his teeth with the extra toothbrush I keep and getting his clothes on to get to work.

"So, are you going to tell me how you managed to talk Kyle into forgiving you?"

"Still thinking about that, huh?" he asks, sounding amused.

"Thinking about it? I'm dying to know. What was the magic word?"

He laughs. "There was no magic word. I simply told him that I wouldn't leave until we had everything out in the open and fixed. I told him that it meant a lot to you, and if I was willing to do it, he should be, too, given that you're his sister. So, we sat down and talked things out."

"Did you tell him that we're sleeping together now? Or that we did in the past?"

He chuckles. "Oh, hell no. I'm trying to make him forgive me, not hate me more."

"So we're still a secret then."

"That we are. I figured we needed to talk about some things before anything like that came out."

I shut off the water and climb out, wrapping a towel around me. "So, when do you want to do that?"

"What? Talk?" he asks, tightening his tie.

I nod.

He shrugs. "Whenever you're ready. In the meantime, I'm more than happy to continue doing what we've been doing." He pulls me against him and plants a kiss to my lips. The kiss is soft but strong. When he pulls back, he's wearing a sexy smile. "I have to get to work. I'll call you later?"

I smile and nod, watching him walk out.

TEN

LANDON

I'm not sure if I should be happy that Kyle and I are friends again, or if I should feel bad for sneaking behind his back to fuck his sister. Truth be told, though, I feel a little of both. I never would let myself admit it, but I've been missing Kyle since we went our own ways for college. I've made a lot of friends since then but none as close to me as Kyle was back then. Now that he's back, it's almost like we're just a couple of kids again. I want to cut class and go get drunk. I want to hit up parties with my buddy by my side. I want to cause trouble, the way he did back then. But we're adults now, and our friendship has to be a little different.

At the same time, I also want to explore my options with Kaylee. Before, she and I couldn't get enough time for our hookup sessions to go much further than that. Now, we have nothing but time, and every time we're together, I get a little more addicted to her. There's only one thing that I know for sure. I'm nowhere near ready to let her go again. I don't know where that leaves us or where it could take us, but I know she's my end game.

I plan a date night for the two of us at a fancy restaurant here in town. That will give us the time we need to figure things out. I send her a text telling her I'll pick her up at seven, and then I get back to work. Throughout the day, I get several messages from Kaylee and Kyle. Kaylee is looking forward to our date and is trying to talk me into revealing my plans, and Kyle seems to be on the same page I am. He's happy we've reconciled, and now, he wants to make up for lost time. He's offering dinner and drinks, sports bars, or just watching a fight at his place and ordering in. I decline his offer and promise to make it up to him, telling him I have a special lady who I'm taking out tonight. He isn't happy with my answer, but he lets it go, probably feeling like the friendship is still too new to be guilting me into doing anything yet.

But I do want to better my friendship with Kyle. He's the key to getting what I want: Kaylee.

WHEN WORK ENDS for the day, I go home to shower, shave, and get ready for our dinner date. I dress in a nice black suit with a white dress shirt and a black tie. I comb my dark hair and style it into place. Then I add the cologne that Kaylee loves. On my way to pick her up, I stop and pick up a bouquet of flowers, and I take them to her door. I raise my hand to knock but hear voices on the other side of the door that makes me stop. It's Kaylee and Kyle. I freeze, listening as they talk.

"Come on, Lee Lee. This fight is supposed to be epic. Call your date off," Kyle says.

"I'm not calling off my date because you don't have anyone to play with tonight. Call one of your friends... or call Landon and see what he's up to tonight," Kaylee says.

"I already tried. Everyone has plans."

She laughs. "Well, so do I. Now, my date will be here any minute. I really need you to leave so I can finish getting dressed."

"Maybe I should stick around and meet this guy. Where'd you meet him at anyway?"

"His name is James. He's the contractor who I hired on to do the work at the hotel. And it's not a date date. It's a business meeting, and I can't miss it. It will make me look like a horrible businesswoman."

Kyle scoffs. "Fine, go do your work. I guess I'll go home and be alone."

She giggles. "Maybe you need to find yourself a woman, Kyle. Then you wouldn't have this problem."

I hear him repeat the same thing she said but in his high-pitched, mocking voice. I hear his steps get closer to the door, and I rush down the hall and around the corner so he doesn't see me.

The door opens. "See ya tomorrow, sis," he says.

"Love you," she calls after him.

"Love ya too," he replies, shutting the door. His footsteps are silent on the carpeted floor of the hallway, but I hear the elevator ding and the door opens then closes. I peek around the corner and find the hallway empty. With a long breath, I rush back to her door and let myself in, locking it behind me so he can't come back in without us knowing.

"Hey," I call out from the living room.

"Hey," she says, sticking her head out of her room. "I'll be a few more minutes. You're lucky. You just missed Kyle."

"Yeah, I was about to knock on the door when I heard you two talking. I had to hide around the corner until he left."

Her bedroom door opens now, and she comes walking out in a black dress that hugs her hard little body. Her heels are high, giving her legs a nice shape.

"These are for you," I say, holding out the flowers.

She smiles and her eyes light up. "They're beautiful. You didn't have to do that."

"What kind of guy would I be if I showed up for a date without flowers?"

She giggles but takes them to the kitchen. I hear the water turn on, and moments later, she's back with the flowers in a vase. She sets them on the entryway table before grabbing her coat and pulling it on.

"So, where are we going?"

I laugh. "To eat. Are you ready?"

She rolls her eyes, but her smile doesn't falter as she grabs her purse and keys.

She shows me out and locks the door behind us. I lead her to the elevator and we ride it down. I take her to my awaiting car and open the door. She slides into her seat, and I take my place behind the wheel. The ride to the restaurant is quiet, but we talk briefly about the day we've each had. At our table, after we're given a glass of wine and while we're waiting for our meal, I decide it would be a good time to bring up the subject of our relationship.

"So, I think we have some things to discuss."

She takes a sip of her wine. "I believe we do," she agrees.

"Do you want to go first, or shall I?" I ask, feeling the nerves rising up inside of my chest. It's making my heart race and my breath quicken.

She motions for me to continue, so I raise my glass of wine and take a sip.

"Kaylee, I've had an amazing time with you these last couple of weeks, and I've been thinking more and more about where this relationship of ours could be heading. I didn't know if I should treat it the same way we did in high school or if this was more serious. So I had to look inside myself. The one thing that's different from high school is that we're older and can make our own choices. That's why I wanted to work things out with Kyle. My hope is that if we become friends again, he'll be a little more inclined to listen to our side of things. Because, Kaylee, I don't want to make the same mistake we made in high school. I screwed up and let you walk away once. I don't want to do it again."

Her eyes are wide as she listens, taking in every word. "Are you saying that you want to date? Like seriously date?"

I nod once. "Date, get married, have kids. I want all of it, and I only want it with you."

She lets out a nervous giggle. "I'm glad to hear you say that, Landon, because I feel the same way. I feel like we lost so much time. It's like we should already be married. But I have no problems starting over with you."

I reach across the table and take her hand in mine. "And I understand if you want to keep things between us for now while I continue building my friendship back up with your brother. Plus, no sense in jumping the gun or rushing into anything. We can take our time, get to know one another on a more personal level instead of just... in bed." I laugh and she giggles.

"I like the sound of that," she replies, cheeks flushing pink under my stare.

Dinner is great. Conversation is never lacking; the food is delicious, and the drinks are smooth. I pay the bill, and we leave the restaurant behind us as I drive her home. I pull up in front of her building and lean in for a kiss goodnight. She kisses me long and slow, and by the end, there is so much more on my mind. She pulls back, and her eyes have darkened. She bats her lashes and gives me that shy smile. I can tell she's only moments away from asking me to come up, but then her eyes dash off in the opposite direction.

"Is that Kyle's car?" she asks, squinting into the darkness.

I look. It does look like the one he drives. "It might be."

"I better get up there before he realizes I'm not there and comes back down here to catch us." She gives me one more quick peck and jumps out, rushing to the door of the building. I back up and pull out onto the street, driving myself home.

When I get to my quiet, lonely apartment, I pour a drink and take it back to my bedroom with me. I set it on the dresser, and I begin to take off my jacket, tie, and shirt. My phone chimes, and I see it's a text from Kyle.

Kyle: *How'd the date go?*

Landon: *Great. She's a lovely girl. I can't wait for you to meet her one of these days.*

I grab my drink and phone and take it to the bathroom to get ready for bed. I strip out of my pants, socks, and shoes and pull on a pair of sweatpants. My phone chimes again.

Kyle: *You know what we should do? Boozie movie night like we used to. Remember how fun that was with the three of us?*

Landon: *Yeah, why don't you two come to my place tomorrow night? I have a huge TV.*

Kyle: *Awesome. I'll get the booze and Lee Lee can bring the food.*

I wash my face and brush my teeth before climbing into bed. I never thought about how hard it will be to keep my hands and feelings to myself with Kyle around. I guess I'll find out how hard it is tomorrow. I refuse to out us before we even get started.

I lie in bed and force my eyes to close, but behind them, I see Kaylee. From the time we were just a couple of kids, up through high school, and to now, she's always been more special to me than I could understand. Now I know why. She isn't just another girl. She isn't a childhood friend or my best friend's twin sister. She's the woman I'm supposed to marry, the woman I spend my life with. Now the only challenge is figuring out how to make that happen.

ELEVEN

KAYLEE

The elevator door opens and Kyle is inside, ready to step off. He looks up, finding me trying to get on. "Oh, hey. You just now getting home?"

"Yep," I say, stepping into the elevator and standing at his side. "What brought you back?"

"I think I left my phone in your kitchen, but the door was locked, and I don't have my key to get in. Care if I check?"

"Of course not," I reply just as the door opens and I step off, leading the way. I unlock the door and we both go in.

"Nice flowers. Your date buy them for you?"

I look over my shoulder. "Yes, but it wasn't a date. It was more of a 'thank you for hiring my company' present." I smile, hoping that I'm selling the lie. I feel guilty about lying to Kyle, but the truth is that I'm not ready to let anyone into this new relationship just yet, especially not him with his and Landon's recent rekindling of their friendship.

"A dozen long-stemmed red roses seem like a little more than a thank you," he points out, walking into the kitchen.

I follow him in and get to work on making a cup of tea for bed. He finds his phone on the island, and he checks it before slipping it into his pocket. "You know what would be fun now that Landon and I are friends again?"

"What's that?" I ask, dipping the tea bag into the hot water.

"Boozie movie night. What do you think?"

I force a smile. "Yeah, that would be fun," I lie. Not being able to touch, cuddle, or kiss Landon during a movie sounds almost painful, but if it's what needs to be done, so be it.

He smiles. "Okay, cool. I'll run the idea by him. I'll bring the booze and you bring the food?"

I nod, agreeing. "Sounds great. Now, don't take this personally, but get the hell out. It's late, I'm tired, and I have too much work to do in the morning."

He chuckles at my bluntness but heads for the door. "Night, sis."

"Night, bro," I say, changing my voice to mock him.

When he shuts the door behind him, I lock it and turn off the lights as I make my way to my room. I set my tea down on the bedside table and strip out of my dress and into my pajamas. I crawl into bed and turn on the TV for noise as I scroll around on my phone and drink my tea. I sigh, wishing that Landon could've come home with me tonight, but there will always be tomorrow night and the next and the next.

"ARE YOU SURE YOU GOT EVERYTHING?" Kyle asks over the phone as I load everything into the car to head to Landon's for our movie night.

"Yes, I have pizza, cheesy bread, wings, popcorn, and candy. I have it all. Now, send me the address. I'm climbing behind the wheel now."

I don't need his address, but if I didn't ask, Kyle would wonder how I knew. This way saves time. A little while later, I'm carrying everything up to Landon's apartment. I knock on the door, and Landon pulls it open with a smile. "Hey," he says, quickly leaning in to kiss me. He pulls back just as fast. "Kyle, Kaylee is here," he shouts into the living room.

"Cool. Now we can eat," he says, rushing up to me and taking a few of the things from my hands. He sets everything on the coffee table before picking up the remote and getting the movie started.

"You want a drink?" Landon asks, pointing at me.

"Thank you," I say with a nod of my head as I slip out of my coat.

Kyle is already sitting on one end of the sofa, eyes glued to the TV above the fireplace. I take the seat in the middle, hoping and praying I'll be able to keep my hands off of Landon. When he comes back into the room, he turns off the lights so the room is only lit up by the glow of the fire burning and the blue light of the TV. He sits next to me and hands me a beer.

Kyle is already digging into the pizza. He puts a little of everything on a plate and passes it to me, which I hand over to Landon. When we all have our food, we focus on the TV and the movie playing before us. A little while in, my eyes glance from Kyle, whose eyes don't seem to be moving from the screen, to Landon, who looks just as uncomfortable as I feel. His eyes are moving from the TV, to the fire, to me, and back. He sets his hand between us, and I see his fingers twitch like he wants to take my hand but has to stop himself.

I let out a deep breath and sink into the couch, trying to settle myself. By the end of the movie, I'm not even sure what I've watched because I didn't pay a bit of attention to it. All I know is that I'm ready for Kyle to leave so I can be normal with my boyfriend again.

Boyfriend?

That's the first time I've ever thought of him that way. I like it. I have a boyfriend. Landon is my boyfriend. I smile to myself.

"Happy the movie is over?" Kyle asks, looking at me.

It's only now I notice the credits rolling up the screen. "Oh, sorry. Nah, I was just thinking about something Andrea said at work today. You know me, always in my own little world."

"You guys want to watch another one?" Kyle asks.

Landon and I both jump to deny him. "I have an early day tomorrow," Landon says.

"Yeah, and I still have some sketches to finish up before an early morning appointment, so I need to get home."

Kyle scoffs. "Man, look who's getting old."

I stick my tongue out at him but scoot up to sit on the edge of the couch to clean up. Kyle gets up and retrieves his movie, then turns to both of us. "Need help cleaning up?"

"I'll be fine," I say, closing the lids on the boxes.

"I'll help," Landon says, taking a pile of empty beer bottles and standing up to walk to the kitchen.

"Alright, good night, sis," Kyle says, dipping down to hug me, "and good night, bro." He gives Landon a head nod.

Landon walks him to the door, and I stand to take things to the kitchen. In the kitchen, we're both alone. He drops the bottles into the trash, and I set the pizza boxes on the island. When he turns around, his eyes land on mine and we both freeze.

"That was harder than I thought," he says, taking a step closer.

"What?" I ask.

"Keeping my hands off you." He closes the distance between us and presses his lips to mine as his hands draw me closer against his body.

"Hey, guys. Forgot my—"

We pull apart quickly just seconds before Kyle comes into view.

"Phone," he finishes. He looks at us with his brows pulled together. "Everything okay?"

"Yeah," I say, nodding. "We were just talking about how I should have gotten pizza from the place around the corner."

"It's my favorite," Landon adds on.

"Oh," Kyle says, turning and heading back to the couch. "Well, next time." He grabs his phone off the table, slipping it into his pocket.

"You seriously need a leash for that phone, you know?" I joke, walking over to the table and gathering up more of our mess.

He laughs. "You're telling me. I lose this thing about twenty times a day. Night, guys." He walks out, and this time, Landon walks over to the door and locks it.

I pick up the rest of our mess and take it to the kitchen. Walking back into the living room, I find Landon on the couch. The room is still dark, and the TV is now off, so only the soft glow of the fire lights the room. He's stripped off his T-shirt and is now just lounging across the couch in his loose-fitting jeans. I walk around the couch. "Getting comfy while you still have guests?" I ask, straddling him.

His hands land on my hips. "I was hoping that you'd join me for the evening." He runs his tongue across his bottom lip, and it glistens.

"Were you now? That's a little presumptuous of you." I give him a flirty smile.

His hands on my hips tighten as he lifts his head slightly, trying to reach my mouth with his own. "What will it take to get you to stay here tonight?"

"Oh, I don't know," I say, teasing him. "Mind-numbing sex, for one." I begin to lean down, pressing a soft, featherlight kiss to his lips, but I pull back too quickly for his liking. "And maybe some coffee and breakfast in the morning." I kiss him again the same way.

"I think I can handle both of those things," he says, getting tired of my game as he sits up and captures my lips with his. His hands move up to cup my face, keeping me from pulling away, but this time, I don't want to pull away. I want to stay right where I am, with my lips pressed against his soft ones, with my tongue dancing with his, with my core pressing against his hardening cock. My mouth waters, needing more. And when he stands with me in his arms, I know I'm going to get it and everything I could ever want.

TWELVE
LANDON

Kaylee and I have been dating for three months now, and so far, we've been good about keeping things secret and covering our tracks. Every night I spend with her stretching around me is another night of happiness I get. Kyle got sent out on his first job to design and oversee the building of a hotel he recently drew up. The job is in New York, so he's one less thing to worry about when it comes to planning our dates. We meet up for lunch nearly every day unless one of us is too busy to get away. Every night is spent either at my place or hers. We have dinner and spend the rest of the night wrapped around one another. Everything has been perfect, but I have this nagging feeling. I want to take things deeper. I want her, all of her, for the rest of my life, but before we can do that, we need to break the news to Kyle.

We make a plan to have a big family dinner at her place with the two of us, Kyle, and her mom where we can break the news to them without fear of a fight breaking out in a crowded restaurant. The only thing is that Kyle won't be home for another week, and I'm dying to make her mine in every way right now. I've already bought a ring, and I've carried it in my pocket every day since, just waiting for the right moment. I've made several failed attempts at asking her, always changing my mind at the last minute. Kaylee seems perfectly happy living in the little world we've created, but I'm tired of biding my time. I want her now. I want to start living our lives now. I want our future now. I want the stress of planning a wedding. I want the excitement of our honeymoon. I want the overwhelming happiness of learning that she's carrying my child.

I've never been so sure of anything in my entire life, and that thought alone scares the shit out of me. I mean, what if I'm wrong? What if things change between us? There are a thousand what-ifs in my head, but I try not to listen to any of them because I know how sure I am of her, of us. If the two of us were never meant for one another, I wouldn't have this need to make her mine despite all that's against us.

I feel like her mom will be the easy one to convince. Kyle, on the other hand, will be a royal pain. I know because that's what he's been his entire life. Why change now? What I'm most afraid of, though, is not getting his approval. Will that make Kaylee change her mind about me? Only time will tell, and I feel like I'm holding a ticking time bomb until I know for sure.

I get to her place around six thirty, and she's already in the kitchen starting on dinner. It's nothing fancy, one of those mail-order boxes that send you everything you'll need to prepare a meal for two people. I toss my coat on the table and wash my hands to help.

"Have you figured out what we're cooking the night of the family dinner?"

She lets out a long breath and rolls her eyes. "Honestly, I have no idea. I'm not the best cook, if you can't tell." She holds up the directions for the food she's cooking. She has to follow them step by step.

"We could order in. If you place the order, I can swing by and pick it up on my way over."

She offers a small smile. "Thank you. I'm actually really nervous. I don't know how Kyle is going to take it."

"We'll just have to give him time to come around. It doesn't matter what he has to say. It's not changing my mind. I'm sure of us."

Her eyes meet mine, and I can see them glistening with tears that don't fall. "Okay," she whispers, going back to cooking.

When everything is finally done, we make our plates and take them to the living room couch to watch TV and eat. She's flipping through the channels on the TV, and suddenly, I can't wait until after our dinner next week. I can't wait one more second. So I turn to face her. "Kaylee?"

"Hmm?" she asks, not bothering to pull her eyes from the TV screen.

"Kaylee," I say again. This time, she turns her head and looks at me. "I know you're nervous about next week. I know you're afraid that your brother is going to stand in your way, but I'm not, and I don't want you to be afraid either. Because I only know one thing for sure."

Her eyes stay locked on mine.

"I love you. I've loved you since we were kids. I loved you when we'd sneak away as teenagers. I loved you when I had to stand back and watch you go off with some other guy. I loved you when we went our own separate ways for college. I've loved you these last ten years that we didn't even see one another. And no matter what your brother says next week, I'll still love you. I'll love you for the rest of my life, and I know that because I also know that you're the woman I'm supposed to spend the rest of my life with. Will you marry me?" I pull the ring from my pocket and show it to her. Her eyes stretch wide as she takes it in. Her lips part with her heavy breathing. Her eyes don't move from the ring as she stares at it and thinks it over.

Finally, her open mouth turns into a smile. "You want to marry me?"

I smile. "I do."

"I love you too," she breathes out, wrapping her arms around my neck and hugging me close. I have to catch the plate that's on my lap, the sudden movement making it slide.

"Of course I'll marry you," she says, pressing her lips to mine.

When she pulls back, I take her hand in mine and slide the ring into place. We both look at it, and she smiles as her eyes move from her hand, to me, and back.

"I can't believe this," she whispers, moving her hand to watch it catch the light.

"So, after next week when we tell your family, we can start planning a wedding. We can start planning the rest of our lives," I say, pulling her against me one more time, planting kisses along her lips, cheeks, jaw, and neck.

WHEN I WAKE in the morning, Kaylee is already out of bed. The bathroom light isn't on, and the bedroom door is closed. I hear muffled sounds coming from the kitchen. I push back the blankets and exit the room, finding her pouring coffee into her to-go mug and packing her lunch.

"Hey, why are you up so early?" I ask, resting my chin on her shoulder.

"I have a lot of work to do today. I was going to mention it to you last night, but then we got carried away celebrating and I totally forgot." She spins around and presses a kiss to my lips quickly. "Take your shower and get ready for work." One more quick kiss, and then she's pulling away from me and walking across the kitchen floor with her things in her hands. "Lock up before you leave, please?"

I nod and wave. "I'll call you later," I say just as the door closes between us.

I turn off the coffee pot and go back to the bedroom where I gather my clothes for a shower. The hot water feels good running over my body. I'm always cold in the mornings and this morning especially. I got a frosty feeling coming from Kaylee today, and I can't help but think it has something to do with that ring I put on her finger last night. She seemed excited last night, but has sleeping on it made her change her mind? She seemed like she couldn't get away from me fast enough, or maybe I'm just overthinking the whole situation. Maybe she really did need to get to work early this morning and she forgot to bring it up last night. Between the proposal and the sex we had afterward, there wasn't a whole lot of room for talking. Not that kind of talking anyway. I push my worry, doubt, and fear away and focus on what I do know. Kaylee agreed to marry me. She's wearing my ring on her finger now. And next week, everything will be out in the open. We'll be able to move on, plan our future, plan our life. That's good enough for me.

After I'm dressed and ready for work, I turn all the lights out and lock her apartment behind me as I leave. I climb behind the wheel of my car and make my way through the drive-through, getting some breakfast and coffee before going to work. I eat at my desk and complete my morning tasks, but my eyes keep falling back to the phone sitting beside me. I have the urge to text her to see if everything is alright, but I hold it back. I don't want to be overbearing or distracting if she's really busy like she claimed she would be. I shake the thoughts from my head and bury myself deeper in work.

The day drags by, and I manage to make it the whole day without calling or texting her even though this is the first day we haven't met up for lunch in months. That's something we usually agreed upon in the morning before we go our separate ways, and since we didn't talk about it today, I took it to mean that she would be too busy to take a lunch break. After work, I go across the street and order a drink, waiting to see if I get a call or text from her asking me to come over for dinner. Craig ends up walking in only minutes after me, and he takes the empty barstool to my right.

"How was your day?" I ask, getting my drink and taking a sip.

"Same old, same old. You?"

I nod but don't reply.

"What's going on? You're looking very serious over there."

I take a deep breath and catch him up on all things Kaylee and me. I tell him how we've been sneaking around her brother's back after I managed to save our friendship. I tell him how I asked her to marry me last night and how she happily accepted, and then I tell him about her coldness this morning as she was in a rush to get away from me.

He shrugs. "Maybe she really is just busy today."

"Maybe," I mumble, "but it seems like more than that. I'm worried that she's changed her mind or something."

"Oh, there's no point in worrying yourself sick. Just chill out and talk to her. I'm sure you'll see that everything is okay."

I nod. That's the same thing I've been telling myself all day. Only problem is that it doesn't work. Even when I try keeping my mind on my work, I find my thoughts always drifting back to her.

I finish off my drink and say goodbye to Craig as I make my way outside and across the street to my car in the bank parking lot. I climb behind the wheel, start the car, and take my phone out of my pocket in case I get a call as I'm driving. I look at the blank screen, willing her to call, to text, something, but nothing happens. I place the phone in the cupholder and shift into reverse.

At home, I feel almost lost, like I don't know what to do if I'm not with her or preparing to be with her. I change out of my work clothes and replace them with jeans and a T-shirt, then I pour a drink and have a seat on the couch. I turn the TV on and go through a stack of mail, reading each paper, each envelope, and each magazine as a way to occupy my brain and kill time.

I look at the clock a little while later and see that it's going on seven. I'm usually with her by this time, and I still haven't heard anything. I look at my empty glass and debate on pouring another. I've only had three since I got home, four if you include the one I had at the bar. I push the thought away when I notice how blurred my vision is already. My stomach growls, reminding me that I haven't eaten since breakfast, so I go to the kitchen and find some leftover Chinese food. I pour it out of the carton and onto a plate before tossing it into the microwave.

My phone rings and I race to answer it. In my haste, I don't even think to check the caller ID. "Hello?"

"Hey, buddy. What's going on?" Kyle asks.

I let out a breath I didn't realize I was holding. "Nothing much. Just warming up some leftover Chinese food for dinner. What are you doing?"

"Just got back into town."

"You made it early!"

He laughs. "Yeah, I finished my first job for The Mason's Group. Thought we could celebrate. Wanna grab some drinks?"

"Yeah, sure," I agree.

"Sweet. I just called Kaylee, and she's going to meet us at Berry's. Say an hour?"

"Sounds good. See ya then," I say, hanging up. I toss the phone onto the island, wondering why she's been too busy all day to call me but she's suddenly free enough to go for drinks. Something is definitely going on. I have to get to the bottom of it.

THIRTEEN
KAYLEE

"Good morning. Why are you here so early?" Andrea asks as she sets her things down and walks into my office.

"Because I needed an excuse to get out of the house this morning."

"Oh, the secret relationship getting rocky?" she asks, walking farther in and sitting across from me.

"No, things are going good. Great, actually. He asked me to marry him last night."

"What?" She sits up tall, her eyes wide and full of excitement as her mouth hangs open.

I nod. "I said yes."

She smiles. "That's awesome! So why are you looking for excuses to leave?"

I look up at the ceiling. "Because everything was great last night. We had dinner, he proposed, we made love, then he held me until he was fast asleep."

"But you weren't fast asleep?"

I shake my head. "I was too excited at first, but then my excitement changed to worry and panic. I mean, first of all, isn't it too soon? We've only been seriously dating for three months."

"True, but you've known one another like your whole lives, so that changes things."

"Okay, well, what happens if we tell my mom and brother next week and he flips his shit? I can't pick between Kyle and Landon."

She tilts her head to the side. "It sounds like you're just looking for excuses to not be happy. Why can't you just enjoy this?"

Is that what I'm doing? Do I not want to be happy?

No, I do want to be happy, but I want my brother to be happy, too, and I won't put my own happiness above his. I can't. He's only just gotten his friendship with Landon back. This will change it for sure. For better or worse, I'm not sure. But nothing will be the same.

And what's going to change between Landon and me? I like the way things are going. I like going over to his place or him coming to mine. Married couples typically share one place. Who will have to give up their apartment? Him or me? It's not like my apartment is all that great. His is much nicer, but I chose my apartment because of its close proximity to the office. I like being able to rush around the corner if I've forgotten something. I like not having to leave until ten minutes before I open. I like my life and my routine, all of which will change if we get married. I don't know why none of this ran through my head before I said yes. Would it have changed my answer if it did?

I don't know and I'll never know for sure.

Maybe I just need a little break. I need to push it from my head and bury myself in work for the day. I'll see Landon later, and we can have a grown-up discussion about what we're willing to give up or change about our lives in order to fit two into one.

But even with that plan, there is still one wild card: Kyle.

How will he take the news? Will he think we tricked him into becoming friends with Landon again? I mean, we sort of did. We both thought the way to getting what we wanted was for him to befriend my brother first, that with their friendship would come understanding. But now I'm not so sure. Now I'm worried that he'll think we used him or tricked him somehow. He'll be mad that we've been sneaking around instead of just telling him what was going on, but that might be something he'll be able to overcome. Either way, my brother's approval is all I really want. I mean, I've approved of all the stupid things he's done or wanted to do. Why can't he support me the same way? I guess he might, but first, I'll have to give him the chance.

I avoid my phone for the entire day, not wanting the extra temptation. When work ends, I go home and get cleaned up. I haven't talked to Landon all day, and I'm sure he's probably freaking out. I plan on showing up at his place and surprising him so I can talk to him about how nervous I am. Maybe if I confess all these feelings, he'll understand where my head has been at all day. Hell, he might be feeling the same way.

When I get out of the shower, my phone is ringing. I answer it and find my brother on the other end.

"Hey, Lee Lee. I'm back!"

"You're early!" I breathe out cheerfully. Really, it's more panic than anything.

"Yeah, I finished my first job. Want to come celebrate with me?"

I know if I say no, he'll never let up, so I agree in hopes of getting it out of the way so I can go to Landon's and talk with him about all of this.

Before I leave the house, I notice the ring on my left hand. The princess cut diamond sparkles when light hits it, and I know this sucker is so big that a blind person could see it a mile away. I have no choice but to take it off until news of the engagement is out. I remove the ring and set it on the table.

I WALK into the bar and find Kyle and Landon already at the table. When I approach, Kyle stands and pulls me in for a big hug. I look at Landon from over his shoulder. His eyes are on me, burning with all the questions he wants to ask. His mouth is in a straight line even though it's clear that he's trying to smile.

Kyle releases me, and I slide into the booth across from Landon. The waitress brings over another glass, and I pour from the pitcher of beer that's already on the table. When I do this, Landon's eyes watch my hands. When he notices that I'm not wearing his ring, his eyes double in size as his back straightens and his chest puffs out.

"So, what's new with you two?" Kyle asks.

"Nothing," we both say at the same time.

"Ooookay," Kyle says, picking up on our weirdness there. He taps the table. "I think I'm going to go put us in an order for the sampler platter. Sound good to you two?" He looks between Landon and me, and we both nod our heads.

The moment Kyle walks away, Landon leans in slightly. "Why haven't I heard from you all day? God, I was worried you were changing your mind on me." He rakes his hands through his hair.

"Sorry," I breathe out. "I was busy, and I've kind of been trapped inside my own head."

His brows pull together. "So you are having second thoughts. That's why you're not wearing the ring?"

"No," I say. "I'm not wearing the ring because I didn't want Kyle to see it before we tell him."

He's back, and so our conversation stops. "What are you two talking about?" he asks, looking between us.

"Uh," Landon says, taking Kyle's attention, "we were just talking about how proud we are of you getting this new job and rocking it. Way to go, man." He smiles wide, and Kyle is willing to buy it anytime a compliment is thrown his way.

"Thanks. Honestly, I'm pretty proud of myself too."

"Cheers," I say, picking up my glass and holding it out for the two of them. They clink their glasses off mine, and we all drink.

Kyle talks through most of our celebration time, telling us about every shot he called on the job. I don't listen to a word of it, and I don't think Landon does either. Every time I look up, his eyes are on me. Our appetizers come and we all dig in. With our mouths full, it's hard to talk, but that doesn't stop Kyle. He's on a roll, talking about nothing but himself, and since neither Landon nor I stop him, he keeps going for hours.

By ten o'clock, I excuse myself to leave for the evening, and I give both of the guys a hug. I whisper in Landon's ear, "Come by the house when you escape."

He doesn't reply, but I see the acknowledgement in his eyes as I pull away and turn for the door. Back at home, I waste no time getting in my pajamas and plop down on the couch in the living room. It takes about an hour for him to show up just as I'm drifting off to sleep. The door opens, and I hear him lock it behind him. I sit up and spin around. "God, you scared me," I say, covering my heart with my hand.

"Sorry," he slurs.

"Are you drunk?"

He plops down next to me. "After you left, your brother insisted on shots. I kept saying no, but he didn't listen. Blame this on him," he says, motioning toward himself and his current state.

I laugh. "You ready for bed?"

He looks over at me with bloodshot, droopy eyes as he slurs his words. "Don't weeee have some thingssss to talk about?"

I smile. "It can wait. Come on, let's get you to bed." I stand up and help him to his feet. He leans on me as we walk to the bedroom, and when we get to the bed, he lies back across it. I drop down to my knees to remove his boots, and he says, "Yes, you give the best head."

I laugh. "I'm not giving you head, dumbass. I'm taking your shoes off so you can sleep this off."

"Okay, that works. I'm soooo drunk I probably couldn't get it up if you paid me."

I shake my head but help him to get straight in the bed, and then I take my place at his side. He throws his arm over me and yanks me back against him. His heat engulfs me, and his heart beats steadily on my back. It's in this moment that I know that nothing could change us. Things can change around us, but nothing will ever change us. He's the same guy he's always been, loving, protective, and goofy. And I'm the same girl I've always been, headstrong, a little spoiled, and totally in love with him. I don't know what will happen, but I know that everything will work out in the end. I won't give it any other choice. I know what I want. I've known since I was a teenager. Nothing has every changed that and nothing ever could. I hate that I wasted a whole day of talking with him, having fun with him, and kissing him, but at the same time, I know that it's okay because we have our whole future for that.

FOURTEEN

LANDON

When I wake up in the morning, I'm regretting every choice I've ever made in life. My stomach is rolling; my head is pounding, and my entire body is sore like I've gone all twelve rounds with the best boxer on the planet. My eyes open, and the early morning sun comes pouring in. My head screams in pain, and it feels like I'm being burned from the inside out. A wave of nausea hits me hard, pulling me under and drowning me.

"What the fuck did I do last night?" I mumble to myself.

I hear her giggle, and I force one eye to open as I lift my head toward the sound. She's walking out of the bathroom, looking perfectly fine and beautiful. My eyes close with shame, and I feel the bed dip like she crawls up beside me.

"I take it you're not feeling well today."

"Shh, stop yelling," I whisper, joking, but her normal speaking volume is too much, and it creates a ringing in my head.

She silently laughs. "What do you need to feel better? Food? Sleep? Sex?" she whispers, moving her hand to my stomach and gliding it back and forth across my stomach, hip bone to hip bone.

"Mmmm," I say, smiling as I cover my eyes with my forearm. "Show me what you got." I lift my hips as she climbs on top of me. Her fingers hook my boxers and start tugging them down. "Wait, you're not calling off our engagement, right?" I ask, not bothering to lift my head or uncover my eyes.

"Does this answer your question?" she asks, wrapping her hot mouth around my dick.

I take a hissing breath, expecting her to slide down on me, not take me in her mouth. Her tongue swirls around me as she sucks me further and further down into her throat. As her mouth takes care of my dick, her hands massage my balls. It's like being touched everywhere all at once. My muscles begin to tense as my release begins to build. I try holding it off, not wanting this to end, but it's too early to have any kind of control of myself.

I lace my hand into her hair. "Kaylee, stop. I'm going to come."

She doubles her efforts, pushing me over the edge and swallowing me down. I'm tugging her hair as I try to catch my breath, but she keeps sucking, and I can't do anything but freeze as shock and pleasure wash over me. After several long seconds, I'm able to pull her up my body and flip us over so I'm hovering over her. The sickness hits me, but I push it back. "Where the fuck did you learn to do that?"

She smiles with her swollen, glistening lips. "Do you really want to know the answer to that question?"

I laugh. "No, I guess not. But it's nice to know that those talents will only be used on me and nobody else." I press my lips to hers.

The two of us end up playing hooky and skipping out on work for the day. It's nice getting to lie in bed, make love, sleep, talk, giggle, and just enjoy one another without any interruptions. We eat in bed, we watch TV, we nap, we hold one another, we have sex again and again, and by dinnertime, I'm feeling like a human again, so we get up to shower. As I stand in the back, watching as she rinses the shampoo out of her hair, I can't help but feel incredibly lucky.

"Kaylee?" I ask.

"Hmm?" she says, peeking one eye open.

"What made you freak out on me yesterday? What scared you?"

She takes a deep breath, and I notice the way it makes her naked chest rise and fall. "It was a little of everything, I guess. I was scared of change, you changing, me changing, our lives changing. Then I was worried about Kyle. I'm still scared of that actually, but now, I know that it doesn't matter what he has to say. You're the one I want, and he's just going to have to come to terms with it." Her eyes open and lock on mine.

"So, you're in? Fully in, through thick and thin?"

She offers up a small smile. "I'm in."

My hands grab her hips, pulling her mouth to mine. I kiss her deeply. "I love you, you know that?"

She nods, her forehead resting against mine. "I love you, too, Landon. Always have and always will."

Then we start all over again, hands on each other's bodies, lips kissing over every inch, our bodies, hearts, and minds tangled together, just like we've always been.

"HERE'S THE FOOD," I say, walking into the kitchen and setting the bags on the island.

"Thank you," she says, grabbing the plates and taking everything out of the bags to plate it perfectly. "Will you get out the wine, glasses, and silverware and take them to the table, please?"

"Absolutely." I gather the items and take everything into the rarely used dining room. She has the table set beautifully. There's a white tablecloth over the table with a cream-colored runner across the center. There is a small bouquet of flowers in the center with a candle on either side. Each place setting is set with a cloth napkin and a water glass, and now a wineglass. I set out the silverware.

Someone knocks on the door, and I go to answer it while she

finishes plating the food. I pull open the door, and her mom is standing on the other side, not looking a day older than the last time I saw her ten years ago. Her blond hair matches Kaylee and Kyle's, and she keeps it long but always in some fancy updo. Her makeup is perfect and complements her manicured eyebrows and bright-red lips.

She smiles as she takes me in and holds out her arms for a hug. "Landon! It's been too long," she says, pulling me against her.

I hug her lightly. Her tiny body feels breakable pressed against me. "It's good seeing you again, Mrs—"

"Mom," she insists like she always did.

"Mom," I correct. "Come on in and get comfortable."

She walks inside and makes herself at home, putting her purse and coat on the back of the couch as she looks around. "I swear, it changes every time I come in here."

I chuckle. "Well, you raised an interior designer, so..."

She laughs. "True. She used to dye her hair every other week. Now she decorates rooms," she jokes.

Kaylee is bringing the food from the kitchen to set on the table. "Hi, Mom." She smiles in her direction as she places two plates on the table.

"Hi, dear. Don't you look like you're glowing," she says, walking over with her arms out, ready for a hug.

The door opens and Kyle walks in. He walks up to me first. "Hey, bud," he says with a handshake.

"How ya been?"

"Good," he says with a nod. "Mom, Lee Lee." He nods in their direction.

"Come on, guys. Sit. Let's eat," Kaylee says, waving us over.

Kyle sits at one end of the table with his mom and Kaylee on either side. I sit at the opposite end, which is probably where I'll want to be when she drops the news. I won't want to be in arm's length, not that he can punch hard.

We all start eating, and her mom goes on and on about the books she's been reading, the shows she's been watching, and all about her new boyfriend. Kaylee thinks it's great her mom has found someone she can spend her time with. Kyle, not so much. In fact, every time she mentions his name, Kyle sighs and shakes his head. The girls have caught on, but neither of them pay him any mind.

I get asked about practically everything since I left high school. College, jobs, moves, girls—

all of it comes up.

"So, are you seeing anyone special now?" her mother asks.

I swallow down the bite of chicken I just took and nod. "Yeah, I've been seeing someone. I think she's pretty special." I quickly glance at Kaylee, and she glances at me with wide eyes.

"Oh, well, isn't that nice. I wish these two would settle down. I'd like to have grandchildren while I'm still young enough to enjoy them."

"You're plenty young, Mom," Kyle says, rolling his eyes.

"What about you, Kyle?" I ask, changing the subject. "You seeing anyone lately?"

He nods. "There's a woman at work I've had my eye on, but I haven't asked her out yet."

"Well, why not?" his mom asks.

He laughs. "Office romances are frowned upon, Mother."

She waves her hand through the air. "Oh, everything great is frowned upon. I say just do it. Do whatever makes you happy."

That sounds like our cue. I look at Kaylee and nod. She returns the nods. I see her swallow down her nervousness, and she takes a sip of wine to prepare.

"I'm glad to hear you say that, Mom, because..." She stops, and I feel like I've been left hanging.

"What, dear?" she asks, looking up at her with a worried expression.

"It's just that, I didn't ask you two here just to have dinner. I actually have a little announcement to make."

Her mom nods, and Kyle sits so still, I'm not even sure if he's breathing.

Kaylee looks at me, and I reach over and hold her hand under the table, giving her the strength she needs to continue.

FIFTEEN
KAYLEE

"I'm engaged!" Yep, I just blurt it out.

Mom's mouth drops open in surprise, and Kyle just sits still. The only thing that moves on him are his eyebrows when he drags them together in confusion.

"You're engaged? I didn't even know you were seeing anyone," Mom says.

I nod. "I've been seeing someone for a few months now."

"Well, honey, forgive me, but I think for a marriage to be successful, you should date them for more than a few months."

"I agree, Mom. It's just that in this case, that doesn't really apply because the guy I'm engaged to, I've known and been friends with my whole life."

"Your whole life?" she repeats quietly to herself. Suddenly, everything clicks into place for her, and she slowly turns her head to look over at Landon. Her eyes light up, and a smile spreads on her face. "You?" she asks him.

He smiles nervously and nods his head.

Mom squeals and stands up, quickly pulling him in for a hug.

"Oh, I always thought you two would be the perfect couple. Why on earth did you wait so long?" she asks, moving back to her seat.

"Well," I say, not sure how to answer.

"It's because of me," Kyle says, and all our eyes move in his direction.

His jaw is cocked, his eyes trained on Landon, and his nostrils are flared. His face is growing redder and redder by the second.

"Kyle," Landon starts, but Kyle pushes his chair back, the legs screeching against the floor as he gets to his feet.

Landon jumps up and walks with him toward the door. "Kyle, just hear us out," he says, but Kyle spins around.

"Don't." He points his finger at him. "Don't fucking go there. I don't need to hear about how the only reason you befriended me as a kid was to get to my sister or how, twenty years later, you've done it again." He looks at me. "You know that, right? I didn't bring him into your life. You brought him into mine. I wasn't cool enough for him to be my friend growing up. He wanted you, and he used me to get to you. You'd think I'd be smart enough not to fall for it again, but of course, I gave him the benefit of the doubt." He shakes his head. "Well, I'm tired of being used. Enjoy your life." He turns and walks out the door, slamming it behind him.

―――

MOM ENDS up leaving soon after, assuring me that Kyle would come around in his own time. Landon helps me to clean up the dining room and kitchen, and then we shut the apartment down and head to the bedroom. I've been quiet since Kyle's explosion. I'm sticking to my word: his reaction isn't going to change my mind, but it doesn't make me feel any better about my decision either.

Landon runs me a bath, and the two of us sink into the tub full of hot water and bubbles. He's behind me with his strong arms wrapped around me, and I'm leaning my head against his chest.

"You okay?" he asks.

"I will be," I tell him. "I'm just feeling sad."

"He'll come around," he assures me.

I nod. "I don't feel sad for me. I feel sad for him. Why does he think that about you? That your friendship isn't real and that it's all based around me?"

He lets out a long breath. "Back then, after the fight we had, I was pissed. We were in a screaming match, and I wanted to beat the shit out of him, but I didn't want to kill him and I didn't want you to kill me. So I was trying to hurt him any way I could. I told him that I was only friends with him to get to you. That's what really ended our friendship."

"Why did you lie to me?" I ask, sitting up and spinning around to face him.

He shrugs. "I didn't want you to know how horrible of a person I am. And it wasn't a total lie. Everything I told you was true. We caught your boyfriend and best friend together. I tricked her into bed to screw her over. Then Kyle and I got into a fight about it all. All the elements were there. They were just out of order."

I shake my head. "I get that you're trying to protect me or whatever, but a marriage cannot work on half-truths."

"I know," he agrees. "I swear, I'll never do it again. All my secrets are out in the open. Now, I just gotta figure out how to fix what I broke with Kyle."

I spin back around and lie back in the bath the way we were before. Don't ask how I can believe him so easily, but I don't doubt what he said. He has no reason to lie about any of it now or, I guess, give me half the truth.

"We will figure out Kyle. Let's just give him some time to cool off."

He presses a kiss to the top of my head. "I never should have said that. I was just so mad, and you know how he argues. There is no talking sense into him."

"Oh, I know. I've only been arguing with the guy since we shared a womb." I take his hands in mine. "But look at the bright side. We get to plan a wedding." I smile just from saying the words.

"Yes, we do," he replies, and I can hear the excitement in his voice. "We have the rest of our lives together."

Once we crawl into bed, sleep finds me easily. Landon holds me against his strong chest, his arms wrapped around me, and I feel warm and safe.

"This is stupid," seven-year-old Kyle complains as he stands in front of us under the big oak tree in our backyard.

I stomp my foot. "You guys said we could play anything I wanted, and I want to play wedding. Now, get on with it," I demand.

"Fine," he grumbles.

Landon lifts the lace curtain so it's no longer covering my face, and he smiles when his eyes find mine. I can't hold back my own smile. Even if this wedding is just pretend, at least I get to marry him.

"Do you, Landon, take this girl to be your waffley wedded wife?" Kyle asks.

"It's lawfully, dum-dum," I say, rolling my eyes.

"That's what I said, stupid," he replies but then looks at Landon for his answer.

"I do," Landon agrees.

"Do you, Kaylee, take this boy to be your lawfully wedded husband?"

"I do," I say around a smile as I look at the boy whom I can't get enough of. His dark hair is messy, his face dirty from playing outside all day, and his skin browned from the long summer days.

"Great. You're both married. Enjoy," Kyle says.

I smile, happy.

"You forgot to say you may kiss the bride," Landon reminds him.

Kyle scoffs and rolls his eyes. "You may now kiss the bride."

Landon leans toward me, and my eyes are stretched wide. Is he really going to kiss me?

He chuckles. "Close your eyes, Kaylee," he whispers when he's only an inch away.

I do as he says, and in a moment, his lips are pressed against mine. They're dry but soft and somehow feel completely different from my mom's kisses. After he pulls back, my eyes open and we are both wearing big smiles.

"Gross," Kyle says. "I'm outta here." *He tosses the book over his shoulder and goes off running for the tree line.*

"Thank you for playing with me," I tell Landon.

He smiles. "No problem. We'll consider it practice for when we really get married one day." Then he turns and chases after Kyle.

I can't move. All I can do is stand there and watch him run off. Marry Landon for real one day? Can I really get that lucky? God, I hope so.

"Good morning, sleepyhead," Landon says, squeezing me gently and kissing the top of my head.

My eyes open, and a sleepy smile stretches across my face.

"What?"

"You know what I just dreamed about?"

"Me?" He's being cocky.

I nod. "That time we got married in my backyard when we were seven. You remember that?"

His smile stretches wider. "Of course I do. I believe I told you that we'd end up married one day for real."

I nod. "You did." I rest my head back on his shoulder.

"We're written in the stars, Kaylee. You've always been mine, so there isn't really anything to fight. He'll figure that out one of these days."

He's talking about my brother again, but I push away the sadness that forms when I think about him. Hell, he didn't even want us to play wedding when we were kids, so the thought of a real wedding must really be eating at him.

After getting up and getting ready for work, I manage to talk Kyle into meeting me for lunch. Maybe talking to him one-on-one will help. I'm praying it does anyway. My brother has been by my side my whole life, and that's a pain in the ass I've gotten used to. I'm not ready for him to stop now.

I get a cab and go across town for lunch. Kyle agreed to meet me, but he wasn't going to make it easy for me either. He refused to leave his side of town. Whatever, I'll go to him. I walk into the sandwich shop and find him eating without me. He's sitting in the far back corner, all alone. I make my way over and sit across from him.

"I'm surprised you made it," he says, picking up his napkin and wiping his mouth.

"I'm surprised you showed. I was expecting you to stand me up."

"Maybe I should have."

I tilt my head as my eyes lock with his. A long breath leaves my lips as I sit in the chair across from him. "What's it going to take to get you to accept this? To stop throwing a tantrum so we can all be a family again?"

His facial expression doesn't change. "Kaylee, how do you think you'd feel if you found out that your best friend was only friends with you to get to me? That would hurt, right?"

"Of course, but that isn't true. He didn't mean it."

"Yeah, okay," he says in his sarcastic voice.

"I'm serious, Kyle. When Landon said that, what were you guys doing?"

He thinks back. "Fighting."

"Exactly. He was just trying to hurt you. The same way I say that I should have eaten you in the womb. The way you tell me my ass is too fat for white pants. It's all just to get under each other's skin."

"That last one isn't a lie. Your ass is too wide for white pants."

"Fuck off, Kyle," I breathe out as I sit back in my seat and prop my head up with my hand.

"Look, Landon was supposed to be my friend. We're twins. We've had to share everything our whole lives."

"Get over it," I say, sitting up. "He's a good guy. He loves me. He works hard. He's not an alcoholic or drug addict. He doesn't hit me.

He doesn't cheat on me. Why isn't that enough for you? Shouldn't you want me to end up with a guy just like him?"

"Yeah, just *like* him. Not him!"

"Would it make you feel better if I hooked you up with Lauren?"

He frowns. "You still talk to her?"

"No, but I found her on Facebook, and who knows, maybe her husband is down for sharing."

He laughs and shakes his head. But he laughed. That's the first step.

"This doesn't have anything to do with her. This is about how my best friend went behind my back to get to you."

"Did you ever consider that we were together and that's why you got your best friend back?"

He freezes as he sits up straight. "Well, that makes more sense. All those questions about what happened, it was because you were already seeing him, wasn't it?"

I nod. "Landon and I are meant to be together. I know it. And I'm ready for us all to be a family again. He loves me, I love him, and we both love you. Do you think that one day you'll be able to get behind us?"

He's picking at the food on his plate. "You remember that time when we were kids and I married the two of you in the backyard?"

I laugh. "I just dreamed about that."

"I just remember being so grossed out, like why would you want to marry my sister? But he really did. Even then. He was the one that talked me into playing that stupid game."

I smile. "Really?"

He nods. "He loved you then."

"I loved him too. So it only makes sense that this is where we are."

"I guess I'm just going to have to get used to my best friend being my brother-in-law."

My smile breaks free. "Really? We have your blessing?"

He nods. "Yeah, it's not really any of my business anyway, I guess."

I snort and roll my eyes.

"But don't tell him I've forgiven him yet. I want to have a little fun with him first."

I laugh and stand up, showing him my palms. "Whatever you want, weird one."

SIXTEEN

LANDON

"Come on, man. You know I wasn't serious when I said that. I was just mad," I tell Kyle as I chase him from room to room through his apartment.

He goes into the kitchen and pours a glass of milk. "I don't want to hear your excuses. It doesn't matter what you say 'cause I'm going to think you're just saying it to get my sister all to yourself."

I roll my eyes and growl. "What do I have to do to make you believe me?"

He looks from me, to his glass of milk, and back. "You say you're sorry?" he asks, nodding in my direction.

"Yes," I breathe out.

"Then drink my milk." He pushes the glass toward me.

I look at it, then him. "If I drink that, I'm going to be stuck in the bathroom all day. You know I can't have milk."

He shrugs. "Well, I guess you aren't as sorry as you say." He leans against the counter and crosses his arms over his chest.

He's doing this shit on purpose. I know he is. Our whole lives, I've never drank milk. It makes my stomach hurt, and I end up stuck in the bathroom for hours as my stomach cramps and twists and turns. But making Kyle happy would make Kaylee happy, and making Kaylee happy means being happy myself.

I pick up the glass and chug it all down. As I tip the glass up, my eyes lock on his. He's smirking, looking cocky as hell as he watches me punish myself. I swallow down my last drink and set the glass on the island between us. His smirk turns to a full-blown smile.

"We're cool," he says.

I breathe a sigh of relief. "Thank God. I can marry your sister now?"

"I talked to her earlier and gave her my blessing."

My jaw ticks as I grind my teeth. "You did?"

He nods. "Yep."

"So I just chugged that milk for no reason then?"

"Oh no. There's a reason, and it's because you were being a giant douchebag. I think you'll learn your lesson this time. Right?"

My stomach is already gurgling and twisting. "Fuck you, man," I say, running to the bathroom with the sounds of his laughter filling my ears.

HOURS LATER, I'm still sitting on the toilet when I hear the front door slam shut. "You made him drink milk? You know how sick that makes him," Kaylee yells.

"I know. That's why I did it." Kyle laughs.

"Sometimes, you can be a real asshole," she says. Moments later, she knocks on the bathroom door. "Landon, you okay?"

"I'll be fine," I reply. My stomach hasn't rumbled in a while, so I wash up and open the door. She's waiting on the other side. She sees my appearance and sticks out her bottom lip. "Why did you do that?"

"I had to get him to forgive me somehow."

"I had already done that."

"Yeah, I learned that after I drank the milk. Next time, give a guy a heads-up."

She giggles and pulls me in for a hug. "I'm sorry my brother is an ass."

"Hey!" he shouts from his place on the couch.

"It's fine. I knew better."

"Want to go home and take it easy the rest of the day?"

I nod. "Yeah, and maybe you can show me some more of those mouth skills you have." I say it loud enough for Kyle to hear.

"Man! I'm right here!" he says, leaning over the back of the couch to look down the hallway at me.

I smirk. "I know."

He shakes his head, annoyed. "I take it back. I don't forgive you."

"Sorry, pal. It's too late for that," I say, walking by and patting him on the shoulder.

With my stomach still upset, I opt to leave my car at Kyle's place and climb into Kaylee's. She drives us back to her place, and I throw myself onto the couch. She brings me a cup of hot tea.

"It's peppermint. It'll soothe your stomach."

I take it. "Maybe pour a little Pepto in there for good measure."

She laughs but brings me back the bottle of chalky pink liquid. I take a swig straight from the bottle. She lies down with me, and I hold her close as I drift in and out of consciousness.

"What kind of wedding do you want?" she asks and I force my eyes open.

"Hmm?"

"Do you want a traditional wedding, destination, to elope?"

"Oh, uh, whatever you want, I guess. I don't even care if we go to the courthouse."

She giggles. "You know what I was thinking?"

"What's that?"

"If we had the wedding in my mom's backyard, under that big oak tree like we did when we were kids."

That makes me smile. "I like the sound of that."

"And maybe we can make Kyle get online and get certified so he can marry us."

"That sounds great," I agree, sleep tugging at me once again.

She laughs. "Go to sleep."

My eyes pop open. "What about those mouth skills?"

"I thought you were sick?" she asks, looking at me from over her shoulder.

"I'm never too sick to enjoy a mouth like that."

She jabs me in the ribs with her elbow, and I cough but turn it into a laugh. "Fine, I'll behave," I tell her, settling back down to take a nap.

A few hours later, I wake up when I feel the zipper on my jeans being lowered. My eyes open enough to see the top of her head as she hovers over my lap. I try to hide my smirk and close my eyes, pretending to be asleep, but even as I fake it, my dick is getting harder and harder, knowing that it will soon be in her mouth.

And just like I predicted, she wraps her glorious lips around me and sucks. My eyes pop open as I twitch with the sensation, and she giggles around my dick. It's the sexiest thing I've ever fucking heard.

Her tongue is like a tornado as it spins around me, and her sucking never slows or pauses as she takes more and more of me into her beautiful mouth. My hips begin to lift with her movements as my body hardens and tenses, ready for its release. Within minutes, I come, riding out every last wave of pleasure.

When she pulls back, I flip us over and settle between her legs. She's giggling and breathless, her lips glistening and swollen.

"My turn," I say, my hands moving to her sweatpants as I push them down her legs. I lower my mouth to her clit and run my tongue between her slick folds. She lets out a soft moan as I spread her wetness with my tongue. She tastes sweet, like the ripest strawberry I've ever had. As I suck her bundle of nerves into my mouth, flicking my tongue against it, I slide two fingers inside her, rubbing that magic little spot up top. She goes stiff beneath me as her breathing increases. Her legs begin to shake on either side of my head, and her moans get louder. Finally, she comes undone, and I feel her muscles relaxing and tensing around my fingers as I keep pushing her closer and closer to the end of her release. When she's limp beneath me, I crawl up her body, pushing my jeans down as I go. I'm already hard again, and when I get to her glistening pink entrance, I slide right in. We connect as one, and we both let out a relieved moan. She fits me snugly. She's so hot wrapped around me, so wet that I have no choice but to thrust into her over and over until we're both lost in bliss again. My hips become erratic as I empty myself into her.

When neither of us can move, I rest my head against her chest and wait to calm my heart and breathing. Her fingers lace through my hair as she hugs me to her chest. Her heart is beating steadily in my ear, and it's a sound that grounds me, making me feel alive, excited, loved.

"I love you," I whisper against her neck as I press a kiss to her skin.

"I love you, too," she replies, squeezing me just a little tighter.

EPILOGUE
KAYLEE

"I can't believe my baby is getting married," Mom gushes as I stand in my childhood bedroom, looking over my dress in the mirror. My dress isn't a typical wedding dress. It seemed silly to waste all that money to buy a dress for such a small outdoor ceremony. The dress I ended up choosing is white and made up of lace, but it's more of a summer dress. It has baby-doll sleeves and buttons up the front. The bodice of the dress is tight around my chest and flares out at my hips, ending just below my knees.

I smile at her in the mirror as she pins up a misplaced curl. "I can't believe it either," I confess.

"And who would've thought that you'd be marrying Landon? Ah, it's just like a fairy tale. It's all too perfect."

I snort. "Yeah, tell Kyle that."

Mom's busy fluffing my dress and adjusting this or that. "Kyle is happy for you too. Sure, it took him a while to accept it, but he finally has."

"I'm surprised you haven't set him up yet."

She grins. "I have, but don't tell him that."

My eyes grow in size. "You have?"

"Well, I invited one of my friend's daughters to the wedding. I hope that's okay. I just didn't want him to be alone."

"Hello, we're here," someone says, sticking their head into the room. I look up and find Landon's mom, Vicky.

I smile. "Hi, how are you?" I ask, moving across the floor to hug her.

She hugs me tightly. "Oh, look at you. You're beautiful."

"Thank you."

"The guys are already out back," Mom tells her.

"I'll go out and see my son then. See you soon," she says, turning and heading for the back door.

"I'm good in here, Mom, if you want to go outside."

She fiddles with one last thing on my dress. "Okay, I'll go see if all the guests are here." She walks out of the room, leaving me by myself.

Left in my childhood bedroom alone, I'm hit with all this emotion. It feels like we've all come full circle. This is the house where I fell in love with the man I'm about to marry. This is the bedroom he'd carry me to as a teenage when I'd get too trashed at a party. In fact, this is the room where we had our very first kiss.

I was standing at the door and he was on the other side after he walked me home after a football game. He looked at me and I looked at him. Something was exchanged, and all I remember wishing for was him to kiss me. Then he leaned in and pressed his lips to mine softly. When he pulled back, I yanked him back in and kissed him like I wanted to. It wasn't sweet. It wasn't soft. It was full of all the love, passion, and need I could wrap my head around at the age of fifteen.

I smile as that memory drifts away.

Mom calls out for me, and I take it to mean that everyone is in place. I grab my bouquet of flowers and head for the back door. Mom starts the music, and it plays softly as I walk down the porch steps and into the yard. There's a white runner that takes me to where he's waiting. I look up and find him watching me. He's dressed in a pair of black slacks with a white button-up shirt and black tie. His dark hair is combed nicely, and he's freshly shaven. He looks handsome and sexy as hell all at the same time. My stomach tightens when I think about how this man has been mine for all our lives and now how I will tie myself to him in every way possible.

When I get to the end, Mom shuts off the music and Landon takes my hand. "You're breathtaking," he whispers.

I smile and my cheeks warm up. "Thank you," I whisper.

"Ladies and gentlemen," Kyle starts, looking a little annoyed to be doing this, but I twisted his arm until he agreed, literally. "We're gathered here today to bear witness to these two coming together in holy matrimony. This spot was chosen because twenty years ago, the three of us stood right here, beneath this oak tree, where I married these two. Now, that wedding wasn't lawful, it was waffle—I was only seven."

Everyone laughs.

"But today, we're here to do this again the right way. The couple has prepared their own vows. So Landon, if you will."

Landon pulls a ring from his pocket with one hand and holds mine with the other. "Kaylee, I was five years old when I fell in love with you. It took me another twenty-three years to make you mine once and for all. I vow to stand by your side for the rest of my life. I vow to love you, cherish you, and take care of you for as long as I'm alive. I've waited this long to get you. I'm never letting go. I love you." He slides the ring onto my finger.

"And Kaylee," Kyle says.

I take the ring off my finger and hold it as I prepare my vows. "Landon, I don't remember falling in love with you. I don't remember it ever being a choice. All I know is that I was born to love you, and you've always been by my side. I vow to stand by your side the way you've stood by mine. I vow to make you proud every single day, to love you, to take care of you, and to honor you in everything I do. I love you and can't wait to discover this next phase of our lives together." I slide the ring onto his finger.

"With the power vested in me by the state of Illinois, I hereby pronounce you man and wife. You may kiss your bride."

Landon pulls me in faster than I can process. The next thing I know, his mouth is pressed against mine, and everyone is clapping and cheering. He holds me close while his lips and tongue move with mine. When he pulls back, I smile and my cheeks are hot.

He runs the tip of his finger across my cheekbone. "I love making you blush," he whispers with a grin.

We turn and walk back down the aisle. This time, I notice the yard is full of people I don't know or haven't seen in years. The only person I invited was Andrea, and she's sitting in the back, smiling and clapping.

Landon takes me back into the house and pulls me back to my old bedroom. "Hurry," he says, pulling me in and shutting and locking the door behind me.

"What are you doing?" I ask.

"I've always wanted to fuck you in this room," he confesses, his hands rushing to push my dress up.

"What if my mom tries coming in?"

He's got me bent over the bed with the dress up around my hips. "Who cares? She can't stop us now. You're my wife."

His hands pull my blue panties down my hips, and moments later, he's sliding into me. He feels bigger than ever in this position, and it doesn't take long before I'm clenching around him. I tried to cover my screams with the pillow, but every time I do, he thrusts in harder.

"I want to hear you, baby," he says, reaching around and massaging my clit as he works me over. Just as his release washes over him, someone knocks on the door.

"We're ready," Mom says.

"Just a sec!" I call out, hoping that she doesn't press further. My voice sounds breathy, and I'm sure she knows what's going on in here. But like Landon said, what's she going to do? We're married now.

THE TWO OF us walk back outside. The chairs from the wedding have been rearranged around tables now, and everyone is seated, waiting for us. When we walk down the steps, everyone stands and claps. One by one, everyone comes up to us to wish us a happy life together, to give us a gift, or just to say congratulations.

Champagne is popped open, and everyone is holding a glass, making toasts, and this is the time I pick to turn to Landon. "Will you drink mine for me?"

He looks at me, confused. "You don't like champagne?"

"I do," I tell him, feeling my face grow warm.

"Then why?" he starts to say but stops as he puts the pieces together. "Are you...?"

I smile and nod. "I'm pregnant."

He lets out a loud cheer that gets everyone's attention as he picks me up and twirls me in a circle. Everyone is watching confused.

"We're going to have a baby!" he yells loud enough for everyone to hear.

This is reason enough for everyone to join in, cheering and clapping.

His hand cups my face as he looks into my eyes. "We're going to have a baby."

I nod, and he pulls me in for a long, soft, slow kiss.

"I love you, Kaylee," he whispers against them.

"I love you, too, and I can't wait to start this new life with you." He pulls me back in while everyone crowds around us, cheering, clapping, and tipping their glasses our way. I finally get my happily ever after, even though this is nowhere near the end.

GABBI AND EASTON'S STORY

ONE
GABBI

As I step from the shower into the steam-filled bathroom, I use my hand to wipe the moisture away from the mirror. I'm not even sure who's staring back at me anymore. This too thin girl with straggly blond hair that hangs to her bony shoulders, dark circles under her glistening blue eyes, and tears running down her gaunt cheeks couldn't possibly be me.

I've always been almost unnaturally beautiful. Too beautiful, some would say. My naturally blond hair is the color people pay thousands for in a salon, never quite reaching the perfect shade. My blue eyes are big and round, making me appear like some elegantly painted doll, and they're framed in thick, dark lashes that people envy. My face is angular with high cheekbones, big pink, pouty lips, and perfectly straight white teeth.

Back home, my looks were the main topic of discussion everywhere I went. You'd think looking the way I do would have made my time in school easier. However, my family didn't have the money it required to hang out with the "cool kids," and my beauty became something I was tormented for.

High school was the worst years of my life, and I celebrated the day I got out of that hellhole. It took exactly five years of working at the corner market to save up the money I needed to leave that town behind me. I thought I'd put these good looks to use and come to California where all the most beautiful people go. I would become a famous actress, and then everyone back home would regret treating me the way they did. However, things haven't been working out according to plan.

I was in California for exactly two weeks before I met my long-term boyfriend, Dean. We hit it off automatically, and it was only a month before we decided to move in together. He works at an employment agency here in town, and with his ties, it wasn't long at all before I landed a job as a barista at a local coffee shop. The job wasn't great, but it did give me a little money to pay my bills, and I had plenty of time off to pursue my acting career. I auditioned and auditioned, never landing a role. I guess I should have known that getting famous would take more than a pretty face.

After being rejected from job after job, my dreams of becoming an actress fizzled out, which meant that I needed a better job if I ever wanted to survive in this town. Going back home with my tail between my legs has never been an option. Now, I have waitress, cashier, and assistant to the stars on my resume. I thought that if I couldn't be a star, I could at least work with them. I've been a personal shopper to the award-winning actress Jackie McGee. I've cleaned up after Grammy winner Anthony Wells, and been a personal assistant to the hottest influencer around, Jessica Vaughn. Which leads me to my current job. I have no idea who the celebrity is since that information is withheld, but I have an address and a time to be there. And due to a recent turn of events, I need this job more than ever.

My boyfriend, Dean, got a promotion a few months back and decided to celebrate by moving us to a nicer apartment. It has three bedrooms. Since we only need one, the second was converted into an in-home gym and the other into his home office. There is a full-sized living room with a balcony, a nice sized kitchen, dining room, laundry room/pantry, and two bathrooms. I tried to tell him this place was too big for us, but he wouldn't hear of it. He yearns to make it to the big leagues and live well above our means. Everything was great until yesterday.

"We need to talk, Gab," he says, walking into the gym as I'm running my heart out on the treadmill.

I slow my speed to a brisk walk as I pull my AirPods out of my ears. "What's up?" I ask around my labored breathing.

He holds his head high and squares his shoulders, looking well prepared for whatever he has to say, but then he runs his hand through his dirty-blond hair, making it spike up in all directions. "I'm leaving you," he blurts the words out.

I'm shocked. It feels like I've just ran as fast as I could into a brick wall. I hit that wall going one hundred miles an hour, and it tears me to shreds. My feet stop moving on the treadmill, and I almost fall. I quickly hit the emergency stop button as I hang on to the handles for dear life. "You're leaving me?" I ask, wanting to make sure I heard that correctly.

He nods. "This just isn't working out," he starts, but my anger is getting the best of me.

"Well, it seemed to be working out just fine a month ago when you insisted on moving us to this apartment," I point out.

"I know. I'm sorry. I didn't mean for this to happen."

"For what to happen?"

"Mandy, my assistant—"

"You're cheating on me with your assistant?"

"I'm sorry. I didn't mean for it to happen. Look," he says, running his hands through his hair again and raking them down his face. "I'm leaving, okay? I'm moving in with her, which means that this place is all yours. Okay? You can have it." He turns for the door, but I chase after him.

"And how am I supposed to pay for it, Dean?" I yell, following him to the door.

He bends down and picks up his bags. "I... I don't know. I guess, if nothing else, you have a month until the rent is due again. Make the arrangements you need. I'm sorry, Gab." With a shake of his head, a shrug of his shoulders, and an apologetic look, he turns and walks out, leaving me alone.

Just thinking of that memory has more tears pooling in my eyes. I ignore them and go about brushing my teeth and combing my hair, hoping and praying that this job works out. I know it's impossible for me to make rent every month, even with this job, but my plan is to save every dime I make this month, sell a few things from the apartment—if Dean is going to fuck me over, I'm selling his expensive furniture out from under him—and find me a reasonably priced apartment that I can take care of on my own. I will not give in. I will not go home. I will press on like I've always done, and in the end, I'll be fine. I know it.

After blow-drying and fixing my hair, I add a little makeup and go to my room to get dressed. I settle on a pencil skirt that ends just below my knees and a white short-sleeved top that I tuck into my skirt. I pair the outfit with a wide black belt. I slide my feet into a pair of knockoff designer heels. I stand back and look myself over in the mirror. My blond hair is pulled into a sleek bun, my contour makes my cheeks look razor-sharp, and my red lipstick pops, making my plump lips look sweet and juicy.

I grab the LV bag that Dean had bought me and drop in my phone and keys before heading for the door. I climb behind the wheel of my Nissan. I set my things in the passenger seat and pull out the paper with the address. I type it into my GPS and start my drive to Santa Monica. The drive isn't long, but traffic isn't the greatest, and it takes me longer than I thought it would.

All the houses here look like they've come straight out of my dreams. Most of them are gated for privacy, and they're perfectly landscaped. Each one has palm trees, pools, and large glass walls that provide plenty of interior light.

When I pull into the drive at the address I was given, I stop at the front speaker and hit the doorbell button. Moments later, a man's voice rings out. "Yeah?"

"Hello, I'm Gabrielle Jones. The agency sent me over as an assistant."

"Pull around," the man says moments before the iron gates begin to open.

I hit the gas and ease through the gates. The brick driveway winds through trees and well-maintained grounds. After what feels like forever, the house comes into view—if you can call it that. The Spanish-style house looks to be three stories. There is a covered porch attached to the front with archways leading down to three steps. All the windows are big and welcoming, and the front doors are large and glass, not providing much privacy. I park my car—which just looks stupid sitting next to a house this fancy—and climb out. I walk up onto the porch and notice all the Spanish tiles. As I'm reaching my hand out to knock, the door opens, and an older gentleman in a suit answers the door.

"Ms. Jones?"

I nod. "Yes, sir." I hold out my hand, but he looks at it with disgust. "This way. Mr. Perez is in his office, and he asked me to bring you in right away."

I follow him through the house, taking in the stark white walls, high wooden beams across the ceiling, and the iron railing along the stairs. "Mr. Perez?" I ask, wondering which one I could be working for and holding out hope that it's not the one I went to high school with.

He turns and comes to an abrupt stop. I nearly walk into his back, but my eyes move over his shoulder to find Easton Perez sitting at his desk.

Easton fucking Perez.

My high school tormentor, the reason everyone hated me and

picked on me, the reason I fled from home to begin with is sitting right in front of me with a smug smile on his handsome face. My blood runs cold as I get the overwhelming urge to run from this house and never look back, but the money. I need it. I can't blow this job no matter how much I'd rather tell Easton Perez to shove his Spanish-style home, all this money, and bad attitude up his taut ass.

TWO
EASTON

The agency sent me Gabbi Jones, the one thing I've always wanted but never got. I may have had some influence in her position here, but she doesn't know that, and she better never find out. She hates me with a fucking passion. She's always hated me ever since our first day of kindergarten when I sent a spit wad heading her way. It got her right in the eye and she cried. But hey, I was five years old and in love. I was smitten with her the first day she walked into class, wearing shiny black dress shoes and a little pink dress that barely touched her knees. Her blond hair was to her ass then, and it was curled perfectly, the top half pulled back out of her face by a matching pink bow. I remember being stunned by her blue eyes, round cheeks, and curvy lips. I had no idea what had happened to me, but seeing her changed something inside of me even at five years old.

As we grew, she only got more and more attention from me. Unwanted attention to say the least. She was bound and determined to hate me no matter how badly I tried to get on her good side. By high school, everything had changed in a sense. I had become the star basketball player, and with that came girls and popularity. Still, she wanted nothing to do with me. I mean, what's wrong with this girl? Everyone wanted me. Everyone. But not her and that made me hate her. If I couldn't have her, I was going to make sure nobody else wanted her. The tormenting got out of hand. By our senior year, she was the laughingstock of our class despite how fucking beautiful she is. And she is fucking beautiful.

She's changed over the years though. Her hair looks shorter now, even though I can't be sure since it's pulled up into a bun at the back of her head. She's thin and tall but still curvy in all the right places. I'd guess her chest measures at a C-cup; her waist is probably twenty-nine inches, hips around thirty-two. I've got a good eye for sizing up my women. Her blue eyes sparkle. They're bigger than most women's, giving her an innocent appearance that makes me want to ruin her. Her fucking lips are made for sucking dick. They're thick, plump, and curvy, teasing and sexy as fuck. She reminds me of one of those stupid Bratz dolls that my sister used to play with.

When I saw her name on the list of assistants available, I knew I had to have her. But now it's time to change tactics. I can't be the rich, good-looking, cocky movie star. That shit will never fly. No, I have to reel her in slowly so she doesn't get spooked. I have to trap her without her realizing she's being trapped. And when I have her, I'll have to take things slow. She's grown used to always having to be prepared when it comes to me. I'm going to show her that's not the case anymore.

I look up from my desk when she walks in, and her eyes double in size. I made the agency keep my info private. Her mouth is hanging open in surprise, and her body is stiff, on high alert.

I stand up and hold out my hand to shake. "Ms. Jones, is it?" I ask.

She wipes the expression off her face, but it's quickly replaced with a look of annoyance and hate. Her brows pull together, and her lips form a straight line as she nods.

"It's nice to meet you. If you wouldn't mind having a seat." I motion toward my desk, and she turns her body sideways to squeeze between me and Charles, a member of my staff. She's careful to not let even a hair brush against me on her way past. She takes her seat and I dismiss Charles. He closes the door to my office as I make my way back behind my desk.

"Ms. Jones, why don't you tell me a bit about yourself?" I'm trying to play it cool in hopes of giving us a new beginning, if you will. No sense in picking up where we left off.

She raises her chin in defiance. "You are a good actor, aren't you? Pretending that you aren't the one who ruined my life in high school."

Well. I thought we could start over. I hang my head. "I'm sorry. I was hoping you wouldn't remember that."

"Who in their right mind wouldn't remember being tormented for four years of their life? A stroke victim?"

The corners of my mouth begin to lift up at her anger, but I'm able to control myself. I level my eyes on her. "As most people do after high school, I have changed. That person I was then, that's not who I am today."

She snorts. "Yeah, right. You were popular then. Now, you're rich and famous. I don't see that bettering anyone, let alone you."

"I'm completely willing to start over here," I point out.

She lets out a bitter-sounding laugh. "Yeah, I remember the last time you said that. It was right before you pulled my pants down in front of the whole school." She crosses her arms over her chest. Her jaw is cocked in anger, making it appear sharp enough to cut glass. Her brows are pulled together, making two little lines appear between her eyes. Her eyes are blazing as they take me in before her.

"I know I was an asshole back then. I know. But I swear, I'm not like that anymore, and I'll prove it to you… if you stay, that is."

"Stay?"

I nod. "If you'll accept the job even though I'll be your boss."

Her blue eyes roll. "Of course I'm going to accept this job. I don't have the luxury of turning down work." She sits up straight and uncrosses her arms. "So, what will I be doing?"

I sit back in my chair and shrug. "Basically, just hanging out until I ask you to do something. You'll handle my work phone and deal with my agent, making sure I get his messages and that you're writing all my appointments and appearances down in my date book. I also like things moved from my date book to the calendar in my phone."

She's pulled a notebook out of her purse, and she's taking notes. She's fucking sexy as hell as her hand scribbles across the paper like a good little student.

"You'll also be in charge of going to the grocery store for me. The chef will have a list for you of the items he'll need for the week, and I usually have a few things to add to it. You will be handling the dogs, taking them on their walks and to the groomer."

"This isn't very much work. I don't see this small list keeping me busy every day. You are wanting me here five days a week, yes?"

I nod. "Like I said, you'll just be hanging out until I need you. You'll have your own room here so you'll be comfortable on your slow days, but I expect you to be here at eight every morning and stay until five every evening. I want you to make yourself at home. You can eat here. Anything in the fridge is up for grabs. Feel free to use the grounds. There is a pool and hot tub outside, along with tennis courts if you play. I expect you to join me on all my outings, so you will be given an expense account to go shopping with. I expect you to look professional at all times. No tennis shoes and sweatpants."

"Okay, I think I got everything."

I hit the call button, and Charles comes back into the room. "Yes, sir?"

"Charles, please show Ms. Jones to her room and give her the necessary items she'll need to perform her job here."

He nods. "Right this way, miss."

She rolls her eyes but stands up and follow along behind him.

"See you in the morning, Ms. Jones." I smile and wave.

She looks over her shoulder at me, and even from here, I can see her annoyance. I don't know why that brings me so much pleasure still to this day. That's something I should have outgrown long ago. I think just causing her to feel anything is enough to make me smile. It doesn't matter if it's hate or annoyance. Soon enough, I'll have her feeling a way she's never felt before... as she's calling out my name from underneath me.

A smile breaks free across my face at the thought as my body comes alive with tingles. I'm straining against my jeans as I watch her perfect ass move from side to side in that tight black skirt. I guess I should have asked if she's seeing someone, but it really doesn't matter. Nothing is going to stop me from getting her this time. I've done my time. I've paid my dues. And Gabbi Jones, she's going to be my dirtiest fantasy come to life.

I rub my hands together as I picture having her spread out on the bed before me, me moving between her parted legs, watching those eyes of hers light up the moment she realizes that she wants me, the guy she hates. My whole life, I've wanted one thing: her. And now that she's in my sights, in my home, working with me day in and day out, I'm going to get what I want once and for all.

I turn to my computer and watch as Charles shows her around the property. He takes her out back and shows her the grounds. She smiles when she takes in the pool and hot tub, and my heart begins to flutter. He brings her back in and introduces her to my dogs, Lola and Journey, both American pit bulls. She seems a little nervous meeting them. I mean, they both look mean as hell with their cropped ears, square heads, and muscular bodies. They each weigh over fifty pounds. Any person in their right mind would be scared, but she pets Lola, and Lola overloads her with kisses. Gabbi falls down to her knees, smiling and petting both of them as they roll onto their backs for belly rubs. I'm glad to see her getting along with my girls. Charles shows her the kitchen and the rest of the downstairs area, but then he shows her to her room, and my show is over. The bedrooms don't have cameras like the rest of the house, but for the first time since moving in here, I wish they did. What I wouldn't give to watch her when she thinks she's alone. I'm sure that's the only time she lets her guard down. I want to see the easygoing nature that she used to have before my friends and I stole it from her. It's been a long time since high school, and now, I want to give it back. Hopefully, she finds it with time.

THREE
GABBI

Charles opens the bedroom door for me, and I walk in, gasping when the room isn't what I thought it would be. When Easton said I'd have a room here, I was thinking bedroom. I expected a bed in the center of the room filled with untouchable knickknacks and pristine white carpet, but this room isn't a bedroom. It's a suite. When you walk into the room, there's a seating area. There are couches, tables, chairs, a TV on the wall, and a fluffy rug that I want to feel under my bare feet. There's an archway, and when I walk through it, I'm taken to the next section of the room, the bedroom. There is a bed, but it's not in the center of the room. It's pushed up against the two walls in the back corner. There are sliding doors, like two sets of barn doors, that allow you to close off the bed. The center of the room holds a massive desk, computer, and all the usual items a desk would have. There's a landline phone, a speaker box that I'm assuming is for the house's intercom system, and a stack of paperwork already waiting on me. Behind the desk are two large French doors that open up to a balcony.

"That door there is a walk-in closet, and that one there is your private bath," Charles says, pointing at the two doors on the far side of the room. "This stuff here, we'll need you to fill out. It's just a nondisclosure agreement stating that you cannot and will not talk about anything you see, hear, or experience here. This is the phone that we expect you to keep on you at all times. If Mr. Perez needs to contact you, he will call this phone. And this phone," he says, pointing to the other iPhone, "is a business phone that you must keep on at all times. His agent will call this phone. All the other business calls you'll need to handle for Mr. Perez will also come through it."

I nod, taking in all the information he's giving me.

"This is the card to your expense account. Since you're his assistant, you get a higher amount than the rest of us since you'll need to buy clothes and shoes that are suitable for you to be seen in public with him. You get five thousand dollars to spend on such items every month, and you are expected to use it. Mr. Perez doesn't like to be photographed in the same clothes twice, and he expects you to be the same."

"I'm going to be photographed?"

He nods. "Mr. Perez doesn't go into public without being photographed, and if you're with him, you'll be photographed too," he answers. "Here are your keys. These keys open every lock on this property, including rooms and outbuildings. You'll also have a car to use. This car is to stay here. It's not your personal car. It's the car you'll use to run errands for Mr. Perez. You'll drive your car here every morning and park it in the back with the rest of the staff, and if you're sent on an assignment, you'll take the car provided. Do you have any questions?"

"So many," I mumble, trying to wrap my head around everything.

He lets out a soft chuckle. "It will get easier. In the meantime, you're free to go today, but he expects you back at eight a.m. If I were you, I'd spend the day shopping. Those knockoff shoes won't make it past paparazzi." Without another word, he walks out, leaving me alone.

I look around the room again, and it feels too big for one person. I open my purse and put the two new phones into it, along with their chargers that are sitting next to them. I toss in the keys and pick up the credit card and slide it into my wallet. I can't believe all this. He not only gave me a room in his mansion, but a Tesla to drive, a credit card that I only get to spend on clothing, shoes, and accessories, and a bigger paycheck than I've ever earned before.

Before taking off for my day of shopping, I sit at the desk and sign the contract. Once that is done, I grab my purse and hit the door, not seeing anyone on my way out. Stepping outside, I suck in a large gulp of oxygen. For some reason, I felt like I couldn't breathe in there, not as freely as I can breathe out here anyway. I climb behind the wheel and drive straight to the mall. So apparently, I need better shoes than my favorite pair of knockoffs.

AFTER A DAY OF SHOPPING, I've nowhere near spent my allotted amount on clothing, but I did score some designer shoes and a new purse because God forbid I have my picture taken standing next to a famous actor while I have a Target purse on my arm. I also picked up a few outfits from name-brand stores instead of Old Navy or Gap. But returning to my empty apartment only leads me to remember why I had to take this job to begin with, and the sadness settles back over me. I never escape it for long. His absence is everywhere I look. Literally. I wouldn't be in this apartment if it weren't for him. How he talked me into putting my name on the lease is beyond me.

I shake the thoughts from my head and drop all my purchases onto the floor of the entryway as I go to the kitchen and pour a glass of wine. I take the glass and the bottle to the bathroom where I start a nice, relaxing bubble bath. Sinking into the hot water, I let out a relieved breath. I sip my chilled wine and lean my head back. Easton's face pops into my head, and it makes my head hurt. He's your typical good-looking asshole. You know the type: tall, dark, and handsome. Not to mention he has a killer body with muscles toned in places that I didn't even know existed. I know from a nude scene he did a couple years back.

I wonder if he's really changed as he says he has or if it's all some kind of act. He is an actor after all. It's the one thing he's always been good at: tricking people into thinking he's better than he is. Better, nicer, more charming. Apparently, I was the only one who ever saw the real Easton.

I guess I shouldn't discredit him so soon. It has been ten years since high school, but some things never change. And I can't just forget every horrible thing he's done to me. Hell, I don't even know if I can forgive him. I mean, how do you forgive the person who's tormented you for most of your life? What have I done that was so bad for karma to give me this load of shit luck? I lose my long-term boyfriend, end up getting stuck with an apartment I can't afford, and I have no choice but to take a job working for the man I hate the most. I'm sick of men and the way they think they can walk all over me.

My phone chimes and I pick it up to see a text from Dean.

Dean: *Have you figured out what you want to do with the apartment?*

I sigh and roll my eyes.

Gabbi: *I can't afford it, so I have to be out by the end of the month. Better come get the rest of your stuff.*

I pick up my glass of wine and finish it off. My phone chimes again.

Dean: *I've been talking to Mandy, and since that place is so much bigger than hers, we're willing to take it off your hands. That is, if you plan on moving out.*

My brows furrow together. Not only did he leave me for her, he wants to move her into our apartment? The apartment that has my name on it?

Gabbi: *You want the apartment after you talked me into putting my name on the lease?*

Dean: *You can sublet it. We can do this legally, have contracts and* everything. I hate that we ended the way we did. I'm not trying to fuck you over on this.

Well, that's the first nice thing he's said to me since he walked out on me. But I guess I could put this shitty situation to good use. I mean, it would get me out of the lease so at least I wouldn't be sued. I'll just have to find a new apartment, but that was already on my list of things to do. Then an idea hits me.

Gabbi: *Okay, you can take it. I'll draw up the agreement and be out by the end of the month.*

Dean: *Okay, great! Since I'll be moving back in, you can just leave my stuff there.*

Gabbi: *I'll mail you the agreement and you can mail it back. If I don't get it before I find another place, I won't be leaving. I'm not putting myself into a position to get fucked over again.*

Dean: *I completely understand. I'll sign it and mail it back same day. Sorry again about all this.*

I don't bother replying this time. There's no reason to. But now that I have a plan in place, I feel much better. I crawl out of the tub and dry off, ready to put everything into motion.

I take my half-empty bottle of wine to the living room with me. I turn on the laptop and set it on the table as I move around the apartment, taking pictures of all the furniture I want to sell. If Dean is going to fuck me over like this, I'm going to sell every bit of his shit and use that money to get the apartment I need. "The treadmill, gone!" I snap the picture. "The mirror, sold!" I snap another picture. I finish up in the home gym, which is mostly yoga mats, free weights, and a stereo system, then I move to the dining room, taking pictures of the dining room table and chairs, the hutch that holds the fine china, and the dishes inside. I move from room to room, snapping pictures before sitting on the couch and uploading them to Craigslist. Lastly, I find a contract online that I put our names into, then print it out. I seal it in an envelope and plan on dropping it into the mail tomorrow on my way to my shitty job.

As I stand back and look at the envelope, drinking my wine

straight out of the bottle, I smile to myself. I've never been the type to get revenge. I've always let everyone walk all over me and get away with it without ever having to deal with the consequences. But not this time. It's time to welcome in the new me. I'm no longer a girl who takes shit from everyone and cries herself to sleep. Now, I'm a badass woman who will fuck you just as hard as you fuck me. Dean thought he wanted to leave me. Well, all his stuff is going to leave him. And if Easton wants to go back to how things used to be, he's got another thing coming.

I look over and find my bags in the hallway that I dropped. I giggle and run to them, sitting down on the floor and going through everything one by one. The fabrics are softer than anything I ever would've found at Target. The heels are shiny and gorgeous. The purse smells of expensive leather. I hug it to my chest. I almost feel like Anne Hathaway in *The Princess Diaries*. My life is changing, and instead of fighting against the pull, I'm going to ride the waves.

I stand up, taking everything with me to put away. I change out my purse and look at it on my arm in the mirror. I slide my feet into my new expensive shoes and add on the sunglasses I bought today. I look myself over and smile wide, now ready for this new chapter in my life.

FOUR
EASTON

I slide behind my desk at seven fifty-five and pull up the video surveillance. I see her car make its way up the drive and pull around to the back where the staff parks. I change cameras to watch her. She parks, gathers her things, and then gets out, walking across the concrete to the back door. She's wearing a dark pair of sunglasses, and her shoulder-length blond hair is curled, blowing in the breeze. The fitted pair of dress pants she has on hug her thighs, hips, and perfect ass. Her white dress shirt is tucked into her pants, and she has a few buttons unbuttoned, showing some cleavage. Her tits bounce with every step her new black shoes take. Fuck, she's gorgeous.

She lets herself into the house using her new set of keys, and I shut the computer so she doesn't know that I was watching her. A knock comes at the door and I smile, ready to lay my eyes on her. "Come in."

The door opens and she walks in, her shoes clicking on the hardwood floor as she comes to sit in front of me. "Good morning," she says, dropping her purse onto the floor by her chair.

"Good morning. You look beautiful today." I look her up and down, trying my best to hold off a smile.

She takes off her sunglasses and rolls her eyes. "Please," she breathes out.

"Please what?" I ask, sitting up to be closer to her. Her sweet scent makes its way up my nose, and I savor it, wishing I could bottle it for my own personal pleasure.

"You're not going to win me over by telling me that I'm beautiful. I wasn't beautiful when you made my life a living hell, now was I?"

I let out a long breath, letting my head fall.

"Either way, this is a job, and I'm in serious need of a job. So, I'm willing to put all that behind us and get to work. Deal?"

I look up and find her holding out her hand. I smile as I slide mine into it. "Deal."

She offers up a tight smile as she nods her head once. "Now, what's on the agenda for today?"

"Well, according to my calendar, I have a photoshoot. Remind me later to give you permission to view and change my calendar."

She nods as she writes down a note for herself.

"Ready to go?" I ask, standing up.

"Oh, I'm going with you?" She seems surprised, her eyes wide as she looks up at me.

I nod. "Of course. I'll drive though," I say, walking around the desk and heading for the door. I hear her shuffling behind me, gathering her things and rushing to catch up.

I walk us through the house and to the connected garage. What should I drive today? I think the sleek black Lambo will do the job. I grab the key off the hook on the wall and hit the fob, unlocking it. I climb behind the wheel, and she sits in the passenger seat.

"Whoa," she breathes out, looking around the car.

"What's wrong?"

"I've never been in a car this nice. I'm scared to touch anything."

I chuckle. "It'll be fine. Buckle up," I insist, starting the car. It roars to life and purrs like a mean little kitten. I glance over at her before opening the garage door and shifting into reverse. Her seat belt is on tight and her hands grasp the seat, holding on for dear life. I chuckle.

"What?" she asks, her eyes cutting in my direction.

"We haven't even moved, and you're sitting there like I've already broken the sound barrier or something."

"Well, won't you?"

I shake my head but give the car gas. Slowly, we back up. I hit the button and close the garage door before shifting into drive and starting down the driveway. Before we get to the gate, I hit the button for that, too, and it's open by the time we arrive. Pulling out onto the street, I close the gate and start toward the studio where my photoshoot will take place.

The windows in the car are darkly tinted, and every car we pass, the passenger is trying to look in. I watch her taking this all in for the first time, and she's wearing a smile, amused by it all. I notice that her hands are no longer holding on to the seat. Small crescent moon shapes are indented into the leather from her fingernails. I don't point it out though. I know she'll only lose her mind, thinking she's damaged my car. What she doesn't know is that I don't give a shit about this car. She could have it if she asked. What I'm more concerned with is her and the fact that I have her in my car, so close I could reach out and touch her if I wanted. But I won't. I know how slow I have to take this. I want to talk with her, but I'm not sure how to go about it. Do I bring up the past or try avoiding it altogether? Do I talk about what's going on in our lives now?

"So, why do you need this job so badly?" I ask, wondering if this topic is a safe one or not.

She takes a long breath. "My long-term boyfriend broke up with me only a month after insisting we get this new, bigger, more expensive apartment. Because my credit score was higher than his, I put my name on the lease. Now, I can't afford it on my own, so I have to save up as much money as I can so I can find a more affordable place by the end of the month," she says, sounding a little angry but honest.

"What an asshole. You said long-term. How long?"

"I met him soon after moving here five years ago."

"Damn," I mumble. The longest relationship I've had was only like three months. Being a famous actor isn't good for my dating life, not unless I'm just looking for someone who just wants to hook up or to use me for my money, fame, or name.

She nods. "Yep. But we've come to an agreement. He's going to sublet the apartment from me for him and his new girlfriend. That gets me off the hook, but I still have to find a new place."

"Well, if it helps, there is a pool house that you can crash in if you'd like," I offer. Hell, I'd let her move into the main house, but something tells me she'd never go for it. Actually, something tells me she won't go for the pool house either, but I have to try.

She laughs, but it comes out sounding like a scoff. "Thanks, but I think I can handle it on my own."

I shrug, trying to pretend that it doesn't bother me. "Have it your way, but just know the offer stands."

"What got you into acting? I remember back in high school you didn't do anything but basketball. You weren't in drama club or anything."

I weave in and out of traffic, but with her eyes on me, waiting for an answer, she doesn't notice. "I went to college and got into modeling as a way to make some money. Modeling brought me to acting. I took a few small roles that eventually led to bigger and bigger roles, and here we are. It wasn't my dream or anything, but it turned out pretty well, I think."

She nods, accepting my answer before turning to stare back out the windshield.

"Why did you move out here?"

She lets out a nervous laugh and rolls her eyes. "To try my hand at acting, of course."

"Really?" I ask, raising my brow.

She nods. "Yeah, but I took a few jobs through the temp agency that my ex worked at to keep me fed until I hit it big. It never happened though. I never landed a part."

"Your ex works for the temp agency now? The same one that I used to hire you?" I ask, already forming a plan in my head.

She nods. "Yep. He got a promotion, and that's why he decided to get a bigger place. But the promotion also gave him an assistant, and that's who he left me for."

"I can't believe you're so well adjusted with all this," I joke.

"Oh, I'm not." She smiles. "Once he signs that contract and I move out, he'll find that I've sold all of his things. He'll have a completely empty apartment by the time he moves in." She laughs and I join in.

"At least you're getting some kind of revenge."

She nods. "Still haven't figured out how I'm going to get my revenge on you, but rest assured, your time will come too."

I smile. "I look forward to it."

Something flashes in her big blue eyes. Determination? Vengeance? I'm not sure, but I look forward to finding out. I exit the highway and turn through the streets until I find the place we need to be. I show the guard my pass and he opens the gates, allowing us to drive through the lot. I park the car and turn it off. The two of us climb out as I lead her to the door.

Inside, everything is almost completely set up and ready to go. People are finishing setting up the backdrops and preparing the camera. The moment I'm inside, a woman rushes up to me.

"Mr. Perez, how are you today, sir?" she asks, holding a clipboard to her chest.

I smile. "Great. Where do you want me?"

"Follow me, and I'll take you back to your dressing room where we'll go over wardrobe, hair, and makeup." I follow after the woman, and Gabbi follows along behind me in complete awe as she takes everything in around her. We're led down a hall and taken inside a room to my left. Inside, there is a couch, TV, snacks, drinks, and rows and rows of clothing next to the vanity where my hair and makeup will be done. I walk in and flop onto the couch. Gabbi hangs out by the door, looking like she's ready to take off sprinting at any moment.

The woman with the clipboard stands in front of me, going over everything, but I tune her out as I watch Gabbi instead. She's holding her purse tightly against her, and her blue eyes are wide. She's nervously shifting her weight from one foot to the other as she moves her eyes from one thing to the next. They never settle long. Finally, they move in my direction and they meet mine.

I stand up. "Will you please give us a moment?" I ask the woman.

"Of course," she agrees, walking out of the dressing room and closing the door behind her.

I turn to face Gabbi. "Is everything okay?" I ask, feeling my brows pulling together.

"What? Yeah, I'm fine. Why?" she asks, stumbling over her words.

"You just... look like you're ready to puke or run. Or both."

She waves a hand through the air, and I see how it's shaking. "No, I'm fine."

"Nervous?" I ask, tipping my head in her direction.

She nods as her eyes fall to the floor.

"Want to know what I do when I'm nervous?"

"What?" The word is a soft whisper as it leaves her lips.

"Close your eyes," I direct, walking closer.

She squints at me.

"Trust me. And give me this," I say, taking her purse off her arm and dropping it onto the table. "Now, close your eyes."

She does as I ask. Her arms are resting at her sides, but her hands are balled up into fists.

I take one fist in my hands and smooth her fingers out. "Breathe. Slowly. Deeply. Relax."

She lets me smooth out her fingers as she takes deep, even breaths.

I step up behind her and whisper in her ear. "Slow your breathing. Slow your heart rate." I know she feels my breath against her ear, and she drags in a ragged breath. "Listen to my voice and let it calm you." I push some hair behind her shoulder so her ear is exposed. My nose moves closer to her ear and I breathe her in. She smells like peaches and something else. Coconut? Not a mixture you'd think would work, but on her, it totally does. "Do you feel better?" I ask, running the tip of my nose along her ear.

When I do that, her eyes fly open and she steps away. "Yep. Yeah. I'm fine. All good," she rushes to say. I smile as I watch the nerves that I just melted away reform and multiply.

I shrug. "That's what I do anyway."

Her eyes are wide as she nods her head. "Yeah, totally works," she agrees as she moves to sit on the couch and put as much distance between us as she can.

Someone knocks on the door. "Mr. Perez, it's Lidia, hair and makeup. Are you ready for me?"

"Come in," I direct, still looking at Gabbi.

The door opens and in walks a woman with black hair and enough makeup to paint up an entire drag show. She introduces herself and shakes my hand before asking me to have a seat in front of the mirror where she starts to get me ready for the photoshoot.

I can see Gabbi from the mirror. She looks bored and out of place, like she isn't comfortable. So I decide to give her a job. "Hey, Gabbi?"

She looks up and our eyes lock in the mirror.

"Would you mind grabbing me some breakfast? Maybe a coffee and some kind of sandwich? I think I saw a Starbucks down the street."

"Oh, okay, sure," she agrees, standing up.

"Make sure you get a pass at the gate to get back in," I tell her, watching her go.

FIVE
GABBI

Before walking out, Easton gave me the keys to his car. I don't think anything about it until I walk up to it. He wants me to drive this? This! I was scared to even sit in the thing, and he expects me to operate it? Fuck. I pull out my phone and Google the nearest Starbucks, wondering if it's possible to just walk there. Turns out, it's not even a half mile down the road. Walking it is.

I get my pass in order to get back in and start in the direction of the Starbucks on foot. As I walk, I think about the way my body tightened to the point of being sore because of him. I never expected him to touch me. I never expected him to be close enough to smell his aftershave. And I never expected his mouth to be so close to me. He ran his nose up my ear! He said he was trying to help me relax, but it didn't help me relax in the slightest. In fact, it did the opposite. I never wanted Easton Perez before. Never. But with my eyes closed and his voice in my ear... I probably would have dropped down to my knees if he'd told me to.

Pushing away all the bad memories that he created, I can see the charm other people find in him. He's tall, with broad shoulders and lean hips. He has a killer body and muscles upon muscles but not the big bulky kind that lead you to believe he spends all day in the gym. He's lean, hard, and toned. His face is angular with high cheekbones and a jaw sharp enough to cut glass. He sometimes has a thick dark stubble that makes him appear dirty and rough. His eyes are the color of the darkest chocolate with tiny flakes of gold you can only see when he's mad. And he has thick, luscious auburn hair with natural highlights. Okay, if I'm being completely honest, he's fucking sexy as hell. Too bad all these bad memories live on in my head.

I make it to Starbucks within minutes, and I order us both some coffee and get him his breakfast sandwich before starting my walk back. With my pass, I get in easily and find my way back to the studio the photoshoot is being held in. When I walk back into his dressing room, he's still sitting in his chair, but the woman has moved on to perfecting his hair instead of covering the dark circles under his eyes that were barely visible. I guess the lighting and the camera would have really brought them out though.

"Ah," he says when I walk in. "Thank you. Did you have any trouble with the car?"

I hand over his items. "I walked. No way am I driving a car that costs more than my entire life." I pull his keys out of my purse and drop them into his hand.

He laughs and his eyes light up. "One of these days, you'll be driving that thing like a pro. Mark my words."

"I highly doubt it," I disagree, taking my coffee over to the couch. While the makeup artist puts on her finishing touches, I pull out phone after phone, checking all the emails and moving things to his calendar that I've been approved to change.

He gets called onto set, and while he does his thing, I stay back in the dressing room. I get bored and turn on the TV only to find that it's live broadcasting the photoshoot. I watch as he stands in front of an all-white backdrop, dressed in all black. His dress shirt is unbuttoned, and every time he moves, his abs flex. I feel my muscles tighten as I watch him. He smiles and I swear it lights up the room. I don't know what annoys me more, having to work with him or having to pretend that I'm not attracted to him. Both are infuriating.

I watch the TV screen for several long minutes, burning my favorite poses into my brain, then I shut the TV off, not wanting to get caught ogling my boss. He doesn't need to know that I'm attracted to him. He'll never let me live it down. I have a feeling he's on his best behavior, not wanting me to quit. But why does he care anyway? If he hated me as much as he did back then, he wouldn't want me to have the job, right? Why is it important to him that I'm here? I should ask. I mean, he asked why I needed this job so badly. If he can be forward and direct, so can I.

The photoshoot lasts longer than I thought it would, and it's going on noon by the time we leave. He's back behind the wheel, and I watch as he drives with ease. He's not scared or cautious when he drives. He holds the wheel firmly but also lazily at the same time. His muscles in his arms are nice and relaxed. I have a feeling if I were driving, my back would be ramrod straight. I'd be a mess of nerves, anxiety, and fear. Not him though. If he is, he doesn't show it, and while he's a good actor, he's not that good.

"Want to stop for lunch?" he asks as he drives down the freeway.

"I'm not all that hungry," I lie. I'm actually starving, but it's important that I save every dollar I can, and since I just spent sixteen dollars on coffee and his breakfast sandwich, I can pass on lunch. I'll get to go home in a few hours anyway, and I already have a frozen meal waiting on me.

"Okay," he says. "So, what did you think of the shoot?"

I shrug. "I don't know. I didn't see much of anything. It felt kind of weird and awkward though. I just felt like everyone was staring at me."

He lightly laughs. "You'll get used to it."

"Can I ask you a question?"

"Sure."

"Why did you give me this job?"

His eyes cut to me but quickly flash back to the road.

"I mean, I'm sure you didn't know who the agency was sending over, but why didn't you call it off when I showed up yesterday? I mean, don't you hate me or something? Isn't that why you gave me so much shit in school?"

"You want me to be honest?" he asks. His body is now tensing up. He squeezes the steering wheel tighter as he repositions himself in his seat so he's sitting up.

"Yes. That's all I ever want."

"I don't hate you, Gabbi. I've never hated you."

"Then why put me through so much hell?"

He swallows, and his Adam's apple bobs in his throat. "Because you're the one thing I've always wanted."

My mouth instantly goes dry. My tongue feels thick, too thick to talk. Goosebumps prickle my skin, and my ears ring as my blood begins to race around my body, my heart only pushing it to go faster. "Excuse me?" I manage to get out. Maybe I didn't hear him right. No, I know I didn't hear him right. *Chill, body. Don't freak out on me yet.*

He nods. "I remember the day you walked into our kindergarten class. You remember that?"

I nod. I remember exactly what he was wearing: jeans with a red-and-blue-striped shirt. His hair was lighter then, almost blond, and it was combed neatly to one side.

"You were wearing this little pink dress, black dress shoes with ruffly socks, and your hair was long, blond, and full of curls. You had a bow that matched your dress, and even though I was only five years old at the time, I knew I wanted you. I didn't even know what that meant, but I wanted you. Then I shot you in the eye with a spit wad and fucked up the rest of our lives. You wouldn't look at me after that, and when you did, it was with hate. I wanted you and you hated me. So, at some point, I decided that if I couldn't have you, I didn't want anyone else to either. I know, I was a complete asshole and there's no excuse for that. But that's what it was. I didn't hate you. I wanted you. I still want you."

We're pulling back into the drive now, and my heart is racing so fast, it feels like it could lock up and freeze at any moment and completely give out after working so hard. I don't know how to respond. All this time, pretty much my whole fucking life, I was convinced that Easton Perez hated my guts. And now I find out that he doesn't hate me. He wants me. I don't know what to do with that information. I don't know how to respond. It's like living your whole life and thinking the earth is flat, only to learn that it's round. It's mind-altering, earth-shattering, life-changing.

He parks the car and looks over at me, but I'm still frozen, staring at my hands in my lap. I swallow down my fear as I lift my head and shake it. "I have to go," I say, running from the car. He doesn't stop me or call me back. He just lets me go. I climb behind the wheel of my car, back out, and throw it into drive. As I'm speeding around the garage to the front of the house, he's exiting the garage and watching me drive away. His jaw is cocked, his eyes warm and smoldering as he watches me go.

I hit the button on the key fob to open the gate before I get to it, and it's open by the time I get there. I stop just outside the gate and watch it close before continuing on. My mind is a mess on the drive home. What am I supposed to do now? Am I supposed to go back there tomorrow and act like nothing happened? Am I supposed to use this time to figure out how to respond to what he just told me? Is there any way to go back and not ask that question? I highly doubt it.

When I get home, I find several messages on my voicemail of people wanting to buy the items I listed online last night. I return the calls and set up a time this evening for the items to be picked up. I pour a glass of wine as I sit on the couch. I turn the TV on, hoping to drown out my thoughts, but nothing works. I can't get my mind off Easton and the secret he revealed. I mean, how different would my life be right now if I hadn't started hating him in kindergarten? If I accepted his apology for the spit wad? Would we have become friends? Would I have been part of his inner circle in high school? Would I be where I am now? All the what-ifs do no good, and there's no point in thinking about them. No, what I need to think about now is what I'm going to say to him tomorrow.

SIX

EASTON

I'm drinking a cup of coffee as I sit in the theater, watching the morning news. The door opens and she comes walking in. I smile as I watch her walk closer and closer. She's wearing tight pants that hug all her curves, high heels that make her legs appear shapely, and a white short-sleeved dress shirt. It's ruffly around the arms, and it reminds me of that dress she wore when we were little. The top of the shirt fits her chest snugly while the rest of it is looser. She walks with determination as she comes closer. Finally, she makes it down to me and sits at my side.

"I forgive you," she states like the sentence has been burning her tongue and she's finally glad she's said it and gotten it out of her mouth.

I straighten up. "You forgive me for what, exactly?"

"The spit wad," she states.

"Oh." I chuckle. "That's good. I mean, it's only been what, twenty-five years?"

She lifts one eyebrow and it arches perfectly. "I was thinking last night. All this time, I thought you hated me. So when you said otherwise yesterday, it threw me through a loop. I mean, how differently would my life have been if I had just forgiven you for the spit wad back then? Would we have been friends? In high school, would I have been the one by your side instead of Lexi?"

Hearing that name makes me flinch as acid boils in my stomach. Lexi was my high school girlfriend. We broke up my freshmen year in college. I broke it off. We were just too far away from one another and turning into different people. Since then, she's mildly stalked me, determined to get me back any way she can. It didn't get out of hand until I moved to California and started making a name for myself. Then all she saw was a cash train she wanted to ride.

"I don't know, Gabbi. We can't ever go back now. There's no way we could possibly know."

She nods once, then sits back and turns her eyes to the TV. "What are you watching?"

"The news."

Her nose scrunches up.

"What? You don't watch the news?"

She shakes her head. "No way. It's depressing."

"Then how do you know what's going on out there in the world?"

"I read articles, unbiased ones that only state the facts and not the opinions of others. And I only read the articles that interest me. *Family man of four kills himself*, I skip. *House fire in Georgia*, I skip. *Devastating bombing leaving seventy dead*, I skip. It's too sad."

I laugh as I shake my head. "It is sad, but it's real. That can be hard to come by these days."

She looks over at me like she's surprised that I even said that. "You of all people are talking about being real?"

"I get it, I do. In high school, I had everyone fooled into thinking I was some kind of god. Even now, I'm an actor who pretends to be someone I'm not. But I think that's what changed me. I played so many different characters that I needed to be sure of who I was, and when I sat down to think of who I was, I didn't like what I saw. So I changed the things I didn't like and forced myself to be a better person."

She crosses her arms over her chest. "So, who are you?"

I shrug. "I'm Easton, a guy who likes watching the news to see if there is anyone who needs my help. I like putting my money to a good cause instead of just pissing it all away. I like to volunteer at animal shelters and soup kitchens. I like spending my days with people I genuinely like, good people, not fake, judgmental people who think they're better than anyone else. And I like changing people's perception of me. Like you. I'm really enjoying watching you learn who I am all over again." I smile. "So, Gabbi. Who are you?"

Her cheeks turn pink from being put on the spot, but she sits up and rubs her hands together. "I'm the same girl I always was, only now I'm stronger and refuse to let people walk all over me. I like to spend my time at home, curled up on the couch with a good book and a warm blanket. I like to let loose every once in a while. And I like it when I see the people around me change for the better. It makes me believe that I can do it too."

"You can," I tell her. Our eyes are locked, and somehow, we're both slowly leaning in, so slowly that I'm not even sure she's aware of it. I wet my lips, and her eyes flash down to them and back to mine. She pulls her bottom lip into her mouth, biting down on it for a moment before releasing it, leaving behind teeth marks on the soft, pink flesh. I want nothing more than to smooth them away with my own lips. I can practically taste how sweet her lips will be.

Someone knocks on the door, and we both straighten up quickly.

"Mr. Perez, I was supposed to remind you of an interview you've had set up for a few months now."

"Yes, thank you," I tell him.

He leaves and I look back at Gabbi. She now has a phone in her hand. "Interview today at one, and the rest of your week is clear." Her blue eyes meet mine.

"I guess I better go shower and get ready." I stand.

She nods. "I'll go and get to work." She turns quickly and walks up the aisle of the theater.

"Gabbi?" I call out after her.

"Yes?" she responds, stopping at the door and turning to look over her shoulder at me.

"It's your life. You can change, be who you want to be, and do what you want to do."

She offers up a half smile before nodding and darting across the hall to her room.

I go to my room and into the connected bathroom. I stand at the sink and shave before moving to the shower. Standing beneath the hot flow of water feels amazing, relaxing, and grounding. I can't help but think of her. She seems to be coming around, but she also seems to be holding something back at the same time. I'm sure she's probably trying to decide if she can trust me or not yet. But that's okay. I can wait because I know the prize will be worth it.

Once I'm done with my shower, I pull on some clothes and fix my hair. Exiting my room, I'm walking down the hallway when I hear Gabbi's voice on the other side of her door. She's talking on the phone. I know I shouldn't, but I pause, wanting to know what she's talking about.

"I'm serious, Ash. I'm his assistant."

Ah, I'm the topic of discussion. I want to see where this is going.

"I know. The first day, I wasn't sure how I could make it work, but he really does seem to have changed. He's grown up. He seems more thoughtful, careful. And yes, he's fucking hot as fuck." She giggles. "Oh, I've thought about it, but the truth is that I'm dealing with too much right now with the breakup. I mean, it was only a week ago. I can't be jumping into bed with the first guy I see. Not to mention, I still have to find a new place. I can't afford to stay where I'm at. He offered up his pool house, but I turned him down. It just doesn't seem right to accept."

"Mr. Perez?" Charles says, causing me to jerk my head away from the door. When I look at him, his brows are drawn together in confusion. "Your meeting starts in ten minutes, sir."

I nod. "Right. I was just on my way down." I push myself forward, rushing past him and down the stairs to my office. I turn on the computer, and while it starts up, I pour myself a cup of coffee and a glass of water, taking both back to my desk. I go through my emails and look for the private link I was sent to do the interview. I find it and click it. It takes me to a secure video chat room, and after being welcomed, the interview starts.

AN HOUR LATER, the interview is finished, and I log off and exit my office. With nothing else going on today, I head up to Gabbi's office to let her know that she's free to go if she'd like. I knock on the door.

"Come in," she calls out.

I open the door and walk in.

She looks up with a smile. "Hey, how was the interview?"

"Good," I reply, sitting down in the chair across from her. "Listen, I don't have anything else going on, so if you want to take off, you're more than welcome to."

"Okay, great. I went through all the emails and added things to your calendar for you to approve. I didn't know if you usually did everything or if you pick and choose. So just keep what you want to do, delete the rest, and I'll confirm or deny the appointments tomorrow."

"Sounds good. Thank you."

"No problem," she says, spinning in her chair and picking up her purse from the floor beside her. "I have a ton of people coming over today to buy some of Dean's furniture, so I better get going. See ya tomorrow." Without another word, she stands and walks from the room.

I hate to admit it, but I feel a little let down. I was hoping that she'd choose to stick around, that the two of us could just hang out and get to know one another better, but I guess we can do that kind of thing any day. This is only our third day working together. Even though I know I have to go slow with her, I can't help but want to push forward. I remind myself to step back, slow down, and take my time.

SEVEN
GABBI

I hop in my car and start the engine. It sounds rough, a little louder than usual, but I don't pay much attention as I shift into drive and start down the driveway. Pausing at the gate, the motor almost seems like it wants to give out, but I give it some gas and she roars to life. I check my gauges and don't notice anything out of the ordinary. My tank is half full, so I'm not low on fuel. The harder I push the gas, the louder the engine gets, and it doesn't feel like it's reaching top speed either. I'm about halfway home when the car makes a loud banging sounds and slows to a crawl. Luckily, I'm able to steer it over to the side of the road. Smoke is coming out from under the hood. The car is completely dead.

"Just fucking great," I mumble to myself as I pop the hood and climb out. Cars are speeding past me, making my hair whip around into my face as I open the hood. More smoke comes billowing out and I fan it away. I look down at the motor, hoping something jumps out at me, but I have no idea what to do. Everything looks fine to me.

"What am I going to do now?" I close the hood and get back behind the wheel, trying again and again to start the car, but it doesn't make a sound. Normally in this situation, I'd call my insurance and get it towed away to a shop that can look it over, but I dropped renting and towing when Dean left as a way to save as much money as I could. This really is the perfect time. I don't have any friends here with a car that could come get me. Dean is a no go. Insurance is shot. Who else can I call?

His name floats through my head, but I push it away immediately. No way can I call him, asking for a favor. Maybe I'll get lucky, and someone driving by will take pity on me and stop to help. I chuckle. With my luck, it will be some serial killer who will abduct me. As I think over my options, time ticks by. It will probably be dark soon, and I've had to cancel all my appointments for today, meaning I've lost out on money if the people can't come tomorrow.

Giving in, I call his cell.

"Hey, what's going on?"

"Easton, I need help."

Concern fills his voice. "What's going on?"

"My car broke down on the side of the freeway. I've been sitting here for hours."

"I'm on my way," he says, hanging up.

I let out a long breath, annoyed that he's being so friendly and that I had to call him to begin with. Less than twenty minutes later, he's pulling up behind me. He climbs out of the car and walks up to the driver's side window, rapping his knuckles against it. I grab my things and open the door.

"I called a tow truck. It's on its way. Come on. We'll wait in my car." His hand lands on the small of my back as he leads the way to the passenger door of his car. I take a seat, and he rushes around to join me in the car.

"I can't afford a tow truck. I just canceled renting and towing on my insurance."

"It's fine, Gabbi. I'll handle it."

His words are a relief, but they also make my anxiety go through the roof. "I'll pay you back," I tell him, trying to figure out how much this will set me back.

"Don't worry about it," he says, not seeming bothered in any way.

"I am going to worry about it, Easton. You don't owe me anything, and I'm not taking a handout. I will pay you back."

He smiles. "If that's what you want," he finally agrees.

We sit in silence as we wait. The tow truck finally shows up, and Easton climbs out to talk to the driver. I watch as they exchange a few words and shake hands. He comes back to the car and takes his seat. "They're going to take it to a garage to be looked over. I'll take you home and have the car delivered after it's fixed." He shifts into drive and pulls out onto the road.

I give him directions to my place, but other than that, it's quiet. He pulls into the parking lot and shifts into park before looking over at me. I feel like I should at least invite him up for a drink or something.

"Thanks for saving me. I would've sat there all night if you hadn't."

He smiles. "It's no problem, Gabbi."

I reach for the door handle and open the door but stop. "Would you like to come up for a drink or something? It's the least I can do."

His dark eyes meet mine and they sparkle. "Sure," he agrees, shutting off the car.

We both climb out, and I lead the way to the door and up to my apartment. I unlock the door and let us in. I drop my purse and keys down on the entryway table before sliding out of my shoes.

"This is a nice place," he says, following me down the hallway and into the kitchen.

I snort. "It's nothing compared to your place. Plus, it won't be mine much longer. What's your poison? I got beer, vodka, and tequila."

"A beer is fine."

I grab two beers and hand one over. Then we sit down on the couch in the living room. I pick up the remote and start the fire. I love sitting in front of the fire. It's the thing I'll miss the most when I move out.

"So, how much does this apartment cost?" he asks, looking around.

"Why? You want to move in?" I joke.

"No, but I could give you a raise so you can afford it and won't have to move."

I shake my head. "That's very nice of you, but you've already done more than enough. Plus, I wasn't the one who wanted this place. Dean was. And now, it only reminds me of him, so I'm more than happy to leave. I just gotta find something else first."

"You must have really loved the guy, huh?"

I nod. "I thought we'd get married." My eyes start to tear from thinking about it, but I will them away. "But that's over now and it's time to let go, move on. What about you?" I ask, needing to change the subject.

"What about me?" he asks, taking a drink.

"Well, you see all these Hollywood couples in magazines. Why don't I ever see you?"

He leans forward, setting his beer on the table. "I haven't been in a relationship since high school."

"Really? Why?"

He shrugs. "It's hard when you don't know if the person you're with is only with you for money or fame or whatever. I've dated a few girls, but nothing ever worked out and eventually, I gave up completely."

I nod. "Yeah, I get that. That would be hard. Maybe you should try dating someone who's already famous," I suggest.

"I've done that, too, but it doesn't feel right. It just feels like they are with me to make headlines or something. None of which I'm concerned with, so"—he shrugs—"it's just me and probably always will be."

"Don't you miss the sex though?" The words just fall from my lips. I don't know where they came from, and embarrassment heats my face. I can't believe I just asked him that. "I mean..." I try to think quickly to cover my tracks. "It's only been a week of being single for me and already I'm a little—" *Okay, Gabbi. Shut the fuck up. What is wrong with me?*

He laughs and nods. "I do miss the sex," he says, his eyes darkening.

I tip my bottle back and chug half of it. He smiles as he pulls his eyes away from me, picking up his own bottle and taking a drink.

"Shit. I've made this awkward, didn't I?" I say, closing my eyes and shaking my head at myself.

"It doesn't have to be awkward," he says, making me open my eyes and look in his direction. "I mean, I'll pretend you didn't just tell me you were horny," he laughs, making my face only heat more.

I laugh and cover my face with my hands. "I'm sorry. I was just thinking that if it's this hard for me, it must be really hard for someone who hasn't been in a relationship since high school."

He points at me. "I said I haven't been in a relationship. I didn't say that I haven't had sex."

"Oh. Duh." Fuck, I can't stop humiliating myself tonight. "Clearly, I just need to call it a night and go to bed."

"Nah, don't do that. I like watching you blush." He lifts his hand and runs his index finger along my cheek, right where it's burning. It feels like he sets fire to my skin. Our eyes lock, and his eyes are darker than usual, that hint of gold shining bright, making them look like there's a fire burning behind them.

My mouth opens, but no words come out. I'm not exactly sure how to respond to that.

"You're so beautiful. You know that?" he asks as he starts leaning in. This is the third time I've found myself leaning into him, and I can't help but be confused by it all. I hated him for most of my life. Has all that just gone away? I just got out of a long-term relationship and it's still hurting, like there's still a hole in my chest. But when I'm with him, the hole seems to disappear. How is that possible? Not to mention, he's my boss. My boss! I need this job. I can't jeopardize it by giving in to some kind of sick, twisted urge I have to feel his lips against mine, to feel his body against mine.

And even though all these things are running through my head faster than the speed of light, I can't stop what's about to happen. All I do is freeze as I watch him getting closer and closer to my face.

I should expect it, but a part of me thinks that he'll pull away at the last second. He doesn't. His lips press against mine, and it feels like I'm being shocked. A spark hits my lips, and it ignites a fire that burns a trail from my mouth all the way down to my stomach, which tightens with excitement. His lips are soft but strong as they press against mine. When his tongue comes out, parting my lips, I allow him to slip inside. His hot tongue finds mine, and a soft whimper escapes. His hands move up to cup my face, holding me to him as he deepens the kiss. Our lips move together. Our tongues move in sync, and something breaks inside of me, washing through my body like a heavy wave of need.

My hands move up to fist in his shirt, wanting to pull him closer, wanting his body pressing against mine. One of his hands falls from my cheek down to my hip. His fingers dig in slightly, pulling me closer. As our kiss grows in urgency, he releases my face altogether as he picks me up by my hips and sets me on his lap so I straddle him. His hands stay on my hips, squeezing, massaging their way around to my ass. When he squeezes there, the fire in my belly is met with a flood of my need. You'd think one would put the other out, but no. The fire only spreads, meeting the waves of need. They join forces as they take me over. I want this. I want this with him, but it's wrong. It's bad. I can't remember why right now, but I know it has to stop. We're about to cross a line that can't be uncrossed. I have to pull away. But maybe I could enjoy this for one more minute first.

Before I can break off the kiss, he's laying me back against the couch while his body covers mine. I feel his excitement as it presses into me, right where I need it the most. His strong hands are touring my body, my thighs, my hips, and making their way up my stomach where one settles on my breast with a firm squeeze. I'm breathless, and my lungs are screaming for oxygen. He must sense it because his lips fall from mine, trailing down my neck in hot kisses and soft nips across my skin. I'm burning from the inside out, and only he can put out the fire he's lit inside of me. No, I was supposed to stop this. I have to stop this.

"Easton," I breathe out, "we have to stop."

His mouth only moves back to mine, and my hands betray me, pulling him closer instead of pushing him away. Fuck, he kisses like a god. He tastes like the earth smells on a warm summer day. He tastes like fucking sunshine, dew drops, and the sweet smell of wildflowers blooming nearby. His body is hot pressed against mine, and his weight pressing against me is perfect, not too much but not too little either. It's like we fit together perfectly. This has to mean something, right?

No. It doesn't mean anything. *You're just hurt and confused and attention from any man right now would feel this good. Stop this before you can't go back.*

"Easton," I say, shaking my head. "We have to stop. We can't do this." I somehow get control of my hands, and I manage to push him away.

He sits up, his chest rising and falling quickly with his heavy breathing. He hangs his head as he rests his elbows on his knees.

I push myself to sit up beside him, working to control my breathing, my heart, and my nerves. "You're my boss and I need this job. I can't jeopardize it. Not for some random hookup."

He lifts his head and looks at me with blazing eyes. "Nothing with us has ever been random, Gabbi. You'll see." He stands up and straightens his shirt. He looks back down at me. "I'll wait as long as you need. See you in the morning." Without another word, he turns and walks out, leaving me alone and all kinds of confused.

EIGHT
EASTON

I walk out of her apartment and straight to the elevator. I hit the button and the doors open. I step inside and hit the button for the ground floor. When the doors close, I lean against the wall and let out a long breath I didn't realize I was holding. Fuck. She's better than I ever could've imagined. I knew kissing her would feel like kissing an angel. Her lips are so fucking soft, and she tastes of the sweetest, most delicious, most coveted wine known to man. She's sweet but also complex. She's a million little things all rolled into one. Holding her against me felt like heaven. My body is still betraying me when I think about how perfectly she fit against me. Sliding into her would be like a dream come true. And the fact that she's going to make me work for it instead of throwing herself at my feet like most women do is going to make claiming her that much sweeter.

    I'm halfway home when I get a call from the shop, telling me that the motor in her car is blown. I have Charles drive over a car for her and leave the key under her welcome mat. I write out a note for him to slide under her door. Fuck, I wish I could get her to move into the pool house so I could keep an eye on her, so she'd be so much closer to me. Knowing that she's sleeping so close, I'd probably never get rid of this boner though. It's aching in my jeans, and I know I'll have blue balls by the time I get home.

I go for a shower, and that's when the thoughts of her slip back in. I think back on our kiss, the way she felt against me, that little whimper she let out when my tongue touched hers, and I wrap my hand around my angry cock. My hand begins to move up and down as I picture her naked and sprawled out before me, begging me to take her. I imagine sliding into her, feeling her warmth and tightness wrapped around me. I imagine the sounds she'd make. I imagine her begging me to let her come. I imagine the face she would make when she comes on my dick, and before I know it, I'm spilling every last drop inside of me onto the shower floor.

My lungs are pumping hard and my heart is racing as I drift back down into my body. I thought I wanted her badly before, but that feeling has only multiplied now that I've kissed her, felt her body against mine, and heard her whimper because of me. Now I know I have to have her. There are no ifs, ands, or buts about it. Gabbi will be mine. And once I've had her, I'll make damn sure to ruin every other man for her. She'll be so blinded by me that she'll never want another man as long as I live.

I WAKE in the morning and go down to the dining room where breakfast is already on the table. Charles is standing by the door, newspaper in hand. He hands it over as I walk by. I take my seat, and he gets to work, pouring me a cup of coffee.

"Good morning, sir."

"Good morning. Did you get the car over to Gabbi's last night?"

He nods. "I did. Left the key under the mat and slid the note under her door just like you instructed."

"Great. Thank you."

He nods as he picks up my plate and begins filling it with food. "If you don't mind me asking, what is it with her?"

I look up at him, meeting his eyes. "What?"

He shrugs as he adds bacon to the plate. "I was just wondering. It seems as though you've been waiting for her. Did you know her before she accepted the job?"

Charles has been like a father to me since he started working for me. He's given me advice over the years, and he's whipped me into shape when I needed it. I feel like brushing off his question would be disrespectful.

"I knew her growing up. I've always had a thing for her, but she hated me in school. I guess I'm kind of hoping to introduce her to the new me and cross my fingers that I'm someone she can see herself with."

He nods once. "Ah. I see."

"Do you think it will work?" I ask, feeling like a little kid asking his dad for girl advice.

He laughs. "Only time will tell," he says, turning to walk out.

I hear the back door open a little while later and look up in time to see her go flying by. "Gabbi," I call out.

She takes a few steps back. "Morning," she says with her smile in place.

"There is plenty of food here. Would you like to join me?"

"Oh, I already ate. I have some emails and calls to return, so I'll be upstairs if you need me." She quickly rushes off.

Fuck. I think I scared her off last night. Now I have to figure out how to undo it, fix it. How in the hell am I going to do that? I toss down my napkin and push my chair back. I'm going to talk to her, tell her that there is no reason things between us have to get awkward. We can forget it ever happened if that would make her happy.

The door to her office is open, so I walk in, tapping my knuckles against it as I pass it. She looks up, her eyes wide.

"Look," I say, leaning against her desk and looking down at her. "Last night was..." A long breath leaves me. "Well, it was great, but it doesn't have to be awkward. If you want to, we can just forget that it ever happened."

Her eyes move down my body slowly. It's only now that I realize I'm only wearing a pair of jogger pants and a blue T-shirt. Her eyes slowly move back up as she wets her lips. "Can you really forget?"

Fuck. The way she's looking at me, I'm about ready to throw her down again. "I will do my best," I say, my mouth suddenly dry.

She nods, wets her lips, and looks up at me from beneath her long dark lashes. "I thought I wanted to forget, but..." She stands up, "I don't know if I can." Her eyes move up, locking on mine now. "Last night, all I could think about was losing my job, but then you left and I was kicking myself. As much as I hate that I want you, I can't deny this pull you have over me. I know we shouldn't cross that line, but I don't think either one of us will be happy until we do."

I wet my lips as I look into her eyes. There's something there that's pulling me in. Those big blue eyes of hers look so innocent. All I want to do is sully her, make her mine and nobody else's. My hands have a mind of their own as they reach out and pull her lips to mine. She gives in immediately, her body conforming against mine. Her arms move up and wrap around my neck, deepening our kiss. I drop my hands down to her hips and then around to her ass. With a firm squeeze, I pick her up, and her legs wrap around my hips, and that's how I carry her down the hall to my bedroom.

I kick the door closed and press her back against it. Her legs slowly release me to stand on her own. Her hands fall away from my neck, moving down my chest and stomach to pull my T-shirt up over my head. Our kiss breaks for only a moment as I tear it away and toss it to the floor.

Her dress shirt is tucked into her pants, and I pull it out, my fingers working quickly over the buttons until the shirt is wide open. I pull back and open my eyes to see what I've uncovered. The shirt is open, each side lying across one breast. I see a sliver of her toned stomach, her teardrop-shaped belly button, and no bra beneath.

Each of my hands takes a section of her shirt, and I push it to the side, revealing her naked breasts to me. Fuck, they're perfect. Perfectly shaped. Perfectly perky. Perfectly hard pink nipples that are already standing at attention. As I look at her, her eyes are on mine. I look back up, watching the expressions change on her face as I lower my mouth to her breast. I suck her nipple into my mouth and lash my tongue across it. The moment I do, her fingers thread into my dark hair as her head dips back, resting against the door. A soft moan escapes.

While my mouth teases and tastes, my hands massage. When I'm done with one breast, I move on to the other, my hands exploring more of her at the same time. I kiss down between her breasts to her belly button. That's when I stop. I look back up at her while I unbutton and unzip her pants. I push them down her hips, and she steps out of them.

"Take off your shirt," I demand, wanting to see all of her. She does as I ask and doesn't say a word. No, she just stands there, letting me take her in. I look from the tips of her black-painted toenails, up her long shapely legs, over her toned stomach and perfectly sized breasts, to her face. She's worrying her bottom lip, and her big blue eyes are glistening. She's nervous but fucking sexy as hell. I want nothing more than to slide into her, defile her, tarnish her, make her mine. But at the same time, I want to take my time with her, savor this, make it last. We'll only get one first time, and I want it to be fucking perfect.

I stand before her and pull her back to my chest. Her naked breasts press against me, and it makes tingles rush through my body. I dip my head down, pressing soft kisses along her jaw over to her ear where I whisper, "Go to the bed and take off your panties."

She steps back and looks up at me, unsure, but then she does as I ask.

I take a moment to breathe deeply and clear my mind, not wanting to get too excited. I talk myself down and turn around to face her. What I find is enough to bring me to my knees.

She's on my bed completely bare. Her head is on the pillows, her blond hair fanned out around her. Her blue eyes are wide and watching me. Her thick, plump lips are parted with her heavy breathing. Her chest is rising and falling, her nipples still hard and pink from my mouth. Her legs are bent at the knee, and they're spread open, ready and waiting for me. I don't allow myself to look between her legs yet. I know if I do, there will be no stopping me from taking exactly what I want.

NINE

GABBI

How did I get here, sprawled out completely naked on a movie star's bed with him stalking toward me? His eyes take in every inch of me, and they only darken. He doesn't smile. His jaw is cocked and flexing as he moves toward me. As he approaches the bed, his hands push his running pants down his legs, and his big, hard, erect cock springs free, pointing right in my direction. It looks angry as it swells wider and wider and grows longer and longer. There are thick veins that run along his shaft, and the tip is almost purple. His balls look heavy as they swing between his legs, but oh my God. This is no man. This is the body of a Greek god, hard, trimmed, and toned.

He climbs onto the bed and rests on his knees between my parted legs. He looks from my eyes down my body, wetting his lips. When his eyes land on the junction between my legs, his cock twitches with excitement, a drop of come forming on the tip.

My eyes are glued to his massive length. I have never actually seen one this big in person before. I want to wrap my hand around it and see if his size prevents me from making a closed fist. I want to lick that drop of come off his tip. I lick my lips as I sit up to do just that. I reach for him, but he levels me with one look. I freeze.

"Do you want this, Gabbi?"

I nod my head.

"I want to hear you say it."

"I want you," I say, my voice thick with need.

"Did you want me last night when I had you underneath me?"

I nod and his jaw twitches, so I say, "Yes."

"Did you think of me after I left?"

"Yes." I nod my head. My blood is so hot, it feels like it's boiling under my skin. I feel exposed, and for the first time in my life, I like it.

"Did you touch yourself after I left, pretending it was me?"

My lips part as I suck in a loud breath. I can't believe he asked me that, but what I can't believe even more is that I'm dying to answer. "Yes."

"Show me," he demands.

I swallow down my fear as I lift my hand and start moving it down my body. It's shaking as he watches me with lust-filled eyes. I close my eyes and think back on last night. How I went to bed directly after he left. How I couldn't sleep because I couldn't stop thinking about him and how good he felt against me. My fingers gaze my hip as they move to the junction between my legs. My fingers slide between my folds, finding my wet entrance. I spread the wetness between my folds, finding my sensitive nub. I work my fingers over it, and my knees begin to shake.

I open my eyes and find him watching me intently. His hand is wrapped around his shaft as he works it up and down painfully slowly.

"When I got home last night, I was so painfully hard that I had to jack off in the shower. I came thinking of you, and now I'm going to make you scream my name as I make you come." He grabs my hand and pulls it away. It happens so fast, I don't know what's happening. The next thing I know, his mouth is where my hand just was. His hands hold my hips as his tongue flicks against my bundle of nerves. A moan leaves my mouth as my eyes flutter closed.

"Oh, fuck," I whisper, enjoying each brush of his tongue.

"The only word you're allowed to say is my name. Got it?" he asks, pulling his mouth away but sliding a finger into me. He presses upward, right against my G-spot, and I nod.

His mouth is back, but his hand never leaves. My eyes close as passion floods over me.

"Easton," I whisper his name, and his tongue moves faster.

Oh, fuck. My muscles begin to tighten as tingles take over. Fuck, fuck, fuck. My orgasm begins to build, and his name falls from my lips again. He sucks my clit into his mouth, tongue circling around, pushing me closer and closer to coming undone.

"Easton, I'm going to…"

He pulls away. "What did I say?" he asks with a smirk. My release starts to evaporate, but he's right back to work, winding it up again.

"Easton," I say as I feel like I'm about to snap. I say it again and again and again. The last time, my release washes over me, and his name becomes one long chant in my head. I ride out the wave as it washes through my body, turning every bone and muscle to ice. The ice heats and turns to flame, burning hotter and hotter until it smothers itself.

My body begins to loosen and relax as he pulls his mouth away from me. He runs his arm over his lips, wiping my arousal from his lips. "I hope you're not done with me yet," he says, getting back up on his knees. His body presses against mine as he moves in for a kiss. I like that I can still taste myself on him. I wrap my arms around his neck and pull him closer, wishing we could become one already.

His hard cock is pressing against me, and all it would take is one roll of my hips for him to slip inside. I wiggle them against him, and he pulls away with a chuckle. "In a hurry, are we?" he asks, reaching between us.

"I want you inside me."

He slides his tip between my folds, teasing me. "Are you going to beg?"

"Do you want me to?" I ask, twitching every time his tip touches my sensitive bundle.

"Oh, I want you begging me to fuck you." He's wearing a cocky smile, and even though I've never been turned on by cocky guys, I find him undeniable right now, playing with me like this.

"Please, Easton. Fuck me?"

He positions himself at my entrance but doesn't push forward. "You have no idea how long I've been dreaming of this moment. It's almost bittersweet." Instead of pushing in, he slides himself up my folds again. "You have no idea how badly I want to fuck you, how hard this is for me to hold back like this."

"Then don't hold back."

He gives me a lopsided grin. "Oh, but I want this to last as long as fucking possible." He runs his tip along my entrance. "You're perfect, you know that? I knew you would be, but I wasn't prepared for this, to watch my dick running between your blushing lips, spreading your wetness. How many men have you let see you like this?" He tilts his head and watches me with questioning eyes.

"I've only ever been with two men but never like this," I confess. My first time was with a guy back home when I was eighteen. He was quick and to the point. Dean, he was much better and made sure I got what I needed, but he didn't make a show of it like this. He didn't tease himself or me. Easton is the first to ever torture me this way before.

He moves his dick to my ass. "And how many have been here before?" he asks, pushing just slightly, not enough to enter me but enough that I can feel the pressure. It lights every nerve ending in my body.

"None," I tell him.

"Hmmm. Maybe we'll save that for another day then." He moves his dick back up, and the tip slips in. I suck in a breath, more than ready to feel all of him. Only his tip is inside of me, and I can already feel how much I have to stretch to accommodate him.

"Fuck, you're so tight. I can tell already," he says, closing his eyes and letting his head fall back while he gains control. I try moving my hips downward so it pushes him into me more, but his hands grab my hips and he squeezes, halting my movements.

"Please, Easton," I beg. "I need to feel you inside of me." Tears are building in my eyes from the overwhelming need pumping through me.

Without warning, he lets out a growl as he shoves into me. I call out, feeling as though I'm being ripped in half. The tears slide out of my eyes, running down toward my ears. I open my eyes and find him watching me, his eyes dark and full of need. He lowers himself to me now, his thumbs brushing the tears away from my face as he rolls his hips inside of me. I bite his shoulder to stifle my cry.

"Oh, fuck," he whispers, thrusting back into me.

More tears fall from my eyes, but it's not because of pain. It's all the emotions running through me. The need, the passion, the yearning, the pleasure, the pain, and the way they all mix together to create this delicious cocktail.

"Fuck, Gabbi. I don't think I can hold back. You feel too good, so fucking tight. Perfect."

Without warning, he rolls us over so I'm on top. I look down at him as I place my hands on his chest. Slowly, I lift myself up and let myself fall back down. His hands move around to my ass, squeezing as he lifts me up and pulls me down with even more force. I call out and his eyes roll back. His lips part as his breathing picks up. Within minutes of repeating the same action, I'm shattering around him, calling out his name until I run out of breath and can't make another sound.

He picks me up and flips me onto my stomach. He jerks my hips into the air until my knees are beneath me, then slams into me from behind. I let out a scream into the pillow. As he pounds into me from behind, his hand moves around the front of me until his fingers are between my folds. He spreads the wetness there until his fingers glide with ease. Then they run circles around my clit until I'm breaking again. My release sneaks up on me, blinding me with its force. I can't do anything but ride out its waves.

His hands are on my hips, pulling me into his thrusts. His movements get jerky as his breathing gets more labored. He lets out tiny moans and whimpers until he can no longer hold back. Then he comes with a load roar, a sound so deep I didn't know it was possible from anything other than a lion. His hips become erratic as he pumps every last drop into me.

He collapses on top of me, resting his head between my shoulder and neck. I wrap my arms around him, holding him close as we both work at settling our bodies. After several long moments, he pulls out of me and crumples at my side. He lies on his side and pulls my back to his chest. His arm stays wrapped around me, and I take a deep breath.

My body is tired and content, but my mind is racing. What did we just do? What are we supposed to do now? Why isn't he freaking out too? I can hear his deep, even breathing, like he's drifted off into a peaceful sleep. Fuck. What am I supposed to do?

I wait several long moments until I'm sure he's asleep, then I push the blankets back and try to sit up, but he doesn't release me.

"Where do you think you're going?" he asks, his rough voice cutting through the silence of the room.

"Oh, I thought you were asleep."

"So you thought you'd sneak out?"

I roll over and see his smirk. "No, not sneak. Just... walk."

He laughs. "There's no way I'm done with you yet." His hand moves up to cup my jaw. "After waiting for you all these years, I don't think I'll be done anytime soon." He leans in and presses his lips to mine.

TEN

EASTON

Oh my fucking God. She's perfect. Everything about her is more perfect than I ever thought possible. I knew being with Gabbi would be amazing, but I wasn't prepared for how life-altering it would really be. I thought that having her once would be enough. Now I see that it will never be enough. I want her again and again and again. In every fucking room of this house. In every fucking position possible. I want her wrapped around my dick every minute of every day. I want to call her body home. And she thinks she can just get up and walk away from me, like I'm fucking done with her? Ha.

I pull her back to me and cover her body with mine again. I settle between her legs, but I haven't recovered from the first round yet, so I just settle between her parted legs. With my mouth on hers, I wrap my arms around her.

"So, what now then?" she asks against my lips.

"What now?" I repeat, lifting my head to think. "Shower?" I suggest. "No, bath in the Jacuzzi tub." I offer up a smile.

She giggles. "No, I meant, what happens now? With us? Do we just go back to work like normal? I mean, not that there's been much work. It literally took you four days to get me into bed. That has to be some kind of record."

"Oh, it is. It's never taken me this long before," I joke.

She rolls her eyes. "Well, I never gave in so soon before. Even with Dean. It took him three months of dating before I let him go all the way."

"Three months?"

"Mm-hmm," she says, nodding her head once.

"I would've waited that long, but think of all the fun we can have now that we got the first time out of the way."

She laughs. "Don't you dare think of giving me a raise. This is not being added into my job description."

I smile. "I've never had an assistant who took their job and making me happy so seriously before. I think you do deserve a raise," I joke.

She laughs but smacks me. "Fuck off." She runs her hand through her hair. "I'm just a mess, Easton. Seriously, you'll see it one of these days."

"Well, then we'll be a mess together 'cause so am I," I tell her, pressing my lips to hers.

THE REST of the day is spent together. I go down to the kitchen and get us some lunch and some wine, and we eat in bed, laughing and talking. When the food is gone, we take a nap, and I sleep better than ever with her in my arms. When we wake up, we go for round three, then get up for that bath I suggested earlier. I fill the tub to the brim, and we slide down in it, with her in front of me and her back against my chest.

"You're different than I thought you'd be," she says softly.

"How's that?"

She shrugs. "I thought you'd be some pain in the ass who just bossed me around and had an endless parade of girls coming in and out. I'd thought you'd be a pig, basically."

"And what's changed your mind?"

Her head lulls to the side as she side-eyes me. "Who says I have?" she asks around a giggle.

I laugh and attack her sides, tickling her until she gives in.

We settle back down and she says, "Thanks for the loaner, by the way. Any idea when my car may be fixed?"

"Actually, I was meaning to talk to you about that. The motor blew."

She groans. "That's just great. I'm never going to be able to afford to fix it." She sits up and turns to face me.

"It's fine. You can keep the car as long as you need."

She rolls her eyes. "That's not the point. I can't just keep taking from you. You're not supposed to be like this. You're my boss."

I flinch at her words. "Oh, I didn't realize that's what we were, boss and employee." I shake my head and climb out of the tub.

"Easton, that's not what I meant," she says.

I wrap a towel around my hips and leave the bathroom, going back to the bedroom and walking into the closet for some pants. I pull on a pair of sweatpants. She's standing in the middle of the bedroom floor when I exit the closet.

"Easton, you know that's not how I meant it," she breathes out, looking guilty.

"How did you mean it, Gabbi? You have issues with me giving you a ride; you have issues with the expense account, and now the car? But it's completely okay for us to sleep together?"

"No, that's not what I meant. I just meant that it's not your responsibility to make sure I'm..."

"What? Taken care of?" I ask.

"Yeah, basically."

I'm starting to see through her now. She doesn't have a problem with me giving her things or help. She has a problem accepting help from anyone. She's been on her own practically her whole life, and that's mostly my fault. If I hadn't cast her out in high school, she wouldn't be so guarded. She can't just accept help when she needs it.

My anger melts away as I pull her against me. "Don't push me away, Gabbi. Let me help you. What's so wrong with me helping you?"

She shakes her head, but no words come out. Instead of arguing or fighting or even talking, she lets me hold her, kiss her, touch her. Our kiss grows in urgency, and before I know it, she's pushing my pants down and falling to her knees before me. Her hand wraps around me, and I feel huge in her small hand. Her fingers don't even touch as she works me up and down. The moment she sucks me into her mouth, my eyes roll back in my head. She takes me deeper and deeper, deeper than any woman has ever been able to before. I look down at her and am stunned. She's like a perfect angel on her knees with my cock in her mouth. Her thick eyelashes are wet, and tears are running down her cheeks, smearing her mascara. The image is enough to have me ripping apart at the seams. My release washes over me, and I empty myself into her mouth. She swallows me down and keeps sucking. I officially feel like I've defiled her, but it only makes me want her more. I want her wanting more; I want her appetite for me to never be satisfied.

When I have control over my body again, I place my hand on her jaw and pull her to her feet. I kiss her hard, her teeth knocking against mine as I lay us down on the bed and thrust myself inside her. I'll never get enough. Never.

"I HAVE TO GO. I need a shower and clean clothes," she says, pulling her clothes back on.

"Stay. I'll buy you new clothes."

She giggles. "No. I'm going, and I'll be back in the morning." She leans down and presses her lips to mine. "Dream of me," she says, pulling away and rushing out before I can stop her.

I lie back and stare up at the ceiling. I've slept in this bed alone for years. Why does it feel so empty now? I stare up at the ceiling for what feels like hours. Sleep never finds me even though I couldn't be more tired after my day. I push the blankets back and grab my sweats off the floor. I pull them on and go down to my office. I pour a stiff drink and sit down, looking around the dark, quiet room. My eyes land on a bookshelf, and I stand up and walk across the room, pulling down my old high school yearbooks. I take them back to my desk and turn on the lamp. I flip through the pages until I find her.

I don't know how in the hell I could have treated her so badly. She was fucking breathtaking, even back then. Her blond hair was long, always down to her ass and always perfectly curled. She never wore much makeup, and her clothes weren't name-brand, but they hugged her curves like they were painted on her. What kind of asshole treats an angel that way? Even if I was an asshole, what was wrong with everyone else that they'd listen to the shit I said instead of looking at this girl once?

I close the book and pick up the one from our senior year. I flip through, reliving old memories. The pages are filled with pictures of my friends and me, but her picture is only in this book one time. She stares at me from the page, and even the picture of her can see into my soul. I don't know what it is I'm doing. I don't know how in the hell this can ever work. All I know is that I've been in love with her since I was five years old, and now that I've had her, I only love her more. There's no way I'm letting her walk away. She's mine. I've branded her. My name is written all over her through the kisses I trailed across her skin, the burning trail of my hands as they toured her body. She's mine. I wonder how long it will take her to realize it. Hopefully sooner rather than later. I know she's mine, but I want her to know it too.

I study her picture a little while longer and finish off my drink. Shutting the book, I turn off the light and head back to bed. I don't know what tomorrow will bring, but I know she'll be here and that's enough for me.

ELEVEN

GABBI

Tonight may have been wrong, but it felt so perfect. Everything about it. His hands on me, soft but strong and controlling in a way that I didn't even know I needed. His words, raspy and thick with need. His lips and hands. His whole body touching me, making me crave more of him. It's literally the best day of my life, but it still leaves a sour taste in my mouth. What is this with us? How am I supposed to go to work now? Is he going to expect me to keep sleeping with him? Do I want to keep sleeping with him? If it's anything like today was, then yes! But that scares me.

I've been so wrapped up in Dean that I don't even know how to be with anyone else. Don't get me wrong, I wouldn't take Dean back now if he paid me to. We're done. But he is really the only boyfriend I've ever had. He was my first love. That's not something you get over in just a couple of days.

When I get home, I'm surprised to find an envelope on the floor like it was slid under my door. I put my things down and pick it up. Opening it, I find the signed contract that gets me out of this apartment. It's time to put this place behind me. The gym has been emptied out, and the dining room is in the same condition. All that's left is the living room furniture: the couch, love seat, tables, TV, and lamps. The appliances came with the apartment, so I can't do anything with those, and the bedroom furniture is mine. Even though I have to get up early in the morning, I'm too wound up to sleep. I go into the kitchen and start packing away the things I won't need anytime soon. I pour a glass of wine and play some music to keep my mind busy as I pack box after box full of dishes, drinkware, and silverware. Tomorrow, I'll make sure to pick up some plastic utensils and paper plates—not that I eat here all that much. It's going on midnight before I finally get to bed.

MY ALARM GOES OFF ENTIRELY WAY TOO soon, and I smack it off the table as I sit up. I yawn and rub my eyes before pushing myself out of bed and heading to the bathroom for a shower. It takes me an hour to get dressed and ready. I decide I need a little caffeine boost, so I make some coffee and pour it into a to-go cup before heading for the door. I lock up behind me, then walk down the hall and hit the button for the elevator. The doors open, and I go to step in but pause when I bump into Easton.

"Oh, hey. What are you doing here?"

He smiles down on me, making my body come alive in ways it never did before him. "I checked over my schedule and saw that I was free today, so I thought that maybe we could do something fun. What do you think?"

I smile and nod. "I'd like that."

"Great. Let's go." He steps back into the elevator and holds his arm in front of the door so it can't close. I join him, and he hits the button for the ground level.

The elevator is quiet as we ride it down. I have my arms crossed over my chest, and he's standing at my side, his feet shoulder-width apart and his hands clasped in front of him. "So, how'd you sleep last night?"

"Good once I finally got to sleep," I say, glancing up at him. "When I got home, I found the contract signed and slid under my front door, so I stayed up and packed the kitchen until midnight."

"About time to move then, huh?"

The doors open and I step out. "Yep. I really need to find a place."

He follows me out and leads the way to the door. "Move into the guest house," he insists. "Hell, move into the main house, but at least move into the guest house."

I smile. "I can't. It's too much."

He opens the door for me, and the two of us step out into the warm, sunny day. He leads the way to his car. "Well, if it comes down to it, the place is yours. There's no sense in stressing yourself out. Move in until you find a place that's acceptable." He opens the passenger side door for me, and I slide in with a smile.

"Thank you."

He takes his seat behind the wheel, and he turns to face me. His hands move up to cup my cheeks, and he slowly leans in to press a kiss to my lips. The kiss is soft and slow and teasing. When he pulls away, he says, "I've been thinking about that since you left last night."

I don't know how to respond, so I just offer up a smile.

"Now, let's get this day of fun started." He fires the car up, shifts into drive, and hits the gas, leaving my apartment building behind us.

I don't ask where we're going or what we're doing. I just sit and enjoy the ride. The windows are down, and the warm air is blowing through the car. The sun is shining down on us, and he's holding my hand between us. Right now, it's easy to pretend that we're a real couple and that this is just how life is now. I'm so relaxed that I fall asleep, but then the car stops and I look out the windshield to find the ocean.

"That one is mine," he says, pointing to a very big, very expensive-looking yacht. "Come on."

We both climb out of the car, and he takes my hand, pulling me out onto a dock and then over to the boat. The captain is standing in front of the boat, dressed in a dark suit and hat. "Mr. Perez, it's good to see you again," he says, holding out his hand.

Easton shakes it. "Nice to see you too. This is Gabbi. She's a close personal friend. Are the staff already on board?"

The man nods. "They are. We're all ready to set sail."

Easton turns back to me with a smile. "Ready to take off?"

"Ready as I'll ever be," I say, climbing on board.

Easton takes me inside and down to a bedroom. "I got you a bathing suit in case you didn't want to wear that all day. It looks a little uncomfortable."

"Thank you."

"There are towels in the bathroom. I'll be up top, mixing some drinks." He picks up my hand, kisses the back, and slips out the door, leaving me alone.

I smile to myself as I turn around and find the bathing suit he's laid out on the bed along with a lace cover-up. I change quickly and go into the bathroom to check my appearance. The string bikini is red and fits perfectly. I pull the white lace cover-up on, and it ends just above my knee. My blond hair is shining more today, and my blue eyes have a sparkle to them that wasn't there before yesterday. I feel sore but a good sore, the kind you get after reaching a goal at the gym. I push my curled hair behind my ears and head up to the top deck.

I find Easton mixing drinks on the deck. He looks up and smiles. He's gorgeous with the sun shining down on him. His skin has always been naturally tan, but he's even more bronze than usual. His dark hair has a hint of blond highlights to it, and his scruff is growing thick on his jaw. Talk about tall, dark, and handsome. He holds out a glass, and I walk over and take it.

"Thank you."

He holds his up and softly clinks it against mine. "To a day of fun and relaxation."

I tip the glass back, and the chilled liquid runs down my throat, cooling my warming body. The martini is made perfectly, and despite the cold drink, it warms my stomach.

We take our drinks to the lounge chairs, and we both stretch out. I remove my cover-up and let the sun kiss my skin. I notice his eyes on me, but I try not to let it distract me. They start at the tips of my toes and travel up my legs. The trail his eyes leave feels like a fire burning on my skin. It follows his eyes up over my stomach and breasts and settles on my face.

"Move into the pool house," he says with a grin.

I laugh. "Why is it so important to you? Don't you think this is moving a little too fast?" My eyes are closed against the bright sun, so I can't see his expression to that question.

"Moving too fast? It's not like you're some woman I met on the side of the road. We've known one another since kindergarten."

"Yeah, and I hated you until recently," I point out with a smile.

"Did you ever think that maybe you didn't really hate me?"

"No, I hated you."

He laughs. "I hated you, too, but it was because I wanted you and couldn't have you."

"I just hated you." I giggle.

"Alright, alright. Let's just say that it's for work purposes. You're my assistant. I may need you in the middle of the night. You'd hate to have to get up and drive all the way over, wouldn't you?"

I crack open one eye and look at him.

"What if it was a job requirement? I mean, Charles lives in the guest house."

"How many houses do you have on that property?" I ask, but he waves me off.

"Tell you what. You move into the pool house, and I'll double your salary for the inconvenience of moving."

I shake my head.

"Come on. There's got to be something you want. Name it."

"There's really not. I just want to work, have my own place, and live my life."

"Well, you can do that from the pool house."

"No, I can't," I argue.

"Why are you so against this?"

"I want my own life, Easton. I don't want my life splashed out on magazine covers and talked about on the highlights segment of *The Talk*. You're okay with having everything out in the open. You signed up for that. I didn't. I don't want fame. I don't want your life."

"Let's get in the hot tub."

"There's a hot tub on this boat?"

"Yep." He stands up and leads me to the deck out on the front of the boat, and sure enough, there's a hot tub. We both climb in and enjoy the silence for a moment. There's a light breeze blowing from the boat pushing through the water.

He grabs my wrist and pulls me over to him. When I'm close enough, his hands find my hips, and he pulls me onto his lap. We're nose to nose when he says, "I promise we'll be discreet about this. You want your privacy and I respect that. But I want you, and I'm not going to stop pursuing you." His lips land on mine and the kiss is hard, passionate, intense. My toes go numb and start to tingle. The longer we kiss, the more I forget about what we were talking about. My arms wrap around his neck, pulling him closer.

"Be mine," he whispers against my lips as his hands start to touch my body.

I don't answer. I don't want that. I don't want labels and strings. All I want is this. This feeling that's running through me right now. This feeling that I've never gotten from another person, not even Dean. These butterflies—or whatever you call them—are addicting. I crave the flutter of their wings. I yearn for the tingles their wings create. And when everything mixes together and I combust under the pressure, it's the highest I've ever been.

"Say you're mine, Gabbi," he whispers, his lips moving to my neck and ear, his hands running under my breasts with featherlight touches, thumbs brushing against my hardened peaks.

"I—" I start, but the words drift away. I want to be his. I do. But I don't want to belong to the world. What's his isn't just his. It's everyone's. It's for everyone to watch with curious eyes. It's for everyone to examine under a microscope. And when things end, they don't just end. They're splashed all over the TV, the internet, and magazine covers.

"Say it." His hands move up to cup my face, and he tilts it back until my eyes lock in on his rich dark-chocolate eyes. "Tell me how much you love being under me, how much you love it when I'm sliding into you, branding you as mine. Tell me you never want this to end." Between each sentence, he's kissing me and touching me until it feels like every spot on my body is stimulated at once. "Tell me who you belong to, Gabbi."

"You," I breathe out the word, and his mouth crashes against mine. His left hand falls from my face down to my throat, and his long fingers wrap around it. He holds firm but doesn't squeeze, and that's when I know that no matter how much I don't like his life, I do belong to him. I'm his now. He could tighten his fingers around my neck and squeeze until I stop breathing, but he doesn't. He holds me, owns me, dominates me, and the scariest part of this all is that I like it.

TWELVE
EASTON

Hearing her say that she belongs to me after all of these years has my body rock-hard. Every inch of me is taut and straining to hold back my excitement. My dick is tenting my swim shorts, straining so hard, it's almost painful. When she brushes against it, I bite down on her lower lip, and she moans into my mouth. I tug her bottoms down and then mine, then pull her back onto my lap where she glides down onto me. Becoming one again is like heaven.

My hands stay on her hips, lifting her up and pulling her back against me. "Who do you belong to?" I ask, needing to hear it again.

"You," she says, and I pull her against me harder. Her head falls back and her eyes close. I can't do anything but watch her face as I repeat the same actions as before. Her lips are parted with her heavy breathing, her eyes clenched so tight, wrinkles form around them. Her blond hair is blowing in the breeze, and it's like gold as the sun hits it. I feel her muscles begin to tighten around me, and I move my thumb over to her clit to push her over the edge. She comes undone in soft whimpers and moans, and I explode into her. We ride out the waves of our pleasure together, not stopping until neither of us can move.

She rests her head against my shoulder to catch her breath, and I can feel the way her heart is pounding against her chest, beating because of me, because of the way I made her feel. It feels like my heart leaps out of my body and flies to heaven. I don't know how I've lived my entire life without her, but I know I can't go a single day without her again.

BY THE END of the week, we've managed to sell the rest of the furniture in her apartment and put the rest in storage. The only things she brings to the pool house are her clothes and bathroom items. I help her unpack and make sure that she gets settled before inviting her over for dinner. We head inside where dinner is already prepared and laid out on the dining room table. We both take our seats and fix our plates full of steaks, baked potatoes, steamed vegetables, and freshly baked dinner rolls.

"Do you always eat at the table?"

I shrug. "Usually. Why?"

"I like to eat on the couch while watching a movie."

"Well, come on." I take my plate and walk to the living room. We both sit on the couch and turn the TV on. Neither of us want to take control of the remote, so the TV stays on the original channel. We end up eating while watching some kind of murder documentary.

Her phone chimes a little while later, and she picks it up and reads the message with a smile.

"What's going on?"

"Dean is going to be moving into the apartment tomorrow, which means that he's going to walk in thinking everything is just how he left it only to find that everything is gone." Her smile gets wider.

I laugh. "Remind me to never fuck you over."

She snorts. "You already have."

"High school doesn't count," I argue, pulling her against me and tickling her sides. She fights me off. Eventually, we settle, lying on the couch as I hold her against me. The house is dark and quiet, only the light from the TV lighting up the room. Right now, it's easy to imagine how our lives could play out, and I want nothing more than to live like this for the rest of time. I don't want to work. I don't want to leave or even move. I could die a happy man right now.

I wake a little while later and find that she's still dead to the world. I get up and pick her up, carrying her against my chest up to my room. I lay her across the bed and cover her up. Then I climb in and lie beside her. She rolls into my chest, one arm wrapping around me and one leg thrown over my hips. I wrap my arms around her and pull her closer, breathing in the smell of her hair. Peaches and coconut, a weird combination but a mixture I absolutely love.

We both wake up in the morning with the sound of her phone ringing over and over and over. When it ends, it immediately starts back up. I rub my eyes, wondering the in the hell is going on. I don't even remember bringing her phone in here last night. That's when she reaches under the blanket and pulls it out. She must have put it in her pocket and it fell out sometime throughout the night.

"It's Dean," she mumbles.

"What the fuck does he want?" I ask, running my hands through my hair.

"I don't know." She taps the button and brings the phone to her ear. "Hello?"

"What the fuck happened?" he asks loud enough that I can hear from beside her.

"What do you mean?"

"Where is all my shit?"

"What shit?"

"My shit? My furniture? My desk? My couch? The gym? I spent a fortune on that shit. Now where is it?"

She smiles. "Oh, well, you only signed a contract for the apartment, not its contents."

"Why would I have to sign a contract for its contents when it all already belonged to me?"

"That's where you're wrong, Dean. You moved out and left everything with me, meaning it all became mine. I didn't need all that stuff, so I sold it."

"You sold my stuff?"

"Yes, yes, I did. You wanted to fuck me over, so I fucked you over."

"You really are a fucking bitch, aren't you?"

That's when I take the phone from her hands. "Dean?" I say into the phone.

"Who is this?"

"This is Easton, Gabbi's new boyfriend. Listen, if I hear you talk to her like that again, I will do more than sell all your shit. I'll make sure you can't pick up a phone to call her again. Got me?"

"Fuck off, man. I hope you enjoy my leftovers. God knows she doesn't put out enough to be a real girlfriend."

"I don't know what you mean there, man. We've only been together a fucking week, and I can't get her off my dick long enough to take a piss." She frowns at me, but I ignore it. I'm not trying to put her down in any way. I'm just making my point. Like maybe if your dick was big enough, she would have wanted it more.

"Yeah, whatever, man. Enjoy my sloppy seconds." He hangs up the phone, and I let it fall to the pillow under my head.

"He's a dickwad," I tell her and she giggles.

"Yep, but it's nice knowing that I pissed him off."

"It's nice knowing that you'll be here where I can keep my eye on you so I don't have to worry about him trying to fuck with you over some stupid-ass furniture." I pull her against me, and she snuggles close.

"Yeah, that is pretty nice."

"Are you finally admitting that moving into the pool house was a good idea?" I look down at her.

She laughs. "Yeah, I guess so. Although my first night didn't go as planned. How about tonight we stay at my place?"

"Are you inviting me to stay the night?"

She smiles. "I am."

"I don't know. I don't believe in staying over at some girl's house after only a week of dating."

She smacks me across the chest but laughs.

We eventually manage to get out of bed and get dressed for the day. She goes into her office to check the calls, texts, emails, and calendar while I go down for some breakfast and coffee. I'm halfway through when she comes into the room. Her brows are pulled together, and her lips are in a tight line.

"What's wrong?"

"Look at this," she says, dropping the phone onto the table.

I pick it up to see the headline—*Who is Easton Perez's Newest Fling?*—followed by a picture of the two of us in the hot tub on the boat. In the picture, she's on my lap with her arms around my neck. My hands are beneath the water, but I know exactly what I'm doing. I'm pulling her down on my dick. We're kissing, both of our eyes closed. The picture is taken from somewhere up high, but we were in the middle of the ocean, so there weren't any buildings around. I didn't hear or see a drone either. That means one of the staff snapped it from the balcony of the boat.

"I'll get to the bottom of this," I promise her.

She shakes her head as she pours her coffee. "What's the point? What's done is done. It's out there. The media won't stop until they figure out who I am and my whole life is out there for them to pick apart. There's nothing we can do."

"There's plenty I can do, starting with finding whoever snapped this picture and firing them."

"Firing them?" she asks, her brows drawn together.

"It had to be a staff member on the boat. That's the only explanation. Every employee had to sign a gag order. This is a breach." I push away from the table and go straight to my office to get to the bottom of this.

It doesn't take me long to figure out who leaked the picture, and I call my lawyer and smack them with a lawsuit within the hour. I'm absolutely livid that one of my staff would fuck me over like this. At least it wasn't one of my housing staff. They know better, and I've made damn sure to create a connection with each one. The ones I employ for my yacht, though, not so much. I don't spend much time there. I don't know what pisses me off more, my staff fucking me over or that my girlfriend, for lack of a better term, now has her sex life splashed all over the internet. I can only pray that this doesn't make her change her mind about me. I promised her we'd keep this secret between us, that I wouldn't let our relationship become the talk of the town. Already, I've broken my first promise, and it's not something I take lightly, especially when it had nothing to do with me. I pour a drink and take my time sipping it, wanting to calm down before I see her. When the glass is empty, I feel like I have a handle on my anger, and I push away from my desk and head for the stairs, wanting to let her know that this is handled and will never happen again.

THIRTEEN
GABBI

My phone rings, and I see Hannah's name flashing on the screen. "Hello?" I answer with a smile. Hannah and I haven't talked in a long time. I'm excited to hear what she has to say. Surely, she's calling to tell me that she and Jeff are finally engaged. They've only been together for six years.

"It's you!" she says the moment I answer.

"What? What's me?"

"On the cover of *Celebrity Style Magazine*! That's you wrapped around Easton Perez."

"Ugh." I hang my head.

"It's you, isn't it?"

"Yes, it's me," I confess.

"What the... How... When... Oh my God. I can't even form a sentence. Tell me. Spill."

"Spill what?"

"The how, when—really, *how*? I mean, this is Easton. You two hated one another, like, your whole lives!"

I want to laugh at her excitement, but the seriousness of the situation makes me hold back. "I took a job as his assistant, and things just happened. What do you want from me?"

"But you hate him," she points out.

"I used to hate him," I correct.

"He hated you."

"No, he didn't hate me. He hated that he wanted me."

She laughs. "I can't believe this. So now what?"

"Now we hang up and forget we had this conversation."

"No, Gabbi. What happens now? I mean, do you think you'll get married? Were you having sex in that hot tub?"

I laugh. "What do you think?"

She squeals. "Oh my God, you were! Ugh, I'm so jealous. How is he? Good? Of course he's good, what am I saying? Is he big?"

"Sooo big," I say quietly into the phone.

He walks into the room. "Who's big?"

I smile at him. "You are," I tease.

He smiles smugly. "Yeah, I am." He drops down to his knees before me and starts kissing my throat. My eyes flutter closed with the sensation as his hands move up my thighs.

"Ugh, I gotta go. Bye." I hang up the phone and toss it onto the desk in front of me. My arms wrap around his neck, pulling him closer as he attacks my neck, ears, and lips with his mouth.

"It's taken care of," he whispers as he presses kisses to my skin.

"What's taken care of?" I ask, breathless as his mouth trails down my neck to my chest. My shirt cuts him off, and he pulls away to unbutton it.

"I found who leaked the picture. My lawyer is filing a suit."

I freeze. What? Someone is getting sued? I push him back slightly so I can see his face. "You're suing someone over it?"

"Well, yeah. Don't worry though. I won't take everything. Just their job and everything they sold the picture for."

"I don't know if I like that," I confess as his lips go back to my skin.

He pulls back. "What am I supposed to do, Gabbi? I can't let people think they can sneak around, taking risky pictures of you and then selling them for a profit. You're mine and I don't like to share," he says, pulling my lips back to his.

Despite all the sex we've had over the past week, I find myself wanting him more and more each and every time. We drop the subject as he pulls my pants down and bends me over my desk. Yes, this is the best thing I've used this desk for to date.

———

DAYS TURN to weeks and weeks turn to months, and I only get more and more wrapped up in him. Thanks to that picture, our relationship is known around the world now. We can't go out together without being recognized. In fact, the only time I can go out without a hoard of photographers following along behind me is when I go by myself and play it safe. By safe, I mean hats, glasses, and staying away from high-profile places.

My life has changed drastically, and even though I resisted at first, it no longer seems that bad. I was never one of those girls who liked to go out all that much, so staying locked away in the house isn't that bad. Not to mention, the longer we stay locked in our bedrooms, the more time we spend with one another. We've managed to sneak off a few times and take little vacations to Hawaii, Paris, and even Japan, places where we don't have to hide as much. It's safe to say that we're no longer hiding our relationship. Now, we're just hiding away from the world.

Easton takes a part in an upcoming psychological thriller about a man who stalks his way into a woman's life. He gets to play the bad guy, and he's totally psyched about it since he's only ever played the hot boy next door type. The movie is going to be huge, and I'm just as excited to see it since I read the script. I stayed up all night reading it, unable to put it down. I've been running lines with him and practicing every night. But every day, he has to leave and be on set by four every morning. Letting him go is hard, but I remind myself that I'm the one he's retiring to every evening, and it all seems alright.

One thing that I haven't been able to wrap my mind around, though, is his costar. Her name is Jessica Athena, and she's absolutely gorgeous. She's tall, thin, and has the perfect body with round hips, a firm ass, and big boobs. Her hair is long and dark, and she has these almond-shaped eyes and full, pouty lips. I can't help but compare myself to her. I know from reading the script that there is plenty of kissing in this movie and one rather graphic sex scene. It makes me wonder how the spouses of actors do it? How can he spend all day with her, kissing her, touching her, pretending to be in love with her, and then come home to me, a regular person? I try to push the negative thoughts away. I know no good will come of them. I know that all it'll do is drive a wedge between us, and that's the last thing I want.

Tonight, we're having a dinner with a few of the actors from the movie and the director. I'm hoping that seeing everyone as a normal person, being their usual selves, will squash all these thoughts I've been having about Jessica.

The dinner is being held at an upscale restaurant I've never been to. Easton hires a limo, and we both dress to impress. He wears a sharp suit that's tailored to fit him perfectly, and I wear a custom-made gown he ordered just for me. Someone comes to do my hair and makeup, and I feel like the whole thing is rather silly. If it's just a dinner amongst friends, why couldn't we have had it here and ordered pizza? I accept that there is a lot I don't know about actors, making movies, and building relationships, but I humor him, going along with this whole Cinderella story.

We get to the restaurant, and word must have leaked that something was going on here because men armed with cameras are hanging out by the doors, ready to swing into action. When they see the limo approaching, they all raise their cameras and have their trigger finger ready.

"Fuck," Easton says as he prepares to open the door. He turns to face me. "Don't look directly at them and don't answer any of their questions. Got it?"

I nod, and he takes my hand before opening the door. He leads me from the car to the door so fast that I hardly process that my photo was taken. I wouldn't have even noticed if it weren't for the flashing lights that seem to be a permanent part of my vision now.

We're led to a private room and shown to our table. Immediately, I recognize Jessica, the costar, Jacque Forrestor, the actor who plays the therapist, Jeanine Bradly, Jennifer Cooper, and Anderson Miller —all A-list actors. Jeff Brags, the director, is at the head of the table.

Easton pulls out my chair and I have a seat. Then we go around the table, introducing everyone. Easton sits between Jessica and me. I keep my back straight and head held high, reminding myself that these are just people who are doing a job, but as dinner goes on, I can't help but notice the way that Easton and Jessica talk. She throws her head back and laughs when he says something funny, and when she talks about Easton, she reaches out and squeezes his bicep. Is this normal behavior? I don't want to be the jealous type, but I've never been the kind of girl who's okay letting another woman touch her man. Should I excuse it because she's a famous actress? Or maybe because they're costars?

Halfway through dinner, I can't take it anymore, and I get up to go to the bathroom. I use the toilet and wash my hands. I'm checking my makeup when the door opens, and Jessica walks in. She looks perfect as always in her skintight black dress. She stands at my side and leans into the mirror to check her makeup.

"Easton is great, isn't he?"

I force a smile. "That's why I'm with him."

She seems taken aback. "Oh, you're together like together together? He told me you were his assistant." Her brows are drawn together.

Mine don't pull together. They skyrocket. "How many people do you know that bring their assistants to dinner? Not to mention, at the table when we did introductions, he introduced me as Gabbi, his girlfriend," I remind her.

"Oh, I guess I didn't hear that part," she says, shrugging it off. "Nevertheless, he's a great guy. You're a lucky girl." She flashes me a smile before turning to go into the stall.

I'm seething as I leave the restroom and take my place back at the table. Easton leans in.

"Everything okay?" he asks, placing his hand on my thigh.

I force a smile and nod. "Mm-hmm." Now isn't the time to talk about this.

The rest of the dinner is pretty uneventful other than the fact that telling Jessica that Easton is mine isn't enough to keep her hands off him. We all say our goodbyes and leave the restaurant with more cameras shoved in our faces. When we climb into the limo, I feel like I can finally breathe.

"Well, that was eventful, wasn't it?" Easton says as he sits at my side.

I'm not quite ready to talk yet. I need to calm down and form my thoughts, so instead, I just force a smile and nod.

He talks the whole way home about the dinner, the movie, and the relationships he's formed with everyone at our table. I don't put much into the conversation. When we get home, I go straight for the pool house, but he catches my hand and stops me.

"Where are you going?"

I nod toward the pool house. "To get undressed."

"Come up to my room," he says, moving closer.

I shake my head. "I'm really tired, and I'd just like a little bit of peace to relax. I want this dress off, and I want to soak in the tub. I'll see you in the morning when I go back to being your assistant."

He frowns. "What's that mean?"

I shake my head, regretting that I said anything. "Nothing. I just don't feel like talking right now. Okay? We'll do this tomorrow."

"Do what?" he spits out. I'm sure he's just confused. To him, we had a great night, and he's ready to finish it off like we do every night.

I shake my head, close my eyes, and take deep breath, trying to relax and push the negative away. "Just give me tonight. Okay?" I turn and head for the door.

FOURTEEN
EASTON

I don't know what's suddenly upset her, but I have to find out. She tries walking away, but I grab ahold of her wrist and turn her to face me. "Do what?" I repeat my question from before.

"Argue," she finally says.

"Why would we argue?"

She lets out a long breath as her head falls back and she stares up at the ceiling. "How do you think tonight went, Easton?"

I feel my brows pull together. "I thought it was a great night. Why?"

"That's because you only saw things from your point of view. What about mine?"

"What about it?"

She holds up a finger. "Let me tell you what I saw." She walks over to the drink cart and pours a glass of bourbon. I've never seen her drink straight liquor, so automatically, I know this isn't a good sign. "First, we pull up to this fancy dinner where my picture is taken and my privacy is intruded upon—something I told you from the beginning that I didn't want. And what did you say? We'll be discreet, we'll keep this a secret. Then I get to sit at this table and watch a woman who is better than me in every fucking way touch you, flirt with you, laugh at all your jokes. And when that became too much, I went to the bathroom where she followed me to make sure I knew that you told her I was just your assistant. Can you even imagine how I feel right now?" she asks, tipping the glass back and having another swig.

My shoulders fall as my breath leaves my mouth. "I didn't know that."

"How would you feel if Dean was at that dinner and he kept touching me and calling me babe?"

I nod. "I'd be pissed. Hell, I'd probably be in jail right now 'cause the first time I saw him touch you, I would've kicked his ass."

"Exactly. And you expect me to be okay with all of this?"

"I didn't even realize it was happening, Gabbi," I promise.

"You didn't realize that she kept touching you?" Her eyes are wide. "If you don't realize when she touches you, what are you two doing on set? Do you meet in each other's dressing rooms and 'run lines,' practicing all the kissing scenes?"

"No, that's ridiculous, Gabbi," I breathe out.

She shakes her head. "I don't think I can do this, Easton. I mean, I knew I couldn't and I tried anyway. I guess I shouldn't be surprised." She tries to walk out, but I grab her again and pull her against my chest.

"Don't do this. We had a bad night, that's all."

"No, that's not all, Easton. I told you I didn't want a life in the public eye, and that's all I've had since I got with you. I mean, we can't even leave the house together. I can't leave the house without being followed, for crying out loud. I told you what I didn't want, and that's exactly what I got. Plus, after Dean and the way that relationship ended, I don't have it in me to sit and watch another woman touch you like that. It... it fills my head with all these bad thoughts that I just don't want."

I reach up and cup her face, forcing her to look at me. "I swear, Gabbi, nothing is going on with her outside of work. Nothing is going on with her at work other than work. You're all I want." I press my lips against hers and she kisses me, but it's different. It's guarded. It's soft and holds no emotion. I lift her up against me and set her on the dining room table. "You're mine. Only mine," I say, kissing my way down her neck.

She shakes her head. "Not anymore, Easton."

I freeze with her words and pull back to study her face. It's like stone. No emotion.

"I can't do this anymore. It's too hard. I mean, am I your girlfriend, or am I your assistant? I don't know anymore." She slides off the table. "I think it's time to go back to how things are supposed to be. I'll be your assistant, but this relationship, it's over." Without another word, she walks away, out of the door and to the pool house.

I'm left standing alone, angry, and wondering how in the hell I lost everything I've ever wanted in one night.

I pour a drink and toss it back. I pour another and throw it back just as quickly. I pour one more, and the edge finally seems to dull. I drink this one slowly, thinking everything over. I know that Gabbi has every right to be angry. I would be angry if I was in her shoes, if my whole life was taken away and changed into something I didn't want. If I had to sit and watch someone I considered better than me touch her. I would be fucking livid. But it wouldn't be enough to make me want to end things. Nothing would be enough to do that. I meant what I said. She's mine and she always will be.

I finish off my third glass, and my vision is doubling after the drinks I had at dinner too. I hear a splash, and I move over to the glass French doors, looking out. She's in the pool, and there's a bottle of wine sitting by the edge. Her head pops up out of the water, and she swims over to it, taking a long drink straight from the bottle.

I loosen my tie and yank it off. I toss it onto the table along with my jacket. I kick off my shoes and socks and remove my belt. All that's left is my pants as I walk outside. Her big eyes lock on mine, and she watches as I make my way over to the pool and step in, still in my pants.

"What are you doing?" she asks as I walk across the pool to her.

"I meant what I said, Gabbi." My sights are set. "You're mine, and there's no way I'm letting go this easily. I'm fighting for you." I reach out and grab her by the hips, pulling her against my chest as my mouth finds hers. She's completely naked beneath the water, and I take advantage of the opportunity, touching all of her. Her arms wrap around my neck, pulling me closer as I press her back to the side of the pool. I free myself from my pants and thrust up into her. She lets out a moan the moment we become one.

"We're not over," I tell her, thrusting into her again. "We'll never be over." I rock my hips against her and she whimpers. "I'm in love with you, Gabbi." I feel her tighten around me with her rising orgasm, and I push into her harder and faster, wanting her to feel how I feel. "I love you," I say, my hips stilling as one hand moves to tangle into her hair, gently pulling at the root. The other wraps around her throat, owning her. "Say it," I demand, moving my hips again slowly, teasingly. "Tell me who you belong to." Her big eyes lock on mine, and they look to be glistening with fresh tears. Her lips are swollen and parted. "Who's the only one who can make you feel this good?" I push into her harder, deeper. "Tell me," I demand.

"You," she says and it's like a dam busting. The emotions come rushing out, toppling over me, pulling me under, holding me captive, and bashing me along every hard surface. I drown in her.

My mouth crashes back with hers as I continue to push her closer to the edge I've kept her teetering on. Her nails dig into my back, clawing, as she cries out my name. Once her release has ended, I hold her close as I walk us out of the pool and into the pool house. "I'll never hurt you," I promise, laying her down on the bed, still completely wet and naked. "I'll never betray you," I promise, moving my hips again and rocking against her. "I'll never stop loving you." I smash my lips against hers. "And I'll never be able to let you walk away." I roll us over so she's on top, looking at me with those big innocent eyes of hers.

"Show me how much you love me, Gabbi." My hands squeeze her hips, and she begins to move back and forth, grinding her clit against me. "Show me how badly you want me." She moans as she rides my dick. "Do you want to leave me now?" I ask, picking her up. She shakes her head and I pull her back down, making her call out. "Am I going to have to bury my dick in you every time you get jealous?" I lean up, catching her nipple in my mouth and biting it gently. She moans.

"Answer me," I demand.

"Yes, fuck... Don't stop."

"If I have to fuck you into exhaustion every time, I will," I promise, sucking on her nipple as she grinds against me. Her orgasm washes over her and she moans, whimpers, and calls my name again and again until she's completely limp on top of me. When she can no longer move, I flip her over and position her on her knees. I slide in from behind and move my hand around to her front, coating my fingers in her arousal. As I'm slamming into her, I slide the tip of my middle finger into her ass, and her back arches.

"You're mine now, Gabbi. All of you. Forever." Hearing the words leave my lips and believing them, I finally let my release wash over me, stronger than ever. I pump into her at lightning speed, riding out every last wave of pleasure until I'm too weak to keep myself upright. We both collapse onto the bed, and I pull her against me. My heart is racing, hammering away in my ears, and the only sound I can hear is our labored breathing. It doesn't take long before we're both completely out.

I WAKE in the morning and, for a moment, don't know where I am. I look around the room, finding the bed empty. "Gabbi?" I call out, rolling over onto my back. My stomach rolls, and a headache makes itself known. I had entirely way too much to drink last night.

I force my eyes to stay open as I sit up and let the room stop spinning. I climb out of bed and kick the sheets around, looking for some clothes. That's when last night hits me. The dinner. The fight. The pool. I grab a sheet and wrap it around my hips before I explore the house further, finding it empty.

I walk out into the bright sun and see that my pants and the bottle of wine have been picked up. Inside my house, all traces of our night have been erased. I make my way upstairs in my sheet. I expect to find her behind her desk, but the room is empty. I almost walk past until I see the cell phone sitting on the desk on top of a sheet of paper. I walk in and pick it up. It's a note.

Easton,

I'm sorry that I have to do this this way, but it seems to be the only way I can make you hear me. Last night was great, don't get me wrong. I enjoyed every minute of it, but that doesn't change anything I said beforehand. I can't live this life with you. I wasn't meant to be famous and have my personal space invaded. I wasn't made to be okay with another woman touching my man. Know that you didn't do anything wrong. I'm not leaving because of you. I'm leaving because I can't be the woman you need. I'm not strong enough to stand by your side in the spotlight. I meant what I said last night. I do love you, but that doesn't mean this can work. I refuse to give up who I am and what makes me me in order to be that for you. I called a cab and I've packed my things. I can't live here anymore. At this point, I'm afraid all I can offer you is to be your assistant. I can't play both roles for you anymore. I'm sorry.

Gabbi

I wad the letter up and throw it at the wall. Where did she go? I have to find her. I get up and rush to my room. I pull off the sheet and throw on some clothes. I grab my keys, wallet, and phone and run for the garage. I have no idea where to start looking, but I'll never give up. I'm desperately in love with her, and there's no way I'm letting her run away from this.

FIFTEEN
GABBI

Hannah opens the door, and when she sees me, her eyes stretch wide. "Gabbi, what are you doing here?"

"I need a place to crash. That cool?" I ask, walking by her. I fling myself onto the couch and cover my eyes with my arm. I'm hungover and my head is killing me. Why did I mix wine and bourbon last night? Such a bad idea. Although the after-party was fun. But that thought only makes my heart hurt as bad as my head.

She closes the door and comes to sit at my side. "What's going on? Why do you need a place to crash? Did something happen with you and Easton?"

"I broke up with him."

Her mouth drops open. "Why in the hell would you do that, Gabbi?" Her voice is high-pitched and squeaky.

I cover my ears. "Stop yelling. My head is killing me."

"Then you better start explaining what's going on. I just saw you two online, leaving some fancy dinner with a million other famous people. Your life is looking pretty good to me right now, so why did you just run away from it?" she demands.

I scoff as I push myself to sit up. "You don't understand. That fancy dinner was crap. Jessica"—the way I say her name says it all—"has serious issues with keeping her hands to herself."

"Well, of course she does. You've seen Easton. I have a feeling every woman on the planet has a problem keeping their hands to themselves when he's around."

"You've seen her! She's fucking perfect. How am I supposed to compete with that?"

"Who says you're supposed to?"

I shrug. "Nobody, but still. How can Easton love me when he's around beautiful, rich, famous women like her all the time?"

"You're jealous. Seriously? That's why you just ruined the best opportunity you've ever gotten?"

"No, I'm not jealous. I'm insecure," I point out, but that's not really any better. "Not only that, but I don't like the whole being in the spotlight thing. I mean, what happened to having a little bit of privacy?"

She rolls her eyes. "You have as much privacy as anyone else. Nobody is sneaking into your bedroom to film a secret sex tape! Who cares if you go out and get noticed? No other celebrity seems to have a problem with it."

"I'm not a celebrity, Hannah!"

"You're with one. That makes you one by association."

"That's not what I want though. I want to fall in love, get married, have kids. I don't want fame."

She shakes her head. "So picky! Look at what you're doing, Gabbi. You found a sexy as fuck man who adores you. And it doesn't hurt that he's loaded. You got something that most people go their whole lives without, and you're just going to throw it away because it's not the way you want it?"

I never thought of it like that before. Is she right? Am I being stupid? I do love Easton and he loves me. Does it really matter than I can't go to the mall without having my picture taken? Does it matter that he gets asked for autographs every time we go out for dinner? He loves me. That should be enough. So why do I feel so horrible?

"You're more than welcome to stay here for as long as you need, but by doing so, you're also going to have to listen to me. And I'm telling you right now that I have plenty to say on this subject matter. You need to think long and hard about what you want. Do you want an extraordinary life with a sexy as fuck man who adores you, or do you want a normal, boring life with a guy who may never love you as much as Easton does? And even if he does, I bet there won't be nearly as much passion between you. Passion like that only comes around once in a lifetime, Gabs."

I rest my head against the back of the couch and think everything over. I know deep down that she's right, but how do I get over these issues I keep getting hung up on? How do I handle the man I love being around gorgeous women all day? How do I handle the fame that comes along with being Mrs. Perez? All I know is that I'll have to figure it out because what Easton and I have is too good to just throw away. But right now, I'm too tired and too sick to do much of anything but sleep it off. My eyes shut as sleep pulls me under.

I wake later and look at the clock on the wall. It's going on two. I better get back. I can't believe I freaked out like this. I can't believe I snuck out while he was still sleeping or that I left that note. I lug my bag back downstairs when the cab arrives, and I have him take me back to Easton's. Since I left my phones and keys on my desk, I have to ring the bell.

"Can I help you?" Charles asks.

"Charles, it's Gabbi. Can you let me in please?"

"Certainly," he says and the gates begin to open. The cab takes me to the front doors, and I toss him some cash before running inside. Charles is standing by the door, and I nearly run him over.

"Where is he, Charles?"

"I'm afraid he's not here at the moment."

"What? Where is he?"

"He went looking for you this morning."

Of course he did. I nod. "Okay, I'm going to go upstairs to his room. Will you send him up when he arrives, please?"

"Of course, ma'am."

I take my bag up to his bedroom and collapse onto the bed. I wait and wait and wait, but he never comes home. I give up and take a shower, hoping it erases the memory of last night from my head. It doesn't, but it does make me feel almost like a person again. I pull the blankets back on his bed and crawl beneath them, not caring that my hair is soaking his pillow. The sun sets and the room grows dark. Sleep tugs at me, and I force myself to stay awake, but I lose the battle and drift off to the land of nod.

I don't know what time it is when I wake up, but the room is pitch-black. "Easton?" I call out, feeling the bed, only to find it empty. I get up and use the bathroom, finding his robe hanging on the bathroom door. I pull it on and head out of the room, needing to go to the kitchen for a drink. I'm walking down the dimly lit hallway when I pass by the room where I left my keys and phones. In the corner of the room is a lounge chair, and it looks like someone is asleep in it. I frown out of confusion as I walk through the door. I'm only a few feet away when I see Easton. His feet are kicked up on the stool and his head is held up by his fist, elbow bent and resting on the arm of the chair.

I fall to my knees and cup his cheek. "Easton?"

His eyes pop open and lock on mine. "Gabbi?" he slurs, sitting up.

"What are you doing in here? I told Charles to tell you I was here."

"He was asleep when I got in. I saw his note that said to call him, but I didn't want to wake him." He rubs the sleep from his eyes. They open and find me again. "What are you doing here?" His hands move to cup my cheeks.

"I'm sorry. I wasn't thinking. I was stupid." I shake my head.

"You came back?" he asks.

I nod.

"I've been out looking for you all day. I didn't give up until a few hours ago when I stumbled into a bar." He cups the nape of my neck and pulls me closer and kisses me softly. "If this is a dream, it's a damn good one," he says, pulling me back in.

I smile into his kiss, wanting to tell him this isn't a dream but not wanting to break away from him long enough to say the words. He pulls me against him and picks me up, carrying me into his room where he kicks the door shut. His hands push the robe open, and he falls to his knees before me. "Fuck, you're perfect. Just like in real life," he says, moving his lips to my stomach.

"I'm real, Easton. I love you." I thread my fingers into his disheveled hair.

"Mmmm, I love hearing those words." He kisses my hip. "Let's see if you taste as good in a dream." He yanks my leg up over his shoulder as he moves his mouth to my clit. His hot tongue runs between my folds and I call out. "You do," he whispers. "You sound just as heavenly too." His face moves back in, his tongue working my clit over as his fingers thrust inside of me. It doesn't take long before I'm shattering to pieces in his hands. When my release ends, he pulls away, taking me with him over to the bed. He rips his clothes off and settles between my knees.

"You taste good, you sound good, now let's see if you feel as good." He thrusts into me and I cry his name, digging my nails into his back. He thrusts once, twice, three times, and he lowers his face to mine. "Gabbi?"

"Yes?" I reply.

"You're real? This isn't a dream?"

I giggle and shake my head. "No, this isn't a dream. I'm really here, and I love you." I move my hands to cup his jaw.

He smiles and lets out a relieved breath before moving his lips to mine. He kisses me deeply and passionately, like I'm the air he needs to breathe. His hips start moving again, and it's only moments before we're both tearing apart at the seams. When he releases his seed into me, he rolls to his side and pulls me against him.

"You're really back?"

"I'm really back, and I'm not leaving this time. Hope that's okay with you."

"You're fired," he says and my back goes ramrod straight.

"What?" I ask, turning in his arms.

"You're fired. I don't want you to be my assistant anymore. I want you to be my wife."

SIXTEEN
EASTON

She shakes her head, her brows drawn together, and her blue eyes glaze over. "You...what?"

I press a kiss to her forehead. "I wasn't lying when I said I love you. I've loved you since I was five years old, and now that I have you back, I don't ever want to let go. Fuck the world. Fuck the fame. Fuck the money. I'd give it all up for you. Marry me." I kiss her neck and trail my lips up to her ear. I push her hair out of the way with the tip of my nose. I breathe her in, burning her scent into my memory. "Marry me, baby," I whisper, pressing my lips below her jaw.

She laces her fingers into my hair and pulls until I'm looking her in the eye. "You're drunk." She smiles, flashing me her bright white teeth.

"But I know what I want," I say, not denying that I'm drunk out of my mind. I thought she was a fucking dream. Hell, I may still be in a dream. But either way, I want her. Forever.

"Well, let's see if you still feel that way tomorrow, huh?"

I lay my head on her chest and listen to her steady heartbeat as it lulls me into a deep, dreamless sleep.

I FEEL the bed move and my eyes open. The room is filled with bright morning light since I was too drunk to pull the curtains closed last night. I roll to my side and find her still beside me. "It wasn't a dream," I whisper, my voice thick with sleep.

She smiles and shakes her head as she rolls over to face me, her big eyes lit up by the sun. "It wasn't a dream."

"Why'd you come back?" I ask, needing to know.

"I just realized how much I love you. And even if I don't want your life, I do want you. Can't have one without the other, right?"

I want to smile, but I'm too sleepy, too hungover. "Marry me," I ask again.

She laughs. "Still with this?"

"Always with this," I reply.

"Don't you think it's too soon? We've only been together for three months."

"Three months, three years... hell, three hundred years, I want you to be mine. I knew it after one second when I was five. I've known it ever since. Marry me. I swear, I'll make you happy every single day. I'll prove my love to you every minute." I roll on top of her and press my lips to hers. My body comes alive, and my dick prods her between her legs.

She wiggles her hips against me, sliding my length between her needy folds. "I think it's going to take some convincing."

I smash my mouth against hers while my hands wrap around her throat. One roll of my hips and I'm sliding inside. "Marry me?" I ask, thrusting into her.

She moans, and I tangle my free hand into her hair. "Marry me, Gabbi." I push into her again. "You're mine. You've always been mine. Now, let's make it official." I kiss her as my hips continue to move, but she doesn't answer me. Her body starts to tighten around me, and I know I need my answer. I slow my hips. "If you marry me, we can do this every day. Would you like that? Would you like me moving inside you every single day?" I ask, pushing into her slowly. "Sliding into you inch by inch? Do you want that?"

"Yes," she pants out. "Please, I'm going to come. Let me come," she begs.

"Marry me," I throw back, kissing her. "Will you marry me, Gabbi?"

"Yes," she screams, and I thrust into her as hard as I fucking can. I don't stop, don't slow. I pound into her until we're both coming undone and I'm filling her with every drop. I slow to a stop on top of her and kiss her until I can't breathe. Wetness hits my nose, and I open my eyes and pull away to see tears leaking from her eyes. I wipe them away and kiss her cheeks. "I love you." I kiss her forehead. "I'll always love you." I kiss her chin. "I swear, I'll never stop." I kiss her lips, and her tongue slides into my mouth, dancing with my own as her arms wrap around my neck, pulling me closer.

"I love you too," she replies.

After thinking that I'd lost her for twenty-four hours, hearing those words leave her lips is better than anything I've ever felt. It's like being starved for air and finally getting to take a breath. It's like being in the desert, feeling the water drain from your system and finding a glass of ice-cold water with condensation running down the glass. It's like being starved and then getting to eat your favorite meal. It's more than just a want. It's a need. I need her at my side. I need her in my arms. And I need her love. It's no less important than food, water, air.

I pull away. "Come on. We have something to do today."

Her brows furrow together. "What do we have to do?"

"You'll see," I say, dragging her into the bathroom to shower.

We take a long shower, cleaning each other, kissing, talking, and giggling. We finally emerge an hour later, and we both pull on our clothes, hers from her bag.

"I'll have the staff clean out the closet and put your things away while we're gone today."

"So I'm moving into the main house, huh?"

"Well, we are engaged now," I point out.

"Engaged isn't married. You wanting the milk for free?"

I smile. "I've already had the milk, and it's worth every penny I have."

She laughs as we exit the bedroom and head for the car.

"You're seriously not going to tell me where we're going?"

"Nope," I say, climbing behind the wheel.

"YOU DON'T MOVE SLOW, do you?" she asks with a smile as we come to a stop outside of Tiffany's.

I grin. "Not my style," I say, killing the engine and climbing out. I rush around the car and catch the door as she opens it. I offer my hand. She takes it and I help her out. We walk into the jewelry store hand in hand.

"Mr. Perez, what can I do for you today?" a saleswoman asks the moment I step into the store.

I lean in close. "There will be a very big tip for you today if we can do this discreetly."

She nods. "Follow me." She leads the way into a private back room. There's a desk and a large window that looks out onto the sales floor. She walks around the desk and smiles as she places both hands on it. "Now, what can I help you find today?"

Gabbi and I glance at one another. "We're looking for an engagement ring."

The woman smiles wider. "I'd be more than happy to help. Any certain cut or metal that you want to see more than the others?"

"Rose gold," she answers.

"Have a seat and I'll bring out some options for you. Would you like anything to eat or drink? Some wine or champagne, maybe?"

"Yes, we'd love some. Thank you," I say, pulling out a chair for Gabbi.

The woman leaves us alone, and the two of us sit and wait.

Gabbi shakes her head. "I can't believe this."

"What?"

"That you can just walk in here, and everyone falls over themselves to help you."

I chuckle. "Well, it's not all me. She'll get her cut after selling me a rather expensive engagement ring."

She smiles but gets up and walks over to the window, gazing through the glass to the sales floor. "I can't believe you even got me here. How do you trick me into doing these things?" She spins around to look at me.

I get up and walk over to her slowly. "I can be very persuasive when I need to be"—I press a kiss to her lips—"when it comes to something I want." My hands pull her closer while our lips explore one another's for the hundredth time today.

I grab her ass and pick her up against me. She squeals but wraps her arms around my neck. "Easton, we can't do this here."

"We can do this anywhere we fucking want, Gabbi." I lay her on the couch that's on the far side of the room and cover her body with mine.

The door opens and the saleswoman walks in. "Oops. So we need a few minutes?" she asks, blushing.

"No, not at all," I say, sliding away from her and pulling her up with me. "We have the rest of our lives for this, right? Let's get that ring on your finger."

The woman comes in and sits behind the desk, spreading out the rings in front of us.

"This is all the rose gold we have in the store, but we could always customize something for you if you don't see anything here you like."

Gabbi looks from the rings to me and I nod. She smiles as she scoots closer. I watch her blue eyes move from one ring to the next and to the next, all the way down the row and then on to the next one. She picks one up and tries it on. She holds her hand out and scrunches up her nose. She takes it off and puts it back before continuing her search.

After what feels like forever, she settles on one. "I think this is it," she says, her smile wide and her eyes glowing. "What do you think?" She flips her hand around for me to see.

"I think there is one thing missing," I say, taking her hand in mine and pulling off the ring at the same time. I drop down to one knee and show her the ring. "Gabbi, I've loved you for what feels like my entire life. Will you marry me?"

She smiles and nods. "Yes," she agrees, and I slip the ring onto her finger. I have to admit, it's nice to hear without my hand around her throat and my dick buried inside her.

She leans in and kisses me deeply, a long, slow kiss. When I pull away, the woman is smiling. "Should I wrap it up, or will you be wearing it out of the store?"

"I think I'll be wearing this ring for the rest of my life," Gabbi says.

"You better," I joke, though I'm completely serious.

"Okay, I'll ring you up." She turns to the computer on the desk and scans a barcode on the ring's box. She scoots the card reader closer to me, and I pull my card out of my wallet, swiping it without concern. The receipt prints, and she hands it over with the box and the warranty. "My business card is in there too. You know, for the wedding bands."

I take the items. "Thank you very much." The two of us stand, and Gabbi walks through the door. I hang out a second longer, passing five one-hundred-dollar bills over to the saleswoman. "Thanks for your help."

She bows her head. "Thank you. Best wishes for a happy union."

I catch up to Gabbi quickly and open the door for her. We step into the warm sun of the day and get back in the car.

I look over at her as I start the car. "How about we stay lost a little while longer?"

She smiles. "A bikini and martini sound pretty nice right now."

"You're reading my mind," I agree.

I drive us straight to the ocean where we climb onto the yacht and set sail. We have drink after drink as we celebrate together and watch the sun set over the horizon. This is the beginning of a very happy life. A life that we'll live together. A life I'll never stop celebrating.

EPILOGUE

GABBI

"Do you even know how to drive this thing?" I ask my husband as we climb into a speedboat to zoom to our honeymoon destination.

He chuckles. "I've been boating longer than I've been walking." I believe it. His parents always had boats growing up. He'd hosted lots of parties on them that I was never invited to.

I take my seat and the boat roars to life. "Where are we going?"

"I rented us our own private island."

My mouth drops open. "You rented us a whole island?"

He laughs. "Yep. Are you impressed yet?"

I shrug it off. "Meh, buy an island and I'll be impressed."

He shakes his head. "The longer we're together, the harder you're getting to impress."

"What can I say? I'm spoiled," I joke, laughing, and he pushes the boat forward at an alarming speed.

As we soar over the ocean, I take a moment to burn every aspect of this night into my memory. After a quiet wedding, we hopped onto a flight and then a boat. The sky is dark, like a mix of black and midnight-blue oil paint, speckled with white stars. It's cloudless and beautiful. The water is warm as it splashes up over the boat, misting into my hair and making it stick to my skin. I look over at my new husband and thank God that he was strong enough to fight for us when I wasn't, when I was ready to roll over and give up. I look back at that time now and can't believe I almost passed on all of this just because my life was turning in a direction I didn't foresee.

I'm happy that he seemed to know me better than I knew myself, that he was able to fight for both of us, even though it was me that we were fighting against. I don't know where this life will take us, but I know it will be someplace beautiful and that, if nothing else, we'll be together, the two of us against the world—even if that means we're fighting against ourselves.

Up ahead, the outline of an island comes into view. I can see the silhouettes of palm trees and a house. The closer the boat gets, the more I can make out. The house is a big two-story home made up of cedar or some kind of wooden siding. It fits perfectly among the scenery. There's a large wraparound porch, and the big white moon is high in the sky, making the water below glisten like diamonds.

The boat goes silent when he kills the engine. He hops out, tying it to the dock. He stands up and looks down at me with a smile, his hand outstretched. "Ready to get our honeymoon started?"

I smile as I take his hand, and he helps me from the boat, pulling me into his arms. With some kind of smooth swing, he's cradling me against his chest.

"What are you doing? You can't carry me the whole way."

"I can and I will," he says, walking up the dock and onto the sand that leads to the porch. He takes two steps at a time until we're at the front of the house. He uses the hand under my legs to open the door, and he steps inside. "Welcome home, wife," he says, pressing his lips to mine.

"Home?" I ask, pulling back.

He shrugs as he sets me on my feet. "Home for the next month."

I feel my eyes stretch wide. "A whole month?"

He chuckles. "If you want. If you get sick of me, we can leave sooner."

"I highly doubt that will happen," I say, pulling him back in for a kiss.

"Why don't you turn on some lights and get comfortable. I'll go out and grab our bags."

He rushes back out the door, and I walk through the house, turning on all the lights. I walk into the kitchen first and flip the switch. It lights up, and I find marble counters and top-of-the-line appliances. I follow the light to the dining room, which holds a massive table, and I follow that beam of light into the living room. The living room is done up in hardwoods, whites, and shades of cream. There's a big fireplace, brown leather sofa, and a wall made entirely of glass. I open the glass door and walk out onto the back porch. There's a light breeze, and the sound of the ocean is relaxing.

He walks up behind me and kisses my bare shoulder. "So what do you think of the place?"

"It's perfect," I breathe out, spinning around to wrap my arms around him.

He pulls me against his strong chest and kisses me. "You up for a midnight swim?"

I smile as I pull away and run down the steps into the sand, ripping my sundress over my head as I go. I toss it onto the sand and strip out of my panties before running into the lukewarm water. It practically feels like bathwater while the sand beneath my feet is like the finest, softest powder. I turn around to find him still standing on the shore, watching me. "Come on in. The water is warm."

He smiles as he unbuttons his shirt.

"If you're not going to come play with me, I'll just have to play with myself," I tease.

His face turns serious. "Don't you dare touch what's mine. I'm not much for sharing my toys," he says, pushing his pants over his hips and kicking them off his feet. Moments later, he's rushing into the water, gathering me in his arms. His lips find mine as I wrap my arms and legs around him, holding him close.

His kisses move down to my neck, and I whisper in his ear. "I love you."

He lets out a quiet growl. "I love you too." His lips find mine as he carries me out of the water and back to the house.

"Hey, I thought we were going to swim?"

"If you expect me to do anything but have sex when you're naked, you're sorely mistaken."

I giggle. "Noted. If I want to swim..."

"Wear a bathing suit," he finishes for me.

THE NEXT MORNING, he's still dead to the world, so I pull on a bathing suit and head to the ocean. The water is a few degrees cooler than it was last night but not by much. It's perfect for waking me up and making me feel alive. I swim for about twenty minutes before I find him watching me from the back porch with a cup of coffee in his hand. He sets it on the railing and walks toward me, pulling his boxers off as he comes. He's in the water and pulling me against him a moment later. Under the water, his hands rip my bottoms off.

"Hey, I thought if I was wearing a swimsuit, you could control yourself."

"I lied," he says, thrusting into me.

THE MONTH WAS PERFECT, and I'm sad when it ends, but I'm also happy to get back to real life. We make it home, and I don't do anything but sleep for the first three days. I wake up long enough to use the bathroom, eat, and drink, but then I'm right back in bed. Easton comes home from set one day and finds me back in bed. He crawls up the bed and gently shakes me awake.

"How are you still sleeping?"

I shrug. "Traveling takes it out of me."

"I've made your doctor's appointment first thing tomorrow morning."

I groan.

"I know, but I want to make sure you didn't pick up a parasite or something on the island. Do this for me, please?" he begs.

"Fine," I agree.

In the morning, I'm still tired and just feeling under the weather, so Charles drives me to the doctor since Easton had to be back on set. I sign in and get called back immediately. I step on the scale before taking the urine cup and stepping into the restroom to leave a sample. I step into the exam room and the nurse wraps the blood pressure cuff around my upper arm. Then I'm left alone to sit on the bed to wait for the doctor. Someone knocks and the door opens.

"Good morning, Mrs. Perez," Doctor Roney says. "How are you today?" He shakes my hand.

I shrug. "I'm okay. I'm just tired, really."

He leans against the counter and opens my file. "I'd say so. Did you know you were pregnant?"

My head snaps up, my eyes locking on him. "Excuse me?"

"You're pregnant. Based on the date you gave the nurse, you should be around ten weeks. Did you notice you were late?"

I nod, but in my ears, I hear this long buzzing sound. "I just thought it was all the stress and travel. It's not the first time I've missed a period."

"Well, it is the first time it's due to pregnancy. I would like to do a pelvic exam and get a heart rate on the baby, if that's okay with you."

I nod, my thoughts racing.

"I'll get the nurse and we'll be back in a moment."

He leaves, but I don't notice as I try to think back on when we could've conceived. Easton and I have never used protection. We didn't think we needed to since I was on birth control. He and I, we've never talked about starting a family or having children, and I don't know how he will take it. Worry eats at me, but excitement bubbles in my stomach. I've always wanted a family, children of my own to watch grow, to guide them in ways my mother tried guiding me, to know what it feels like to love someone more than myself.

The doctor performs the exam, and I even get some pictures of the little baby that's growing in my stomach before I leave. I tuck the photos into my purse before walking out, not wanting Charles to know before Easton. Keeping this secret is the hardest thing I've ever done, but I won't breathe a word of it to anyone before Easton.

I plan on telling him during dinner, which I asked to be served in our room for added privacy. When he gets home, there's a small table set up in the bedroom with candles and our dinner already plated up. I'm in his favorite silk nightie, and my hair is down and in soft curls as it hangs past my shoulders.

He walks in and doesn't even notice the table, the candles, or the nightie. "Hey, what did the doctor say?" he asks seconds after kissing me hello.

I smile. "I'll tell you, but first, look. Isn't it romantic?" I ask, showing him the table.

"Yeah, it's great, but what did the doctor say?"

I pull out a chair for him. "Have a seat."

He lets out a long breath but sits down and waits for me to sit across from him. "Are you going to tell me?"

"I will, but first, look. I got some pictures printed off from the honeymoon." I hand them over, the sonogram pictures mixed in.

He takes them. "What is this?" he asks, flipping through the first couple.

"Aren't they great?"

"Yes, and I'd love to go through these with you another time, but right now, I just want to make sure my wife is okay. Now, what did the doctor say?"

I peek over the stack of photos. "Flip two more."

His chest puffs out, and a vein in his forehead starts to throb, but he humors me and flips two more pictures. His eyes land on the sonogram, and he freezes. His eyes move from the pictures, to me, and back. "What... what is this?"

"That's what the doctor gave me. The reason I've been so tired lately."

He smiles. "You're... pregnant?"

I grin and nod. "Ten weeks!"

His smile falls as he looks at the picture again.

"Are... are you okay? Is this good news?" I ask, feeling my anxiety rise.

There's a long pause as he looks at the photo. "Of course this is good news. Are you kidding me?"

A laugh slips past my lips. "I... I didn't know. We've never talked about this and—" My words are cut off when he flies out of his seat and pulls my mouth against his. He kisses me feverishly, passionately, hard and long. It's a kiss that I can feel in the pit of my stomach. It makes my toes tingle with excitement and my muscles tighten with need. We haven't been together romantically since we've been home. I've been too tired, and he's been working so much that there hasn't been a good time, but now, now is a good time.

I wrap my arms around his neck and pull him closer. His hands land on my hips, and he pulls me from my chair and into his arms. Picking me up against him, he turns and lays me across the bed, kissing his way up my body. He pushes my nightie up to my breasts and then pauses to look at my stomach.

"I can't believe it," he whispers, his hands moving to my stomach but not touching me, like he's afraid to hurt me or the baby. "This is real?"

I nod. "It's real. We're going to have a baby."

His smile breaks free now, and he presses his lips lightly to my stomach, right above my belly button. Slowly, his kisses fan out, moving over my stomach, hips, and breasts. His hands are everywhere, massaging, caressing, touching, and kissing every spot at once. He pushes my nightgown out of the way, and his clothes follow soon after. He works himself between my knees and positions himself at my entrance. With his hand around my throat, he pushes into me and fills me completely. It's like his body was made for mine. We fit together so snugly, like two puzzle pieces.

I call out as he slowly moves inside me. "I love you, Gabbi."

"I love you, too, Easton," I whisper against his lips.

As his body moves with mine, I can't think of anything but us and how I never expected this. It scared me when my life started to change, but now, I can see how silly all that was. I never expected the guy I hated in high school to be the man I was meant to be with. I never expected to lose the person who meant the most to me only to find out that I was meant for another all along, a person who loves me, takes care of me, and gives to me in every sense of the word. Our past was rocky, our present is perfect, and our future? I don't know anything for sure. Nobody ever does. But I know one thing like I know my own name. Easton Perez is the one I'm going to spend the rest of my life with, from now until forever. Wherever life takes us, we'll be okay. We'll be together. And really, that's all you can ask for in life.

When I come, he kisses me and absorbs my cries into his mouth. Moments later, he's releasing inside of me. He stills on top of me, pressing soft kisses to my skin as he brushes the stray hairs away from my face. "I don't know how this happened, but I'm glad it did. You're all I ever wanted, and now, look, you're giving me so much more than I could have ever asked for."

"I'm not giving you this baby, Easton. This baby is ours. We created it out of love, something I've never had so much of in all my life." I cup my hand around his jaw.

His eyes darken, the gold flakes lighting up and practically glowing under the candlelight. "I love you, baby."

"I love you too," I say as he pulls me to his chest and wraps me in his arms.

He presses a kiss to my shoulder and says, "You can't sleep yet. Eat." He gets up.

I sit up. "What?"

He smiles as he brings my plate over to the bed and feeds me a bite.

I laugh and shake my head as I chew. "I don't want to eat. I want to sleep and I want you with me."

"After you eat." He feeds me another bite, and we talk about the baby and how I felt when I heard the news. We talk about how this could turn out, what we think the baby's sex is, and what we could name him or her. After I've eaten my dinner, he crawls back into bed, and I instantly relax against him. I sigh out of happiness as the warmth takes over. My eyes close as I feel his breath against my cheek, his arms around me, and I drift into a deep, dreamless sleep, knowing that no matter what happens, we'll be okay and happy. Easton and I finally get our happily ever after, even when neither of us thought it would work out. I guess the world is funny like that, giving you exactly what you need when you need it most.

The End

IF YOU LOVE SMALL TOWN BOXSETS CHECK OUT THESE TWO BY ALEXIS WINTER!

**Grand Lake Colorado Series
A Complete Small-Town Contemporary Romance Collection**

Welcome to Grand Lake, Colorado—Where the men are hot, alpha, and a little downright dirty.

Fall in love with them in this never before published collection of four steamy, small-town romances from best-selling author Alexis Winter.

[The Slade Brothers: A Complete Small Town Contemporary Romance Collection](#)

Meet the Slade Brothers. Brooding. Protective AF. Rich and drop-dead delicious.

If you love small-town love stories full of alpha men who will stop at nothing to claim the women they love then grab this complete best-selling Slade Brothers Series in one steamy collection.

GRAB A FREE BOOK FROM ME!

SIGN UP FOR MY NEWSLETTER AND GET *MY BEST FRIEND'S BROTHER* FREE!

It's no secret I've always had a crush on Damon Strickland.
My best friend's older brother and the center of every single one of my fantasies.

He's a walking, talking temptation.

That cocky grin and those broad, athletic shoulders.
You know what they say about a man with big hands right?

Growing up, we always tormented one another.
I was the nagging, annoying little girl he hated
And he was the man-whoring, douchebag I couldn't seem to get over.

Now as adults he actually came through and helped me land a job at my dream company.

How the hell am I supposed to focus when all I can think about is tearing that tight suit from his tempting body!

What's even worse?
He forgot to mention, he's my boss.

SIGN UP HERE AND GET A SECOND FREEBIE SENT RIGHT TO YOUR INBOX!

ALSO BY ALEXIS WINTER

Slade Brothers Series
Billionaire's Unexpected Bride

Off Limits Daddy

Baby Secret

Loves me NOT

Best Friend's Sister

Castille Hotel Series
Hate That I Love You

Business & Pleasure

Baby Mistake

Fake It

South Side Boys Series
Bad Boy Protector-Book 1

Fake Boyfriend-Book 2

Brother-in-law's Baby-Book 3

Bad Boy's Baby-Book 4

Mountain Ridge Series
Just Friends: Mountain Ridge Book 1

Protect Me: Mountain Ridge Book 2

Baby Shock: Mountain Ridge Book 3

Make Her Mine Series

My Best Friend's Brother

Billionaire With Benefits

My Boss's Sister

My Best Friend's Ex

Best Friend's Baby

ALL BOOKS CAN BE READ AS STAND-ALONE READS WITHIN THESE SERIES

ABOUT THE AUTHOR

Alexis Winter is a contemporary romance author who loves to share her steamy stories with the world. She specializes in billionaires, alpha males and the women they love.

If you love to curl up with a good romance book you will certainly enjoy her work. Whether it's a story about an innocent young woman learning about the world or a sassy and fierce heroine who knows what she wants you,'re sure to enjoy the happily ever afters she provides.

When Alexis isn't writing away furiously, you can find her exploring the Rocky Mountains, traveling, enjoying a glass of wine or petting a cat.

You can find her books on Amazon or at https://www.alexiswinterauthor.com/

Follow Alexis Winter below for access to advanced copies of upcoming releases, fun giveaways and exclusive deals!

Made in the USA
Coppell, TX
03 April 2021